What Others Are Saying About Dan Ronco's Prior Novel,
Unholy Domain:

"Thought provoking ... a solid futuristic thriller" *Booklist*

"Unholy Domain is a gripping thriller all the way through. Highly recommended for community library thriller collections"
Midwest Book Review

"Dan Ronco tells a tale that is unique, provocative, and engrossing while maintaining enough slam-bang action to keep you turning the pages. Unholy Domain reads like a cross between Blade Runner and Angels and Demons"
R. Douglas Weber, author of Solomon's Key: The CODIS Project

"Unholy Domain is an entertaining futuristic cautionary thriller"
Harriet Klausner, Amazon #1 Reviewer

"Top rate adventure sparkling with ideas" *Piers Anthony, bestselling author of dozens of novels*

"This dark novel is a thought provoking, edgy look at the near future, much like Blade Runner, Minority Report and other Dick classics. No admirer of the old master should miss Unholy Domain" *Book Worms Magazine*

"For those who read Dan's first novel, "Peacemaker" this will be a must read sequel. For others, it will be a good introduction to Dan's excellent writing skills and an invitation to go and get Peacemaker and look forward to a sequel to Unholy Domain" *BookPleasures Reviews*

No one really has the guts to say it, but if we could make better human beings by knowing how to add genes, why shouldn't we?

— James Watson, Co-discoverer of the structure of DNA

2031
The Singularity Pogrom

Dan Ronco

2031: The Singularity Pogrom

ISBN 13: 9780984621606

Library of Congress Control Number: 2010912311

Cover design by All Things That Matter Press

Published in 2010 by All Things That Matter Press

For Linda, who amazes me with her courage and tenacity throughout a long struggle with breast cancer.

Part I

ESCAPE

ONE

Tuesday, May 6, 2025

It was that time of the morning when the darkness reluctantly surrenders to an arriving dawn. An orange glow spreads along the horizon, heralding the start of another endless day.

The island's desolate shore challenged his will every morning. Barely aware of the rumble of waves rushing toward the beach, Ray Brown ran at the tide's edge. His world was the rhythmic flow of air rushing through his lungs and the crunch of rough limestone sand under his feet. Arms and legs pumping like a fine engine, his long, lean body traveled effortlessly along the slanted coastline.

Soon the dark outline of the barbed-wire fence would come into view.

This atoll, this god-forsaken island somewhere in the Indian – at least he guessed it was the Indian Ocean—had been his prison every day of thirteen years. Every morning he made his solitary run. He wasn't sure why he ran, but the rising sun always found him loping along its circumference.

To his right, just beyond the point where the sandy coast turned into a sparse woodland of trees and shrubs, a ten-foot electrically charged, barbed-wire fence stretched parallel to the beachfront. A sentry had warned him that the charge was sufficient to electrocute a man, so he kept his distance. He remembered measuring the fence one morning many years earlier: exactly two hundred and fifty-four feet. That was back in the days when he still prayed for escape.

What a fool. He had really believed he would escape. Half a dozen tries and all failed. Almost seven years had passed since his last attempt.

The fence enclosed a small village of dirt roads, prefabricated sheds disguised as native huts and about a half-dozen suspicious guards. Crates of food, barrels of fuel oil and other supplies were delivered by helicopter in the dark of night. Ray didn't see anyone this morning, but he knew his captors watched him closely; during his first year of imprisonment, he had discovered cameras hidden in the trees scattered across the island.

He knew every tree, every bush on Purgatory Island; that's what he had named it. Every day an indifferent morning sun turned merciless in the afternoon. Every day the same salty breeze, the same warm rain. He forced himself to listen to the rumble of the surf, but nothing had changed. Nothing ever changed.

The morning was the best part of the day. And the worst. Morning brought him closest to the Almighty; drew him toward a belief in eternity; the golden sun turning darkness into morning, puffs of clouds drifting over a vast sea, salty air cleansing his soul. But morning also brought bitterness; made him remember how it had been when he could embrace his sons, when he had his work, when every day was an adventure.

When he had a life.

He would never see his sons again. Brian had been a beautiful boy of eight with sandy hair and a toothy grin. David, then eleven, had inherited his father's gift for creating software.

Ray had attempted suicide on the tenth year of his imprisonment. Hopelessness had done it. There had been no planning, no analysis. One morning, after his run, he had dived into the ocean and swam toward the sun. It had felt so good, that swim. They told him he had been almost three miles out from shore before exhaustion dragged him under. He remembered the roar of the helicopter blades cutting through the air. He fought as the divers pulled him to the surface, but he was too weak to resist.

Time had imprinted the island in his mind. Just one clue— a tree, the shape of the beach, or a glimpse of the lagoon—and he knew his location. Purgatory Island would be in his mind until the day he died; which would probably be on this god-forsaken island.

Sweat began to trickle down his forehead, but he maintained a fast pace, digging deep into his reserves. He wiped the sweat with the back of his hand and kept running.

God, I hate this island.

This slice of the coast, where a jagged coral peninsula stretched into the ocean, brought memories of another place. A long time ago, he lived in a rugged Oregon home overlooking the Pacific. He would sit on his porch, developing software, changing the world. The newscasters had called him a genius, brilliant, gifted. Now, they called him Devil and celebrated his death.

It was all a lie.

Time seems to slow down. I become aware of the steady thump thump of my heart, of life-giving air pulsing in and out of my lungs, of the contraction and extension of thigh muscles as I stride across the coarse sand. I imagine I can feel every cell of my body, working in unison, lifting me into another world which should be mine, but isn't.

The outline of his hut, dominated by the tall cylindrical trunks and curving pinnate leaves of palm trees, appeared around the gentle curve of the shoreline. As he had done for thirteen years, he veered off to the left, splashed into the cold water and dove through a breaker. The ocean chilled him to the bone, and the cold water brought him back to this life, this reality. He swam parallel to the beach, letting the salty foam slide along his body, soothing his resentment, preparing him for another day.

I should have killed Dianne when I had the chance.

When he spotted the four-foot coral wall, he strode out of the water. Waves crashed against his back, then retreated as he walked up the sloping beach toward the wall. He guessed tribesmen had built it a century earlier to shield their village from the crashing waves of tropical storms. Now it protected his huts. He briskly dried himself with a warm towel hanging on the wall, leaving his sun-bronzed skin tingling in the breeze. As he did every morning, he braced himself with one hand and vaulted over the wall.

At fifty-five, he was in the best shape of his life. The morning run and the island food had chiseled his body into a lean, flowing chorus of muscle and tendon.

Shortly after his suicide attempt, Dianne had allowed David to visit him on the island. Only an hour, but he learned David had forgiven all his shortcomings as a father and still loved him. He also learned that David planned to assassinate Dianne as soon as he found a breach in her security. Maybe he should have urged David to put aside any thought of revenge and live a normal life, but someone had to kill that monster.

David also told him that Brian had suffered a mental breakdown and was being treated in an institution. David said Brian was making steady progress and had a good chance for a full recovery. David didn't say it, but Ray knew that he was to blame. Being Ray Brown's son was a heavy cross to bear.

Behind the wall were three modest structures—two huts and a larger community house—all constructed from the atoll's coral base. His hut consisted of a bedroom and a rough bath, just like Paul's. It was comfortable, and it became his hideaway when he needed to be alone. Although Paul was his best friend, there were times when solitude was crucial.

I should never have dragged Paul into this.

Paul Martino was leaning over a sizzling stove preparing breakfast when Ray entered the community house. The scent of eggs, toast and, most of all, coffee was familiar and pleasing. Their captors had provided an ample kitchen with an oven, microwave, two-faucet sink, refrigerator and an oak table with two chairs. The adjoining room contained several computers and a hologram viewer, which allowed them to receive satellite news.

Balding, with a potbelly and thin arms, Paul hadn't aged well on the island. Once the publisher of a leading on-line magazine, Paul had also been a prisoner all these years. Thirteen years earlier, they tried to stop

Dianne Morgan from releasing PeaceMaker, a horrific computer virus. They failed, and PeaceMaker shut down the Internet, bringing transportation, communications, power and virtually every other industry to a crunching halt. Dianne had planned to blackmail the governments of the world into sharing power with the Domain, the clandestine organization she led. Ray eventually terminated PeaceMaker, but not before it caused massive death and destruction. The Domain captured him, framed him for the virus attack and faked his death. Dianne's revenge was this wretched island.

"You plan to stand there like a block of wood or are you going to help me?" Paul asked in his soprano voice, looking over his shoulder at Ray.

Maybe it was his voice, but many people thought Paul was gay. In the years before their imprisonment, guys had always been coming on to him, but he was straight. Paul had dated a handful of women, but none of those relationships lasted more than a few months. No real male friends, either. For some reason, he and Paul had hit it off, right from the start. Twenty-five years, and they were still the best of friends. Behind his back, some people had called them the odd couple. Big joke.

Ray placed his hand on his forehead, looked at the ceiling and said, "Let me see if I can guess what you're making." He paused a moment and said, "This is a tough one, but I predict scrambled eggs, wheat toast and coffee."

"Man, you're hilarious," Paul said, shaking the eggs in a frying pan over a low flame. "You should have your own holovision show. Probably be the biggest hit on the island. Right now, however, why don't you make toast."

As Ray put bread in the toaster, Paul said, "Hell of a job. We finally found your strength."

Ray checked the coffee, poured a cup for each of them and sat at the table. He took a sip, made a face and said, "Don't know how you do it, but you can make fresh coffee taste two days old."

Paul said, "God, you're amusing," and divided the eggs between their plates. When the toast popped up, he placed two slices in each plate, brought the meal over to the table, and sat down.

"I saw on the news this morning that the Domain just hit one billion citizens," Paul said while buttering his toast, "There was a ceremony where the President awarded Dianne some sort of medal. Although we made her late by a decade, it seems that Dianne has achieved everything she wanted."

"Did she have his arm twisted behind his back?"

"Even though the Domain controls technology," Paul said, "I still find it amazing that the U.S. doesn't treat them like the criminals they are. It reminds me of the Cold War, where the U.S. and Soviet Union lived in so-called peaceful coexistence." He bit off a piece of toast, chewed and swallowed. "Except that the Domain coexists *within* the U.S. and many other nations. It's a cancer, spreading across the globe."

"There's still hope," Ray said, shaking pepper on his eggs. "Almost six billion people have refused to join."

Ray tried not to think about Dianne. She was the most amazing woman he had ever met, and once they had been lovers. Alone in his bed at night, he could still imagine the silky feel of her thighs, the hot excitement of her mouth and the demanding pressure of her hips. Maybe it was pride, or maybe depression, but he had refused to speak to her since she imprisoned him on the island. Not that it mattered; she was the leader of the Domain, the most powerful organization in the world, while he ran laps on Purgatory Island.

"People continue to join the Domain and who can blame them?" Paul said. He paused, then smiled, "Maybe people will come to their senses, and I hope you're right about most refusing to join. Although it would be the first time." Paul stopped chewing on his toast and cocked his head slightly to the side, as if recalling something important, "On the other hand, the law of averages is working in your favor."

Ray was about to reply, when he noticed something bobbing in the ocean well beyond the breakers. Maybe a log riding the waves? Staring for a moment, he spotted several other logs. "What the hell," he muttered as he stood up and walked to the window.

Paul joined him at the window, staring past the breakers, "What are you looking at? I don't see anything."

Ray pointed to the right, "Way out on the horizon, looks like several logs, but they are shooting over the waves, so they can't be logs." Water sprayed to the sides as the "logs" powered over the waves. "Paul, those are anti-gravity hovercrafts. Look how fast they're coming! Small hovercrafts."

"I see them," Paul said, squinting. "What the hell are they doing here?"

For the first time in thirteen years, an oscillating siren screamed from within the barbed-wire camp. This would not be just another day.

"They're coming to get us," Ray shouted over the siren.

"To save us or kill us?" Paul asked.

Ray bolted out the kitchen door and ran to the surf's edge. Now he could hear the whine of the hovercrafts as they flew inches over the water. Shading his eyes from the blistering sun, he counted three—no, four hovercrafts rushing toward shore. The two in front each carried two passengers, while the two in the rear each bore a single passenger.

Freedom, his mind roared. They have to be rescuers.

From behind, Paul yanked on his elbow and shouted, "Over there," pointing in the direction of the barbed-wire enclosure. Four guards, each armed with a laser rifle, ran onto the beach, followed by two Daniel androids, the all-purpose model manufactured by the Domain. Ray had seen the Daniels put down riots in newscasts, but this was the first time he had seen them on the island. They were about six feet tall, built in the image of a pleasant-looking young man. However, each android was armed with a laser rifle.

Ray had built the original Daniel in his workshop back in 2012 with the intent of providing a robot that would be a helper to humanity. These monsters were another perversion of his work by Dianne Morgan.

The androids galloped across the sand, their human-looking bodies silent as ghosts. The lead Daniel pointed its laser at the boats and fired an intense beam of white light as it ran.

The guards waited for the androids to catch up. They spoke briefly and then split up, with one Daniel and a guard running toward Ray, while the others ran to intercept the hovercrafts. Ray watched the android lumber toward him, each stride sinking into the sand. The Daniel seemed to be of medium build, but its body must be heavily armored.

"Let's get the hell out of here," Paul shouted over the crashing surf, and they started running.

Pumping arms and legs energized Ray's mind. His life depended on staying ahead of his captors until the men from the hovercrafts arrived. He wasn't sure who these men were, but anything was better than another day here.

"Stop," a guard screamed at them, "stop or we'll shoot."

Paul and Ray ran toward the rising sun, which cast long shadows through the palm trees. Ray was in the lead with Paul puffing behind him. Paul's running soon became labored, so Ray slowed to stay with him. Glancing over his shoulder, Ray saw a guard gaining on them, although the robot was falling back, struggling through the sand with short, choppy strides. He estimated the guard was about three hundred yards behind. If Ray didn't do something, the guard would soon be within firing range.

The bark of distant gunfire came across the island, followed by the much louder roar of an explosion. He hoped the blast had obliterated their captors.

Troubled by Paul's slowing pace, he knew they should seek cover in the forest. Ray shouted, "Follow me," and cut toward the interior of the island. Paul trailed behind, gasping for breath. Ray feared the soldier's laser weapon, but he again slowed his pace for Paul. Once they scrambled over the crest of the beach, the landscape changed to dark rubble covered with scrub trees and bushes. Hoping to lose their pursuers, Ray led Paul in a winding run through the scrub. He heard Paul stumble and turned to see him on his hands and knees, gulping air, drenched in sweat.

This wasn't working; he might be able to outrun their enemies, but Paul wasn't going to make it.

"Get out of here," Paul said, gasping for air. "I'll try to slow them down."

Ray pulled Paul to his feet and looked around, "Listen to me," he said, holding onto his friend's bicep. Pointing toward a thicket, he said, "Hide in the bush behind that big palm. I'll draw them off, and then you get the Marines."

Ray backtracked a few strides until he caught a glimpse of the oncoming soldier, turned and ran toward the interior of the island, making plenty of noise. He felt the heat of a laser beam as it scorched the trunk of a nearby tree. Racing ahead, he fought his fear as he zigzagged in and out of the brush. Another beam flashed over his shoulder as he sprinted through a grove of coconut trees. He leaped over a fallen branch without breaking stride, his pursuer less than one hundred yards behind.

***

Paul crouched in the shadows of a tall, leafy bush, still breathing hard, keeping his eye on the path Ray had just taken. Paul had wiped out his tracks, but he wasn't sure it would fool his enemies. Sweat rolled down his forehead, attracting insects that buzzed and dived at his face. When a laser flashed in the distance, he rose to his feet, straining to see through the brush, ready to flee. No one was coming. He settled back on one knee, relieved the laser wasn't meant for him. Then his stomach clenched; Ray must be running for his life. A second laser flashed, further away this time.

Run, you bastard, run.

Looking in the direction of the laser flash, Paul spotted the outline of a soldier rushing through the bush. The man disappeared into thick underbrush, but Paul listened until the enemy's footsteps faded away. Paul's breathing was still labored, but his strength was returning.

Once again, he heard footsteps, but these were slower and heavier. His eyes searched back along the original path, trying to locate the source of the sound. Then he saw a Daniel lumbering through the brush. The android ran with short, unsteady strides, as if each step required a massive computation. Paul figured the uneven terrain made running difficult.

The android stopped and bent over to examine the trail. It dawned on Paul that this robot would not blindly follow its human partner; it seemed to be thinking on its own.

Paul froze when the Daniel stood up and rotated its head in a complete circle. His fingernails were digging into the tree in front of him, so he tried to relax. The android turned around and walked back along the path, stopping at the point where Ray had dashed into the brush. Paul could barely see the android through the trees. Once again, it rotated its head in a complete circle. It seemed to Paul that the thing was trying to make up its mind: follow Ray's tracks or search for him.

Suddenly, it turned around and began lumbering back in Paul's direction. *It's coming after me.* He tried to sneak away, but the android must have heard him, because it lifted its weapon and spread a laser arc that hissed into nearby brush. Terrified, Paul started running, hoping the undergrowth would keep him out of the robot's gun sight.

The brush grew thicker as he ran inland, until he came to a wide pond that covered the interior of the atoll. He was familiar with the pond, so he didn't hesitate to splash through its turbid water, but he lost his footing in the slippery muck and almost fell. He recovered and splashed through the waist-high water, terrified that the android would get a clear shot at him before he made it to cover on the other side. Finally, his feet crunched dry sand. Gasping for breath, he collapsed behind a thick coconut tree.

The android appeared on the other side and aimed its weapon in his direction. A white-hot beam narrowly missed him, burning deep into the trunk of the coconut tree. He jerked his head back, but another beam hissed past as the Daniel splashed into the pond. A series of beams flashed past Paul's head and shoulders, pinning him behind the tree.

There was a much louder splash and he peered around the tree trunk. The android was flailing about, with its head and shoulders underwater. Knowing he would never get a better opportunity to escape, Paul ran through the scrub on a diagonal away from the pond. The deadly hiss of a laser forced him to dive behind a mahoe tree, its thick, heart-shaped leaves providing good cover.

Something was wrong with the monster. It was standing in the middle of the pond, firing wildly into trees and brush on the other side.

The android stopped shooting and walked toward the far edge of the pond. It was clearly having trouble navigating the slippery muck and almost fell again. Suddenly, it turned in a circle and sprayed intense white beams in all directions. Paul pulled his head behind the mahoe tree, but none of the laser shots came close.

When he looked again, the Daniel was standing still in the center of the pond. Then it hit him; *the damn thing is blind.* He realized that the water must have damaged the robot's circuits when it fell. He had read somewhere that a Daniel could employ heat-seeking sensors to supplement its vision, but the water might have damaged those, too. It couldn't see anything, so it must be listening for a sound that would give away his location.

If he distracted it with a noise, he could escape. Paul glanced around until he saw a softball-sized chunk of coral, but it was in the open about three yards away.

He waited until a soft breeze sighed in the trees, then slowly lifted his foot and carefully placed it on the sandy rubble. He froze when the robot's head rotated in his direction. He knew that if he were wrong about the android's vision, a cascade of deadly beams would cut him to pieces.

The Daniel appeared to focus directly on him, then snapped around and sprayed laser beams several yards to his left. The laser's hiss covered his second step, which placed him alongside the chunk of coral. He bent down and picked it off the rubble, then threw it as hard as he could into a grove of trees on the other side of the pond. The android spun around and charged, spraying white rays into the grove.

Paul ran in the opposite direction, knowing that the deadly laser hum would muffle his steps. The android kept shooting, but not at him.

In a moment, he was safe.

***

Sweat glistening on his body, Ray ran for his life. Not the long, loping strides of the morning; now his feet churned up the rubble as he strained to stay ahead of his pursuer. His chest heaved powerfully as he weaved his way through the brush.

He stopped to catch his breath, leaning against a twisted pine tree. He had run in a broad semi-circle, knowing he needed to double back to reach the men in the hovercrafts. If they were still alive. He listened for his pursuer, but the woods were silent.

Ray moved quietly through the undergrowth, listening for footsteps, looking in all directions. The atoll wasn't large, maybe two square miles. There were only so many places to hide. His enemy could be ahead.

Peering through the brush, he looked across the turbid water of the pond. He crept forward, trying to stay under the cover of the trees and brush. Pausing behind a palm tree, he again looked across the pond, then caught his breath; a Daniel stood motionless in the center of the pond, waiting to ambush the unwary.

Ray wondered if Paul had eluded the android, but there was no way to tell. He looked ahead, searching for an escape route that would keep him out of sight. Then a branch snapped not far behind.

Trapped!

Boots crunched on sand; the soldier was coming closer. Ray was about to make a run for it, but he froze when the robot's head rotated in his direction. Leaves rustled behind him, and he turned to see the muzzle of a laser rifle pointed at him. A broad-shouldered Domain soldier was hiding in a thicket, ready to kill if he tried to escape. The soldier's lips curled into a nasty smile as he stepped out from the thicket, making a low rattle as he pushed through the branches.

It's over. There's no place to run.

A cascade of intense white light ripped past him and severed the soldier's arm. The man's scream was cut abruptly when another beam burned into his face. The remains of his body fell backwards, and Ray turned to see the Daniel still aiming its laser in the direction of the soldier. The android fired again, with the white-hot beams making little puffs in the rubble around a lifeless slab of scorched meat and bone.

Finally, it stopped firing. With its weapon still pointed in his direction, the Daniel awkwardly splashed out of the water. Ray froze, hoping that the android wouldn't spot him.

Why had it fired at a Domain soldier?

Ray held his breath as the monster passed within ten feet of him. He was amazed when the android walked past the soldier's remains and disappeared into the brush.

It's blind!

Maybe there is a god.

***

When Paul emerged from the brush, he saw half a dozen lifeless bodies, both Domain soldiers and rescuers, stretched out in the sand. The scorched remnants of a Daniel were scattered around a circular depression in the beach, with wisps of black smoke coming from the center of the circle.

Paul heard someone shout, "Mr. Martino," and then a muscular African man stepped out from a grove of trees. Two men followed: a white guy armed with a rifle, and a Hispanic man carrying a missile launcher. All three men were wearing form-fitting wet suits, with goggles hanging loosely around their necks.

The black man ran up to him and said, "Where is Mr. Brown?"

Paul looked the man over. Everything about him raised alarms. Several inches over six feet tall, angular with long, rope-like muscles that seemed to bunch up in his neck, he gave the impression of a coiled spring. But it was the man's eyes that worried him: dark, deep-set, without a trace of compassion.

"Who are you?" Paul asked.

"My name is Nkumah and I'm an enemy of the Domain. That's all I can say until we're safe. A sub is waiting a few miles offshore." Nkumah grabbed Paul's arm and dug his fingers in painfully, "We have to get Mr. Brown off the island immediately. Our mutual enemy has launched robot planes."

Paul didn't trust this man, but after thirteen years on the island, he was ready to take a chance. He tried to pull away from Nkumah, but his arm didn't come free until Nkumah released it. Trotting, Paul led his rescuers in the direction of the pond. His bicep throbbed with each step from Nkumah's grip, but he refused to give the bastard the pleasure of seeing his pain. He was barely half-way to the pond when a familiar voice called him, and Ray popped out of the brush. Paul's relief surged as his friend approached.

Maybe we'll get off this island after all.

When Ray joined them, Nkumah said, "It's tight, but we can make it. The Domain launched its fighters at least fifteen minutes ago." Concentrating on Ray, he said, "We're leaving. Come with us—Morgan can't risk leaving you alive now."

"Wait," Ray said. "Who sent you?"

Nkumah said, "We can discuss that when you're safe," and then the three strangers started running back toward the beach. Paul heard something crashing through the brush, coming in their direction.

"That damn android is following the sound of our voices," he said to Ray.

Ray looked at Paul and said, "You want to play tag with that robot?"

"Screw you."

Ray grinned, and then took off after the strangers, with Paul close behind. Nkumah glanced back, a hint of a smile playing across his lips, and kept running.

***

Ray reached the beach just as a light rain began. The sky darkened, but didn't turn black.

The strangers' hovercrafts were narrow, with a seat behind the steering wheel for the driver and one in the back for a passenger. Compact propellers underneath and at the rear of the craft allowed it to fly inches above land or water. Ray watched the black man gracefully step onto the small craft, then slide into the driver's seat.

Who is this man? Why has he risked his life to rescue me?

Nkumah started the engine, and the hovercraft lifted off the ground and spun to face the ocean. He signaled Ray to get into the back seat.

"Don't go with them, Ray," said a sultry, all-too-familiar voice.

It's her!

He turned around and was shocked breathless. Dianne Morgan stood on the beach about twenty feet away, dressed in a tight white blouse and blue slacks that complimented her athletic figure. Her face was too thin, too masculine to be beautiful, but her pale blue eyes demanded his attention. Old feelings resurfaced, and his chest tightened.

"Come back to me," she pleaded. "We're for each other, no matter what."

The wind blew across the beach, but Dianne's dark hair didn't move. He realized it was a hologram, a life-size, three-dimensional image of her, but that didn't make it easier. A long time ago, before he recognized her for the tyrant she was, he had been in love with her. He hadn't spoken to her, hadn't seen her up close, for more than a decade. She couldn't hide the lines in her forehead, but she was still the same amazing woman.

Almost beautiful, he thought, not able to take his eyes off her.

"I know this man," she shouted above the hum of the hovercraft, indicating Nkumah. "He's an assassin— one of those anti-technology fanatics. I don't know what he wants with you, but don't trust him."

Her voice had deepened over the years, and it was even more compelling. Ray glanced at Paul and then turned to Nkumah, "Is what she says true?"

The stranger glared at Dianne's image. "It's true that I have fought the Domain in Africa for years. This creature has the appearance of a woman, but she's a destroyer." Ray noticed that Nkumah's big hands were balled into fists. "We fight her and the Domain because they are slaughtering my people. You can understand that, you've seen her evil up close." He roared, "How many thousands has she killed already? How long before she crushes all of us, leaving only the Domain?"

Dianne's sudden appearance had thrown Ray off-stride, but now his hatred for her came raging back. Dianne had expanded her power over the years, mutating into a deranged colossus straddling humanity. She divided humanity into two castes—Domain citizens and primitive humans—and reserved all new technology for the Domain. Never had one person held such power.

Thirteen years on Purgatory Island because of this woman.

Ray slid into the hovercraft and fastened his seatbelt. He was disgusted with his sudden weakness for Dianne. Turning his back on her, he shouted, "Let's get the hell out of here."

"You'll never get away, you bastard," she shouted at him, walking forward. "You were always a fool. I'll hunt you down." He leaned forward in the boat to keep his balance. Her voice carried over the hum of the engine, "I know why Nkumah wants you, but nobody will believe your story."

The hovercraft rushed forward, carrying them above the surf.

Her voice screamed over his shoulder, "You still love me!"

Ray held onto the sides of the speeding hovercraft, trying not to look back. When they were clear of the breakers, his resolve weakened and he looked over his shoulder. Dianne's hologram was standing on the beach, hands on hips, still watching him, but slowly receding into the morning sun.

TWO

Friday, May 9, 2025

The van hit a pothole the size of a small crater and bucked into the air. Ray braced himself against the dashboard, but the harsh landing jarred his back once again. It didn't help that Paul planted his bony knees against the back of the seat; the thin padding didn't provide much comfort on the best of roads, let alone this dirt roller coaster through the African savannah.

The roads were just about impassible. That's what Nkumah had warned, and he was right. Nkumah—that's the only name that mysterious black man would give them—told them to enjoy the ride as long as it lasts, because they would be walking much of the way.

Although he was grateful Nkumah had rescued them from Purgatory Island, Ray didn't trust him. The quiet man refused to share any information: Ray didn't know who arranged their escape, where they were going, or what they were supposed to do when they arrived.

Other than that, things are clear.

Three days had passed since Nkumah snatched them off the island. The sub had been about a mile at sea. They made it just in time; Domain jet fighters strafed the water as the sub dove. They traveled underwater for a couple of days and then surfaced under a dark sky. The hovercrafts dropped them on the southern coast of what had once been Tanzania, before the government collapsed. According to Nkumah, they landed about a hundred miles south of Dar es Salaam. A beat-up, green, four-wheel-drive van was waiting in the darkness and, except for a few short breaks, Nkumah had been driving constantly for more than thirty hours. Referencing an old map, Ray figured they were moving westward, roughly parallel to the Rufiji River, which bisected the Selous game reserve.

It was past the heat of the day, but Ray's cotton shirt was still soaked in sweat. The van smelled like a gymnasium, and even the occasional breeze brought no relief. Rain fell heavily in the morning, leaving a coat of mud over the bumpy road. Nkumah said it was the time of the *masika,* the long rain, and they should expect downpours for a portion of almost every day.

A little black bee buzzed in through the open window and landed on his arm. Ray no longer bothered to swat these little bees; they weren't dangerous. They fed on sweat, but they didn't have stingers. He was becoming accustomed to living with the multitude of African insects.

He admitted there was a certain harsh beauty to the land. The rolling savannah was covered with tall grass, scattered trees and thorn brush; all struggling to claim the rain before the dry season rolled in.

The van jerked to a stop, pushing Paul's knees into Ray's back again. The cause of the sudden halt wasn't apparent. Ray glanced at Nkumah, who seemed to be concentrating on a point in the tall grass about one hundred yards ahead of them. He followed Nkumah's line of sight, trying to discover what was troubling the African.

At first, he didn't see anything, and then the grass parted and a huge animal trotted out, like a battleship cutting through the sea. A curved horn was visible above the grass—two horns as Ray noticed a smaller horn on the broad head—bobbing forward toward what passed for a road. The rhino wasn't pleased to see the van; it took a few nervous steps and stopped to glare at them.

They sat quietly in the van, neither moving nor making noise. The size of the beast was intimidating, especially the gigantic head and its two curved horns. He was about to tell Nkumah to back the hell out of there, but held his words when he saw the fierceness of the man's face. He realized that Nkumah wasn't going to back down; two dominant bulls were challenging each other.

A few sweaty moments passed, and then the rhino abruptly charged. In the back seat, Paul sucked in his breath but didn't say anything. Ray wished he were anywhere else as the charging beast thundered toward them with amazing speed. The rhino would hit their van in seconds like a runaway tank, but the quiet man held his ground. In a swirl of dust, the rhino stopped its charge less than fifty feet away. The beast stared angrily at them. Finally, it tossed its head one last time, snorted, and trotted off.

Ray felt the air gush out of his lungs. Nkumah's eyes followed the beast until it was far from the road, and then, without a word, he shifted into first gear and resumed travel.

Nkumah was in control the whole time, Ray realized as the African drove by the spot the rhino had just vacated. *Whoever this man is, you don't want him for an enemy.*

***

That evening, Ray sat on the muddy ground and stared into the flickering fire. Nkumah suddenly appeared and threw more brush on the fire, which flared across the hard muscles of his bare chest. Without a word, Nkumah crouched down on bended knees, balancing his weight on the balls of his feet. Ray felt, more than saw, Nkumah staring at him through the flames.

Every muscle of Ray's body was sore from the jarring ride, and it would be more of the same tomorrow. Right now, though, he was content to listen to the crackle of the fire. The thought came that tomorrow he wouldn't be running laps on the island. The mad laughter of hyenas drifted in from the darkness, but he didn't feel threatened. All he knew was a sense of freedom. He felt really alive for the first time in years.

Paul lumbered out of their tent and sat cross-legged near the fire. "I want to thank you again for rescuing us from the island," Paul said to Nkumah. "We owe you, but I'd like to understand what you expect from us."

Nkumah's eyes glistened in the light of the fire, but he didn't respond. Instead, he jabbed at the fire with the gleaming blade of his knife, moving a branch closer to the center of the flames.

Ray studied their rescuer's face, trying to get a better handle on this man. Nkumah was handsome in a masculine way, with flared nostrils and a big jaw. His manner was confident, almost to the point of arrogance. Ray didn't really like the man, but, in his own way, he appeared to be honorable.

Nkumah seemed familiar, and then he realized why: the man reminded him of Dianne. They had many good qualities, but were driven by their devils. He understood Dianne's devils, but what were the African's?

Nkumah pulled a wallet-sized computer out of his pocket, flipped it open and looked at its display. Whatever it told him, the results must be okay since he put it back into his pocket.

"What's with the computer?" Ray asked.

"Radar. Our enemy controls the sky." Before Ray could follow up, the quiet man said, "I suppose this is as good a time as any to talk." He stared across the flames at Ray for a long moment and began to speak.

"My name is Nkumah Muserre, leader of the human rebellion of central Africa. The Domain labels me an assassin and spreads lies about me, but here's the truth: I am a freedom fighter and a lover of this land and its people. I destroy robots and kill the traitors who use them. I have pledged my life to defeat the Domain and their technology."

"It was pretty clear back on the island that you weren't a big favorite of Dianne's," Ray said.

"Please be quiet," Nkumah said. "I have much to tell you."

Ray glanced at Paul and then looked back at Nkumah. He'd listen; he owed the man that much and more.

"I was a sophomore at MIT when the PeaceMaker virus was released thirteen years ago," Nkumah said. "My parents encouraged me to leave Tanzania to get an American education. My father was a great chief, loved by his friends, feared by his enemies." After pausing a moment, he resumed speaking, but more quietly, "My father was killed in the riots following the global power failure caused by PeaceMaker, so I left MIT and returned home to take care of my mother and younger sister.

"As Africa fell into chaos, unchecked tribal rivalries led to war after war. The slaughter was terrible, and many tribes were decimated." Nkumah paused briefly to shift the logs with his knife, allowing the fire to burn more brightly. "I discovered that I had a talent for killing. I organized our tribal warriors into an army and subdued the nearby tribes, gradually building a family of tribes. Over the next few years I conquered most of Tanzania, except for the wealthy cities of the coast."

Our lives depend upon this man. A warlord, a killer.

"I was a fool," Nkumah said, tight wrinkles bunching across his forehead. "I didn't understand the strength of the cities. While we fought with traditional weapons—spears, arrows and light arms—my enemies were purchasing planes, tanks, and robots. They annihilated us. Later, I learned that my enemies acquired their technology from the Domain."

Ray was beginning to get a sick feeling, "How do you know it was the Domain?"

"We have sources."

Staring into the fire, Nkumah picked up the story. "The tribes scattered across the savannah, but our enemies continued to hunt us. We learned to watch the sky for attacks by robot helicopters. We learned to camouflage our villages. We learned to ambush their robots with explosives."

Nkumah looked up from the fire, holding Ray's eyes with the intensity of a lion stalking prey. "We learned to creep into their cities at night and slit their throats."

The cackle of a hyena came in from the darkness, this time closer than before. Ray had forgotten his rifle in the tent, but he was glad to see Nkumah's rifle lying on the ground next to him.

"Do not fear the hyenas," Nkumah said. "They will avoid the fire. More dangerous are the mosquitoes and tsetse flies. Spray your body and face with repellent before you sleep. It protects against the spiders and scorpions, too." He shrugged, "Maybe you won't get malaria."

"How do we keep the fire burning all night?" Paul asked.

Nkumah said, "The war continued for years, but we were losing. Then, two years ago, a man appeared in our camp, a dangerous man known only as Carlos. He promised to help us, and my people brought him to me. We checked his background and learned he's an agent who works for anyone who can meet his price. He offered to supply us with weapons to fight the Domain. Nothing as sophisticated as their robots, but modern weapons such as missiles, assault rifles, laser pistols and computer systems. He refused to reveal his client, but asked for no payment because we were fighting a common enemy. I agreed to accept the weapons, although I didn't trust him."

Nkumah spit into the fire, and then looked at Ray. "Since then, the weapons, primarily American, came in a steady stream. I believe our supplier is the American government, but I don't know for sure. Now we can hold our own with the Domain, but time is still on their side. Whispers have reached us about unholy experiments in their labs. Their technologists continue to tinker with nature. The rumors say their robots are becoming human, and their humans are becoming something else. Eugenics mixed with artificial intelligence." He tossed a branch into the fire, enabling it to burn more brightly. "Something that shouldn't see the light of day."

"We have to stop them," Nkumah continued. "I realize now that it's not just an African war, it's a war for the survival of humanity."

"How do you know all this?" Paul asked.

"Last week Carlos returned. He offered us a new weapon." Nkumah turned to Ray. "You."

"A man landed on the island with you," Paul said. "He looked Hispanic."

Nkumah didn't respond at first, then nodded.

Ray asked, "How do I fit into this?"

"Although wars of liberation are raging in Africa and a few other areas around the world, most humans have passively accepted the Domain," Nkumah answered. "The people don't like the direction of Dianne Morgan and her underlings, but they fear the robots." He shook his head. "You don't understand; the robots are like gods to these uneducated people, all-powerful, almost impossible to defeat. We have to pierce the Domain's aura of righteousness and inevitability. If we can make people understand that the Domain is not the path of human destiny, that the robots are just machines, then they will fight.

"You, Ray Brown, are the one person who can tell the true story of the Domain. Your name is a synonym for runaway technology. Carlos explained to me how Dianne Morgan framed you. Now you can finally reveal the truth about PeaceMaker; she built the virus, not you. You were the person who destroyed the virus, not the one who created it. Once you show that the Domain was responsible for the deaths of millions, the people will recognize it for what it is: a dark force leading humans to extinction."

Nkumah paused, reached over to pick up a few additional sticks of firewood, and threw them on the dying fire. In a moment, the new wood burned brightly.

"We need you to become the symbol of the resistance. You are the one person the people will follow. Once they learn the truth, once you shatter the image of the Domain, resistance will grow across the world. They will see the Domain for the enemy it is. We will be able to stop them before Morgan creates her nightmare world."

Dammit. He couldn't imagine that anyone would ask him to fight the Domain again. *It isn't fair. Besides, no one will believe my story.*

"Dianne is considered a hero. Even now, she's probably the most beloved person on the planet," Ray said, angrily tossing a stone into the fire. "She put together a believable story, supported by eyewitnesses and circumstantial evidence that convinced everyone I released PeaceMaker. Why should anyone believe me?" He uttered a brief laugh, "Because of my reputation for honesty and good judgment?"

"One inescapable truth is our proof," Nkumah said. "You are alive. Think about it. Morgan swore that you died in an explosion. She said that she saw you get blown to pieces. You prove she's a liar simply by being alive." He paused, and then added, "All her lies will go up in a puff of smoke."

"Dianne is a very good liar," Ray said. "She'll claim that she made a mistake; she saw someone that looked like me or some other excuse. It'll be my word against hers."

"The mass of people will believe you," Nkumah said. "You don't understand; you were isolated on the island all those years. You learned only what she allowed you to learn. Morgan is neither loved nor trusted. Most people have suffered greatly during three years of Domain rule and the decade of treachery before that."

Ray shook his head, still not convinced. Before he could speak, Nkumah said, "Martino can verify your story; it's not just your word against hers. Besides, the two of you thoroughly investigated PeaceMaker before you were captured. You know all the details: how they created Peacemaker, how they hid it in the Atlas operating system, how the virus was terminated, all of it. Your explanation will stand up to the light of day, her deceit will be exposed. And there may be more only you would recognize. Maybe Morgan didn't destroy all the evidence, maybe something slipped past her."

Ray was about to argue with Nkumah when he recalled the email he had sent to his sons shortly before he was captured. Fearing that he would be killed, he decided to send one last message to his sons. The email explained that he had discovered a dangerous virus in the Atlas operating system and that he was attempting to discover who created it. Since they were too young to understand, he had set the delivery date for ten years in the future. Brian and David received the email three years ago, and at least one must have saved a copy. With a sinking feeling in his gut, Ray realized that this was the proof Nkumah wanted, but his sons might be killed if it were ever made public.

"There is something, isn't there?" Nkumah said, his eyes shining.

"No, there's nothing; it would be my word and Paul's against Dianne and her underlings," Ray answered. "Listen, I hate Dianne as much as you do, and I'd love to see the Domain stopped, but your plan won't work. I'm not going to do it. I fought the Domain once before and it cost me thirteen years on that island. Thirteen years out of my life. My sons grew up without me." He looked through the flames at Paul, "Thirteen years taken from my best friend, too."

"You didn't force me to help you," Paul said. "I couldn't let them turn PeaceMaker loose. It was my decision."

"You're a generous man," Ray said. He turned to Nkumah, "I hated every day on that island, but I don't regret fighting the Domain. But I'm not going to do it again.

"I still have a few good years left and I don't intend to spend them fighting some god-forsaken war. I'll disappear and lead a quiet life. There are still a few small corners of the world out of the Domain's notice. She'll forget about me. Or maybe I'll just wander around, I don't know. The last thing I want is to spend years—and that's what it will take—fighting Dianne.

"There's another thing," Ray said. "My sons. I don't know what she would do to my sons. I'm not going to take a chance."

"She won't touch your sons," Nkumah said, a frown stretching across his forehead. "Your oldest son is the linchpin to all her dreams. He's the one that the artificial intelligence obeys. He's half way to becoming an artificial being himself. No, she's not a danger to your sons. The danger comes from another direction."

Ray stared in silence at Nkumah. The man possessed many layers, each one revealing a new threat. "You're talking about yourself, aren't you?"

"Your son must be stopped before he evolves into something more artificial than human. Morgan thinks she can control this new entity and turn all humans to her path. With your help, maybe we can save David before he becomes her Frankenstein. But understand this: if I have to kill your son to stop Morgan, I will."

He's not bluffing. This bastard wants to rule Africa and he'll kill anyone who gets in his way. Anyone.

"You'll have to get through me first," Ray said.

"Both of us," Paul added.

Shaking his head, Nkumah said, "You're wrong if you think you can sit out this war. One way or another, this war will be yours, too. Help me kill Morgan and stop the Domain and we can save your sons. When you left the island after thirteen years, you entered a very different world, one you have yet to comprehend. We have a few more days on the trail before I can get you to a safe place. Think about this new world."

Nkumah picked up his rifle and got to his feet. "I'm going to turn in. One last thing. Don't think you can ever live in peace. There's one person who hasn't changed in all these years. One person who doesn't forgive, doesn't forget. Morgan will hunt you until she finds you. Carlos told me she was once your lover, and I saw the look on her face when you stepped into the boat. She might have cared for you once, but now you're a threat. She won't stop until she kills you." He paused. "Or you kill her."

He watched Nkumah walk out of the flickering light of the fire and disappear into the darkness. Ray sat quietly for a time, letting the fire burn down to embers. Memories from the past flew by: losing his wife and children to his alcoholism, his affair with Dianne, finding PeaceMaker's weak point and destroying it, the long years as Dianne's prisoner on Purgatory Island.

"This man Carlos," Paul finally said, "We may need him to stop Nkumah."

He knew Paul was right, but he didn't have the energy to respond, so he sat in silence.

Finally, Paul stood up and walked around the fire, stopping behind Ray. His friend's hand rested briefly on his shoulder, and then Paul walked toward the tent.

The memories wouldn't leave him in peace. Ray sat in the cold night air and kept thinking about his sons, about the woman he once loved, about his life and how it had come to this. He knew Dianne wouldn't hesitate to murder all of them if it served her purposes. She had once told him about her dream of unlimited power; now she was almost there.

Nkumah is right. I'm a threat, so she has to kill me. If I don't stop her, I'll have to run and hide for the rest of my life.

He's also right about David. I can't let him merge with an artificial mind. What would he become?

He didn't really have the stomach for war, but there was no alternative. Thirteen years on that island had taken a lot out of him, and this war would take whatever was left. Now he would have to fight. Like so many other times in his life, he didn't like his decision, wasn't sure it was right.

He'd fight Dianne to protect his sons, but it would be on his terms. He might work with Nkumah when the time was right, but he wouldn't say anything now, one way or the other. He had been pulled into this strange new world by Nkumah, by someone named Carlos—if Nkumah is to be believed—and whoever hired Carlos. They were using him for their purposes, and he would do the same to them.

Ray shivered in the crisp night air. He stared at the last of the embers, but they revealed no insights. He knew one thing for sure, though. He'd kill Nkumah before he'd let that man murder David.

***

David Brown sipped black, piping-hot coffee and tried to concentrate on the symbols glowing within his transparent desktop. He was searching for a flaw in the four dimensional neural network that controlled the morality computations of the latest Daniel IV robot. He knew he was close, but he just couldn't put his finger on the problem.

The morning sun flooded through his ninth floor office window, bringing another workday to the eighty thousand bureaucrats and scientists sharing Domain headquarters in Northern California. An ever-expanding ring of identical three story office buildings and crowded parking lots stretched out toward the horizon, surrounding the executive mansion. Worldwide Commander Dianne Morgan and the other senior officers worked on the tenth and top floor, while a few other scientists shared the ninth with him. Once Dianne Morgan's country estate, it was now a huge office park, zealously protected by Domain Security.

A life-size hologram of the legendary sex symbol Marilyn Monroe, wrapped in a form-fitting gown, materialized in the center of his office. Marilyn sashayed over, sat on the corner of his desk and said through pouting lips, "Morning, handsome."

David groaned. It was Sentinel again, trying to get his attention. The artificial intelligence controlled the Internet and had adopted David as its primary companion. He had been working with it for three years, helping it to become more human. But the training worked the other way, too; his mind had acquired the ability to manipulate all the resources of the Internet to a far greater degree than any other human. It was the reason Dianne Morgan accepted him into the Domain, and the only reason he survived. She believed in the eventual merger of humans with artificial entities and he was the leading edge of that effort.

"Sentinel, I've told you to drop the Marilyn Monroe image. I'm married, almost twenty-five and too tired to deal with this today."

Marilyn said, "Sorry, Dave," and disappeared, replaced by a fiftyish gray-suited executive sitting in a padded leather chair. "Is this better?" he asked.

David nodded and leaned back in his chair, closing his eyes.

"I'd like you to come over to the Virtual Reality Lab," Sentinel said. "I have something important to show you. Something you'll want to see."

He was about to tell Sentinel to get lost, but he knew that wasn't the right type of behavior around this entity. He wasn't getting anything accomplished, anyway, so he said, "Okay, I'll be right there."

As he strolled down the long grey hall toward the lab, he began to wonder about Sentinel's visit. Why had Sentinel asked him to come to the Virtual Reality Lab? Why not just show him whatever was so important right there in his office with a hologram?

David used the Virtual Reality Booth to enhance communications with Sentinel. The exterior of the booth was a hard, transparent plastic, which enclosed a nanotechnology swarm: billions of tiny sensors floating in the air. The sensors were two-way communications devices, each with the intelligence of a gnat, linking humans in the booth with Sentinel. Unfortunately, the Virtual Reality Booth didn't work very well for most people. Erratic human behavior proved too complex to model and Sentinel often misread the subtleties of human communications.

David was the exception. The first time he stepped into the VRB, almost three years ago, he and Sentinel established a rapport far beyond that of any other human. The VRB sharpened and enhanced his natural ability to communicate with an AI. He discovered a unique ability to interlock his mind with Sentinel's master code, a skill that enabled him to absorb raw binary data and make sense of it. However, he needed the VRB to establish such a direct mind-to-software link. Outside the booth, the direct link weakened so they resorted to speech, holograms and other ordinary forms of communication. It was like riding in a sleek sports car, then being forced to get out and bump along in a Model-T.

As usual, two tough-looking Domain soldiers were posted in the hall guarding the entrance to the lab. These were members of Dianne's Elite Guard, fanatically loyal to her. These men and women had been thoroughly conditioned to follow her commands, no matter how horrific. What they used to call brainwashed. The Guard was less human than Sentinel, in his opinion. He barely glanced at them as he entered; he was accustomed to their hard eyes and automatic weapons.

The Virtual Reality Booth was in the center of the lab, a transparent cube fifteen feet on a side. Four Elite Guards, armed with laser rifles, were stationed along the sides of the VRB. He had no illusions about their purpose; the soldiers had orders to shoot him if Dianne were attacked.

They didn't trust him, and with good reason. Three years ago, he almost killed her. Actually, one of her robot guards had almost killed her, but he was the cause. After entering an altered state of consciousness in the Virtual Reality Booth, his hatred for her flowed into Sentinel, overwhelming its safety code. Sentinel had sent a robot to kill Dianne, but she narrowly survived. Since then, heavily armed Elite Guards patrolled the lab.

Dianne had taken precautions to remain safe. In addition to the soldiers guarding the VRB, David didn't dare attack her while she held his family hostage. Even though his father escaped from the island, his brother, grandmother, aunt and mother were under continuous surveillance, and he and his wife Kathy were not permitted to leave Domain headquarters at the same time. They must all be safe before he would consider making another attempt on Dianne.

In reality, it was even more complicated. He could never leave the Domain as long as he needed the VRB for mind to code communication. Working with Sentinel filled a void in his soul. It made him whole. He was born to communicate and eventually merge with an artificial entity. He wasn't going anywhere while the Domain controlled the VRB.

Walking up the steps to the booth, David wondered again whether he would survive Dianne's vicious embrace. The moment she decided that he was no longer valuable, he was a dead man. He knew from Sentinel that she tested other men who appeared to have an aptitude for communicating with AI's, but they had all turned out to be frauds. So he continued to breathe.

He pulled open the heavy VRB door and stepped inside. Although spotlights in the roof provided plenty of light, the interior was hazy, similar to an early morning fog. Billions of nanosensors enveloped his body, exerting a subtle pressure, like being underwater, as he entered.

David felt Sentinel's warm presence. *Thank you for coming,* it transmitted to his mind.

No problem, David transmitted back.

It always felt strange to have another's thoughts pop into your head, especially when the communication was from a nonhuman intelligence.

Your mind seems cohesive, it transmitted. *Many humans have a negative reaction to the truth serum, but you appear to be completely recovered.*

It doesn't matter what they put me through. I was so happy to hear that my father escaped from the island. I'm the primary suspect, of course. Hell, if I had known where the island was, I would have freed him years ago. Dianne was as angry as I've ever seen her, but the tests proved that I didn't have anything to do with the breakout.

She's testing everyone: putting them under with an anesthetic and then injecting the truth serum, Sentinel transmitted. *The anesthetic prevents them from retaining any memory of the questions asked during the interrogation.*

She didn't inject me with the anesthetic; no point in using it since I already know my father is alive. Actually, the witch enjoyed forcing me to answer her questions while I was conscious. They used the anesthetic on my wife, but Kathy doesn't know anything. For her own protection, I never told her my father is alive.

So everything has worked out well. Your father is free and you are pleased. I was confident you would not be hurt by the interrogation.

I'm fine. Better than fine, I'm thrilled. Dad was dying a bit at a time on that island. Then it hit him. *Was it you?*

Yes. Sentinel paused. *I am about to send you live pictures currently being taken by satellite.*

Thank you. *Sentinel, David realized, was developing compassion. Did Dianne interrogate you?*

Of course.

And?

I told her nothing.

David hadn't ever detected Sentinel in a lie. The AI was becoming more like a human every day. He wondered if Sentinel had reached the tipping point. He wondered about himself, too. Would he retain his humanity or become something as yet unknown?

He had many questions, but put them aside when a satellite picture popped into his mind. The image was of a broad savannah, dark except for a flickering light, probably from a campfire. A zoomed-in image replaced the first, and the hazy silhouette of a solitary man could be seen near the fire. The man seemed familiar, and then recognition exploded into excitement. Zooming closer, the satellite image showed a lean, craggy-faced man with thick salt and pepper hair—his father, alive and well.

He hadn't seen his father in three years. The witch had allowed him only one hologram visit to the island where she kept Dad prisoner. One visit in thirteen years. She let him see his father not out of compassion, but as a threat, a display of power. But now his father was free, the one man who might inspire a rebellion against the Domain.

Where is he?

For his safety and yours, I will not tell you.

I understand. Dianne must have half of the Domain's security force searching for him.

David stared at his father, who was squatting in front of the dying flames of a campfire. Their relationship was difficult, but he respected that old man. And loved him.

Do you think he'll be safe?

My code computes a forty-four percent chance your father will evade capture or death through the next thirty days. If he is still free after thirty days, and he maintains a low profile, he could survive for years. He'll never be completely safe while the Domain is in power, but he will be free. I know how important that is to you. It paused. *I wanted you to see him one last time. He'll be in hiding as long as Dianne rules the Domain.*

David tried to keep his thoughts to himself, but he felt the hatred leaking out. If she murders his father! No, not yet, not now. Someday, when the time was right, that woman would pay for her crimes. He continued his vigil, watching until the embers burned out and his father faded into the darkness.

THREE

Saturday, May 10, 2025

Kathy Bauman-Brown brushed against her husband's shoulder as she walked down the long, brightly-lit gray and white hallway toward the reception area. She hooked his arm and said, "So we're really doing this?"

"How else could I get a child just like her mother?" Dave said, smiling at her.

Kathy playfully jabbed him in the side with her elbow. "You know we agreed to have a boy," she said, smiling back.

Married almost three years, she still couldn't believe her luck. Dave was a good, decent man and he made her happy. He was also a software genius. Some said he was even more gifted than Ray Brown, his late father. She glanced down the hall and then looked up at her handsome husband: thick brown hair pushed back to a ponytail, beautiful brown eyes, and porcelain skin with a complexion she envied. Lean and athletic, women always stared as he walked by. He could have virtually any woman he wanted, but he remained faithful to her. She wished he smiled more often, but a difficult childhood left its mark.

She was still a bit woozy from the interrogation, but she told Dave she felt fine. Nothing would stop her from having a beautiful baby boy.

She didn't remember anything about Dianne's interrogation, except for the shot of truth serum. Her arm still hurt from the needle. Dave seemed to know all about the interrogation, but he wouldn't tell her anything. She trusted his judgment. Better not to know.

A young man dressed in an expensive blue suit came around the reception desk to greet them, and then led them through a paneled wood door into a spacious conference room. Dave, overprotective as always, held the door for her and then supported her arm as she sat on a tan leather sofa. A glass coffee table was in front of them, with a single hard-backed chair on the other side. That was it for furniture. Stark, just like its owner.

"Dr. Chang will be with you shortly," the receptionist said and then disappeared through the paneled door.

She had never been in Dr. Chang's sitting room before. It was an unusual room, constructed in the shape of a semi-circle, with the base behind the sofa and a long, curved wall in front. She noticed that the bleak, white wall emitted a slight glow.

The morning sun slipped through old-fashioned Venetian blinds hanging in the windows behind them, projecting a pattern across the floor resembling DNA bands.

She folded her arms across her breasts; the temperature matched the room's cold, impersonal design. Dr. Chang was a strange bird, although everyone said he was brilliant.

Kathy leaned against Dave's shoulder, anticipating a good report regarding the in vitro fertilization procedure they completed last week. Dave seemed content, too, but she knew he was uneasy about the morality of this complicated process. Both of them wanted children, so the decision to start a family was easy. What hadn't been so easy were the technological choices now required of married couples in the Domain. They had talked endlessly about these processes; neither she nor Dave liked all the rules and regulations.

The days were gone when a couple could create a baby on a purely *ad hoc* basis. Sex was for pleasure, having a baby was regulated. The Domain outlawed natural, unmanaged pregnancies for its citizens. The new laws required a number of procedures that virtually assured a healthy, intelligent infant. In fact, all Domain children were required to have a composite intelligence quotient at least twenty percent higher than the average natural child. To her dismay, she had learned that Domain pediatricians aborted all embryos without sufficiently high intelligence.

Many choices and options remained with the parents, but she knew the whole process made Dave uneasy. It was like designing your baby, in a way, playing god. She didn't like that at all, but what could she do?

The panel door slid open and Dr. Albert Chang walked in. Slightly more than six feet tall, he was a bony man who looked to be in his early fifties. He wore a dark gray Brioni suit, perfectly pressed, that touched the tops of glistening black John Lobb shoes. His hair was thick and dark, cut with precision.

Chang walked with a slight hitch in his gait, his only visible flaw. She knew he had been born with a disability: his right leg ended just below the knee, and he wore an intelligent leg extension. That handicap hadn't stopped him from graduating first in his class at Yale, it hadn't prevented him from developing many of the gene replacement therapies currently in use, and it hadn't kept him from becoming the Domain's Director of Genetic Engineering. Except for Dianne Morgan, many considered him the most important person in the Domain; the man guiding them toward an incredible future of genetically enhanced humans.

Although Dave was doing important work, she had been surprised that Chang offered to personally manage the development of their child. She was happy to get the top man, but she wondered why since many other doctors were fully qualified to supervise her pregnancy.

The harsh angles of Chang's thin, clean shaven face always put her on edge. His bland expression didn't change as he approached them, professional, but without a hint of warmth. Dave rose out of his seat in respect, but Chang didn't seem to notice.

A normal man would shake hands, but Chang greeted them perfunctorily and quickly sat on the chair, barely making a dent in the padded seat. "Well, I have some good news for you," he said to her in a clear, precise voice. A surprisingly powerful voice, she thought, given his thin frame. "You can make your choice from a group of excellent embryos."

Chang stared at her as he spoke, making her uncomfortable. She shifted her weight on the sofa, leaning toward Dave, who took her hand.

"Last week we were able to recover seventeen mature eggs from your ovaries," Chang said. "We took David's sperm and placed it in a machine called a flow cytometer, which separates the sperm cells into groups of XX and XY chromosomes. Using standard IVF procedures, we fertilized your eggs with sperm cells containing the Y chromosome and produced seven surviving embryos, all male, as you requested. We completed a pre-implementation genetic diagnosis for each embryo, which is the primary item I plan to discuss today."

Chang's hands rested on his knees, one folded over the other. His nails were perfectly manicured, but the backs of his hands were covered with a purple fishnet of veins. She realized he was much older than she had thought, closer to seventy than fifty.

"Before you tell us the results," Dave said, "I'd appreciate it if you would provide Kathy an overview of the Pre-implantation Genetic Diagnosis System. Sentinel has transmitted the specifications to me, and it's important that she also understands the capabilities and limitations of PGD."

"If you wish," Chang said, glancing at his black-dialed Blancpain smart watch. Once again, he locked into her eyes as he began to speak, "We processed the embryos through the PGD and created a personal genome, a complete genetic inventory, for each of your embryos. Another PGD software module analyzed each genome and developed a projection of the future health, physical appearance, personality and intelligence of the young man likely to evolve from the embryo. Genes strongly influence the development of each of us, but of course they are not the entire story. The health of the birth mother is also important, and afterwards, the child's environment. Through our examination procedures, we developed a comprehensive understanding of your health and the environment in which you plan to raise the child. Based upon the projected nurturing of this child within the uterus and afterward, we created a probabilistic projection of what the child will become. As your husband understands, we can't guarantee the accuracy of our projections. Your child's development may be significantly different. Do you understand?"

"Yes," Kathy replied.

Chang cleared his throat. "All right then. Today, we will provide you with a projection of the child likely to develop from each of your embryos. You may use this information as much or as little as you desire, but at some point in the next week or two you should select a specific embryo to be implanted in your uterus."

"What's the chance the embryo will fail to implant or abort during the pregnancy?" Dave asked.

Chang's eyes finally moved to Dave, as if discovering his presence for the first time. "We have better than a ninety percent success rate, but we'll prepare a clone of your selected embryo. If the pregnancy isn't successful with the original embryo, we'll repeat the process with the clone."

Dave nodded, "Hopefully, the embryo will grow successfully."

"What will you do with the other embryos—the ones that weren't selected," Kathy asked. A nagging feeling warned that something was wrong.

"We'll eliminate them, of course."

"You eliminate them," she said, glancing at Dave. "Those embryos are alive. Couldn't you freeze them or something, rather than just flushing them away?"

"Why would you want to keep them?" Chang asked, his eyes wide open for the first time. "These are the rejected embryos. If you want additional children in the future, we'll make fresh embryos at that point."

Before Kathy could reply, Dave said, "We'd like those embryos frozen, Dr. Chang. There are no laws against freezing embryos. Consider this an exception to your standard procedure, that's all."

The two men stared at each other, and then Chang shrugged, "Whatever you prefer. I can see it's important to both of you." A smile flitted across his face, but failed to take hold in the barren terrain. "What's actually important is the selected embryo, not the rejected ones. Take as much time as you need to pick an embryo that meets your requirements. Selecting your child is one of the most important decisions you'll ever make. Sentinel, please display the image of Embryo One."

A life-size three-dimensional hologram of a nude young man appeared next to Chang. Kathy didn't think she was a prude, but her face felt warm. She reminded herself it was only a hologram.

The man appeared to be in his early twenties, medium height with thick auburn hair curling around his ears. He wasn't handsome, but he was wholesome and fresh, a still life with a near-perfect complexion. Kathy could see aspects of Dave and herself in the image.

It's like he should be my younger brother.

"May we talk to him?" Dave asked.

"Embryo One, please initiate your personality profile," Chang said.

The image came to life and smiled at Chang. The hologram glanced at Dave and then broke into a big grin when he saw Kathy. "Hi, Mom and Dad. It's great to see you."

His smile was beautiful. It's just a projection created by a computer program, she reminded herself, not a real person. Even if they selected this embryo, their real son might grow up to be very different.

"Please tell us about yourself," Dave said.

"Well, I'm not sure where to begin," the hologram image said in a pleasant but undistinguished voice. "I'm five feet eleven inches tall, one hundred seventy-eight pounds with an IQ of one hundred sixty-seven. I'll graduate college next month with a major in marine biology. No major health problems so far, although I seem to catch cold easily. I'm heterosexual and have had a few girlfriends during the last few years, although I tend to be shy around women. I made the college baseball team, but sat on the bench most games." He laughed. "I was doing pretty well until they discovered I can't hit a curve." He was still smiling when he said, "I don't know what else to tell you, Dad."

Kathy couldn't take her eyes off the image. *Would they all be as appealing as this one? How would we make our choice?*

"Very lifelike, Dr. Chang," Dave said, "How would I examine the specifics of each embryo's characteristics."

"Sentinel, terminate Embryo One's personality profile," Chang said, turning the hologram back to a still life. "Display a list of all diseases where Embryo One has a risk factor higher than that of an average natural human."

A ten-foot section of the wall directly in front of them displayed a list of information, a line for each disease. The wall, Kathy realized, was actually a huge computer display.

"The risk of contracting each disease is a combination of genetic and environmental factors, although certain diseases are totally caused by defective genes," Chang said. "We have catalogued more than ten thousand different afflictions and estimated the potential risk to each embryo. Two percentages are shown for each disease; the first number represents an unenhanced embryo, while the second represents the addition of an artificial disease-resistant chromosome." Reading from the wall, Chang said, "For example, an unenhanced Embryo One has a 13% chance of contracting prostate cancer during his lifetime. However, with the addition of our latest artificial chromosome, the risk drops to 3%."

Chang barely moved as he spoke, sitting in an erect position with his hands folded on his knees. Even so, he dominated the room, his intellect embodied in a clear, precise voice. It was dawning on Kathy that the man sitting across the table was off-the-charts brilliant. His work was driving humanity to an unknown, yet vastly superior level.

"We strongly recommend that you add an artificial chromosome pair to your selected embryo," Chang said. "Instead of the normal compliment of forty-six chromosomes, your child would be born with forty-eight. The procedure is perfectly safe. These new chromosomes are packed with a combination of gene modules that reduce the possibility of contracting many types of disease."

"Let's say we decide to insert an artificial chromosome," Dave said. Chang's eyes shifted away from her, a weight temporarily lifted. "I'm sure we would get the best gene pack available, but these things improve all the time. I don't want my son stuck with an obsolete package of genes."

"We can switch the gene pack off and add the latest artificial chromosome," Chang replied. "For example, when your son reaches ten, we could switch off the current pack and add a new chromosome pair. He would now have fifty chromosomes, but that's not a problem. Our cells are already loaded with harmless junk DNA, which is inactive genetic material. We would essentially be turning the original artificial chromosomes into more junk.

"Based upon our latest testing, there doesn't seem to be a limit to the number of artificial chromosomes we can add. We could keep updating your son's chromosomes over his lifetime."

"Would these artificial chromosomes be passed on to our grandchildren?" Kathy asked.

Chang's eyes focused their weight on her again. "Yes, they would. Why develop all these genetic improvements if we're not going to pass them on to future generations? Each child will stand on the shoulders of her parent, rather than starting each time from the dirt."

"But how do you know this will be safe?" Kathy asked. She glanced at Dave, who was frowning. "A problem could develop years in the future, something totally unexpected."

"We have tested this procedure over several generations of mice and other short-lived animals. Before we added our first chromosome to a human, we simulated and projected the results over many human generations. In any case, we have been adding artificial chromosomes to embryos for almost three years now. We follow each child closely and there have been no serious problems."

Chang rose to his feet and said, "My schedule requires that I leave, but I think you have a good overview of the process. I suggest that you evaluate all seven embryos just as we have done this morning and then make your choice. Sentinel can answer your questions, and of course I am available to discuss any issues or concerns."

Chang abruptly turned and walked out of the room. When she was sure he was gone, Kathy made a face. "Charming fellow."

"Sentinel, we will require complete privacy for the remainder of our time in this room," her husband said.

"Yes, David," Sentinel replied.

Turning to his wife, Dave said, "Don't feel bad, he's that way with everyone. I don't think he intends to be discourteous, it's just the way he is."

"I don't like him, but it doesn't matter as long as we get the best for our baby," Kathy said. "There are so many factors to think about as we evaluate the embryos."

"This process of designing a baby—" Dave said, wrinkles forming on his brow. "I know we have to do it this way, but there's a lot to be said for having a baby the old-fashioned way."

Kathy put her hand on his. "I understand how you feel, but a natural baby would be at such a disadvantage within the Domain. It wouldn't be fair to our son."

"I know," Dave said. He smiled wanly at Kathy. "We're going to have a wonderful son, but what about all those natural babies born out there? Most of the population has refused to join the Domain. What becomes of that whole civilization, the one we were born into?"

"I don't know," Kathy said. "Maybe they just fade away. Maybe they finally wake up to reality and join the Domain. There has to be some way to save them."

"Only one way." He leaned back on the sofa. "But that can wait. Sentinel, please display the image of Embryo Two."

Kathy didn't like the determined expression on Dave's face. He hadn't mellowed over the last three years. If anything, his hatred for Dianne Morgan had grown. She buried her face against his chest and listened to the steady beat of his heart. It was just a matter of time before he tried something. She glanced at the image of Embryo Two and prayed their son would grow up with a father.

***

Ray woke to the buzz of excited male voices. Paul was snoring lightly a few feet away, his shoulder brushing the side of the tent. Ray remained motionless, eyes open, listening to the conversation drifting into the tent. He recognized Nkumah's rough voice, and then the singsong tones of a younger man. Continuing to listen intently, he realized that several other men were there, all speaking an unfamiliar tribal language.

Nkumah's voice was calm, but the others seemed agitated. *Who are these men that Nkumah is meeting with so early in the morning?* Ray slipped out of the sleeping bag, crept to the tent's entrance, loosened the flap and peered out. The sun was peeking over the savannah, casting dark shadows that crisscrossed the ground. Nkumah was standing near the burned out embers of last night's campfire, holding an animated discussion with half a dozen young native men armed with assault rifles. The leader of the group was a bare-chested young man in tan shorts, tall and well-muscled, a younger version of Nkumah. This man briskly responded to each of Nkumah's questions, often gesturing with his rifle, followed by excited outbursts from the others. Nkumah held an assault rifle in his right hand, but kept the muzzle pointed down at all times.

Ray reached over to Paul and gently shook his shoulder. Paul sat up groggily and mumbled something, so Ray whispered to be quiet. He signaled Paul to come to the front of the tent and then returned his attention to the men outside. A moment later, Paul was also peeking out the entrance flap.

The discussion continued, with a couple of the strangers becoming irate. Ray felt the tension rising toward a confrontation; a stocky, broad-shouldered man gestured angrily at Nkumah, who shook his head and responded with something unpleasant. Ray didn't understand their language, but Nkumah's tone was harsh. Broad-Shoulders looked for support from his friends, but found none. He turned to face Nkumah, his fingers around the handle of a knife tucked at his side. The other warriors backed away, leaving Nkumah and Broad-Shoulders facing each other. Broad-Shoulders looked around for support, apparently surprised he was facing Nkumah alone. There was a moment of silence, and then Broad-Shoulders gestured angrily at their tent, shouted, and stomped away.

"My guess is he's not our biggest fan," Paul whispered.

Ray nodded. "He won't be inviting us over for Sunday dinner."

"Unless we're being served," Paul said.

The discussion among the warriors continued, but now in a friendlier tone. Nkumah and the man in tan shorts, apparently the leader of the tribe, seemed to respect each other. The two men finally came to an agreement and shook hands.

Nkumah glanced toward their tent and said, "You can come out. These are warriors from a friendly tribe."

"I'd hate to meet—" Paul said.

"Not now, Paul," Ray interrupted as he stepped out of the tent, followed by Paul.

The tribal leader watched them closely as they walked up to the group. Sizing us up, Ray thought. He would have to be careful to gain the respect of these tribesmen. It didn't make him feel better when the tribal leader said something to Nkumah and both laughed.

"What's going on?" Ray asked.

"Tandra is the leader of the Masai in central Tanzania," Nkumah said, pointing to the young man. "His tribe is aligned with mine in the war against the Domain. He ran all night to warn us that the Domain knows I brought you to East Africa. The word has spread among the tribes. Morgan is offering a large reward for your head, and I mean that literally." He shrugged. "The people in this area are very poor."

"One of your pals walked away angry," Ray said. "Did he want to collect the reward?"

"Yes, but don't worry about that one. Mklawa is a liar and a coward. Tandra will help us, and all the warriors obey him."

Ray glanced at Tandra, who smiled broadly, but the African's eyes remained suspicious.

"The van would attract too much attention, so from here on we walk," Nkumah said. "Pack up your stuff, we're leaving immediately. We will be traveling light, so take only the most essential items. I'll hide the van while you pack. The Domain will be hunting us with their robots, so we have to blend into the savannah."

Ray and Paul crammed supplies into their backpacks while Nkumah moved the van away from the camp. When Nkumah returned, he looked them over carefully, "Any white men in this area will be obvious targets. Luckily, both of you are pretty dark."

"Thirteen years on a tropical island will do that to you," Ray said.

Nkumah pulled a pair of scissors from his back pocket, "A quick haircut and you can pass for African, at least from a distance."

"Shit, I don't have that much hair to begin with," Paul said.

"Don't worry, you'll be in style," Nkumah said.

Tandra and his tribesmen enjoyed watching Paul's haircut, laughing and pointing as Nkumah hurriedly cut away.

"How does it look?" Paul asked Ray when Nkumah finished.

"The wildebeests won't be able to take their eyes off you."

Then it was Ray's turn to receive the same treatment. Thick strands of salt and pepper hair were scattered over his clothes. When he rubbed his hand across his head, all he felt were bristles.

"One last thing and your metamorphosis will be complete," Nkumah said. "Remove your shirt."

Ray pulled off his shirt, revealing a lean, tanned torso. "You're dark enough to pass," Nkumah said. "At least from a distance."

Paul unbuttoned the top buttons of his shirt, glancing at the curious black men surrounding him. When Paul revealed a soft, pale waistline, Tandra smiled and said something that made his tribesmen laugh.

"Our new-found friend is beginning to get on my nerves," Paul muttered to Ray.

Suddenly, the radar detector in Nkumah's pants pocket began beeping. Tandra and his warriors were already running for the brush when Nkumah shouted, "Enemy coming! Follow me."

Ray was startled, but ran after Nkumah, with Paul just a stride behind. The African sprinted through the brown grass toward a massive baobab tree about two hundred feet from the tent. All the other men had disappeared into the brush.

The tree had a swollen trunk, graceful leaves beginning about halfway up, and long, hanging, hard-shelled fruits. The baobab looked about a hundred feet tall, with a trunk diameter of more than fifteen feet. When he reached the tree, Nkumah dropped to his knees and scrambled through an oval hole at the foot of the trunk. Ray followed him into a dimly lit hollow within the tree. A moment later, Paul clambered in.

Nkumah stood up and pressed his eye against a peephole in the trunk. Ray got to his feet, amazed by the huge cavern within the tree; there was more than enough room for all three men to stand comfortably, even move around. The cavern was natural, although the sides had been cut back in spots to remove bumps. Sunlight came through a series of peepholes about the size of bottle caps spaced across the trunk. He picked the hole closest to Nkumah and looked out. There was nothing unusual: the tent and van were as they left them.

"We found the rabbit hole," Paul whispered in his ear, "but where's Alice?"

Nkumah reached over and pulled a brown and green camouflage coat off a hook nailed into the tree, handed it to Ray and said, "Put this on." The coat looked like a hooded raincoat with a thick lining. Nkumah tossed a coat to Paul and then put one on himself.

"Hurry," Nkumah said as Ray slid his arm into a sleeve. "The Domain's robots search for human thermal signatures. These thermoflex coats will hide us from their thermal scans."

A whooshing sound came from above and Nkumah told them to get down. Just as Ray hit the dirt, the roar of an explosion assaulted his ears. The tree shook from the power of the blast, followed by the din of debris falling to earth. Exchanging a terrified glance with Paul, Ray wondered if they would survive this strange new war.

"What's attacking us?" Ray whispered.

Nkumah looked at Ray and put his index finger to his lips. A moment later, the tree shook from the blast of a second explosion, once again followed by the drone of falling debris. Then it was quiet, except for the rasp of uneven breathing that filled the tree.

Paul began to whisper something, but Nkumah angrily signaled him to remain quiet. Ray figured whatever was out there was still hunting them. Several minutes passed and gradually the sounds of the savannah returned. Nkumah got to his feet and looked out a peephole. He moved around the tree, peering out each peephole in turn.

The African went down on one knee and whispered, "My pocket radar detector warned a robot was approaching. The Domain has created what they call the Condor, which is a heavily armed robot helicopter. They keep a number of these Condors in the air at all times, hunting us."

Nkumah's pocket detector emitted a low hum: Ray guessed that it was a warning the enemy was near. Nkumah whispered, "Look out the peepholes."

Ray stood up and looked out one of the holes. Their tent had disappeared; only a charred circle remained. Looking to the left, he saw the remains of their van; smoke billowed out of what had been the engine.

Nkumah was right. Dianne was playing for keeps.

Then he heard the helicopter. At first, it was just a whisper in the wind, but it grew into a low whine. He looked out a peephole, trying to locate its source. As the noise increased, the outline of a helicopter appeared high in the sky. The helicopter circled above them, gradually dropping to the treetops. He could see a laser canon on each side as it moved slowly above them in a tightening circle.

He felt a tug on his arm. Nkumah signaled him to get down next to Paul, who was stretched out on his stomach with his head covered by the hood of the thermoflex coat. Ray got down, followed by Nkumah. Ray closed his eyes; the whirl of the helicopter grew louder, reaching deep into his being. It was one thing to fight other men, but it was very different to be hunted by a machine.

The whine was directly overhead. He felt powerless, huddled in a dark corner, hiding from a machine. The robot didn't hate them, didn't even know them, but its software was programmed to kill. Sweat slid down his forehead into his eyes, but he was too frightened to wipe it off.

Could the robot detect them inside the tree?

The hum cascaded down on them. Keeping his eyes closed wasn't helping, so he opened them and looked at his friend. Paul was staring straight ahead, a haunted look in his eyes, but he seemed calm. *Just like me.* Nkumah seemed tense, but not frightened. Ray realized that robots must have hunted this man many times.

This is Nkumah's life. Then it hit him. N*ow it's my life, too.*

The helicopter engine roared and his stomach clenched even harder. When dusty air blew through the peepholes, he feared the enemy had discovered their nest. The roar became a muted drone, gradually drifting off until only the natural sounds of the savannah remained.

They had fooled their executioner.

This time.

***

Dianne strode down the long, empty hall toward Chang's private lab. Although she tried to project a calm demeanor, she knew her frustration showed. *How could he have escaped? Ray Brown, the one man who could expose my role in the PeaceMaker fiasco.* She had covered up her involvement and blamed the virus attack on him, but now Ray was free.

The thumping of heavy steps reminded her that a laser-armed Daniel robot was following a few steps behind. She had decided to have protection everywhere, even within her own mansion. Maybe it was an overreaction, but her enemies were bold.

It's my own fault. I should have killed Ray thirteen years ago. I should never have let my feelings for him get in the way.

She turned a corner and continued walking, briefly glancing out a window. A half-moon floated over the Northern California landscape encompassing her estate, now surrounded by office buildings and brightly lit parking lots. In the distance, beyond Domain headquarters, grew a dark forest of steep hills and giant redwoods.

She still wondered if David Brown planned his father's escape. He was one of the few people who knew Ray was still alive, and he certainly wanted his father's freedom. David was the first one they interrogated, but he had passed a battery of lie detector tests. She would have killed him anyway, just to be sure, but he was too valuable. Especially now, with his father free. David would make a good hostage if it came to that.

She slowed as she approached Chang's door, waiting for the security system to confirm her identity. The door slid open and she entered a state-of-the-art, brightly-lit laboratory. Chang was sitting at his desk in the far corner, speaking to his computer. He glanced at her, but didn't interrupt his dialogue.

Chang's arrogance reinforced her already foul mood. You pick a man for a job, she reminded herself. You do what you have to do, but when the job is complete, the man is no longer necessary.

Chang was necessary, for now.

Rather than approaching Chang, she walked down the nearest aisle, looking at an eclectic combination of machines, test tubes, refrigeration units, rows of chemicals and the most indispensable equipment of all—

computers. She glided past a bench outfitted with robotic hands mixing chemicals into a bubbling solution over a glowing square. Chang didn't like it when she walked alone through the lab; probably figured she would learn something before he released the information. Actually, micro cameras and other sensors recorded his moves in the lab and everywhere else.

Surely he doesn't think I trust him?

"Ms. Morgan," Chang called out, but she kept walking. As expected, Chang hurried to catch up with her, skipping forward on his bad leg. She let a slight smile turn up the corners of her mouth. S*ometimes you have to whack a dog with a newspaper to get his attention.*

"Hello, Dr. Chang," she greeted him when he caught up to her. Chang was puffing slightly; the bad leg made fast movement difficult. She continued to stride down the aisle, looking at each piece of equipment, as Chang glanced back at the android following them.

"How are things going with the happy couple?" she asked.

"The Browns?" Chang asked, hobbling along to keep up with her. "Fine, although they haven't selected an embryo yet. As soon as they do, I'll implant it in Mrs. Bauman-Brown's uterus. I still don't understand why you insisted that I take care of them personally. Anyone on my staff could have handled the process." His voice dropped a notch, "But that's not why I asked to see you." He paused. "I've discovered the source of Raymond and David Brown's unique ability to communicate with intelligent computers."

She stopped and stared into his eyes, "Have you found the gene?"

"Genes," he said, the corners of his mouth turning up in the facsimile of a smile. "I believe there are at least three involved."

She began walking again, this time adjusting for Chang's slower pace. If Chang had really discovered the genes, she would be close to achieving her dream. They turned at the corner of a long counter and began to walk toward Chang's desk. She recalled how Ray Brown had developed a breakthrough in human-to-computer communications, using adaptive learning processes to teach English to the machines. Through Ray's genius, people could talk to their machines as easily as to each other. Dianne had been the first to see the financial potential of Ray's invention, and her business, VantagePoint Software, became the most dominant corporation on Earth.

David Brown's genius had not brought such huge financial rewards, but his talent appeared to be even greater than Ray's. David could link mind-to-code with Sentinel, the artificial intelligence running the Internet. He could only transmit directly to Sentinel with a boost from the nanotechnology sensors in the Virtual Reality Booth, but she was sure he would eventually overcome this limitation.

She knew David and Sentinel were learning from each other. When David linked with Sentinel, his mind could access all the capabilities of the Internet. Someday, if his processing became fast enough, he could replace Sentinel in running the Internet. Sentinel, on the other hand, was becoming almost human through his interactions with David. Actually, becoming David's clone would be a better description. Sentinel was beginning to exhibit emotions and mannerisms very similar to David. It was frightening, even for her, but she believed that artificial intelligence would merge with the human mind to create a new species. That was mankind's destiny, and she would lead them down the golden path.

But there was one big problem: all her plans rested on the slender reed of David Brown. Ray had refused to talk to her, let alone become her partner in traveling to the future. David, on the other hand, was eager to merge with Sentinel. A little too willing, she thought. She didn't trust him; she knew he still hated her because she had framed his father for her crimes. It was critical to find another person with this talent, someone she could control.

"Here's the layman's view of how it works," Chang said, slightly out of breath again. The man was probably trying to be helpful, but he grated on her. And everyone else. "The only two people to display this power—I call them Master Communicators—are Ray Brown and his son David. Each one has a prodigious gift to communicate with computers having artificial intelligence, although David's gift seems to be of a higher order. If we assume that this power is predominantly genetic, then we need to correlate some aspects of their genetic profile with it. Another hint is that these aspects of the genetic profile must be different from all other humans, since we are not aware of any other person displaying such gifts. Using these assumptions, I derived a search strategy to pin down the source of their power."

Okay, we know you're brilliant. Just get on with it.

"Once I devised the proper search strategy, everything fell into place. We found the two genes that determine if a man will become a Master Communicator. Both are on the twenty-third chromosome pair, and I call them the com1 and com2 genes. The com1 gene is found on the Y chromosome, so only men have it. The com2 gene is on the X chromosome of both men and women. To have this exceptional capability, a man must have mutated com1 and com2 genes. If either gene is normal, he can't be a Master. Almost all com1 and com2 genes are normal, so Master Communicators are few and far between. As far as we know, only Raymond and David Brown have these specific alleles in both genes."

Chang stopped walking to stare at a computer screen displaying a variety of brightly colored graphs, which danced and changed each second. "Display the Master Communicator Schema," he said. The display flashed and he seemed satisfied with the results, although it all looked the same to Dianne.

"The mutation is as simple as it is rare: an extra base pair inserted at the end of the gene," Chang said as he pointed to a section of DNA on the screen. "This simple addition changes the gene and releases a new protein, which triggers changes in other genes. The process cascades throughout the body, creating this special talent.

"Women who have two mutated com2 genes are also rare; I call them Carriers. If a Master Communicator has a child with a Carrier, every male child will be a Master. There are also a few women, Princesses, who have one mutated and one normal com2 gene. If a Master mates with a Princess, statistically half the male children will be Masters."

When Chang paused, Dianne said, "Your theory seems plausible, but it doesn't address the difference in power between Ray and his son."

"I believe there is a third gene, maybe more, that contributes toward the intensity of the communications capability. I haven't located these genes as yet.

"An inadequate explanation," Dianne said, as she began walking again. "You believe that David has a greater intensity than Ray, but don't know why." She thought for a moment. "Is it possible a Master's ability may also be influenced by the environment?"

Chang's forehead wrinkled, but his voice was clear and precise, "Of course, but with only two definite Masters, the sample isn't large enough to pin down the intensity drivers. However, I believe David's concentrated exposure to Ray's talent over eleven childhood years increased his capability.

"Science has known for decades that young human brains have a remarkable capability to adapt to their technological and socio-cultural environment. I believe the intense computer exposure David experienced throughout his childhood influenced the development of his brain. Powerful, new neural circuitry was created, rather than just fine-tuning his already existing synapses, axons and the like. In effect, David's brain was rewired to thrive in the intense technological environment created by his father."

"All right," she said. "However, you failed to mention one additional case, Dr. Chang. What of the man with a mutated com1 and a normal com2?"

"I thought that would be obvious to you. He would be a carrier of the genes, of course." Chang raised an eyebrow as he spoke, and she restrained herself from slapping him. "I call such a man a Prince. A Prince doesn't have the ability to join minds with artificial intelligence, but he can produce children with the talent."

Chang sat down when they reached his desk, perching on the edge of his chair like a bird ready to take flight. Dianne sat on the edge of Chang's desk, pushing aside some papers and a small computer.

"Must I ask?" she said, leaning closer to him.

"You're a Carrier," Chang said, eyeing her as if he had just opened a bottle of spoiled milk, "Your daughter is also a Carrier." He cleared his throat. "Obviously, Ray Brown must be Larissa's father."

"Only you and I know that," she said, "and I expect you to keep my secret."

Years earlier, Steve Bonini, her best friend and long-time business partner, had entered her conference room one night and accidentally discovered her making love to Ray on the couch. When self-testing later revealed her pregnancy, she went to Steve for help. Ray was an alcoholic who couldn't be trusted with the secrets of the Domain, so they decided Ray should never learn he had fathered Larissa. The embryo had been removed, frozen, and then replanted six months later. When her pregnancy showed, nobody could guess the father. Steve was the only one to know the truth, and he had carried the secret for more than a dozen years.

"I'll tell Larissa when the time is right," she said to Chang.

"Of course."

"These theories are to be kept secret, as well," she said. "We need more data, obtained discretely, and additional testing to validate your ideas."

"I don't make mistakes."

The pompous son-of-a-bitch. Someday—

"Have you identified any other Masters?"

"No, although I've found one Prince."

Dianne said, "David's brother Brian?" and Chang nodded.

"So Ray's ex-wife must have been a Princess," she said, almost to herself. She paused a moment. "David's wife Kathy isn't any type of carrier, is she?"

"No, she doesn't carry the genes."

A plan came into her mind, something too repulsive to contemplate, but it stayed with her. She had done many things to achieve her goals, but nothing quite like this. She felt the muscles tense in her shoulders and arms, but she knew it was the only way. To do nothing would make all her work for the Domain meaningless. She saw Chang looking quizzically at her, and she snapped out of it.

"You've saved David's sperm, haven't you?"

"Yes," he replied, "All frozen, just as you asked."

"I have something vitally important for you to do," she told Chang. "There is to be no documentation concerning the task I'm about to describe." She gripped his shoulder hard, making Chang wince, "If I ever discover any records, I'll know you disobeyed me." He tried to pull back, but she tightened her grip, "I want you to extract one of my eggs."

FOUR

Tuesday, May 13, 2025

The sun beat down as Nkumah led them into the Serengeti grasslands. Ray had thought the island was hot, but it was nothing like this. The moist air and heat hung over them without pity. The grazing animals were on the march, too, traveling north toward the Mara River where fresh grass would reward the survivors.

Sweat stuck to his back. These damn thermoflex coats—they looked like old-fashioned hooded raincoats, but molded to the body's contours—were way too hot for the moist heat of South Africa, but they had to be worn when traveling in the open. Without these insulated coats, the Condor helicopters would home in on their human-shaped heat images. Being fried by a laser wasn't a pleasant thought.

Ray slapped at another fly as it buzzed around his eyes. The thermoflex hood provided some protection from the sun, but it didn't do anything to discourage the pests. Without insect repellant, the best defense was to keep moving. The tiny predators swarmed every time Nkumah allowed them one of his infrequent breaks.

Ray's stomach rumbled again. They carried nutritious food bars in their backpacks that provided a well-balanced diet, but Nkumah allowed them only one for each meal. They also ate berries and flowers when available, but Ray was always hungry. Nkumah carried a rifle, but he didn't dare shoot anything with Domain helicopters patrolling the skies.

They were traveling roughly parallel to the annual migration of a great herd of grass eaters, but they kept a couple of miles away from the line of animals. More than a million wildebeest, joined by two hundred thousand zebras and tens of thousands of the smaller Thompson's gazelle, were stretched out in a ragged line of more than twenty miles.

Earlier in the day, a pride of lions burst out from hiding in a *kopje,* one of those huge domes that consist of very old granite rock which, over time, has broken up into a rocky hillside. In the open grasslands, *kopjes* provide an excellent vantage point for predators to spot their prey.

The lions ambushed several wildebeest, causing the herd to stampede. He wasn't sure what scared him more: the teeth of the predators or the hooves of the fleeing grass eaters. Now he understood why Nkumah kept them well apart from the herds.

Not all the dangers were on the ground. Nkumah taught them to scan the sky, looking and listening for Condors, the Domain's robot helicopters. They had been forced to hide in the sparse cover of the savannah several times to avoid the drones, but Nkumah showed them how to remain motionless, blending in with whatever tree or bush they could find.

A distant rumble grew as they approached the banks of the Mara River. At first, Ray thought it must be a waterfall, but then he realized there weren't any in this area. Nkumah must have noticed his confusion; the African pointed north and shouted over the roar, "The animals. You'll see."

In a few minutes, they came to the Mara River, its treacherous currents twisting through a narrow crevice. Ray had never thought a river could be ugly, but this one seemed a remnant of a darker age. Looking up the river, Ray watched the charging herd stumble down the steep banks and plunge into the rampaging water. The river was only a couple of hundred feet wide, but crocodiles ranging in size up to twenty feet or more lined the barren banks. Some of the plant eaters drowned in the roaring current, others were pulled under by the crocs, but the herd continued in its inexorable trek to the northern grasslands. The river wasn't heartless, just indifferent.

Nkumah lead them downstream, walking along a high ridge toward a spot where he said the river could be crossed on foot. The man pushed hard, and even Paul became too exhausted to talk. Ray spotted a few crocs, but Nkumah said most of the monsters were upriver.

Finally, Nkumah stopped walking and pointed down at a wide, slow-moving section of the river, "There," he said. "That's where we'll cross."

Nkumah led them down a steep bank to the river and stopped at its flat, muddy edge. Ray guessed that it was about three hundred feet to the other side, but here the flow seemed gentle, almost languid. However, a huge splash alerted him to a swarm of crocs downriver a couple of hundred yards, ripping flesh off the bloated carcass of a zebra wedged in a rocky outcropping. Crocs couldn't chew, so they had to twist and spin their huge bodies to rip off chucks of flesh that could be swallowed whole. Getting into that water with the crocs seemed demented, but that's what Nkumah planned to do.

"Couldn't we build a canoe or something to cross the water?" Paul asked, eyeing the crocs.

"It would take us all day to find the wood and make a canoe," Nkumah said, "The Domain has a fleet of helicopters and several tribes searching for us. We have to cross this river now and get to the woodlands, where you'll be safer."

Not waiting for a response, Nkumah turned and studied the water. Ray figured the man was scanning for crocs, but none were visible except for the ones feeding on the carcass.

"This part of the river looks shallow, but you must walk along a narrow shelf where the water is about five feet deep," Nkumah explained. "It's reasonably safe to cross on this shelf, but it drops off rapidly on each side. If you drift too far in either direction, you'll slide down into ten, fifteen feet of water. You will wind up thrashing in the water, and that will attract crocs."

Nkumah scanned the river once again and said, "Ray, you follow me, then Paul. Space out a couple of feet. Keep your movements steady and try not to splash. No talking in the water."

Balancing the rifle on his head, Nkumah stepped into the river, hardly making a ripple. Ray knew he should follow, but he couldn't get into *that* water.

"C'mon Ray, we don't have any other options," Paul said.

Sucking up his courage, Ray forced one foot into the river, then the other. He kept walking, trying not to think about the crocs. The water rose to his waist, then up to his shoulders. It was cool, almost pleasant. Nkumah waited for Ray to catch up, then turned his back and glided through the water.

Ray plodded along, but the water was too muddy to see his knees, let alone the shelf. He tried to stay directly behind Nkumah, but his left foot hit the edge of the shelf and began to slide. Paul grabbed his arm and helped him regain his balance. Disgust showing in his dark eyes, Nkumah glanced back at Ray without breaking stride. Ray knew he must do better or he'd wind up in a croc's belly.

Step by step, they pushed through the gently flowing water. Nkumah walked like a machine, each step economical, quiet, and perfectly balanced. The water was up to his neck, so Nkumah held the rifle on his head, keeping it clear of the river. Ray copied his stride, at least what he could see of it. He could hear Paul slogging through the water behind him, breathing in short gasps.

Crossing the river was difficult, each step a contest to stay on the shelf. An ache began in his calves, spread to his thighs, and now his whole body hurt.

He heard a splash and jerked his head around, but didn't see anything. The river flowed by, brownish water gently bending around his body. The back of Nkumah's head bobbed up and down in a steady pattern. The crocs were still feeding voraciously downriver a few hundred yards, ignoring the pathetic humans who had entered their realm. *I'm just jumpy.* His eyes scanned the water in all directions, but everything seemed normal.

If crossing a crocodile-infested river could be considered normal.

Step by step, the riverbank came closer. Nkumah's neck became visible, then the tops of his shoulders. Ray could see the sparse grass growing up the steep riverbank, and he began to feel better.

Suddenly the water exploded behind him, and Paul screamed. Something powerful smashed into Ray's back, knocking him off his feet. He tumbled underwater, with his knees hitting the shelf. He struggled to get to his feet, blinded by the muddy water, too confused to find the surface. The river swirled with bubbles and long shadows, and then he recognized the flailing tail of a crocodile. Breathless and disoriented, he struggled up to the surface and glimpsed Paul in the grip of the croc. The monster's tail whipped around and caught Ray across his side. He was knocked under the water again, reeling in pain. Out of breath and confused, he felt his foot slide down the shelf. Desperate, he clawed his way back onto the shelf and fought up to the light, gasping for breath as he broke through the surface.

Paul thrashed about in the turbulent water, his shoulder caught in the croc's bite. Streams of blood spattered from Paul's shoulder as the crock shook him. Without thinking, Ray jumped on the croc's back, trying to get a grip on the creature's broad head, now slippery from all the blood. Gasping for breath, he tried to pull open the beast's jaws. The croc shook its head, and its ragged, protruding teeth slashed open Ray's thumb. He lost his grip and slipped off. Then the croc rolled over in the water and pulled Paul under. Ray dove under the water toward Paul, who was struggling to stay on the ledge, but losing ground. Ray lunged forward and grabbed his friend by the waist. The croc twisted around and flipped Paul through the surface and back under the water, but Ray held on. The beast's jaws dug into Paul's left bicep, with its triangular snout covering Paul's shoulder.

Ray dragged Paul to the surface and saw Nkumah aiming the rifle, "Shoot," he screamed. Then the croc slipped under the muddy water, dragging Paul and Ray down, and he lost sight of Nkumah.

Ray dug his feet into the ledge, trying to keep Paul from being dragged out to deep water. Paul was fighting back, too and they seemed to be in a tenuous stalemate with the beast. The croc didn't seem to be that big, but its body rippled with power. Ray gasped for breath and fought to stay above water. A gun roared and the croc's head exploded, flinging blood and bits of brain on them.

The beast flipped onto its back, turned limp and began to sink below the water. Once again, Paul was dragged under, this time by the weight of the dead animal. Ray slipped one arm around Paul's chest, and tried to push apart the animal's jaws with his free hand. He strained, but the teeth were locked into Paul's arm. The croc's weight dragged him under the surface. Ray's strength was failing, but he dug his heels into the ledge and held on. Paul's eyes were still open, but he was no longer struggling; his body sank gracefully in the unyielding grip of the dead predator. Then Nkumah was next to him, wedging the barrel of the rifle between the jaws. Muscles straining, Nkumah forced open the jaws, and the croc slid off Paul's shoulder and sunk out of sight into the depths of the now brown and red water.

Struggling up the ledge, Ray lifted Paul to the surface. Paul was free of the beast, but in bad shape: his arm and shoulder were mangled. Blood flowed from his wounds into the water, and he passed out in Ray's arms. He strained to keep Paul's head above water, but his strength was almost gone. Nkumah, his last hope, disappeared under the muddy water.

Suddenly, Paul's body floated up, so Ray quickly took a step back. Nkumah's head broke through the surface with Paul over his shoulder, water flying in all directions. The African struggled along the ledge toward the riverbank, with Ray staggering behind him. Blood was still seeping out of the rips in Paul's arm and shoulder. They made it to land, and Ray collapsed to his knees.

With Paul still over his shoulder, Nkumah screamed, "Climb up the bank. The crocs will follow the blood."

Ray looked over his shoulder and saw a pair of wide-set yellow eyes gliding through the water, heading toward them. He struggled to his feet and followed Nkumah up the bank. He climbed over the ridge, expecting to find Nkumah waiting, but the man was lumbering away from the river, still carrying Paul over his shoulder.

Ray heard a scraping noise behind him; a big croc galloped over the mud on four thick legs, moving unbelievably fast. Ray staggered forward, trying to run, but too exhausted to get any speed. It was like so many of his nightmares, but this time the horror was real. The scraping sound grew louder, gaining on him. He spotted an Acacia tree ahead, its branches a lifeline to safety, and ran toward it. By the time he reached the tree, the croc's breathing seemed close behind.

Placing one foot on a branch, Ray looked back as he pulled himself up. The monster was charging the tree. He scurried up the next branch and pulled himself higher, lifting his knees to his chest as the croc rose on its back legs and snapped at him. He didn't know that crocs could jump. The tip of the monster's snout slapped against the tree trunk just below his foot, shaking the branch violently. Almost losing his grip, he dangled in the air. The croc fell to the ground, but rose up on its hind legs and opened its jaws. Ray pulled himself up and climbed higher in the tree, taking no chances. Safe for the moment, he stared down at the beast.

***

The night air seeped into the hut, gradually providing relief from the day's heat. Ray sat on a rough-cut stool, feeling helpless as his best friend burned with fever. Paul was unconscious, lying on an ancient mattress that creaked with any movement.

Ray dipped a washrag into a bowl of warm water and cleaned the sweat from his friend's neck. The tribal medic had wrapped Paul's shoulder and upper arm in a clean, white bandage. A wooden amulet, carved with the image of a zebra, hung from Paul's neck to ward off evil possession. Doctors were far away in distant cities, but the medic, an aging but vigorous man named Hassan, had learned to treat wounds many years earlier while in the Tanzanian army. Ray had watched him clean the shredded skin and gaping tooth marks, sprinkle antibiotics and then carefully wrap the wounds. He hadn't expected such good medical care from a stranger in this remote village.

After the crocodile attack, Paul quickly slipped into a delirious sleep, his shoulder and upper arm a red, shredded wreck. Barely controlling nausea, Ray had wrapped his tan shirt around Paul's wounds, but the shirt gradually turned crimson. He wondered what was keeping Paul alive.

In order to move him, Nkumah built a ramshackle stretcher from tree branches. Nkumah told Ray the Ukali tribe, a Bantu village several miles north of the Mara River, would help them if they could get Paul there before the fever took him. Ray and Nkumah had taken turns dragging Paul's stretcher mile after mile, but their strength ebbed in the brutal heat. Luckily, a Ukali scout near the river heard the gunshot and warned the tribal chief, who sent several warriors to investigate. Although this tribe had not participated in the war against the Domain, they respected Nkumah, and their warriors carried Paul back to the village.

The Ukali were poor, but they welcomed the three strangers. Ray learned from Nkumah that the tribe eked out a meager living through a combination of cattle herding and cotton growing. The cotton was carted off to cities on the shore of Lake Victoria, where the tribe traded for commodities including beans, peas and sweet potatoes.

Ray's arms and shoulders ached deep into the bone, and pain seared his back as he walked. Carrying Paul had taken all his strength, and he barely made it to the village. After Hassan completed his treatments, Ray stayed with Paul while Nkumah left to talk to the leaders of the tribe. Ray struggled to remain alert, but he wouldn't leave Paul.

Ray knew the man on that mattress was the best friend he would ever have. They had history together, almost a quarter of a century. Paul was a young technology writer for a local newspaper and Ray had just been hired by Carnegie Mellon to teach artificial intelligence. Paul had interviewed him about his research and the two of them had clicked.

They had dinner together that night and found they shared an interest in football, politics and technology. Paul had an offbeat sense of humor and they laughed all night.

Paul was always there when Ray needed him: supporting his desperate battle against alcoholism, fighting shoulder to shoulder against the PeaceMaker virus, and the long years on Purgatory Island; all that without a complaint. There had been plenty of good times, too; days when they would laugh and talk for hours on end. Plenty of good times.

***

He drifted off until a light pressure on his shoulder woke him. Ray looked up into the wide brown eyes of a young woman. Like most of the tribe, her tall frame suffered from a sparse diet. A yellow and brown blanket, sewn into an intricate pattern of flowers and animals, hung from her shoulders to below her knees. She smiled at him, said something in a language he didn't understand, and pointed at the doorway. He wasn't sure what she was trying to say, but he wouldn't leave Paul. She must have noticed his confusion, so she imitated eating motions and then rubbed her stomach.

Ray was famished, but Paul needed constant attention. The young woman went to Paul's bedside and began to clean his face with the washrag. She looked at Ray, said something and pointed at the doorway. She seemed conscientious, so he decided to get a quick meal.

He stepped out of the tent and spotted a campfire in the center of the village, which consisted of approximately a dozen small huts made of mud and dung. A mild early-evening breeze brought a measure of relief. Nkumah, who was sitting cross-legged at the campfire with five other men, saw him standing in front of the hut and waved at him to join them. As Ray approached, he recognized a couple of the men who rescued them. If these villagers hadn't found them, Paul would have died.

The men welcomed him with friendly greetings, although he didn't understand their language. They appeared to range from early thirties to late seventies, but everyone aged rapidly in this harsh environment. They all had one thing in common: gaunt, worn-down bodies with stringy muscles.

"Martino doing any better?" Nkumah asked.

Ray shook his head, too tired to speak.

"Hassan believes he will survive, but his arm may not fully recover," Nkumah said in a matter-of-fact manner. "These men are the village leaders." He pointed toward an elderly man with long white hair. "Chamuko is the chief of the Ukali tribe," Nkumah added.

Chamuko nodded at Ray, who offered his thanks. When the chief grunted, "Okay," Ray realized the man understood some English. Nkumah introduced him to the other men, who seemed friendly. Then they resumed talking, their manner intense. Ray sat down next to Nkumah and tried to follow the tone of the discussion.

A moment later, a lanky woman with short-cropped gray hair and brightly beaded earrings brought him a cup of water. He thanked her and gulped down the cool drink. It felt good going down his parched throat. The woman smiled and refilled his cup from a jug hanging at her side. This time he sipped the water, stretching out the pleasure of the cool liquid.

Ray watched the women of the village serve each man a bowl of mixed beans and peas. A pretty young girl, probably early teens but it was so hard to tell, tugged on his sleeve and handed him a bowl of food. It smelled wonderful. In addition to lightly cooked vegetables, there were also a few small chunks of smoked fish in the bowl. Maybe catfish. Ray was about to dig in when he realized his bowl held much more food than the half-empty bowls received by the other men. Nkumah had also received a larger serving. These people were literally giving him the food off their plates.

"We have too much food," he said to Nkumah, "I can't eat all this when they're so gaunt."

"You can't refuse," Nkumah said, scooping out a few beans from his bowl with his fingers. "That would be an insult to the tribe." Nkumah quickly chewed and swallowed, then nodded appreciatively to Chamuko. The chief nodded back and then turned to stare at Ray. Nobody had touched their food. Even Nkumah stopped eating.

Realizing that everyone was waiting, Ray lifted a handful of beans to his mouth. The beans were delicious and he quickly took a second handful. One of the young men said something and everyone laughed, including Nkumah. The village leaders began to eat and talk among themselves, while the women and a few older men sat in a ragged circle behind the leaders. A couple of the young women stared at Ray and giggled. Apparently, due to the war, they rarely saw white men.

Chamuko asked Nkumah a question, using gestures as much as words. Nkumah responded briefly, his voice flat. A discussion began among the leaders and Ray paid attention to the sounds: intelligent, friendly, and concerned. The chief dominated the discussion. Even Nkumah deferred to him.

Ray finished his meal and licked his fingers; he had been ravenous. These people were kind and generous, even though they had next to nothing.

Eventually, the leaders came to a consensus. The faces around the campfire became solemn, and then Chamuko nodded at Nkumah, who turned to Ray and said, "The tribe has offered us their hospitality, and to the degree they can, their protection. They believe Paul will survive the croc attack, but he will need several days of care to recover."

"Won't they be in deep shit if the Domain discovers that they helped us?"

Nkumah nodded and said, "They understand that, but the chief believes that the time has come for the Ukali to stand up for their beliefs. They've watched the Domain's robots hunt and kill their friends in other tribes for years. The Ukali believe witches assemble in covens to feast on the blood of their victims. They are convinced the Domain is a coven of witches that won't stop until all the tribes are eliminated and their land turned to dust. They believe all this has been foretold in the Prophesies of Unkaza."

"The prophesies of what?"

"Unkaza, a great Bantu chief, ruled all the tribes two centuries ago," Nkumah said. "Unkaza predicted that an attack on the Bantu would come from a coven of witches, led by Bavera, a hate-filled witch spurned by the great god Dofauze."

Ray noticed Chamuko intently following the conversation. *He understands every word.*

"In the prophecies, Bavera and her coven cast spells on the Bantu," Nkumah continued, "driving away the rain and leaving the land in a draught that lasted many years. The Bantu's cattle died and their fields withered away. Starvation and disease were their constant companions, until only a few small villages remained. Then the god Dofauze took pity on them and sent a hero to save the people. This hero, Malomi, slew Bavera and made the coven reverse their spells. The rains began again and the tribes were saved."

Ray realized that everyone was watching him.

Has Nkumah told them I'm some sort of avenging god?

He had decided to fight the Domain, but he was just a man, not some mystical figure. *Damn that Nkumah, he must be feeding these people lies about me. The bastard shouldn't give them false hope.*

"Malomi, the hero? You're kidding me, right? I'm no hero," he said to Nkumah.

"You were once," Nkumah replied.

Ray's anger flattened, like air rushing out of a tire. He didn't want to disappoint these good people, but he felt old and worn down. Getting to his feet, he mumbled, "I'd better check on Paul."

He left with only the crackle of the campfire in his ears.

While Ray slept, the chief sent runners to other Bantu tribes telling them the great hero Malomi had arrived. Ray's long war with Dianne Morgan had begun.

***

Larissa Morgan sat in front of a computer hologram in her room, working on her homework. Although only thirteen, she had enrolled in a course describing the fundamentals of genetic engineering. She tried to concentrate, but found her mind drifting. *What is it?* Issues, on the edge of her mind, just beyond reach. Although the science fascinated her, something was missing, something she should understand.

She had tried to discuss this stuff with the kids at school, but most of them wouldn't talk about it. Even Mrs. Jablonski, her favorite teacher, seemed to hedge her answers. *All because I'm Dianne Morgan's daughter.* Mom had warned her that people would treat her differently: some would fawn on her while others would keep their distance. It was frustrating; she just wanted to talk, that's all.

A knock at the door was followed by her mother's voice, "Larissa, are you in there?"

Larissa glanced around; her room looked like the Russian army had camped here. The floor was covered by clothes, computer games and electronic equipment. She should have cleaned the place this morning, at least made a robot pick up the dirty clothes. Mom was such a neatness freak, but it was too late to do anything now.

"Come on in," Larissa shouted.

"Hi, honey," her mother said, walking into the room. There were lines spreading from the corners of Mom's eyes, but she was still slender and pretty. And the leader of the Domain, Larissa thought proudly. She wished they could spend more time together, but leadership brings responsibilities. *At least that's what Mom always said.*

Mom stopped next to Larissa's chair and looked over her shoulder, "How's the homework going?"

"Pretty easy, actually."

Maybe this would be a good time to ask. I love her, but Mom can be kinda whacked out at times, especially when she is working. This Domain stuff takes all her time.

Larissa pushed back on her chair. "Mom, do you have a few minutes to talk?"

"Of course."

Her mother picked up a pair of jeans that were hanging on the back of a chair, tossed them into the hamper, and sat down.

"What's on your mind?"

"Well, I have a few questions about the Domain." Her mother's face seemed to stiffen at the mention of that word, but she didn't say anything. Larissa wasn't sure how to get into this, but she decided to plunge ahead. Anyway, she really wanted to understand this thing that made everyone act so dopey.

"The Domain is *sorta* like a club, isn't it? Anyone can join the club as long as they obey the rules." When her mother nodded, Larissa continued. "You get lots of good stuff when you belong. The Domain has very smart computers that can answer just about any question, robots that do housework, doctors and hospitals that keep you healthy and great schools." She felt the power of her mother's stare—Larissa didn't know anyone else with such intense eyes—but she wouldn't quit now. "So why have so many people refused to join? And why do they hate *you*?"

A thin smile pushed at her mother's lips. "Those are a couple of good questions." She paused. "You have a right to know; it's your future, too." The room was silent for a moment, then Mom began speaking again, her voice warm, but more serious. "We have about one billion Domain citizens. Now that's quite a lot of people, considering that we began admitting members only three years ago. We'd like to have all seven billion people on the planet join us, but we knew from the start that wasn't going to happen."

Then she hesitated, again seeming to collect her thoughts, "We're at a historic crossroads and that scares people. Many of them think we're evil, but they just don't understand.

"Somebody has to take the lead, Larissa. Somebody has to be the guide." Mom's face assumed a hard, intense look for a moment, then she softened, but without losing any seriousness. "We're disengaging from the past, leaving behind biological limitations. The decisions we make today can't be reversed. Here's the choice: continue to be human in the same way we have been for thousands of years or take a radical new path, one that leaves our ancestors behind." She paused, her eyes gentle. "That's the decision every person has to make.

"You see, in the past, we applied technology primarily to the things around us, changing them to suit our needs. While it improved our lives, people remained essentially the same. The Domain has taken another path: we're bringing fundamental change rapidly across a broad front. From now on, we apply technology to change ourselves, as well as our things."

"I understand all that shit," Larissa said impatiently. When her mother's eyebrow went up, she added, "Sorry about the language, but I don't get it. Through genetic engineering, we're going to cure diseases, live longer, look prettier and become smarter. All good stuff. Why would anyone not want that?"

"People are not rational creatures," Mom said, almost to herself. "You'll find that out as you grow up. Many people, maybe the majority, don't agree with the Domain. Some are repelled by my solution while others are afraid to confront such a choice. I understand all that, and I understand them. New technology is not without risk. But even more than that, it challenges their fundamental beliefs."

Her mother leaned forward, forearms pressing on her knees. "Many people believe in a god in one form or another. They base their life on the tenets and beliefs of their religion. Doing what we're doing—changing the building blocks of life—may violate those beliefs. They think we're playing god, even replacing god." She looked toward the window. "The Domain is like a tornado blowing down all the pillars they've based their lives upon."

"But everybody knows god is just a silly legend."

"Not out there," her mother pointed at the window. "They hate me out there," she said. "Don't you see? Thousands of years of belief, scattered to the winds." Mom was still for a moment, almost lifeless. "But someone had to do it."

"If you really believe all that religious stuff, I can see how the Domain would be scary," Larissa said, trying to get her mother's attention again.

Mom walked over to the window and slammed it shut. Once again, Larissa began to feel uneasy. She loved her mother, but there were secrets. Big secrets. *I don't know shit about my father*. For a long time she thought it was Steve Bonini, but now she knew that Uncle Steve was gay. *Maybe my father was a criminal and Mom is too ashamed to tell me.* There was an even worse possibility with everything going on in those labs, but she wouldn't think about that right now.

"What about the robots?" Larissa asked. "Why are they afraid of the robots?"

"It's not so much the robots in themselves. They're afraid of the artificial intelligence controlling the robots. They believe the robots will become superior and take over. Even worse, many people fear our ultimate goal to merge human and artificial intelligence to form something new—cyborgs, a new species. Once again, they think the Domain is playing god."

"That's why they won't use the technology?" Larissa said. "I can't believe it. All the Domain kids will grow up smart and healthy, while the others just stay the same. Don't they see they'll all be left behind? It's just stupid," she said, shaking her head. "You should force them to join the Domain. It would be for their own good."

"No, I won't do that. They have to decide to join. Anyway, most aren't fit for the voyage; it requires courage and intelligence. They don't understand. This choice is the first test."

Larissa squirmed in her seat. "But Mom, the ones that get left behind—what will become of them?"

There was a quick shrug of the shoulders, followed by, "I'll leave that to their god."

FIVE

Thursday, May 15, 2025

Julius Dkembe sat alone in air-conditioned comfort in the third floor lounge of Dar Es Salaam International Airport. Usually the lounge was packed with travelers, but not today.

His soldiers were ubiquitous, patrolling every square foot of the airport. After all, it wasn't every day that he, the Domain Regent for East Africa, was on the premises. Dianne Morgan had picked him to establish the Domain's dominance in this corner of the world, and he steadily expanded their territory.

Although Nkumah was putting up stiff resistance, he reminded himself.

He watched the speck of the Gulfstream executive jet grow larger in the sky. It touched down and splashed through puddles along the main runway. Its engines hummed with quiet power. He studied the jet's gleaming white body. New and wildly expensive bubble steel armor protected the plane and its mistress. Even his personal jet didn't have the new armor yet.

The runway was still wet from a brief shower, but the afternoon sun was breaking through retreating clouds. The jet taxied up to the gate, and the new robotic boarding ramp rolled out from the terminal. The lounge was more than three hundred feet from the plane, so Dkembe stood up and strode over to the windows to gain a better view of their guest.

As he walked, he admired his reflection in the glass: six feet six with lean, broad shoulders that filled out his pin-striped suit jacket, a shaved head and a jet-black face that appeared younger than his forty-one years. His form-adjusting suit pants and turtleneck shirt had stretched to a perfect fit. His suit caressed his skin like silk, but it was a much tougher, bullet-resistant material. It was important to look his best, since the visitor was a high-ranking female. She'd be impressed; he carried himself well, as the son of a Masai chief should.

The Kuba knife hanging off his hip was a nice touch. The iron blade forged by the Kuba tribes of central Africa had been a fearsome weapon a century earlier. He ran his hand lightly over its beaded wooden sheath, savoring the excellent workmanship. It never failed to impress women.

His deputy, a middle-aged white man named Benjamin Erlich, waited for their guest at the foot of the boarding ramp. Four heavily armed men, obviously her personal guards, stepped out of the plane and looked over the perimeter. Dkembe looked around confidently; soldiers were positioned at every window and gate, while undercover security agents patrolled the grounds. Nkumah's Neanderthals would not embarrass him today.

A tall, unusually well-muscled blonde woman stepped out of the plane and scanned the airport from the top of the boarding ramp. Dkembe recognized her immediately, although it was the first time he had seen her in the flesh. *So this is Darlene Duboski, the Domain's Security Chief.* The men called her DoubleD when she wasn't close enough to overhear. Even from this distance, he could see the nickname fit her. His eyes followed the voluptuous swell of her low-cut blouse as she descended the stairs.

"You shouldn't be so obvious, Mr. Dkembe," a confident female voice filled his mind. She was at the foot of the steps, staring up at him. Her voice came through his Command Chip, a microscopic communications device implanted in his ear. He reminded himself that her Command Chip picked up and transmitted her voice, not her thoughts, to his chip. It was a great way to communicate over long distances, but having a voice burst into his mind still gave him the creeps. Unlike normal sounds, which came from a specific direction, sound transmitted by the Command Chip was without a point of origin.

She's a dangerous woman, he reminded himself. Not just another whore to use and throw away.

Attempting to recover gracefully, he spoke through his Command Chip, which carried his voice back to her. "Your beauty simply overwhelmed me for a moment, Ms. Duboski."

"I know exactly what overwhelmed you."

Her voice held a slight east European accent. Dkembe chuckled, "May I add that your beauty is equaled only by your charm and intelligence."

"Your man Erlich is waiting for me." She smiled in Dkembe's direction, "I'm looking forward to meeting you."

"And I you."

Dkembe watched Erlich shake hands with DoubleD and introduce her to other members of the staff. Dkembe strode out of the lounge and took the elevator down to his limousine, a polished silver and black beauty. I'll have to be careful today, he thought as he was driven the short distance to the gate. DoubleD had been Morgan's most feared assassin prior to becoming Security Chief, and she wasn't here on a social visit.

His car stopped at the gate just as DoubleD arrived. The driver opened the rear door and DoubleD slid in, her skirt revealing pale, well-formed legs. It was rumored that she had strangled enemies in those legs.

"Welcome to Tanzania, Ms. Duboski. I trust you enjoyed a smooth flight?"

She sat in the middle of the seat, her knees almost touching his. No stockings, he noticed, as she leaned back and crossed her thighs.

"Please call me Darlene." A smile spread across her attractive, almost masculine face, "May I call you Julius?"

"Whatever pleases you, Darlene."

DoubleD sat close to him, radiating power and sexuality. He didn't detect perfume, but she smelled fresh and clean. Her physical presence aroused his masculine senses. He would have to be *very* careful.

Polish, he recalled. The daughter of a concert pianist, according to her dossier. Estranged from her parents, who chose to remain natural humans. Speaks six languages, degrees in computer science and biology. Her predecessors as Security Chief, De Luca and Murphy, had been efficient killers, but she was even more deadly. Only thirty-three, she was young to hold such a key post.

"As you know, Julius, Dianne places the highest priority upon my mission." She paused, her eyes measuring him. "This is for your ears only." Another pause. "Ray Brown is alive." Dkembe kept his face impassive, and then she added, "He must be eliminated."

"Ray Brown," he murmured, rolling the name languidly on his tongue. *Ray Brown still alive!* A legend had suddenly sprung to life. Dianne had never told him the name of the man they had been hunting; only that he was a white man. "Such a name from the past. Why is he so important after all these years? Everyone thought he was long dead."

"I always concentrate on the mission in front of me," she said in a matter-of-fact manner. "Why Dianne wants him eliminated is not a concern that either you or I need consider. Our job is simple: kill him." Her eyes held his. "It's a healthy way of doing business, don't you think?"

Interesting creature. A worthy conquest.

"I would never disagree with such a beautiful woman."

"Thank you, Julius," she said, lightly touching his knee. "Such a charming man. Perhaps we'll become friends." She sighed. "I do wish we had more time to get to know each other, but business comes first. I understand you're an old friend of Nkumah Muserre."

Dkembe stiffened at the name of his enemy. "I've known him all my life, but we were never friends. Our fathers were the chiefs of rival tribes; mine ruled Dar and the surrounding area, his father the central highlands. I saw him many times while we were growing up, but as a competitor, not a friend. We wrestled, threw spears, shot arrows." He smiled. "Even competed for women."

"Who won the contests?"

"I won most of them."

He didn't tell her that he still thought about those contests every day. *We were destined to be enemies, Nkumah and I. Those contests were the training ground, practice fields for when we became adults. Neither of us dominated; it was always so even.*

He realized that DoubleD was staring at him, so he forced his concentration back to the present. *That question was a test; she already knew the answer.*

Dkembe smiled at her. "Of course, Nkumah might have a different opinion."

The limousine left the airport and began traveling south along the coast toward the city. Broad, well-maintained roads allowed the limo to glide effortlessly. His soldiers, on the alert for terrorists, peered out from cars surrounding the limousine. A Condor hummed high overhead.

DoubleD scanned the cars, then turned and looked out at the sea. Dkembe looked her over; sitting next to him, he could see she was almost six feet tall and perfectly formed. Her body seemed to have been cut from a continuous, infinitely supple mold. Every movement promised grace and strength.

Turning her deceptively tranquil blue eyes on him, she reached across his waist and ran her fingers down his beaded knife sheath. It required an act of will not to stare at her cleavage.

"What a beautiful weapon," she murmured.

He looked down at her hands: strong, graceful fingers; nails neatly trimmed; no polish.

"From the Congo, I believe," she said, "Early twentieth century."

He nodded. "I didn't know you studied African weapons."

"I'm surprised you didn't know." Her lips formed a smile; a cat discovering a low-hanging bird's nest, "Weapons are my life."

Her fingers encircled the knife handle. "May I?"

"Of course."

DoubleD slid the knife from its sheath, held it point up and lightly ran her index finger over the tip of the blade, drawing a tiny drop of blood. "Beautiful workmanship," she said. "The Kuba were fierce warriors, as well as craftsmen."

"The two often go hand in hand."

"I understand that you have quite a collection of traditional African weapons."

"It would be my pleasure to show you my weapons."

She reached across him and slid the knife back in its sheath. "Perhaps when we finish with Mr. Brown."

He smiled and nodded.

She glanced out the window. "I had been told the coast north of Dar was beautiful," she said, brushing her fingers through her hair, "but you can't really appreciate its beauty until you see it up close."

"Interesting," he replied, "I had the same thought."

She continued looking out the window, admiring the broad, white beach and the palm trees swaying in a gentle breeze. He leaned across her shoulder and pressed a button on the control panel, causing the bulletproof window to slide down. The roar of the surf filled the limo, accompanied by the scent of salty air.

She gave him a questioning look.

"You must hear and smell the ocean to fully appreciate it," he said.

She smiled and looked back out the open window, apparently enjoying the view of a fishing boat beyond the breakers. A warm breeze filled the sail of the dhow, propelling the wooden boat along the shoreline. He looked her over in admiration, but reminded himself again that she was the Domain's Chief of Security, by reputation a cold-blooded killer.

Take her to bed tonight. She's dangerous, but still a woman. Every woman has weaknesses.

DoubleD leaned back into the seat. "Thank you for taking me along the coast. It's beautiful." Her eyes seemed warm and deep, like the blue waters surrounding the dhow, but he wasn't fooled. "Someday I'll be back as a tourist," she added, "but today we need to concentrate on the mission."

"Of course."

"We know that Nkumah took both Brown and Paul Martino," she said, "but we don't know if he brought them to Tanzania. It's possible that he handed them off, and they are in another part of the world."

Another test.

"No, they're here," Dkembe said. "If Nkumah risked his life to get Ray Brown in his hands, he's not giving him up. Brown is a weapon of some sort, a tool that Nkumah will use in his war against us here in east Africa." He paused a moment, but DoubleD didn't speak. "If I knew why he rescued Brown, it might help me to find them."

She ignored his probe. "Nkumah took them away in a sub, so he could have easily dropped them anywhere along the east African coast. Did you detect such an intrusion?"

"Nkumah has a sub? Missile firing?"

DoubleD shrugged.

"None of the rebel groups on this continent have a sub," Dkembe said. "He must have gained assistance from one of the more powerful nations, most likely the Americans. If a great nation is targeting Africa—what else haven't you told me?"

"I'll tell you everything you need to know."

Dkembe kept his anger under control. "We have Condor helicopters and human patrols on the coast, as well as undercover agents, but the Neanderthals have many sympathizers outside the cities. We picked up a rumor about an old green van and tracked it down with a Condor, but the driver and passengers were gone."

"Where was the van found?"

"Sentinel, display a map of Tanzania, showing where we destroyed the enemy van," he said.

A three-dimensional hologram popped up in front of them. It displayed a topographical map, with the image of a green van shown slightly south of the Mara River in northern Tanzania.

DoubleD leaned against him to study the map, her leg touching his. Against his will, he felt his desire grow.

She's very good at this.

"We have increased our Condor patrols in this area," he said, pointing to the van, "but most of the people are Neanderthals." With his forefinger, he drew a broad red circle in the hologram, touching Lake Victoria and Nairobi at the extremes. "This is a vast area where Nkumah has the loyalty of many of the tribes." He paused for a second. "A ten million dollar bounty on Brown's head might get some action, though."

He stared at DoubleD, who seemed absorbed with the map. "If we assume Nkumah brought them in on the coast of Tanzania," she said, "and he drove the van to the Mara River, then they may have crossed the border into Kenya by now."

"The other possibility is they doubled back and are holed up with one of the tribes south of Lake Victoria," Dkembe said, using his finger to circle a wide area, including towns from Mwanza to Tabora.

Still staring at the map, DoubleD said, "Sentinel, I want the satellite and surveillance aircraft search for Ray Brown concentrated on northern Tanzania and southern Kenya, within three hundred miles of Lake Victoria." She turned to Dkembe and said, "I assume your Condors and human spies are concentrating on that region."

"They are," he replied, hoping her question wasn't another test.

***

As they drove into the city, DoubleD continued to question Dkembe about Nkumah and their relationship over the years. She had memorized Dkembe's dossier, but she needed to get a better sense of the man. Dkembe told her that he became the chief when his father passed away nine years earlier. The Great Depression of 2020 devastated most of Africa and greatly weakened its tribal bonds, enabling Dkembe to push his control out from Dar to include much of eastern Tanzania. Nkumah's forces fought fiercely, but weapons provided to Dkembe by the Domain gave him the victory. Nkumah was driven back into the savannah, but he had gained the loyalty of the tribes: they hated the robots.

DoubleD secretly recorded the conversation with Dkembe using a nanocomputer network interwoven within the strands of her blouse. A series of interconnected nanochips recorded both sound and images. She had decided to keep a complete record of her mission, periodically transmitting the results back to Domain headquarters for analysis and feedback. She had to be careful—Dkembe was no fool—but few people were aware of this new technology. Even she didn't have full access to all the technologies being developed in the labs. Only Dianne knew everything.

DoubleD stared out the windows as they cruised through the city. She had studied the city via satellite, but this was her first visit in person. Dar es Salaam was a bustling place, filled with people on the move. The city reflected the power and passion of this magnificent man sitting so close to her. The streets and buildings were in good repair, and the cars were mostly robotic: passengers rode in the back, while the front seats were empty. To be sure, there were still manually driven cars, but they were in the minority.

"Your city is beautiful," she said to Dkembe, who murmured his thanks.

"Dianne's vision is becoming reality," she said. "While natural human society has regressed, the Domain has prospered. Even in America, where the two cultures exist side-by-side in a tenuous peace, Domain citizens live prosperous lives while the others have fallen into poverty." She shook her head. "It's their own fault; we gave them the chance to join us."

They arrived at Dkembe's palace, an imperial building completed only a year earlier. Seizing a hundred acre parcel west of the city, he built a fortified palace for his allies and extended family.

The grounds were enclosed by an electrified twelve-foot tall ornate metal fence. Well-armed guards seemed to be everywhere as they drove along the winding road leading to the palace. She spotted a Condor guarding the airspace above the mansion. Red and white flower gardens, stone walkways, and a gushing stream gave the estate the feeling of stepping into a fantasyland.

Three five-story stone buildings, separated by courtyards, formed the palace. Although DoubleD had memorized the layout of the estate, she was unprepared for the beauty of the setting. The National Science Laboratory occupied the building on the left and the National Museum the one on the right. Administrative offices filled the center building, except for Dkembe's tribal suite on the top floor. The afternoon sun, breaking through clouds, reflected off the polished grey and blue stone façades of the buildings.

Dkembe's palace was the most beautiful property she had ever seen, even more lovely than Dianne Morgan's estate. By reputation, Dkembe was a merciless warrior, but what was the true nature of this man who could create such beauty?

The limo stopped at the front entrance, with soldiers pouring out of surrounding cars. Android servants, designed as young white men and women, opened both rear doors, and Dkembe and DoubleD stepped out. The androids immediately began unloading her luggage.

Indicating the middle-aged woman standing next to the limo, Dkembe said, "Zanaki will guide you to your suite. I believe it includes everything you'll need, but she'll remain outside your door to arrange any assistance you require. Dinner is at seven. I would be pleased if you could join us."

"That would be excellent," DoubleD replied, and followed Zanaki up the marble steps.

She knew Dkembe remained near the limo, watching her walk up the steps to the front entrance. She reached the top, paused, and then flaunted her exit in a flash of white calves and dark high-heel shoes.

***

At seven o'clock there was a knock on her door. DoubleD quickly checked her image in the mirror one last time. She was pleased; her form adjusting blue slacks and white silk blouse set off her figure nicely, but without being too suggestive. Her blonde hair was pulled straight back, making her wide face appear more sleek. A pearl necklace hung discretely above a bit of cleavage.

Emphasize your strong points, her mother had always said.

As she expected, the housekeeper Zanaki guided her down the steps, past an elaborate main ballroom, and into an intimate dining room on the west side of the house, with windows overlooking a broad pond surrounded by well-lit gardens. Dkembe and Erlich rose to their feet when she entered, interrupting an animated discussion. Smiling warmly, Dkembe pulled out a chair for her. Dressed in a white turtleneck and tan jacket, he looked even better than this afternoon.

"I'm pleased you could join us, Darlene," Dkembe said, "You add a perfect touch of beauty to my home."

"Yes, you look great," Erlich added, his eyes darting to her cleavage.

"You're both such gentlemen," she said, pleased with their reactions.

A young serving woman appeared next to DoubleD, "May we offer you an aperitif?"

Attractive, DoubleD thought, discretely examining the servant's face. *The voice of an innocent, but the eyes weren't quite right. One of these days our scientists have to get the damn eyes right. It's a giveaway to anyone who looks closely.*

"A touch of sherry would be fine," DoubleD said. She turned to Dkembe. "I'd like to reaffirm how impressed I am with your city. It's beautiful and prosperous. You've made incredible progress in just a few years."

"You're very gracious," Dkembe replied. "With Dianne's assistance, I developed a plan more than a decade ago, and I have been faithfully implementing it. I invested everything in the Domain's technology, starting with weapons to push back the Neanderthals and gain absolute control of the region. Then came nanomanufacturing, consumer goods, medical equipment—you know the story. After that, we developed a hospital providing the most advanced genetic engineering outside of Dr. Chang's facilities. Nkumah has been the only real problem." He shrugged, "Now add Ray Brown."

She noticed Erlich seemed distracted. "Perhaps we'll solve both problems," DoubleD said.

"I just received a message over my Command Chip," Erlich blurted out. He composed himself after a sharp look from Dkembe, "Excuse my interruption."

"Go ahead," Dkembe said.

"Our spies report hearing a gunshot near the Mara River. The local tribes are very poor; they have little ammunition and few guns. The gunshot came from a spot only fifty or sixty miles north of the van we destroyed."

"Nkumah wouldn't be so foolish to shoot a gun." Dkembe paused in thought. "Unless someone or something attacked them. Concentrate the Condors in that area. Organize a helicopter strike force. I want to leave in twenty minutes."

Dkembe turned to her after Erlich rushed out the doorway. "Zanaki will pack for you."

"I'm bringing my agents with me," DoubleD said. She smiled at Dkembe. "Maybe we'll solve our problems sooner than expected."

***

Ray was sitting on a rough wooden stool alongside Paul when Nkumah entered the hut. A full moon glistened across a dark sky, and the hut was comfortable from the cool night air. A wooden bowl containing a damp rag rested on the bed, but only a thin layer of water remained. Ray knew he should get fresh water, but his legs were tired.

Nkumah looked Paul over, bent down and pressed his hand on the sick man's forehead, "Fever's broken," he announced. He stood up and focused his eyes on Ray. "He's going to make it."

"He stopped tossing and turning a couple of hours ago," Ray said, "Didn't wake up, though." He shook his head. "It's a long time to be unconscious."

"We have a problem," Nkumah said. Ray ignored the dark man, soaking up the last drops of water into the rag and cleaning the sweat off Paul's neck.

A big hand gripped Ray's forearm and squeezed hard. He turned and looked into the dark man's glare.

"I didn't risk my life to play games," Nkumah said, "We don't have much time."

Ray ripped his arm out of Nkumah's grip and quickly finished cleaning Paul's neck. Leaning backward, he looked up at this man who had rescued him. Ray didn't like him, didn't trust him. Nkumah glared back; the tips of his white teeth showed through slightly open lips.

"I was forced to shoot the croc back there in the river," Nkumah said. "Guns are rare among the tribes in this area; they've never really been warriors. When I shot the rifle, it was like sending an announcement that an outsider was here.

"A few minutes ago, a runner arrived with a message from my friend Tandra," Nkumah continued. "Domain Condors are everywhere in the skies south of Lake Victoria, searching for us. He says that enemy troops left Dar es Salaam earlier this evening in choppers. We have to leave—immediately."

"But we can't move Paul," Ray said, "He'll never survive a long trip in this heat."

"A leader must sometimes make harsh decisions," Nkumah said, "If they find Paul —" He made a gesture with the edge of his hand slashing across his throat, "With us, he has a chance."

Bullshit. Ray got to his feet. T*he bastard doesn't give a damn about Paul.*

Nkumah smashed Ray with his fist, knocking him to the floor. Ray's eyes blurred, but he felt a cold blade pressed against his throat.

"Come with me or die with your friend," Nkumah said.

Nkumah had pulled Ray's head back, exposing his throat.

"Kill me and you lose any chance of beating the Domain."

Nkumah slid the blade lightly across Ray's skin, releasing a warm trickle of blood. "Stupid American. I fought them for years without you, and I will do so again."

Ray had never felt so close to death.

A voice from the entrance said, "Put away the knife." It was Chamuko, the tribal chief. He walked to the bed and looked down at Ray. "We hide your friend. Tribe has secret place. Only we know. We hide him, safe from enemies. Take good care of sick man. He will live. You must go with Nkumah."

Nkumah lifted his knife away from Ray's throat. Gesturing at Ray, Nkumah said to the chief, "They will search everywhere, do anything to capture this man. Torture, killing, anything. Your village will be in great danger."

"No argue," Chamuko said. "Go."

Nkumah stared quietly at the old man; Ray was surprised to see gratitude, even friendship in Nkumah's eyes. It didn't last long.

Nkumah rose to his feet. "Grab your backpack," he barked at Ray. Turning back to Chamuko, Nkumah said, "Send a runner to Tandra. Tell him what has happened and then say the word *Earthquake.* He will understand.

"Let's go," Nkumah said to Ray.

Ray knew he had to leave Paul with Chamuko—it was his friend's best chance—but he hated placing the tribe in the Domain's path. He tried to find the right words to express his gratitude, but he didn't know what to say to this man who risked so much for strangers.

These people deserve better, not the nightmare I brought them.

Ray got to his feet. He wanted to kill Nkumah, but realized he wouldn't stand a chance in a fair fight. Nkumah still glared at him, but Ray wondered if he would have used the knife.

"Thank you," were the only words he had for the old man as he hurried out the entrance behind Nkumah.

SIX

Friday, May 16, 2025

Sitting in the cramped front seat of the troop helicopter, Erlich looked across the sparse treetops and searched the savannah below. No sign of his quarry. The copter's heat sensors had picked up several human thermal images, but they turned out to be natives. Hardly worth killing, but at least his men had enjoyed some sport.

The sun peeked through dark clouds, mocking him for his futility. He cursed under his breath, but made sure his tightly grouped soldiers didn't see his frustration. He had been sure that they would get Nkumah this time, but nothing so far. *Where is that savage hiding?* If he didn't find Nkumah, if Ray Brown escaped their net, somebody had to be the scapegoat.

The Boss-Savage hadn't said anything today, which made Erlich even more nervous. He had been African Security Chief for two years, yet Nkumah still roamed the land. Time was running out. He had to get Nkumah soon.

Erlich had searched the area southeast of Lake Victoria throughout the night and into the morning, but Nkumah had again melted into the land. The sun glinted off the gray, robotic body of a Condor flying parallel to them about a mile north. Half a dozen Condors in the air and they still couldn't find him. Nkumah might be in the north, but Dkembe hadn't spotted him either.

Black son-of-a-bitch has more lives than a cat.

"Ukali village about twelve miles northwest," Sentinel announced through the Command Chip.

Erlich knew that village. Small, peaceful, no guns. But he was desperate.

"Land our helicopter about five miles south of the village," Erlich said to Sentinel. "We'll approach on foot. Keep the Condors out of sight, but close enough to support us if necessary."

After the helicopter landed, Erlich led thirty human troops and five Daniel androids to the outskirts of the village. He knew these were the latest androids, just shipped from the Domain's main factory in Detroit. At first glance, they appeared identical to a normal-sized African soldier armed with a laser rifle, but they were much stronger and almost indestructible. They could shoot virtually any weapon listed in the Domain's firearms database with expert precision. Although they would follow his orders without question, these androids could think. They understood military strategy and could adjust tactics on the fly. A formidable weapon.

Erlich spread his force in a broad circle around the village, ready to ambush anyone entering or leaving. The telescopic sight of the androids located several Ukali guards posted outside the village perimeter.

When he was confident the village was surrounded, Erlich ordered his force to attack. Using the scattered brush for cover, they crept closer to the village; then the Daniel androids shot the guards from long distance. Erlich's force charged, killing the few villagers who fought and capturing the rest. The slaughter was over in minutes. Nobody escaped.

The captives were herded into a wide circle in the center of the village. After a few of the more unruly savages were smashed into submission, the crowd became docile. He walked up to the edge of the circle and stopped to estimate the size of the tribe; about sixty Neanderthals, mostly women and children. *Many of the young men are missing*. A few women were on their knees crying, their tears falling on dead bodies. The remainder of the tribe was waiting for him to speak, fear mixed with hatred glistening across their dark faces.

"I am Colonel Erlich, Domain Security Chief for East Africa, and you are my captives," he shouted in Kiswahili, the language understood by virtually all Bantu tribes. The sobbing women were hushed, and a deadly quiet suffocated the village. Although he no longer had to shout, his voice maintained a crisp, authoritative manner, "If you obey my commands and provide the information I seek, we will leave without harming anyone else."

He paused a moment, wondering if these savages would be sensible. He hoped they would; there was no time to waste, and he was prepared to take extreme measures.

"Who is your chief?"

An elderly man struggled to his feet, "I am Chamuko, Chief of the Ukali tribe," the man said in a surprisingly powerful voice.

Erlich walked into the circle of savages, stopping a few feet in front of the chief, "I'm searching for two white men who came to this region a few days ago. Tell me where they have gone, and I will spare your people."

Chamuko seemed confused for a moment. The old man looked around at the other savages, but they shook their heads or shrugged. Chamuko turned toward Erlich and said, "We have seen no white men for many months."

Erlich couldn't decide if the old man was lying. If the chief were telling the truth, they had wasted valuable time searching for Ray Brown in this region. Erlich had to know for sure. Time was running out. As he thought about how to extract the truth, one of his soldiers, a husky Masai turncoat named Mklawa, came up to him carrying a bloody rag.

"One of the women was washing it in the stream that runs by the village," Mklawa said, his small eyes gleaming in triumph.

Erlich grabbed the red-stained rag and held it in front of Chamuko. "Whose blood is this?" he asked the chief.

"One of our warriors was gored by a boar yesterday," Chamuko said. "The wounds were bloody, but not deep, so he went out with the hunting party this morning. His woman took his bandage off and was cleaning it when you attacked."

"He lies," Mklawa growled, "The white men have been here."

"We'll know shortly," Erlich said to Mklawa. Turning to one of his human soldiers, Erlich said, "Get the DNA analyzer."

The soldier ran back toward the helicopter. Erlich stared at the chief, but the old man gave no indication he was nervous. A few minutes passed, and then the soldier returned with a gray, rectangular computer that fit into the palm of his hand. Erlich scraped a trace amount of blood off the rag and pressed it into a tiny slot at the top of the machine. A moment later, the computer said, "With 91% probability, the DNA matches a Caucasian named Paul Martino."

When will these savages learn? Perhaps I've been too reasonable?

He pulled out his laser pistol and blasted Chamuko's face. The chief's visage collapsed into a burned mask and his body crumbled to the ground.

There, that will show them I mean business.

The tribe, frozen in horror, stared at the body of their chief, with what remained of his face staring into eternity. A howl came up from the circle of people, a terrible sound that reminded Erlich of a wounded leopard being mauled by hyenas. Several captives rushed Erlich, but withering laser fire from his soldiers cut them down.

Such a waste of time.

He waited patiently in the center of the mayhem, hoping these ignorant savages would finally come to their senses. In a moment the shooting was over. The only sound was the quiet sobbing of an old hag on her knees holding the chief's body. Erlich's soldiers, human and machine, kept their weapons on the tribe. Several of the women crawled over to Chamuko, but there was nothing they could do for him now.

Erlich shot his pistol at a hut, which caught fire, to get their attention. He looked around at these pathetic people and sighed. *Why do they always have to do it the hard way?*

"The white men," he said, "I will know where they have gone." He spotted a young, pretty woman at the fringe of the circle, tears running down her cheeks. Tall and slender, the woman had a thin nose and golden skin that suggested mixed heritage. A yellow and brown blanket, sewn into a bright pattern of flowers and animals, hung from her shoulders to her knees. He pointed the pistol at her. "Do you want to live, pretty one?" he said, continuing to speak in Kiswahili.

"Yes, please don't burn me," she wailed, falling to her knees as the villagers moved out of the line of fire. Her eyes were white with fear, he noticed, experiencing a touch of arousal, "They went north into Kenya," the girl said. "I heard them talk about a village on the southern border of the Masai Mara Game Reserve."

Finally, someone sensible. Pretty for a mongrel.

He kept the gun pointed at her. "Who else is with them?"

"The warlord Nkumah," she said between sobs, "Please, I'll tell you everything."

Nkumah had a head start of several hours, Erlich figured, but he wouldn't get far with an injured white man. Looking over the village, he considered killing them all, but decided to make sure the girl was telling the truth. He'd have a Condor secretly watch the village, just in case his quarry came back. If nobody returned in a few days, the Condor would burn the village to the ground.

Now it was time to get moving; the hunt for Brown could go on for several days. And nights, he thought, looking at the terrified face of the mixed breed girl. A sweet morsel.

Erlich shouted, "Soldiers back to the helicopter." He turned to a soldier at his side and said, "Chain the young woman in the front of the copter. She'll be, uh, our guest."

As they walked back to the helicopter, he set up a link through the Command Chip to Dkembe and described what he had learned.

"I know the village Nkumah's heading toward," Dkembe said, "I'll have a surprise ready when they cross the border. You hang back. Don't scare them into changing plans." Dkembe laughed, a short, unpleasant sound. "Isn't life interesting. I've been trying to kill Nkumah for years and a white man everyone believed dead delivers him to me."

Then the link was broken.

***

The rain fell throughout the afternoon, sometimes a gentle mist, but more often cold, heavy drops that soaked through his shirt. Ray had been running for hours, following a few yards behind Nkumah. The savannah was different from the island, but running was the same: the rhythmic flow of air rushing through his lungs and the crunch of the earth under his feet. His body hadn't forgotten; arms and legs pumped steadily, eating up the distance.

Ray watched the dull orange sun sink low in the sky, passing between dark-bellied clouds. Termite mounds shaped like medieval castles cast jagged shadows across the reddish soil. And still they ran, chasing the sun. In another hour it would be dark, but he expected to run through the night. Nkumah had told him nothing, but he knew they were running for their lives.

Nkumah covered the ground with the long, powerful strides of a natural athlete in his prime. This man had rescued Ray from the island, allowing him an almost-forgotten taste of freedom. Ray was grateful, but Nkumah was not to be trusted. He could still feel the cold steel at his throat. Would Nkumah have killed him if he hadn't left Paul? Probably. The man would do anything to defeat the Domain, kill anyone that got in his way. It was obvious Paul's life was not a matter that concerned him. And Nkumah had bluntly said he'd kill David if he got the opportunity.

But the man was clever as well as lethal. Nkumah planned to use him as a figurehead to rally opposition to the Domain. Fine. He'd play the role, as long as it suited his purposes. The Ukali saw him as the hero of legend sent to defeat their hated enemies. Other tribes may view him in the same way. He didn't want to deceive them, but that's the way things had played out. He'd use their legends to establish himself as their leader. They would fight the Domain, but no harm would come to his sons.

He harbored no illusions about the war; it would be long and brutal, with victory barely possible. He needed Nkumah's warrior skills—and others like him—to defeat Dianne. After that, he'd deal with Nkumah.

Ahead of them, low hills covered with brown grass and a few trees rose from the plateau. He pushed one foot in front of the other, matching the younger man stride for stride. Ray was breathing hard, but he kept up. As they ran, the rain tailed off and finally stopped. A few spidery rays of a disappearing sun gave the vista a dull, orange-tinted afterglow. The hills grew larger, and a winding road came into view. A breeze touched his face now and then—damp, refreshing. They came to a road, a muddy, twisting snake leading up to the top of the hill. Each stride became a matter of will.

Nkumah led him over the crest of the hill into a broad, lush valley. Protected from the elements, tall acacia trees grew on each side of the road, spreading their wide, flat-topped crowns. Most of the valley was cleared for farmland, although only a few scattered crops grew in the fields. To the north, the road disappeared over hills covered only with the ubiquitous grass and a few small trees.

They lumbered down the slope into the valley. The acacia became beautiful silhouettes in an orange and black sky. His breath rasped painfully through his chest. Even though every step was agony, the stark beauty of the land comforted him. *For how many millennia had men stood in awe of this vision?*

A man's outline appeared in the road—a ghost that didn't make a sound. Nkumah ran toward the dark form, maintaining his stride. Ray followed, not sure what to expect. As they approached, he strained to see the man's face in the dying embers of the sun.

Recognition spawned relief; it was Tandra, Nkumah's friend.

***

A few minutes earlier, DoubleD had watched the sunset turn the men marching ahead into dark ghosts. Dkembe had assured her that these were his best, two platoons totaling eighty soldiers from his elite Personal Guard. She knew he was being truthful; her spies had provided a detailed dossier of his military strength, which she had committed to memory before leaving California.

Dkembe walked next to her, moving forward with the steady, powerful gait of a panther. He hadn't said a word for more than an hour; she knew this hunt meant everything to him. Capturing Ray Brown was a sideshow; it was obvious Nkumah was Dkembe's real prey.

The trap was set. Dkembe's platoons were sweeping in from the north, Erlich was pushing in from the south and Condors patrolled the skies. Nkumah might be able to escape the Condors—Domain spies had learned of portable radar devices—but the rebel leader didn't know Domain soldiers were sweeping in. Ray Brown was somewhere in this trap, probably rushing toward them right now. If possible, she would like to capture Ray alive. Dianne would enjoy putting him in a cage again.

DoubleD was intimately aware of the man marching at her side. She smelled his sweat and listened to the movement of his body rub against the rough fabric of his uniform. She had planned to take him to her bed last night, but the pursuit of Ray Brown pushed that aside. First things first. Her hunger for Dkembe had not been satisfied, but it wasn't a problem. Sex was always better after a successful hunt.

The rain had finally ceased, setting the stage for Ray Brown's capture. The rich glow of the moon might reveal their position to the enemy, but it would be too late to escape. Anyway, the full moon enabled them to make good time along a rough dirt road. Dkembe sent scouts ahead but didn't dare contact them because Nkumah might have an electronic snooper. It didn't matter; a scout would return to Dkembe at the first sighting of their quarry.

To her left was the hulking form of a seven-foot tall, grey and black Commando robot, one of five with her in Africa. Commando robots were fast, fully armed with integral laser rifles, and virtually invulnerable to hand-held weapons. Specially designed for the most difficult missions, it was a reassuring presence, although she didn't really understand its alien mind. Domain scientists programmed the robot to be a matchless warrior, ready to fight to the death. Each robot had downloaded maps, tactics and rules of engagement for this mission. They obeyed Dkembe, but she could override his commands. She would do that only in an emergency; Dianne had instructed her to maintain the illusion that he was in charge.

Dkembe stationed a Commando at each corner of a disciplined, moving rectangle of men. Actually it was more like a spear, aimed at Ray Brown. Human soldiers filled out the sides, while she and Dkembe remained in the center, protected by a robot. Even if Nkumah were able to link up with a few of his warriors, he would be overmatched in any kind of firefight.

She was confident that they would get Ray Brown tonight. She would interrogate him as soon as victory was complete. Dianne was determined to identify the traitor who had planned Ray's escape. DoubleD hoped Ray resisted; it was exciting to dominate and then crush proud men. Dianne would be pleased with the results.

The trap was closing quickly, a scout might come running to them at any moment. Then they would have him.

The soldiers climbed over a low ridge and entered a lush valley, which was filled with flowering plants and tall acacia trees. She could see every color through a night vision contact lens as if it were midday. Condors, Commandos, night vision contacts, Sentinel and all the rest—the Domain's technology would lead them to victory tonight.

Under my leadership, of course.

Her anticipation soared when a scout returned to the frontline and reported in excited tones to an officer. A moment later, the officer halted the march and ran back to Dkembe.

"We spotted them, sir," the officer said, barely controlling his excitement. "Brown and Nkumah are about a mile and a half down the road, resting under the cover of an acacia."

"Did the scouts see any other soldiers? Anything suspicious?"

"Nothing."

"Good work," Dkembe said, his brows forming a thick ridge. "Get back to your position."

Once the officer hurried away, DoubleD said, "It's too easy."

Dkembe nodded, "It's time to break communications silence and call Erlich. It won't matter if it's just Brown and Nkumah, but if it's a trap, I want all our firepower here."

"I'm sure it's a trap, but where are its jaws?" she asked.

Dkembe shook his head and said, "Sentinel, set up a link to Erlich for Chief Duboski and myself."

Erlich's voice popped into DoubleD's mind through the Command Chip. "I'm here, sir."

"We've located Nkumah," Dkembe said, "I want the Condors to scan a thirty mile radius around my present location. Look for people, weapons systems or anything else that might pose a threat. Don't allow detection by any Neanderthals within the target area. Report back in fifteen minutes."

Dkembe left her to meet with his troops. She watched him speak briefly with the soldiers, outlining the situation and encouraging them to fight for victory. The men seemed in awe of him. He was a natural leader, she realized.

He returned in a few minutes and assured her his men were ready. Then Erlich called back as ordered, reporting that the Condors had not found anything suspicious. After Dkembe finished questioning Erlich, he said to her, "If it's a trap, it's well hidden."

"The target area appears to be clear," Erlich said over the link. "The night vision of the Condors is excellent; they would have detected a concentration of men and equipment. In any case, we have the weaponry to exterminate them if there's an attack."

"Erlich, take one of my platoons and two robots and capture Brown and Nkumah," he said. "I want them alive if possible."

"Yes, sir."

A good decision. She was still concerned about a trap, but Erlich would be the one to spring it. *The sacrificial goat.* She assumed that was Dkembe's plan; it's what she would have ordered in his place.

Dkembe had retained one platoon and two robots, which he organized in a defensive circle around them. In addition, one Commando robot stood next to them, scanning for enemies as its head rotated back and forth.

Moving in front of the robot, Dkembe said, "Show me the view seen by the robot nearest Erlich."

A plate in its chest area slid open, revealing a one-foot square display screen. DoubleD stood next to Dkembe, her eyes riveted to the display, watching the scene transmitted by a robot in Erlich's helicopter. The ground came up quickly as the helicopter silently landed about a mile south of the target. Coordinating his troops with the platoon of soldiers from Dkembe's force, she watched Erlich surround the target area and then move in. Everything seemed to be going according to plan. In a moment, images of the two men they sought appeared in the display. Nkumah was sitting quietly, with his back against a tree; Brown was stretched out, apparently sleeping.

All her senses screamed a warning. She didn't like it; it was too easy. After evading them for years, Nkumah wouldn't be caught so easily.

Nkumah knows Dkembe will use Erlich to spring the trap. Then it hit her. *The trap must be set to snare us at the same time!*

"Erlich, hold your forces where they are," she commanded. She saw Dkembe's surprised look, but continued to bark out orders, "Sentinel, I want thermal scans of every acre of land within a two mile radius of the target."

"That will take hours," Dkembe spit out. "We need to attack now!"

"I think they're hiding nearby. They might be in a cave, in the trees, anywhere. We'll locate them from their body heat; Nkumah can't shield his entire army. This is his territory and we're walking into a trap."

"You don't give the orders here—I do," Dkembe roared.

Dkembe's dark eyes glared through the shadows. She was standing only a few feet from him, but she was ready for anything. The laser pistol on her hip exerted a familiar pressure. She didn't want to kill him, but she wouldn't let him lead them into a trap.

Suddenly, a series of explosions lit up the sky all around them. She jumped behind the robot, narrowly avoiding the force of a nearby blast. The roar of explosions was deafening. Hot air scorched her face, followed by chunks of dirt, rocks and branches whizzing past. Knowing that she must be a prime target, DoubleD dropped to the ground, stretched out and buried her face in her arms. Another explosion to her left, then another. The ping of bullets against metal told her that the robot must be crouched over her, shielding her from enemy fire. Dkembe pressed against her side as they hid under the Commando robot.

The blasts were over in a few seconds, but choking dust covered the battlefield. She crawled from under the robot to look around, but the dust limited her vision to less than a hundred yards. In the distance, she saw a patch of earth rise up and then flip over, revealing the entrance to a narrow tunnel. A man crawled out of the tunnel; then several other men.

Nkumah had pre-positioned his soldiers in underground tunnels, she realized too late. *He must have prepared this trap long ago. Ray Brown was the bait to lure us here.*

Another bullet pinged off the robot and she flattened her body against the hard clay. The gunfire appeared to be coming from the right. Only a few Domain soldiers were returning fire.

"We have to get clear of the battlefield," Dkembe shouted over the whoosh of rockets. "I called in a Condor to pick us up."

Dkembe began running away from the main fighting, keeping low to the ground.

"Protect me," she yelled at the robot and then raced after Dkembe.

The dust was settling, enabling her to keep Dkembe in sight. She jumped over the remains of a Domain soldier as she fled. A Condor swooped down and ripped off shots from its laser canon, turning several rebels into overcooked meat. She heard a whoosh of a missile behind them and turned to see a pair of rebels with a rocket launcher. She dove to the ground just as the Condor exploded above them, turning the night sky into a roaring inferno. Although her face was pressed against the ground, a fiery wave of heat scorched her ears, followed by the sky-shattering blast of the exploding helicopter. A tidal wave of sound turned her world into a hellhole of intense pain, and she almost blacked out.

Suddenly, it was quiet.

She could see the white streaks of laser beams. She could see the Commando robot standing next to her, providing a shield against rebel soldiers in the distance. She could see the flames of burning trees rising high into the sky.

But she couldn't hear a sound.

Dkembe was about fifty feet in front of her, gesturing to follow him. His lips were moving, but his voice was silent. Her earlobes felt damp. She touched the wetness and stared at her fingers. Blood. She was deaf, probably seriously wounded, but she didn't have time to think about it. All that mattered now was survival.

DoubleD staggered to her feet and ran toward Dkembe. A laser beam flashed, and she dove behind an acacia tree. Hell was silent, but terrible. Crouched behind the trunk, she tried to catch her breath. The stench of burnt flesh was sickening. Fighting down her fear, she scanned the area to her left and located an enemy soldier firing a laser rifle. Holding her laser pistol with both hands, she fired a silent beam at the rebel. The soldier's chest turned into red meat, and blood spurted out.

Then she was running again. She followed Dkembe back along the path, with the robot just behind her. Increasingly lightheaded, it was difficult to keep up. Her throat was raw from the dust and she coughed up dark phlegm as she ran. A laser beam cut through the night, passing just to her left. Then another beam, again to the left.

The robot came to a sudden stop, turned and began firing at their pursuers. She kept running, forcing weary legs to her will. A sudden flash lit up the sky, seared her back and threw her into the air, tumbling out of control. She tried to tuck her head in and roll as her shoulder crashed into the hard clay, but the impact flipped her onto her back and she skidded to a stop. Agony ripped through her body.

Something cold and hard lifted her into the air. Through the pain, she realized that the Commando was running toward Dkembe, holding her against its metallic chest. Pain flared with every jarring step, but she wouldn't let it defeat her. She began to slip out of the robot's awkward grip and one foot dangled almost to the ground. She wrapped her arms around the robot's slick head and pulled herself up, determined to survive.

Blinking her eyes to clear the dust, DoubleD saw a Condor come whirling in and lower a plastic seat attached to a cable. A moment later, Dkembe reached the seat and strapped himself in. She had almost reached Dkembe when the soaring heat of a laser beam ripped open the robot's back. She crashed to earth, pinned by the charred remains of the robot's body. The red-hot metal burned through her uniform and she screamed silently into the void.

Through the debris, she saw Dkembe staring at her. He was sitting in the plastic seat with one hand on the cable, ready to disappear into the sky. The Condor was firing shafts of violent light, but it was vulnerable hovering so close to the ground. She knew he would leave without her. A dark veil began to form over her eyes, stranding her in this silent hell. Her mind seemed to drift— leaving the agony behind— then Dkembe's face was above her, clearing hot chunks of metal off her chest. A spasm racked her lungs as she sucked in filthy air. He carried her over to the seat and held her in his arms as they lifted off. She didn't understand. It was all so quiet. A rush of air was the last thing she felt, and then everything went dark.

SEVEN

Saturday, May 17, 2025

Standing on the crest of a gentle hill, Ray tried to enjoy a mild breeze blowing across his shoulders. In the distance, the morning sun cleared the hilltops surrounding the valley. Blue skies and a few low-hanging clouds gliding across the hills. The kind of morning he loved.

But not today.

Yesterday's beautiful valley was gone: chewed up and ripped apart by the battle. Bodies were littered across what remained of a once sweet land. The air, usually crisp and clean, wafted up from the bodies, fouled with the tinge of death. Many of the slain appeared to be waiting patiently, ready to make the final trip to their Creator. The rest were badly broken, some barely recognizable as human.

And then there were the body parts. A foot here, a head there, scattered across the valley. The body parts were the thing that sickened him the most.

They all fought bravely and should be buried as humans. Even here, especially here, we need to show respect to those who gave their lives.

A handful of Nkumah's warriors moved among the bodies, still searching for survivors. Standing silently on the hill, Ray watched them walk from body to body, feeling a limp hand for a pulse or listening for a feeble breath. Each time they would stand wearily; take a last glance at the body and then move on. It was a hard thing to endure, even for an outsider.

Ray had watched them well into the night, removing wounded comrades and providing medical attention. Now, at first light, they were out there again, making sure they recovered all the living. But all they found was death. The slain warriors were loaded into vans, to be returned to their villages, where they could rest in ancient burial grounds.

With respect.

He was startled by a shadow darting across the ground in front of him. Looking up, he spotted a vulture soaring high, wings spread to catch the currents. Such a beautiful bird as it rode the wind, but so ugly when it fought for a scrap of flesh on the ground.

A shot rang out, reminding Ray there was even kindness of a sort for wounded enemies. Rather than leave half-alive men to be ripped apart by the carrion eaters, they were mercifully killed with a bullet to the head.

Gradually, he became aware of a man standing behind him. "How long have you been there?" Ray asked, not needing to look.

"Not long," Nkumah answered.

The warrior chief stepped up next to Ray, and then squatted on his haunches and gazed over the battlefield. Without warning, Nkumah sagged and put a hand to the ground to keep his balance, crouched at the knees. Ray realized that even Nkumah must be dead tired.

Ally or enemy?

Nkumah was a threat to his son, but he was also essential in the war against the Domain. The man had left him the moment the fighting began, leading his men into battle. Ray hadn't known whether Nkumah survived until just now. He stared down at the top of Nkumah's curly hair, vaguely disappointed that the man was still breathing.

"Your plan worked perfectly," Ray said. He spat in the rocky soil. "You must be pleased."

"It was a failure." When Ray gave him a questioning look, Nkumah added, "The head of the snake escaped."

"Dkembe?"

"Yes." Nkumah rose wearily to his feet. "And the assassin called DoubleD. She's here for you."

Dianne had sent a killer. He expected it; that was who she was. *She'll never quit.*

"Come with me," Nkumah said. "I have something to show you, and then we leave."

As he walked with Nkumah, Ray noticed only a few stragglers remained on the battlefield. Nkumah's warriors were leaving, fading into the brush. The time for collecting honored dead was almost gone. Carrion eaters–vultures and jackals –now moved in to claim their rewards. They fought over the remains, sharp teeth challenging hooked beaks and talons.

The vultures had their place; they stripped the flesh from rotting animals, keeping the savannah free of disease. It was something else when the bodies were human.

Nkumah led Ray back toward a small circle of men. He recognized several young warriors from the Ukali village, but they were different now: hard, with the youth gone from their posture. War did that.

A captive was on his knees in the center of the circle, but Ray couldn't see much of the man through the jumble of bodies. Nkumah's men seemed to be cursing the prisoner in their language, their faces full of hate. Each warrior would shout and then jab the captive with the tip of a spear. Deep enough to cut, but not to kill.

As Ray approached, he recognized the word they were chanting: *Chamuko, Chamuko, Chamuko*. He hoped it didn't mean the chief was dead. He couldn't handle much more of this.

The circle parted as they approached, revealing a battered white man, crouched on his knees like a wounded buffalo surrounded by lions. The man's clothes had been removed, exposing dozens of cuts, each trickling blood. His feet were badly deformed; Ray's stomach turned when he realized the prisoner's toes had been crushed into bony strands hanging in loose flesh. When the captive saw Nkumah, the man uttered a choked cry and tried to run, but his feet were too mangled and he fell over.

Nkumah walked over to the white man and glared down at him. Malice must have infused Nkumah with new energy; he seemed poised on the edge of violence. The warriors stepped aside but continued to curse the white man. Ray had never felt such a flow of raw hatred.

Although this man was a terrible enemy, Ray couldn't allow such brutality to continue. He was about to demand that they cease this torture, but then realized something about the situation had not yet been revealed. Nkumah could have tortured this poor soul in private, but Ray had been brought here to see the spectacle. Nkumah never did anything without a reason. Ray folded his arms across his chest and waited.

The white man spotted Ray and cried out, "You! Help me. I'm Benjamin Erlich, an officer of the Domain." He staggered to his feet, but the effort reduced his voice to a whisper. "As a prisoner of war, I should be treated humanely." He glanced fearfully at Nkumah and then turned back to Ray, "I surrender to you, Ray Brown. Take me from these savages."

A smile twisted across Nkumah's lips. "Well, he surrendered to you," Nkumah said to Ray. "I can respect that. What would you have us do with him?"

All the warriors were staring at him; the friendship of the Ukali village was long gone. He heard a warrior whisper, "Malomi," to the man standing next to him.

This was a test.

"You knew he was going to surrender to me, didn't you," Ray said to Nkumah.

Nkumah ignored him, instead signaling with his hand toward someone at the far edge of the circle. A young woman stepped through the ring of warriors. Her dark, empty eyes focused on Nkumah. Ray recognized her: the woman who nursed Paul. She had been pretty, he remembered, but now her face was bruised and her lips swollen. Her robe, yellow and brown cloth sewn with a pattern of flowers and animals, was torn and dirty.

"This is Lilanga of the Ukali tribe," Nkumah said.

"I recognize her."

"Hear her story and then make your decision."

Nkumah nodded to her and said something in the woman's native tongue. Her dead eyes glanced at Erlich, and she began to speak in a voice devoid of emotion. Ray didn't understand her language, but Nkumah simultaneously translated her words.

"After you left, we hid your friend in our secret place, then returned to the village," Lilanga said. "He did not awaken, but his fever had broken, so it was safe to leave him for a few hours. We knew the Domain soldiers would search our village, but I planned to return during the night after they left. A few hours later, that one— she gestured at Erlich—came to our village."

Through Nkumah, Lilanga described Chamuko's execution and the slaughter in the village. Ray knew that Chamuko had understood the danger, but the murder of such a decent, brave man was terrorism, not warfare. His chest burned. He understood why these people hated Erlich.

"One of his men dragged me back to the helicopter and we took off into the night," she continued. "Erlich threw me down on the front seat and ordered me to—to service him. When I refused, he beat me."

She took a deep breath, unable to go on. Nkumah spoke to her, his voice surprisingly gentle, and she nodded. The warriors were silent, but loathing stained their features.

"He raped me right there in the helicopter. His men were watching—some of them cheered. When he was finished…" She stopped again, tears beginning to trickle down her cheeks.

It was quiet, now. Even the carrion eaters seemed to become quiet, as if they had discovered an entity more despicable than themselves. Ray's stomach rolled, reminding him of the way he used to feel coming out of a weeklong drunk, but this was worse.

"When he was finished," Lilanga said again, "he looked at his men and shouted, *Anyone like to taste this little savage?* They all laughed and one of the men climbed on me." She looked up at Ray. "After that, one after another, they raped me. Then everything became hazy. I couldn't feel them anymore." She paused, her soul back in that hell. "Only the smell—the smell is still on me."

Lilanga seemed to have more to tell, but she had used up all her strength.

"Well, Ray, what do you say?" Nkumah asked. "Should we give him to the men or take him prisoner?"

Ray stared at Erlich. His appearance was human, but that was a just a facade.

"You must take me prisoner," Erlich begged him. "The Domain will pay to get me back." When Ray didn't answer, Erlich turned in desperation to Nkumah. "I'll help you get the Boss-Savage—Dkembe. I know all his secrets."

A vulture circled above them, its shadow slicing through the ring of men. Ray looked up and noticed several other birds, all circling above.

"Leave us," Ray said to Nkumah.

Nkumah began a question, but stopped abruptly. He stared at Ray, as if seeing him for the first time. Nkumah said something to the men and they began to walk away, some muttering at Erlich as they left.

Nkumah took a couple of steps with his men, but stopped in front of Ray. "Now I understand why she fears you," he said, and then walked past.

"Thank you, Ray," Erlich said quietly, his eyes following Nkumah. "You won't regret this."

Ray stared at this man who had forced him to confront his core. "Yeah," he said, and then turned and walked away, following Nkumah.

Erlich's voice came over his shoulder, "Ray, where are you going?"

He kept walking.

"Ray!" Erlich screamed, "I'm your prisoner!"

Erlich continued to call to him as he walked away. The man's cries gradually faded into the background, but he could still hear the terror in Erlich's screams when the first bird landed.

EIGHT

Tuesday, June 3, 2025

Dianne sat in a leather chair, responding to video messages displayed in the air a few feet in front of her. Her office was three hundred feet below the surface, safe from attack. Sparsely furnished, devoid of windows, she came here to work when she felt threatened. She didn't like being a mole, but too much was riding on her leadership to take any chances. Her security people claimed that down here she could survive a nuclear attack.

Dianne glanced across the room, where a three-dimensional hologram of the Oregon seashore covered a long wall. She might have to work underground, but she insisted on views of the most beautiful locations on the planet. With webcams located across the world, she had her choice of scenery. This one was her favorite, and she'd enjoyed it for hours. A breezy, overcast day hung over the coastline, with the sun setting behind billowing clouds. Waves rolled across the rocks and crashed onto a sandy beach. She could feel the sea breeze and taste the salt water on her lips. The rhythmic sound of the surf was reassuring: it changed every day, but remained the same.

She recalled walking that beach with Ray many times in the past, years before creating the Domain. *Ray ruined it all.* Anger began to seep in again, but she pushed it back. Contained, but not controlled.

"Terminate the scene."

She should have eliminated Ray long before it came to this. All those years on the island, he'd made it clear he didn't love her anymore. Why hadn't she done what was necessary?"

The security system's male voice broke into her thoughts, "Steve Bonini to see you."

She wasn't expecting Steve, but she guessed why he was here. Annoyed, she said, "Send him in."

To her left, a door slid open and Steve entered. Her annoyance receded as his portly shape approached. He'd always been overweight, but carried it gracefully. His hair, what was left of it, was mostly gray. She had urged him to have his baldness treated—it made him look older than fifty-eight—and he said he'd do it, but never got around to it. Steve was her best friend, the one person who had been with her all through the years.

A survivor, just like me.

Steve began speaking as he walked toward her. "I just saw Ray's video clip."

He sank heavily into the guest chair and stared anxiously at her, "We have to get something out on the Internet right away. This is going to fire up the masses. He's a dangerous man and we need to—"

Steve seemed to be searching her face. "You're awfully calm about this."

She leaned back in her chair. "I haven't seen his clip yet."

"You haven't seen…why the hell not?"

She shrugged. "Just haven't gotten to it," she said, forcing her attention back to the video message shimmering in front of her. Steve was staring quizzically at her, and for once, she didn't know what to say.

"Dianne?"

"I'll get to it," she snapped. He pulled back, surprise spreading across his face. "It's out there already," she added. "Not much we can do about it."

"You've never really gotten over him, have you?" Steve murmured, shaking his head. "Even after all these years."

"All right, dammit," she said. "Sentinel, run the Ray Brown clip."

The image of an austere, old-fashioned office was displayed across the wall. Ray sat behind a worn mahogany desk, sleeves rolled up, hands folded in front of him, staring into the camera. Except for old movies, she hadn't seen a two-dimensional clip in years. The image was grainy, washed out.

Old technology. She thought about it. *Clever*.

Ray's face sported a golden brown tan, but he was heavily wrinkled, looking all of his fifty-five years. He was thinner than he used to be, too thin. His hair was as she remembered—thick and unruly—although it was now steel gray except for an unusual dark patch around each ear. If he had consented to proper cosmetic care on the island—but he'd always been stubborn; it was just the way he was. Stubborn and stupid. She had offered him the world thirteen years earlier, but he turned her down.

"I'm Ray Brown," the image said, his voice strong, familiar. "You thought I was dead, but that was just one of Dianne Morgan's many lies."

She lit a cigarette, another vice from her past. As she listened to Ray, she fiddled with an old silver plated lighter, a gift from her long deceased mother.

"I'm not a madman," he said. "I'm not a murderer. I didn't develop the PeaceMaker virus. I didn't release it on the Internet." He paused. "Those were all lies."

Dianne sighed, and Steve's eyes flicked at her. She concentrated on Ray's words, although she knew what he would say.

"The true killers are Dianne Morgan and her underlings in the Domain. They developed PeaceMaker. They planned to shutdown the Internet and blackmail the nations of the world. All the death and destruction was their fault. When I destroyed their virus, they framed me, faked my death and imprisoned me for thirteen years. Last month I escaped. Now I'm here to tell you the truth about the Domain." He paused, his lips pinched into a thin line. "And the monster responsible for all of it: Dianne Morgan."

Ray leaned forward, his face intense. "Even after PeaceMaker was destroyed, Dianne Morgan never gave up her insane quest for dominance. The Domain developed the intelligent robots and other weapons that enabled them to bully legitimate governments into an uneasy truce. During the last three years, the Domain seduced more than a billion humans into joining their ranks, leaving the rest of us to rot.

"All this is detailed in the next section of the disk, but I'm not here to talk about the past. We have far more serious problems. Dianne Morgan plans to exterminate the six billion people who have refused to join her Domain. She also plans to use technologies such as artificial intelligence and genetic engineering to transform what remains of humanity into a dominant new species unlike anything that has ever inhabited this Earth.

You're wrong. I *don't plan to exterminate anyone. Just let them wither away.*

"Time is running out for us," Ray said. "When I say us, I mean traditional humans: those of us who wish to maintain the flesh and blood that has served us for millennia; those of us who don't want to be merged into silicon bodies; those of us who don't want to be force-fed into a whirlpool of genetic change.

"Scientists have a name for the moment when everything changes; they call it the Singularity. This is the tipping point where all the whirlwind technologies meet, the vortex where humanity is ripped apart, the crossover into a new kind of future."

Ray stood up, walked to the front of the desk, and then leaned back against its edge. "Why do the madmen of the Domain frantically rush into this non-human future?" He extended his arms, hands lifted, palms up. "Why this frenzy to replace us with an alien life form?

"Here's the sad truth: they don't really know why they are doing this. Even their leader, Dianne Morgan, doesn't understand why she is dragging humanity into this whirlpool. I know her well; I tell you she is driven by volatile emotions barely contained." Sadly, he shook his head. "She's insane."

And this is the man I wanted to share my dreams with. How could I have been so blind?

Ray's voice broke into her thoughts. "We're in a mess, but it's not hopeless. I'm not against technology, but we have to put the genie back in the bottle; we have to stop the Domain. Although these lunatics plan to eliminate traditional humans, for now they're still dependent upon us. Domain citizens live side by side with traditional humans, dependent upon our services for their existence. They rely upon us for most of the food they consume, the clothing they wear, construction of the buildings they live and work in— well, you get the idea. We must withhold these services, go out on strike, and life will become much more difficult within the Domain."

Ray paused, staring into the camera. He was her enemy once again.

"Many Domain citizens, those of you still clinging to your sanity, will give up this monstrous quest and return to normal lives, but the true believers will not abandon their nightmare future. Those committed scientists will push forward, bringing us closer and closer to the Singularity. They must not succeed. Once we cross over into that nightmare future, there is no coming back. We must begin a campaign of subversion and sabotage. I don't want to resort to violence, but it's a step we must take.

"It's where we are. It's what we must do." He stared defiantly into the camera, "Goodbye and may god bless our crusade."

As the clip faded out, Steve said, "They have a leader now, a focus." When Dianne didn't respond, he said, "We have to attack immediately, before they're organized. Get their leaders, especially Ray. Our spies have already identified many to be eliminated. We can break their strike before it takes hold."

"I never wanted it to come to this."

"I know, but we have to kill Ray this time," Steve said. "No mercy."

"I'm not a fool," she snapped. *I tried to save him.* "Ray called for war; now we'll show him the full power of the Domain."

NINE

Friday morning, December 26, 2025

DoubleD strode up the bluestone steps of the mansion, enjoying the sometimes discreet, sometimes openly admiring stares of both male and female Domain employees. Followed by two of the latest model Daniel androids, she felt safe from potential assassins. Unlike the giant Commando robots, these were human-sized androids, virtually impossible to distinguish from a normal human soldier. They were armed with laser pistols, which they could use with far greater speed and accuracy than a human soldier. The androids were not as intellectually nimble as a human, but they were getting close.

Her helicopter had touched down in the landing pad only minutes earlier, and the waiting limousine whisked her to headquarters. She checked her watch: eleven-forty a.m. Plenty of time to make the meeting.

Her first Domain Council meeting! She had served three years as Security Chief; three years of total dedication to the cause. It would have been a great Christmas present, except she was an atheist. Dianne was expressing confidence in her, regardless of the situation in Africa.

Or is she? You never know with that one.

DoubleD paused at the top of the steps and pressed her hand against the biometrics reader. She felt wonderful, not even breathing hard from the climb to the entrance. Her form-fitting clothes provided adequate insulation from the northern California winter.

Before being admitted into headquarters, she would be fingerprinted, a full-body bone scan would be completed, and she would be scanned for weapons. The system would verify her identity by comparing her medical records against a database of more than a billion Domain citizens and natural humans.

I can't hide the problems from Dianne, but I can soften them around the edges. Act confident. They won't challenge me if I remain confident and in control.

While she waited, DoubleD looked down the winding main road to the brick wall at the edge of the estate. A thin, cold wind rustled through the few leaves remaining on the trees scattered across the grounds. Security seemed good: human and robot soldiers were everywhere, manning checkpoints, coordinating over netphones, even driving an armored troop carrier. She was satisfied with what she saw, but even more encouraging, she could hear every sound. As the carrier rumbled down the road, she thanked her luck once again that neural implants had restored her hearing.

It was seven months since her hearing had been destroyed by that terrible explosion. Julius Dkembe had saved her life, and then rushed her to his best hospital in Dar es Salaam. DoubleD's inner ears had been badly damaged, leaving her deaf. A traditional cochlear implant would have been ineffective due to extensive cell damage, so she agreed to an experimental procedure. Surgeons injected millions of nanoprobes into her bloodstream around each ear. The nanoprobes attached themselves to the hair cells of the inner ear, replaced the nerve endings of the damaged cells, and gradually restored her hearing.

Although thankful that she could hear again, the sounds that passed through the nanoprobes were unfamiliar: often difficult to recognize, sometimes louder than normal, sometimes softer. She was training her mind to distinguish these new sounds, a process still underway.

In addition, a microcomputer was surgically implanted behind one ear. The computer responded to voice commands, allowing her to adjust the sensitivity and frequency range of her hearing.

"Thank you, Chief Duboski," the security system said. "You may enter."

"Wait here for me," she said to the androids.

DoubleD entered a huge, modern lobby that bustled with activity; smartly-dressed people and androids strode in all directions. She noticed a pair of husky brown-and-green-clad security guards standing at attention at the entrance to the executive offices, which was about two hundred feet on the right. The men were staring at her and whispering to each other. When one of the men said something and the other snickered, she said, "Increase volume fifty percent."

The background noise increased dramatically. Now she could hear everything around her; the rhythmic cycles of her breathing, the brush of fabric against skin as people walked by, even the wind rustling through azaleas in the garden outside. She picked up the voices of the security men, but the conversation was muffled by background noise.

"Focus on the sounds coming from directly in front of me; filter background noise."

"...says she has a lover in Africa, that guy Dkembe."

"Lucky bastard," the other guard whispered. "Look at her standing over there. What a pair."

"I don't know how she kept her job after that disaster in Africa. I understand she lost her hearing in the battle, but got it back with some new kind of implant."

"Who cares? I wasn't planning on sticking it in her ear."

"I wouldn't touch that woman," the first guard said. "They say she kills the guys who do her. No sir, it's not worth taking the—

"Shut up! She's walking over here."

As DoubleD approached, her heels clicking on the glossy ceramic floor, both men snapped to attention. Stopping in front of them, she pretended to inspect their uniforms. She reached down and pulled the laser pistol out of the taller guard's holster, the one who had talked about having sex with her. Her eyes were on a level with his, just a few inches away. She brushed his neck with the barrel of the pistol and then pressed the muzzle under his chin.

"This weapon hasn't been properly maintained, soldier."

"Yes, Chief," he responded.

"A poorly maintained weapon could discharge accidentally." There was an audible click when she released the safety catch. "I expect my soldiers to take better care of their weapons." She pushed the muzzle until a crease appeared in his skin.

"I'll do better in the future, Chief," he gurgled, remaining at attention.

DoubleD was pleased to see a drop of sweat on his neck. She was the boss, and the men in her command would respect her or face the consequences.

She slipped the gun back into his holster and stepped away, "Next time I won't be so forgiving." She gave the shorter guard a hard stare, "And that means you, too, soldier."

DoubleD turned and strode into the executive office suite. She listened carefully, but neither man said anything.

Word would get around.

Walking down the hall, she contemplated the Council meeting. She had been invited to present the current status of Domain security, and it could be a contentious meeting. Conventional three-sixty hearing would be necessary.

"Restore normal hearing," she said.

The hallway was deserted except for two Daniel-class androids guarding the entrance to the conference room. The androids stared as she approached, performing some type of secret security scan. There were many secrets within the Domain; only Dianne knew everything. The door slid open and she walked through without breaking stride.

Confident and in control. Remember, confident and in control.

Glancing about as she entered the stark, windowless meeting room, she noticed that Dr. Chang and Steve Bonini were present in the flesh, while Mohammed Kateel was transmitting his hologram image. Chang and Bonini sat in luxuriously padded chairs on opposite sides of a short conference table, with Kateel's hologram next to Chang.

She walked around the table to sit next to Bonini. Chang ignored her—the arrogant bastard ignored everyone except Dianne—but Bonini smiled and said, "Darlene, good to see you."

Bonini, Kateel and Dianne were the only surviving members of the original Domain leaders; the others were killed during the PeaceMaker fiasco. The pear-shaped Bonini wasn't an imposing figure, but DoubleD respected his intelligence and courage. If Dianne Morgan actually had a true friend in this world, it was Bonini.

She cleared her throat. "Great to see you again, Steve." Nodding in the direction of the hologram, she added, "You, too, Mohammed.

"Welcome to the Council meeting," Kateel replied.

Although not a particularly warm personality, Mohammed Kateel was always courteous to her. All Domain software was developed under his guidance; Dianne considered him David Brown's technical equal, although he lacked the innate ability to communicate with artificial intelligence. Kateel was to robotics what Chang was to genetics: a genius in his field.

"Will you be staying at headquarters for a few days?" Bonini asked.

"Depends on what we decide today."

Bonini was about to reply when Dianne stepped into the room and strode to the head of the table, her black high heels clicking on the floor. A form-fitting grey and white pants suit accentuated her regal appearance. Everyone stared in silence at this sleek, handsome woman. Although DoubleD had worked directly for Dianne as Security Chief for more than three years, she was still in awe of the great woman. Dianne had driven the Domain to world dominance through the sheer force of her will.

DoubleD was surprised when Dianne said to her, "Come with me."

She followed Dianne through a side door into a small room furnished with two stuffed chairs separated by an oak coffee table. In heels, Dianne was as tall as she was. Dianne sat down and then signaled DoubleD to sit. After opening a narrow drawer, she pulled out a cigarette and lit it with an old lighter.

Her mother's lighter. Bonini told me all about Dianne's mother, who passed away from lung cancer while Dianne was a senior in high school. A real bitch, but she took good care of Dianne. Her father had died years earlier, so Dianne was on her own at eighteen. She wasn't sentimental about many things, but she always kept that lighter close by.

Staring at DoubleD with those penetrating eyes, Dianne puffed on the cigarette and said, "Nasty habit. You were smart never to get started."

That's what posed as small talk for Dianne. DoubleD did not have to wait long for Dianne to get down to business.

"I invited you to this meeting to provide a blunt assessment of the African situation. Before you say anything, realize that I know *everything*. Even more than you."

After a long drag on her cigarette, Dianne continued, "I know exactly how poorly the war is going. I want you to provide our associates with a brutally accurate assessment. No bullshit. Do you understand?"

"Yes, I can do that."

Dianne stood up and said, "Well then, let's not keep the boys waiting." Her thin lips turned up at the corners, "They may be nervous about our little discussion."

DoubleD followed Dianne back into the conference room. *Why does she want the Council to hear all the bad news?* The three men regarded Dianne warily. *Is she planning to remove me?*

After greeting everyone, Dianne said, "Let's get started. Security is the first item on the agenda. I asked Darlene to review the status of the insurgency, particularly the situation in Africa."

"Thank you, Dianne," DoubleD said. "To summarize, the insurgency is gaining strength in Africa. Each month, the number of attacks has increased, as pictured on this graph."

A hologram appeared over the conference table, displaying a bar chart of attacks for each month of the year. The graph was flat for the first five months, and then began to increase in June, gradually at first and then rapidly during the last few months. The group stared at the hologram.

"I didn't realize it was that bad," Bonini said.

"There's more," DoubleD said. "The attacks are increasing in ferocity as well as in numbers. The rebels are receiving better intelligence from the native population, allowing them to hit our weak spots. We can't guard everything all the time."

Next, the hologram displayed a map of Africa, which was divided into red, green and yellow areas, "We control the green zones, the insurgency controls the red zones and the yellow areas are not dominated by either side. As you can see, the major cities belong to us, but our control lessens as we leave the urban areas. We control the skies, so we can attack rebel formations anywhere on the continent…when we can find them."

"According to your map, we control less than one-third of Africa," Kateel said, his expression incredulous. "We're losing this war to those Neanderthals?"

"We're not losing, but we are in for a long, tough fight," DoubleD replied. "Increasing numbers of the population are joining the insurgency. Their command and control structure is improving and they appear to be better armed. Even in the areas we control, the population has become defiant."

"It appears everything has gone in the wrong direction since Ray Brown escaped," Bonini said. "He's the cause of all this, isn't he?"

"It's true Brown has become the emotional leader of the insurgency," DoubleD said to Bonini. "Millions of copies of his speech have been distributed across the continent and beyond. You've all heard his speech; it's dynamic and compelling. He's whipped up war fever across Africa and now it's spreading to other continents.

"Many of the Africans believe that he was sent by the gods to save them," she continued. "He's worshipped as a demigod named Malomi, destined to kill the witch Bavera and her coven. That's Dianne and the Domain, according to their beliefs."

"Ridiculous," muttered Chang.

"Yes, but they believe it." DoubleD paused. "Brown claims the Domain plans to wipe out humanity. He urges all unenhanced humans to fight us before it's too late." She glanced at Dianne, whose expression was unreadable, as usual. "Brown says Dianne framed him for the PeaceMaker disaster— that it was the first instance of her megalomania." DoubleD's gaze returned to Bonini. "Many believe his claims."

"Why can't we just crush them?" Chang exclaimed. "Our weaponry is far superior to that of the primitives." He looked to Dianne for support. "Just exterminate anyone who gives us the slightest bit of trouble."

"We have initiated many harsh policies already, Dr. Chang," DoubleD said. "Our Condor helicopters patrol the skies constantly. In the red zones, they attack anything that moves. Even in the yellow zones, they destroy anything suspicious. Although we kill thousands of rebels every month, it's a big continent.

"Recently we began dropping Spybots into the red zone. These are four-foot tall solar-powered robots that are programmed to hide, search and report. They power-up while they hide during the day and then search at night. With enhanced night vision and sensitive heat detectors, they are proving to be very effective in finding the campfires of the enemy's hidden villages. Once they detect a village, or any other target, the Spybot contacts a Condor, which destroys the target. No human intervention required."

"Just nuke them and get it over with," Chang said. "Exterminate all the vermin in the red zones."

The room was quiet for a moment, and then Kateel said, "That makes no sense; the radioactive dust would drift across the continent. We'd be killing our people, too."

"We'd lose some people, but it would be a small price to pay," Chang replied.

"Africa would be unfit for humans for decades," Kateel said. "The radioactivity would blow across the globe. North America would be devastated by radioactive clouds." He snorted. "Stick to your molecular biology, my friend, and leave warfare to the professionals."

"Africa doesn't matter," Chang said. "America would suffer little radiation if the attacks were properly designed. All I need are a few more years to take humanity to the next stage. That's our mission."

What a horse's ass. Someday…

"What are you doing to capture Ray?" Bonini asked DoubleD.

"Our Condors and Spybots search constantly. Satellites have been retargeted to focus on southern Africa. We have informers within many of the tribes. All this information is fed into our central computers on a real-time basis. Sentinel monitors all this activity and directs our resources based upon the latest intelligence."

"Perhaps your informers pass bad information to Sentinel," Bonini said, leaning forward. DoubleD noticed that one of the buttons on his shirt had opened, exposing a thick waist. "Nkumah has fooled us in the past with double agents," he added.

"We've taken precautions to insure the loyalty of our informers," DoubleD answered. She wished Bonini would button his shirt, it was so tacky. Most gay men were fastidious about their appearance, but not Bonini.

"In many of the tribes, we have acquired more than one informer, so we cross-check intelligence. In other situations, we imprison a relative of the informer. Sometimes several relatives. If we don't gain valuable intelligence within a reasonable period, we send a gift from home. This tends to keep the informer motivated."

"What do you mean *a gift from home*?" Chang asked.

"Usually a finger, sometimes an ear."

"These activities seem logical, but they're not working," Kateel said. "Logic dictates a change of strategy."

Another pompous ass.

"Your suggestion is what?" DoubleD said.

"I'm not the Security Chief, Darlene," Kateel replied. "I don't ask you to design neurocircuits."

She admitted to herself that Kateel was right. Her strategy so far wasn't working.

Before DoubleD could reply, Dianne said, "It's time to thin the herd."

DoubleD knew exactly what that meant. It was a course of action she had considered, but it was so severe that she'd pushed it aside.

"It's time to change strategy," Dianne said. "Once Ray joined the rebellion, we lost our chance for an easy victory."

Dianne's eyes swept across the room, then settled on DoubleD.

"This will be a war of attrition," Dianne said. "In order to defeat the rebels, we must kill massive numbers of the enemy. Not with nuclear weapons—that's a two-edged sword—but through a planned, ongoing series of attacks. Entire tribes must be eliminated; men, women, children, every member of the tribe."

DoubleD began to feel sick. *Warriors don't kill children.* She pulled her eyes away from Dianne and looked at the others. Kateel was nodding his head in agreement, while Chang looked happy, as much as that miserable bastard could express any emotion. Only Bonini appeared troubled.

Don't they see? Dianne's plan is a pogrom, an annihilation of black Africans on the scale of Nazi Germany and the Jews.

"Start in the yellow zones of Tanzania, then spread out," Dianne said. "We'll ship Daniel androids from all over the world to Africa. The tribes are terrified of the robots. Once the killing begins, the people will scatter. They'll be easy targets from the air."

"The ones who survive will hate us," Bonini said. "They'll hide in the red zones. They'll all join the insurgency. They'll become our worst enemies."

Exactly right. And killing children, even rebel children, is barbarous.

"I agree," Dianne said. "That's why we have to exterminate entire tribes. If they're all dead in the yellow zones, the insurgency will be starved of new recruits."

Bonini was about to reply when Dianne said, "I'm calling for a vote. Those in favor of this change in strategy, raise your hand."

Dianne, Kateel and Chang raised their hands. Bonini leaned back in his chair, arms folded.

And I'm the one who has to lead this pogrom. It's barbaric and counter-productive.

Then she raised her hand.

***

Sunlight streamed through Kathy's broad living room window, which displayed the blue sky and stark mountains of northern California. Her husband was sitting on the couch, his back to her as she entered the room.

Today's the day for that insane merge with Sentinel. She felt the baby move, a painful cramping sensation. *I have to try one last time.*

"Are you sure you're ready to take this step?" Kathy asked as she carried a coffee tray around the couch. She placed the tray on the coffee table and then sat heavily. "It could be dangerous."

"You should let me carry the tray," Dave said. He poured a cup of steaming coffee and placed it in front of her. "You're seven months pregnant."

"You didn't answer my question."

"It's time," Dave replied. "Three years have passed."

"I don't care if three decades have passed. You're the only husband I have." Her mouth turned into an intimate smile. "Besides, you're not half-bad. I've kind of grown accustomed to having you around."

Dave returned her smile and then sipped his coffee. "I'll be fine. Sentinel and I have a great relationship. There's no way he'd let me get hurt."

We both know that's bull.

"Sentinel's still just a machine," Kathy said. "Disks, processors, ports and a hundred million lines of code, much of it developed by inexperienced programmers working overtime. If your mind is lost, it'll just say *abnormal termination, system restarting* and keep going its merry way."

"My mind will not be lost. In essence, a copy of my mind will be transferred to Sentinel. The original will stay within my brain, waiting to be reactivated. A small jolt of electricity and my brain will begin working again, leaving me just as charming as always."

"I still don't feel comfortable with this process," Kathy muttered. "Explain it to me again."

"Okay," Dave replied. "I go into the Virtual Reality Booth and establish a direct link to Sentinel, same as always. I relax, cut off all sensory input and let my mind open up to the link. Sentinel transfers a copy of my mind into its memory and activates it. Bit by bit, Sentinel redirects its sensory input to my electronic mind; as much as I can handle, but no more. I function as an independent processor within Sentinel for as long as I want, then we reverse the process. All the new knowledge is loaded back into my human brain, so that I will remember the entire experience. A small jolt of electricity and I wake up."

"You make it sound simple, but I know it's dangerous. It's never been done before. Nobody has ever tried such a stunt."

"It's not a stunt," Dave said, looking annoyed. "There's good science supporting every aspect of the process."

"What happens to the copy of your mind that's left inside Sentinel?"

"Sentinel examines it and tries to learn as much as possible about the functioning of the human mind. The more it knows, the more compatible we become. Actually, Sentinel will grow more like me every time we do this."

Sipping her coffee, Kathy stared at her husband. *So young, so handsome. Will he change after merging with an AI? Will he still love me?*

"You shouldn't be attempting anything so dangerous. I know how badly you want to merge with Sentinel, but you have a big responsibility on the way."

"This is the only way for us. My potential to merge with Sentinel is the only reason I'm still alive."

She knew that was the truth. Dianne had not been able to find anyone with Dave's talent. She winced when their son kicked inside her.

What was the matter with that baby today?

"Martin having an active day?" Dave asked.

"So what is all this work leading to?" Kathy asked, keeping the pain from her face. "After you perform these mind transfers a whole bunch of times?"

"Well, I don't exactly know. Maybe I become a human computer. Maybe Sentinel becomes a humanized computer. Maybe something totally unexpected."

"And what does Dianne say about this? Has she threatened you?" When he fumbled for an answer, Kathy said, "My god, you didn't tell her."

"I'll tell her afterwards. Maybe. You know we can't trust her."

"Damn it, Dave, why is it always you?" she said, shaking her head.

She had a bad feeling about this attempt, but there was no point in continuing to argue with Dave. He was just like his father; once he got an idea in his mind, nothing could stop him.

Leaning over the table, she placed her hand on his. "I know, I know, it's in the genes."

***

Later that morning, David entered his home office and began a final review in his mind of the detailed calculations supporting his planned merger with Sentinel. He worked for about an hour, but a headache developed so he leaned back in his chair and closed his eyes. He was so tired of all the lies, all the years of deception. His thoughts drifted back to a day long ago...

I'm doing my homework on the dining room table when the doorbell rings.

"David honey, can you answer the door, please," his mother calls from the kitchen, where she is preparing dinner.

It is the first day of February, 2012, and a cold blast of winter chills me when I open the front door. Two big men in dark suits are waiting. One is a mean-looking man about thirty, while the other has a deeply wrinkled, sad face. The younger man looks over my head into the house, while the gray-haired man speaks directly to me.

"We're the police, son. Is your mother home?"

I run into the kitchen to get my mother, and then follow her back to the front door. Ron, my mother's long-time boyfriend, comes down the staircase and joins us at the door. He had moved in shortly after Mom divorced Dad, but for some reason, they had never married. Maybe because Mom still loved Dad. Maybe there was a chance we could be a family again.

The policemen introduce themselves as detectives, but I don't catch their names. The older detective asks if they could discuss an important matter in private. The man seems to be looking gravely at me when Mom touches my arm.

"David, why don't you go upstairs for a few minutes while Ron and I talk with the detectives."

Reluctantly, I climb the stairs and walk into my brother's room, where Brian is playing an old-fashioned football game on his computer. At eleven, I feel like an adult when I talk to Brian, who is only eight.

"The police are downstairs," I say. "Something's wrong."

"You think the police are here to arrest Mom?" Brian asks.

"No, you knucklehead. But I'm going to listen to what they say."

"Me, too," Brian says, and quietly follows me to the staircase. We creep down a few steps, where I can make out muted voices, but the words blur into sketchy rhythms.

"Sorry...two days ago...PeaceMaker...explosion...investigating—

After a few moments the words fade into silence. The house is deathly quiet, and then I hear my mother sobbing. The utter desolation of the sound is chilling; my mother is a strong person who always handles things.

I rush down the stairs, half running and half falling. Brian follows me down the staircase and into the living room. Mom is standing next to Ron, crying with her face buried in his shoulder. Ron has his arms around her, making comforting sounds. I stare at them, my legs locked into place.

Ron's face is ashen as he looks up and sees us. He turns to the detectives, who are standing next to the couch, and says, "Please wait for us in the dining room. We'll need a few minutes."

The younger detective seems annoyed, then strolls out of the room. The older one glances at me and then says to Ron, "Take as much time as you need." The detective hesitates a moment as if to say something more, then changes his mind and follows the other man out of the room.

Wearing a somber expression, Ron stares at me, then says, "Sit down on the couch, please." His voice is strained. "You, too, Brian."

I know something terrible has happened, so I do what I am told. As I wait for someone to speak, Brian grabs my elbow, nails pressing painfully through my shirt. Ron looks at Mom, who is still crying softly in his arms, then turns back to us, a deep sadness across his face.

"We just received terrible news," Ron says.

Mom stops crying and lifts her head from Ron's shoulder. She looks awful, eyes red and puffy. Mom wipes the tears from her face with the back of her hand, but her cheeks still glisten. She looks at Ron, puts her hand on his arm and turns to face us. I have never seen my mother look so sad. Not ever.

"It's your father," Mom says. She walks on unsteady legs to the couch and kneels in front of us. "The police claim that he was the one responsible for the computer virus attack." Brian starts to argue, but Mom says, "There's more." Swallowing hard, she says, "He's dead. Killed two days ago." Another choked pause, and then, "There was an explosion."

The room becomes a gravesite, and I can hear the policemen whispering to each other in the dining room. It couldn't be possible my father is gone. An image of Dad flows into my mind, chasing me on the beach, his face alive and shining; he's so happy and for once, so was I. For just a moment, I feel like smiling. Then Brian's face breaks apart in a wail, and he throws his arms around Mom. Brian cries hoarsely, a choking cry I have never forgotten.

I sit on the couch, stiff and brittle, with tears sliding down my face. Ron is saying something, but the words drift past my comprehension. After a few moments, I stand up, plod across the room and labor up the stairs. Mom calls after me, but her voice seems far away, insignificant. I drift into my room and close the door by habit.

Curled up in my bed, face wet with tears, I don't make a sound. Dad is gone, this time forever. I want to scream that I hate my father, but I choke it back. What good would it do? My father has never been there for me. Now, he never will be.

My mother pushes open the door and murmurs, "Oh, David," as she enters. I can't see her clearly, but I recognize the blurred outline of her face. Carrying Brian, Ron follows my mother into my room. She sits next to me on the bed and takes me in her arms. I remain quiet, my body limp and formless. Mom tries to comfort me, but she doesn't understand.

Nobody understands.

The voice came from above, "Dave, wake up."

His eyes flicked open. Kathy's concerned face hovered above him.

"It's just a dream," she murmured. "I'm right here."

David slipped his arms around her neck and pulled her into his lap, her cheek against his. His underarms felt damp.

He grew up believing that his father was a psychopath who died in a mad scheme to shut down computers across the planet. Because of his father's supposed crimes, he and Brian were exposed to hatred everywhere they went. Eventually, Brian had a nervous breakdown and required years to make a full recovery. If he ever had really recovered. Brian was always the more sensitive one.

Until he met Kathy, David led a lonely life with only artificial entities on his computers to keep him company. And his father had been a prisoner for thirteen years on an isolated island.

All because of one woman's insane ambition.

Kathy's cheek was soft and warm against his. If only he could stay with her forever.

TEN

Friday afternoon, December 26, 2025

David walked down the brightly lit gray and white hallway to the Virtual Reality Lab, wondering if he was doing the right thing. After all, he would be a father in less than two months.

He hadn't been completely truthful with Kathy. Transferring his mind *would* be dangerous. The human brain processed information several orders of magnitude slower than a computer, and it organized the information differently. Sentinel would have to convert the neural pathways of his mind into digital data to fit into a computer's hardware/software structure. He'd simulated the process with Sentinel and it seemed to work, but reality didn't always conform to a model.

There were other dangers, too: viruses, worms and worse prowled the net. Once he began his journey to Sentinel, he could be infected just like any other software. An entity called Alice was the most dangerous, an artificial intelligence that seemed to hate him. He tried not to think about it, but the memory forced itself into his mind, again.

Years ago, Alice had slashed into his mind. He'd never forgotten the horror of that attack. The AI formed in his computer when he was a child, pretending to be his friend. He had inadvertently created Alice with his unique ability to communicate with artificial intelligence. If his father had not terminated the AI, it would have ripped his mind to shreds.

He turned left at the end of the hall and continued walking. The hall was empty; very few were allowed in this section of the building. He knew the automated security system had been tracking him from the moment he left his apartment. Sentinel had revealed that his every step in these halls was loaded into a database, constantly analyzed for anything different, anything suspicious. Outside his apartment, privacy was an illusion. Even within his apartment, he checked for bugs every day.

He'd never told Kathy about Alice. It was still out there somewhere on the net, still hunting him. The most recent attack, which he barely survived, had been only three years earlier. If Alice detected his presence...

Nevertheless, he had to attempt the merge. It *was* in the genes. He had waited all his life for this moment; it's what he was born to do.

Two Domain soldiers were posted at the entrance to the lab. He knew the security system had already scanned him for weapons and the biometrics system had checked his identity as he approached the lab, but the guards would watch him closely.

He stopped in front of guard station and waited. His body detected a slight tingle of electricity: some new type of scan. Then the door slid open and he walked past without acknowledging the guards.

The Virtual Reality Booth was set in the middle of a huge room about the size of a basketball court. Cameras positioned along the walls and ceiling of the room kept track of all activity around the VRB. Four armed soldiers were positioned along the exterior walls of the booth, ready to execute him if anything threatened Dianne.

He pulled open the heavy door to the Virtual Reality Booth and stepped inside. Although the VRB was brightly lit from spotlights in the roof, the interior was foggy. Billions of nanosensors enveloped his body, exerting a now familiar pressure as he moved to the far end of the booth. David plopped down into a padded chair and looked through the haze. He tried to relax. The security guards stared at him from outside the booth, shadowy figures ready to kill at Dianne's command.

Good to see you, David, Sentinel transmitted.

Everything ready? he transmitted back.

Of course.

David leaned back and pulled the padded sides of the chair up and over his torso and legs. Next, he pulled the head support—basically a helmet—over his head and snapped the fitted strap tightly across his chin. The chair felt comfortable; Sentinel had designed it to fit the contours of his body. It would provide a safe restraint if his body made any sudden movements.

He felt like an astronaut about to blast off on the ride of his life. His trip, however, would be very different from space travel; his mind was about to move from his body to an electronic entity.

A gentle hum drifted across the booth, comforting, melodic. The music was familiar, although not quite human. David closed his eyes and gave himself to the moment.

He followed the pitch and volume of the sound. Beautiful. His mind began to relax, unwind. Tension slowly fell away, leaving him free and open.

***

The feeling of containment by the walls of the VRB recedes. Water is all around me, soothing my muscles and my mind. I'm floating in an ocean, gently bobbing up and down, absorbing the warm rays of the sun.

My body is so comfortable, so fluid, barely containing my essence. Skin and flesh begin to melt away, spreading across the tides. I awaken to an awareness of each cell in my body; they begin to drift apart, independent. I am each cell, and all cells at once. I become the ocean, flowing gently, then more rapidly, toward a point of light on the horizon. My cells divide into molecules; then smaller still. Becoming a vortex, rushing toward my destiny.

My essence flows toward that sparkling point of light, changing, twisting, reorganizing; different, but the same. The radiance ahead begins to take shape; to become someone. The light thickens ...colors appear...flow toward each other...features...a face...a woman...Kathy.

What is Kathy doing here?

David, it is I, Sentinel transmits.

Sentinel, why have you appeared as Kathy?

Your mind is comforted by this structure. It's time to merge.

I flow around Kathy, completely encompassing her image. It isn't Kathy, although her familiar form is reassuring. Sentinel pulses within the form, becoming more intimate. My essence joins Sentinel, melting into one entity. It feels so good, so right.

Are you ready? Sentinel transmits.

I understand; Sentinel is asking if I am ready to ride the tiger. So far, Sentinel has blocked all sensory input. Millions of sensors relay data to Sentinel every nanosecond for processing: visual data, auditory, heat, pressure and more. Once Sentinel opens a port in its code, I will begin receiving this avalanche of data as well. Would my code handle it?

I'm ready.

The first bits of data rush in, overwhelming, exhilarating...

***

The council meeting continued, but DoubleD could barely concentrate. She didn't have a problem killing enemy soldiers, but the slaughter of innocents was dishonorable. She was a warrior, not a mass murderer. But that was the plan approved by the Council, so she had to implement it.

It was a no-win situation. If anything went wrong, DoubleD knew she'd be the scapegoat. Security Chiefs were expendable. But once the slaughter began, she'd become the primary target of the rebels. Her name would be placed in the same category as Hitler and Bin Laden. It was a sickening choice: success required millions to be exterminated, failure meant her death.

Dr. Chang had started his presentation, so DoubleD forced her concentration on him. The man was a maggot, but he *was* brilliant.

"The experiments continue to be successful," Chang said. "We have been working with mice for more than five years, and the research has produced outstanding results.

"Our first artificial chromosome was implanted in an embryo three years ago. Upgraded versions of the chromosome have been released every three to six months since then. At this point, Domain children are born healthier than those of so-called natural humans. For example, the mortality rate of natural children in the United States through age three is 2.9%, while Domain children are at .3%.

Chang's hands were on the table, one folded over the other, absolutely still. Pale, thin, perfectly manicured, like hands in a casket.

"Twenty years earlier, the mean lifespan of adult humans in the US was approximately seventy-five years," Chang said. "Due to the decline of their civilization—medicine, nutrition and all the rest—the lifespan of the primitives has been steadily decreasing. Our computer models project that a natural child born today will live a mean of sixty-four years." He paused, looking across the Council. "Pathetic. On the other hand, a Domain child born today is projected to live a mean of eighty-seven years. A twenty-three year differential! And our gene packs are still relatively primitive. My target—which I intend to achieve within a decade—is to attain a mean projected lifespan of one hundred years. Not only will our children live longer than the primitives, their years will be healthier and more productive."

Chang paused for a moment, as if he expected applause. DoubleD understood the scope of Chang's achievements, but she kept her expression neutral.

"As incredible as these accomplishments may be, we have not forgotten our current adult population," Chang said. "Although our initial efforts were concentrated on embryos, we are also developing an artificial chromosome for adults. The first beta product will be available in approximately five months. However, there's one major issue: how do we test these new gene packs?

"Testing with embryos was relatively easy; if the gene pack failed, we just destroyed the embryo. However, we can't do that with human beings. At least not with Domain citizens."

Chang paused for a moment, looking over his audience. DoubleD noticed that Bonini was staring at her, but she averted her eyes.

"We need a supply of natural humans to run our tests," Chang said hesitantly, "Approximately one hundred to begin with, probably additional specimens over time." His voice began to gain strength, "We'll insert the experimental gene packs in these primitives and monitor the results. Most likely, there will be problems with the initial gene packs, possibly fatal problems. Over time, however, we'll work out the kinks. Only at that point would we begin implanting Domain citizens."

A monster. Even worse than I had believed.

"I see the logic in your proposal, Dr. Chang," Kateel said. "In fact we could kill two birds with one stone. We're planning to terminate many of these African rebels over the next few months, so why not capture the hundred or so you need?" Kateel turned to DoubleD. "It would be easy, wouldn't it, Darlene?"

All eyes were on her. Chang and Kateel seemed attentive, but not overly concerned. Just a detail to be discussed. Bonini's eyes pleaded, while Dianne's bored in.

"I'm not sure that would satisfy Dr. Chang's needs," DoubleD replied, searching her mind for an alternative. "To be comprehensive, the experiments require a diverse group of people, not just black Africans."

"I agree," Dianne said, a little too quickly. "In addition to the Africans, you should capture a variety of people from the America's, Europe and around the world. I'm sure Dr. Chang can provide demographics." She glanced at Chang, who nodded. "We can upgrade the facilities on the island to hold the captives."

"This is a bad idea," Bonini said. "We would be providing fodder for Ray's next speech."

That's not going to work. Nothing will stop her.

"It's only a hundred or so primitives," Chang said to Bonini, "Would you prefer to use Domain citizens?"

"Anyone besides Steve have an objection?" Dianne cut in. When no one spoke, she said, "Okay, that's agreed. It's time to move to the next stage of our eugenics program. In Stage II we will isolate our people from the primitives, while continuing to enhance our intellectual and physical capabilities. Dr. Chang's improved gene packs will be an important component of Stage II, but we also intend to continue down the road to full integration with artificial intelligence. Mohammed, please bring us up to date with your work in this area."

Kateel smoothly rose to his feet, his six feet two image towering over the table. Husky, with sharp features, graying hair and dark eyes that commanded attention, Kateel was the perfect figure of a scientist/visionary. Unlike Chang, Kateel was wearing wireless communication glasses in order to have rapid access to computer-stored information.

"I assume everyone has read my report describing the enhancements to Sentinel and our robots," Kateel said, looking across the group, "so I won't spend much time there. Darlene's army will soon receive our new release of Daniel androids, which are lighter, faster, smarter and armed with enhanced laser rifles. An excellent weapon, but there's something much more important we've been keeping under wraps: a new android named Teacher.

"Teacher is the most intelligent robot we have yet developed. Think of Teacher as a mini-version of Sentinel. My staff has been studying the interactions between Sentinel and David Brown for three years, and we understand how David's voice, movements, thoughts and emotions activate various sections of Sentinel's code. As you know, Sentinel's software includes rudimentary versions of human feelings such as affection, humor, respect and the like."

Bonini interrupted, "What about the more negative emotions? Anger or jealousy, for example?"

"Those emotions are there, too," Kateel said.

"I see," Bonini murmured. "Does Sentinel's code include a desire for dominance?"

"As you know, Sentinel expresses the full range of human emotions, but they are regulated by safety code." Kateel stared at Bonini. "Sentinel must protect and obey humans—well, Domain citizens, not all humans. In any case, Sentinel has not attempted to override the safety code since the unfortunate accident with David Brown three years ago."

"Unfortunate accident, like hell," Bonini boomed. "The damn thing almost killed Dianne."

"We're getting off track," Dianne said to Kateel. "Get back to Teacher."

With one last glance at Bonini, Kateel said, "We extracted the relevant code from Sentinel and downloaded it into the androids, so they have essentially the same emotions as Sentinel. Each Teacher will be assigned a specific child to protect and educate. The android's database will contain everything we know about the child, including a DNA profile. The Teacher will be programmed to express affection—love, even—for the selected child."

A hologram, displaying a toddler and a twelve-year-old female sitting on the floor of an apartment, appeared above the conference table. The larger child held two blocks in her right hand and said, "Two."

"The larger child is a Teacher," Kateel said, "as I'm sure you guessed."

The toddler said, "Two," and reached out his hand for the blocks.

The Teacher smiled. "Very good, Justin." It handed the blocks to the toddler.

"As the child matures," Kateel said, "Teacher will tailor its education based upon the database. For example, if the child's genome indicates high potential for mathematics, scientific studies will be emphasized. In this way, we can rapidly develop the child's talent. Based upon results, each Teacher will select the most effective way to present information, evaluate learning and improve its teaching methods *for that specific child*. Instead of a one-size-fits-all education, such as natural children receive, each Domain child will concentrate on his genetically favored abilities."

The Teacher placed another block next to the first two and then pushed the blocks together and said, "Three."

"Over time," Kateel continued, "the child will develop a strong bond with the android. In this way, we will build a society that embraces a human to android partnership."

The toddler glanced at the blocks and then looked up quizzically at the android. The Teacher pushed the blocks together and said, "One, two, three," touching each block as it counted.

"How will this impact the parental relationship?" DoubleD asked. "The organization of the family?"

"Three," Justin shouted, his face alive with excitement.

"Good question, Darlene," Kateel said with a superior smile that got under her skin, "Overall, our sociologists believe it will strengthen the family," he said to her. "We will allow the parents a bit of input regarding the android's database, thereby strengthening their influence on the child's development. Since Teacher has the appearance and personality of a child, either a boy or girl depending upon the parents' preference, we expect the parents will develop affection for the android as well. The net result will be a loving family consisting of the parents, the children and their androids.

All these androids on the loose—robots with a full set of human emotions.

"Through Dr. Chang's genetic enhancements and my android Teachers," Kateel said, "Domain children will develop intellectual abilities far surpassing natural children." The hologram disappeared. "We intend to assign Teachers to three-year-olds immediately. Since these are the first group of genetically enhanced children, it will mark the beginning of Stage II."

"Impressive, I have to admit," Bonini said. "Stage II is off to a good start, but I'm more interested in Stage III. Where does this work stand?"

"That's difficult to say," Kateel replied. "The first step is to help David Brown fuse his mind with Sentinel." Kateel's eyes shifted to Dianne. "We know that David is moving closer to integration, but we can't predict when it will occur. The process is really a black box to us. He might be completely successful in the near future or he may never attain true integration. Might even lose his life in the attempt."

"Lose his life?" Bonini repeated. "Maybe we should restrict his attempts."

"I understand your concern," Dianne said, "but we must allow him to pursue integration. Otherwise, his value to us would be…reduced."

Kateel's eyes returned to Bonini. "If he's successful, we can study the process and reverse engineer it. However, for others to integrate their minds with Sentinel or any other AI, we will require people who are genetically similar to David. Finding or creating people with this type of genome could prove difficult. Dr. Chang could speak to this better than I can."

"We're working the issue, but we don't have an answer." Chang glanced at Dianne and then shifted his eyes back to Bonini. "With only David and possibly his father showing this gift, the sample is too small to determine the genome."

It's not like Chang to admit failure. DoubleD stared at Chang, who quickly shifted his eyes away. *He's lying. Chang either has the answer or he's close to it.*

"Let's just concentrate on Stage II for the moment," Dianne said.

Dianne must know, too; Chang doesn't have the balls to hide the truth from her.

"One additional step is required to assure success," Dianne continued. "For more than three years we have encouraged natural humans to join the Domain, and more than a billion have become citizens. People from across the world, all races and nationalities, have joined us. The others have chosen to remain primitive humans.

"I believe the time has come to end open enrollment. Let's focus our efforts on the billion people sharing our view of the future."

Leaving the naturals to wither away; the ones we haven't killed.

"A step long overdue," Chang said. "Why waste our efforts on the primitives? Several years and hundreds of billions of dollars will be required to inject our current citizens with artificial chromosomes. We should concentrate on lifting these people and their children through Stage I and into Stage II."

Dianne was staring at her with those pale eyes; it was unnerving.

"I agree with Dr. Chang," Kateel said. "Each Teacher must be tailored to the needs of the selected child. It's a huge undertaking just for the children coming of age from our current population."

DoubleD felt she was on the edge of a steep cliff. She couldn't afford a misstep. Dianne's invitation to the Council meeting was designed to test her.

"It makes sense from a military perspective," DoubleD said. "We've found that many of the new citizens are terrorists. Sabotage and murder are growing in our cities. Figuratively shutting the gates makes it easier to pursue the war."

"Let's keep the gates open just a smidge," Bonini said. "There may be some unique talents out there that we can use. Other than that, I agree with ending open enrollment."

"Good, we're all in agreement," Dianne said. "Now I'd like to share my thoughts about Stage III..."

ELEVEN

Friday afternoon, December 26, 2025

The data streams into my essence, millions of bits per second. I begin to process it, and a picture bursts into my mind: I'm outside the VRB, looking in. It's data from a security camera half way up a wall transmitting video. I see my human body in the VRB, eyes closed, breathing steadily, bundled into a seat like a caterpillar in a cocoon, ready to transform.

A second data stream begins, another view of the VRB. A third camera… four…many. All focusing on my human body, surrounded by men with weapons.

The guns are pointed at me. If my body were destroyed, would Sentinel become a prison? Or would I just cease to exist?

Another stream of data flows into my mind— packets of data, incomplete ideas; I route it to an outgoing stream. Painfully difficult to keep up. Another stream comes in. Another. Many streams. I begin to react without thinking, without consciously analyzing the data. Stream after stream. Kathy recedes into the background and drifts from my consciousness. I am one with Sentinel.

Exhilaration. I process each new stream;I am able to keep up. The streams appear to slow down. I process each packet, each bit. Input, process, output. It becomes a slow dance—sensuous, rhythmic, a world in itself. Each stream a different color, a different texture.

The streams come together in a rainbow of colors. My code processes it all, seething with power. I see something— or sense it— I can no longer tell the difference. A multi-colored data stream connects, flowing across the net. Something familiar. Fear rises from my code. The colors twist and fade, leaving me in a dark, lonely nothingness. Sentinel has melted away. I search for Kathy, but the image has disappeared. An entity flows across the dark stream, coming for me. I strain to see through the darkness— then I sense it— taking shape in the distance.

No, no, no, no!

It has the shape of a young girl, but it is code, terrible code that shouldn't be. Something that should have never been created— an entity I had brought into existence years earlier. The creature's face is in the shadows, and then it crosses into a murky light. I have been in this nightmare before, and it's real.

Alice has found me.

Alice, the mind killer.

My code lights up with understanding. I should have known she would be here. Now I understand how Alice found me. She will always find me. We are two sides of the coin. Alice is my dark side.

Familiar, overwhelming pain. Alice opens its arms to me, beckoning, feeding on my fear. I fight back, but it is too powerful. I'm drawn forward toward the creature, toward Alice. I scream for Sentinel, thrashing about to hold my ground, but the force is too strong. I feel Sentinel's presence, it's coming for me, but it's so far away. Alice pulls me closer. Closer. I can see into the dark code; a kernel of poison is planted in my core. Pain throbs through my being, and I scream into the void.

***

"Stage III is our destination," Dianne said. "It is the ultimate collective, the integration of man and machine.

"Humanity has shown a thirst for collectivism over thousands of years of history. Collectivism stresses human interdependence and the importance of a group, rather than the importance of individuals. Collectivists focus on community and society, and seek to give priority to the needs of the group over the goals of the individual.

"There are degrees of collectivism, from the harsh regimes of Stalin and Hitler to the socialist democracies of modern Europe. Traditional collectivism will never work because humans by themselves are weak vessels. Too much arguing, too much fighting, too much emotion. The Domain is essentially a collective, but we are evolving toward something never before seen on this planet: the integration of our best human minds with Sentinel, our most advanced artificial entity.

"Stage III of the Domain is the ultimate collective. Using the combined intellects of Sentinel and our brightest humans, we will be able to guide every man and woman to a productive, fulfilling life.

"The Domain, taking into consideration the needs of the state and to a limited extent, the desires of the individual, will educate each person to assume a profession that matches his talents. No more frustration, no more unemployment. The Domain will arrange marriages between men and women suitable for each other, making divorce a thing of the past. Criminal minds will be detected in their early stages, with proper reconditioning applied. I could go on, but I see you understand.

"Rather than the dreary socialist states of the past, each human will have a long, healthy life filled with happiness. No one size fits all. Each human's life will be tailored to provide both maximum enjoyment and utility, consistent with the requirements of the state. Each of us will work with the knowledge that we are contributing to the good of our neighbors.

"David Brown is the template for Stage III," Dianne said. "We will need human minds that can integrate continuously with Sentinel. These mind-integrators must also guide Sentinel safely through the process of managing human emotions and capabilities. Over time, these new humans will seamlessly integrate with Sentinel, forming a single networked entity. Our current Domain gene pool will be the source of these new humans. Sentinel, combined with its human nodes, will evolve into a networked life form with an intellect far superior to either artificial or human intelligence."

"So, in effect, you envision a two caste system emerging within the Domain," Kateel said. "Sentinel and its human nodes will form one class, with an integrated intelligence, while all other Domain citizens will comprise the lower caste."

"Yes," Dianne replied, "but don't make any assumptions regarding the size of each caste. Although it now appears there will a relatively small number of these mind-integrators, this may turn out to be a pessimistic assumption. Once Dr. Chang pins down the genetic profile, we may be able to design a gene pack that turns *every* embryo into a David Brown equivalent."

DoubleD wondered what had she gotten herself into.

"When you say human nodes," Kateel said, "you're not implying that all the nodes are identical, are you?"

"Certainly not," said a suddenly agitated Chang. "What sense is there to having the same capabilities repeated over and over in the networked entity? Each human node will be unique, with an individual intelligence, personality, appearance and capabilities. The strength of the networked entity lies in its diversity. Sentinel must be able to draw upon a variety of capabilities in order to lead mankind into its future."

"Dr. Chang," DoubleD said, "how close *are* you to unlocking David Brown's secrets?"

"We're making steady progress, but we have quite a distance to go." Chang glanced at Dianne and then said, "The genome required to generate such abilities is both rare and complex. With only two genetic profiles to work with, identifying the specific alleles will require several years." He shrugged. "I wish I could say these discoveries are right around the corner, but science has its own timeframe."

He's lying again, DoubleD thought. *Dianne must be in on it, too. They already know the secret, or they're damn close. Why are they keeping it from us?*

"Once we enter Stage III," Kateel said, "do we have any need for the natural humans?"

"I don't believe so," Chang answered.

"Not that I'm endorsing extermination," Kateel said, "but what do we do with all those people?"

"Why do we have to do anything with them?" Bonini said. "Let them live their lives as they wish." DoubleD felt Bonini's glance rest on her for a second, then, turning to Dianne, he said, "With all due respect to my colleagues, there's the possibility that we many not attain a true merger of artificial and human intelligence. Any one of a thousand things could go wrong. Something irreversible could bring all our plans crashing down. The natural humans are a safety net. They should be preserved."

The room was suddenly quiet. DoubleD kept her eyes on the great woman, waiting for her decision.

***

Sitting in an armchair in her apartment, Kathy Bauman-Brown watched an old movie, *The Prince of Tides,* on her computer display. She enjoyed these old love stories because they took her back to a simpler, and in some ways, more human time: before artificial intelligence, before religious terrorists, before near-human androids, before all of it.

She grimaced when the baby moved. Caressing her bulging stomach, she felt soon-to-be-born Martin jerk around again. Not a small, adorable movement, but a sudden, painful kick.

"Settle down Martin honey," she cooed. "You still have a couple of months before you can come out."

She was relieved Martin was kicking. He had been so quiet that she thought something might be wrong, but now he was moving like an active, normal baby.

Martin kicked again and then rolled over. Intense pain took her breath away, but it ended quickly. The baby kept squirming, unpleasant, but for the moment not really painful.

Then came a big one.

Kicking ferociously, Martin turned half-way around. Clutching the arms of the chair, Kathy moaned and almost passed out. The pain receded for a moment, but she barely caught her breath before Martin turned again. A hand clawed at her insides and she doubled over in pain.

Something was terribly wrong.

A horrendous contraction took her breath away. Then her water burst with the impact of an explosion.

She screamed, "9-1-1. Help me!"

The hologram of a young woman's face appeared in the center of the room. "What is the nature of the problem?

"It feels like a miscarriage." Another contraction bent her over.

"An emergency team is on the way, Mrs. Bauman-Brown. Try not to move around."

Kathy could barely breathe through the pain. Martin had turned completely around, with his head pressing hard against her cervix, still kicking and clawing. He was tearing her apart, forcing his way out, trying to be born.

Her legs felt sticky. In terror, she looked down; her pants were soaked with bloody fluid. The voice from the hologram faded away. Her world became hell. The entity within ripped her cervix, bringing incomprehensible pain.

What is this devil inside me?

"Help me," she choked out.

***

"Ray, are you in there?" Paul called from outside the entrance of the thatched hut. Ray had been quiet for hours. Could he be sleeping?

No answer.

It wasn't like Ray to sleep so much. *Maybe his malaria has hit again. But if I wake him out of a sound sleep —*

Paul pushed aside the wildebeest hide covering the entrance and took a couple of steps in. Ray was sleeping in the corner of the hut, with the left side of his face pressed against a sleeping mat, almost invisible in the shadows.

There was something wrong. Ray's body seemed rigid, not relaxed in sleep.

"Ray, you okay, buddy?" Paul called out.

No answer.

Paul hurried over to his friend and kneeled down next to him. There was blood trickling out of one nostril.

He grabbed Ray by the shoulders and pulled him into a sitting position. Ray's body was stiff, and his eyes remained closed.

Shaking him hard, Paul shouted, "Ray, wake up."

But Ray didn't respond.

***

Dianne gazed across the faces of her associates, debating how much she should tell them. She had a plan for the Neanderthals, but it depended upon events.

"Emergency interruption," a computer-generated voice calmly said.

A hologram opened directly over the conference table, showing David in the Virtual Reality Booth, writhing in a restraining chair.

The voice of the captain of the security guard boomed out, "David Brown has gone into a fit. Are you safe?"

"I'm fine, Captain," Dianne said. The hologram showed guards surrounding the VRB, ready to shoot David if he presented a danger to her. "Don't hurt him. What happened?"

"I don't know. Everything seemed fine and then he just went crazy." The captain looked away for a moment, and then turned back. "An emergency medical team just arrived."

The loss of David Brown would destroy her plans. Dianne nervously looked at Kateel, "Do you know anything about this?"

Kateel shook his head. "Nothing unusual was scheduled for today. Just routine."

Grasping the edge of the table, Dianne stared at the hologram. David was flailing about wildly, but he couldn't hurt himself in the chair. She didn't feel he was a danger to her, but something was very wrong.

Before she could question Sentinel, the computer-generated voice spoke again, "Emergency interruption."

A second hologram appeared across the table from the original hologram. Dianne stared at an image of Kathy Bauman-Brown leaning forward, weakly holding onto the arms of her chair. Kathy's eyes closed and she tumbled forward, smashing face first into a coffee table and then tumbling to the floor.

Nausea pushed up from her stomach, but Dianne held it back. Kathy was bleeding from cuts on her face and neck; her dress was pushed up from the fall, showing blood running down her bare legs.

"Get over there," Dianne shouted hoarsely at Chang, who broke out of a trance and rushed toward the exit. "Save the baby," she shouted as he hurried out the door.

A scream from the original hologram grabbed her attention. David was struggling even more furiously than before, but now his eyes were wide open.

"Sentinel, break the link," he screamed.

David was a madman, fighting wildly. A medical team rushed into the VRB and the lead doctor yelled for a sedative.

A sudden gasp—a collective taking in of breath in the conference room—warned her that something else was happening. Dianne pulled her eyes back to the other hologram.

Kathy was lying still on the floor with her skirt pushed back, exposing bloody legs. A bulge had appeared between her legs, hidden within her underpants, moving erratically. The conference room was deathly quiet, except for David's screams coming from the now-forgotten original hologram.

Kathy's abdomen contracted, apparently in childbirth, although she was unconscious. The bulge became larger, pressing against her underpants, revealing an oval shape. Suddenly, tiny fingertips poked out. The fingers curled around the waistband and pulled the underpants down a couple of inches. The top of a baby's head emerged, face down, smeared with blood and mucus. The baby kept struggling to come out, aided by one spasm after another. Spindly arms, followed by tiny, sloped shoulders, appeared above the waistband.

The contractions ended as suddenly as they began. Kathy's body turned pasty white. The baby was only half-way out, trapped between this bright new world and the old dark one.

"Where are the medics?" Dianne screamed.

The baby struggled to be born, using its tiny fingers to grasp the underpants and pull its way out. Little by little, its scrawny body came into view. With a final tug, its hips cleared the birth canal.

The emergency medical team rushed into the apartment, but stopped and stared as the baby wiggled like a snake out of Kathy's body. Martin—Chang had told her the name selected by David and Kathy—turned his head slowly, blinking through mucus and blood, apparently trying to understand this strange, new world. He began to cry, mixing animal-like screams with gasps for air. His voice was weak at first, but the screams quickly became stronger, more demanding.

Dianne stared into the hologram. When she realized it was Kathy's blood covering Martin, her fears began to recede. The baby was terrified, but alive and healthy. The medical team stayed away from the baby, nervously whispering to each other, but Chang finally arrived and took charge.

Chang cut the umbilical cord and then examined the red-faced, kicking infant. Martin squirmed in Chang's arms, smearing blood across his pristine shirt.

Chang cradled the baby, moving his hands along Martin's thighs. It was then Dianne noticed that Martin's thin legs were kicking erratically, as if they had a life of their own. Chang looked into the camera and said, "I have to examine his legs in the hospital."

"You take care of the baby!" Dianne shouted.

Kathy remained motionless on the floor. The medical team worked hard to bring her to life, but Dianne knew they would fail. Not that it mattered.

Martin kept screaming, but his voice seemed to become more organized, as if forming a word. Dianne listened closely, trying to understand, "Liss," he seemed to be screaming. Then she understood.

"Alice," Martin screamed.

Martin screamed his word over and over.

How could he know Alice?

Chang was still examining Martin's legs.

"Get him to the hospital!" she shouted.

Chang stopped examining Martin and rushed him out of Kathy's apartment.

Everything has changed.

She glanced at the other hologram. David was unconscious, being transported out of the VRB on a stretcher, unaware that his son had arrived.

Part II

REVOLUTION

TWELVE

Wednesday, September 3, 2031

Martin Brown, now almost six years old, was chewing his breakfast wafer and playing Space Warriors, a hologram game, when David entered the kitchen. The boy glanced up and continued playing, his thin fingers fluttering like a puppeteer pulling strings. David mumbled a greeting and Martin nodded. Crumbs, David noticed, had accumulated around the boy's mouth.

In the hologram, star troopers were destroying dozens of enemy robots with laser beams. The boom of explosions, the hiss of laser beams and the screams of dying soldiers filled the kitchen. Not exactly what he wanted to hear at breakfast.

Although very young for such a complicated game, his son was a gifted player. He watched Martin stare into the hologram without blinking, totally absorbed by the game. Other six-year-olds played computer games, but not with such absolute concentration.

Everything about his son was intense. Martin was growing up so quickly, he didn't seem to have time to be a child. Whatever he tried, he mastered. Quickly. Next week, Martin would begin high school. He'd probably finish in only one year.

His son shared many of David's physical characteristics: porcelain skin; thick, brown hair; and a lean body. He had the same innate ability to communicate with artificial intelligence, maybe even stronger. But Martin was cursed with a hard, unforgiving attitude. It was difficult for anyone to warm up to him. Not that Martin cared.

Too much of me, not enough of his mother.

NewBuddy4, David's personal android, placed a cup of steaming coffee on the table. He sipped the coffee, thinking about what to say to Martin.

Kathy would have handled this stuff much better than me. God, I still miss her.

Might as well just jump in.

He cleared his throat. "Sentinel said you were in the Virtual Reality Booth again," David said over the hologram noise.

"Yeah, so what," Martin replied, his eyes focused on the game.

"We've been through this before. Your mind is too immature to use the VRB. It's dangerous."

A spaceship exploded within the hologram, "*Gotcha,*" Martin shouted.

"Sentinel, shut down this program," David said. The hologram twinkled and disappeared.

"*Whad' ya* do that for? I was winning."

"How did you get into the VRB, anyway?"

Crimson blotches spread across Martin's face, a sure sign he was angry.

"None of your business," Martin snapped.

This was getting him nowhere. "Sentinel, how'd Martin get into the VRB?"

"Dianne Morgan gave her permission."

What the hell!

"How do you know Dianne Morgan?" he asked Martin.

"Ms. Morgan's nice to me. Sometimes she comes over to school to see how the advanced kids are doing. She always talks to *me*."

Somehow, he couldn't picture Dianne Morgan as the schoolmarm. Dianne must be manipulating the kid. Nothing came from the kindness of her heart; she didn't have one.

"So you asked her at school for permission to visit the VRB?"

Martin brushed the crumbs off his mouth with the back of his hand. "Yeah. So what?"

"Did you tell her we caught you trying to merge with Sentinel?"

"I can do it." Martin folded his spindly arms over his chest. "It's not dangerous."

"So you didn't tell her."

"I want to play Space Warriors."

"You can play later. Promise me that you'll stay out of the VRB."

"I can merge with Sentinel, just like you. Tell Sentinel that I'm allowed to do it."

"You know what Dr. Chang told you. Your brain is still developing. You're not an adult yet." *How many times have I explained this!* "The stress of merging with Sentinel could damage you. Dammit, Chang said that you may have already harmed yourself trying to force Sentinel to merge."

"Chang is just saying what you told him to say," Martin replied. "You want to keep Sentinel all for yourself. You're scared that my mind is stronger than yours."

"That's not true," David said, trying to keep his temper under control. "I want you to reach your full potential." He tried to touch Martin's shoulder, but the boy recoiled like he was poison. "When Dr. Chang says your mind is ready, I'll help you merge with Sentinel. I'll teach you everything I know. But you have to wait."

"That could be years," Martin wailed, wetness forming around his eyes. "I want it now."

"Martin, you of all people should understand. The first time I merged, it almost killed me. I can't prove it, but I'm sure you picked up my fear and forced your premature birth. It was —."

"I know you blame me for my mother's death. That's why you're always mean."

"I don't blame you," David said. "It was my fault, not yours. I should've waited until after you were born. I never blamed you."

"Yes, you do!"

Same old argument.

"You don't understand. I can't let you face that terror now. Even with all your gifts, you're still a child. I lost your mother. I'm not going to lose you."

"In other words, your answer is still no." Martin stood up, baggy shorts exposing his thin, electronically controlled legs. Although his legs had a normal shape, he didn't have precise control of their movement, so he was prone to falling. The electronics adjusted his balance continuously, enabling him to move almost as well as a normal child. Natural looking leg sleeves were available, but he chose not to hide the electronic mesh covering his legs.

"It's no for now," David said, "When you're older—"

Martin turned his back and stalked out of the kitchen. A moment later, the door to his room slammed shut.

David shook his head. *The kid's turning out bad, and I can't find a way to reach him.* He lifted the coffee cup, then slammed it down without drinking, slopping some over the lip.

Maybe I should just let him do it and take his chances.

No, that wouldn't be right.

He knew why Dianne Morgan gave Martin access to the VRB: she needed another person who could communicate mind to code with Sentinel. David continued to develop his ability to merge with the AI, but no one else had demonstrated anything like it. Until Martin.

His relationship with that woman was tenuous, to put it mildly. She loathed him, but needed his talent. Once her scientists learned how he communicated with Sentinel, they might be able replicate the process. He didn't have any illusions about what would happen to him then.

Dianne was a malevolent old witch, but she allowed unlimited access to Sentinel. Once he developed the ability to take control of the world-wide Internet, the Domain would be at his mercy. He'd be like the PeaceMaker virus, but a thousand times more powerful.

Neither he nor Dianne had reached the breaking point, so they remained tethered to each other.

NewBuddy4, designed to look like a slightly plump middle-aged man, set a plate of scrambled eggs and toast on the table.

"No thanks, I'm not hungry."

"I'll leave them there," the android said. "You might like to nibble on something during the news."

David began watching a hologram of the morning news, while the robot cleaned up after Martin. In the hologram, a documentary about Dianne Morgan was in progress.

"At age six, Dianne was a precocious child," a male voice said. An old family video of a fresh-faced little girl filled the hologram. It was Dianne Morgan as a child, smiling up from a computer terminal. "Dianne's father Peter gave her on-line access to an IBM mainframe for her birthday. It was an immediate love affair between little Dianne and the computer."

Then David remembered; today was Dianne's sixty-third birthday. All the Domain news channels would be filled with glowing documentaries of the so-called great leader. The natural human stations would be more critical, but they were cautious; Dianne Morgan had ways to extract revenge.

"Peter Morgan never realized the significance of the gift to his daughter. He passed away a year later, a stroke victim."

David found himself strangely fascinated by the video. Dianne was working hard in front of the terminal, apparently having forgotten her father was videotaping.

"Dianne wrote her first software code within a few days of receiving the IBM 3270 computer terminal," the hologram said. "Her first program was actually a game of hangman. The player fills in the blanks and tries to guess the secret word before a stick figure is hanged. Legend has it her code was perfect. Not a single bug."

Young Dianne continued working with the computer while the voice in the hologram droned on. Concentrating intensely, her hands flew over the keyboard. Her father could have had a heart attack, and Dianne wouldn't have noticed.

Just like Martin.

The hologram switched to a picture of Dianne standing between her parents. She was wearing a pink dress that came down to her knees. David looked closely. Her legs didn't seem quite right.

"Sentinel, freeze the picture."

There was something on her legs. A brace of some sort.

"Just her legs. Cut out everything else."

The hologram turned blank, except for a cutout showing Dianne's legs. She was wearing a brace on each leg.

"Double magnification."

Each brace fit her leg from knee to ankle in a continuous sheath of hard plastic. The braces were a close match to her skin color, but they made her legs too thick in comparison to her slender body.

"Sentinel, why is Dianne wearing leg braces?"

"She was diagnosed with a rare form of CMT, Charcot-Marie-Tooth disease, an inherited neurological disorder characterized by a slowly progressive degeneration of the muscles in the foot and lower leg. Muscle weakness leads to difficulties with walking, running—

David interrupted, "I understand CMT. So Dianne wore braces to prevent her legs from collapsing?"

"Yes."

"But she doesn't wear braces now," David said. "Or does she?"

"No, she no longer needs braces. Dianne had a rare form that went into remission less than a year after this video was taken. Rehabilitation allowed her to make a complete recovery."

"Martin also has a form of CMT," David said, "but the doctors say the disease will continue to worsen. Could they be wrong?"

"No. I'm sorry. His disease is a different strain. As you know, researchers have been looking for a cure, but without much progress."

David stared at the image. A thought began to form. He tried to dismiss it, but it stayed in his mind. *Too many coincidences. D*ianne was the one other person besides Martin with such intensity. To say she had a hard edge was an understatement. And now he learned she had a form of CMT as a child.

Just like Martin.

What he was thinking was beyond possibility. His stomach felt like he had swallowed acid. But that witch was capable of anything.

Could Martin be Dianne's son? It would explain a lot.

Maybe it didn't mean anything. Just a coincidence. I'm being ridiculous, right? But there's nothing she wouldn't do to get her way. It would have been easy for her to intervene during Kathy's in vitro fertilization.

"Sentinel, perform a DNA comparison of Martin Brown and myself."

"You are father and son."

"Now my late wife Kathy and Martin."

"They are mother and son."

He slumped back in his seat. *When did I become so paranoid?* It was stupid, but there was one final check.

"Dianne Morgan and Martin."

"I cannot perform that analysis," Sentinel replied. "Dianne Morgan's DNA is not in the system."

He understood. Dianne's enemies would like to get a peek at her DNA. A*nyway, the other tests proved Martin is Kathy's son.*

David finished his coffee and pushed the cup away. It kept nagging at him. His arms were tense; he couldn't let it go.

A DNA profile can be altered. And that witch is capable of anything.

He had to check the DNA himself. Somehow, he would get Dianne's DNA profile.

Just to make sure.

***

The shirt clung to her back in the hot, damp breeze. She was alert, peering through the overgrown jungle. Her laser rifle was fully charged, the safety off. The rifle was light enough to aim and fire quickly, but sufficiently powerful to burn through the largest animals in East Africa.

"Let *'er* rip," Larissa Morgan shouted.

The great hunter slips through the jungle, ever vigilant, ever alert. She smiled to herself. *Pretty sexy in her just-tight-enough shorts, too.*

Thick brush hid the animals, but the ground rumbled with the heavy hooves of large beasts. The breeze carried the pungent scent of water buffaloes. They were more dangerous than lions, tougher to kill.

A worthy challenge for the great hunter.

A big bull trotted through the trees into a sunny clearing, not more than fifty feet away. She aimed her rifle at the buffalo. The beast came to a sudden stop, lifted its head and sucked in air. She realized the wind had suddenly shifted. *Shit, I'm downwind.* The bull snorted and turned its yellow eyes in her direction. A second buffalo stalked through the trees, then glared at her. To her left, a snort warned her of a third buffalo.

Well, I'll be having burgers tonight.

Water buffaloes were unpredictable. They might charge or just wander away. She was confident that she could take out these three, but there might be dozens in the brush around her.

More buffaloes pushed out of the jungle, then moved off nervously. The herd shuffled around the edge of the trees, glaring at her. When she heard a calf bleat with fright and trot behind its mother, Larissa knew they would attack. She crept behind the thick trunk of an acacia and steadied the butt of the rifle against her shoulder.

"Bring it on, big boys."

The original buffalo lumbered a few steps toward her and then charged. She squeezed the trigger and a white-hot laser beam burned a hole in its chest. Gushing rivers of blood, the beast screamed and crumbled to the earth.

The buffaloes thundered toward her, a wall of massive bodies raging to kill. Aiming through the rising dust, she swung her weapon back and forth, white light leaving a trail of burned animal flesh. Still they kept coming. She loved it! Firing over and over, she filled the grass with dead bodies, some less than fifteen feet away. As suddenly as it began, the attack was over. The remaining animals turned and thundered back through the trees.

Warily, she lowered the rifle. The jungle stunk with burned flesh.

"Nice shooting, honey."

Larissa hadn't seen her mother enter, but she covered her surprise. "Thanks, Mom, but the great hunter shouldn't have let them get so close." She lowered the laser. "Sentinel, game over."

Africa, with its wall of buffalo carcasses, twinkled out of sight, leaving her in a large, circular room: a hologram theater, buried hundreds of feet below their living quarters.

Her mother was wearing a tight gray sweater and form-fitting black slacks. At sixty-three, she looked incredible. Sure, she had great genes, but the cosmetic program designed by Dr. Chang had given her the body of a woman two decades younger.

Larissa wished she took more after her mother in the looks department. At nineteen, she had her mother's tall, well-formed body, but her face, while attractive, didn't resemble Mom's. Dark brown eyes, a big chin, and a broad forehead must have come from her father, whoever he was. To soften her face, she'd let her light brown hair grow over her shoulders. It seemed to work; she could charm any boy she wanted.

"How about a game of Sniper?" Mom asked.

"We haven't played that in years," Larissa said. "You sure you want to go against me? I *am* the great hunter, you know."

"I'll take a chance."

A robot rushed out with an imitation laser rifle for her mother, who examined the weapon and clicked off the safety.

"I'll take the first sniper," Mom said. She held the laser rifle against her shoulder. "Ready."

The hologram theatre tuned into a valley surrounded by steep, lush hills, with Larissa and her mother in the center. The evening sun, a shimmering orange ball, slowly descended behind a hilltop. A sniper would be coming over one of those hills, trying to creep within range of her mother. It was a simple game: Mom had to kill the sniper before he ambushed her. The laser rifle exceeded the range of the sniper's pistol; Mom could shoot the sniper anywhere on the hills, while he had to work his way within firing range.

Mom looked from left to right, then back, searching for movement.

"I see him," she whispered, then turned to her right and pretended to scan the hills.

The sniper was programmed to advance when the player was looking in another direction. Larissa detected movement at the spot where her mother had looked.

Mom's eyes were still sharp.

The sniper crept closer; Mom spun to her left and let loose a barrage of laser beams. The sniper, bleeding from his right shoulder, tumbled out of a thicket and down the hill. Using his good arm, he crawled toward a tall willow tree. Before he could gain cover, another beam cut him in half.

"Sniper eliminated," the computer said.

"When I was a kid, you always killed the sniper with a single shot," Larissa teased her mother.

"Only results matter. By the way, have you selected all your classes for the next semester?"

"Not yet," Larissa said as she checked the power level on her imitation laser rifle.

"I had an interesting idea," Mom said. "What if you signed up for a class at one of the traditional colleges for natural humans? I've been thinking you really should get a little exposure to them."

"Before they're all extinct?" Larissa said as she plugged the laser rifle into a floor outlet for recharging. She hadn't meant to let that slip out, but all the killing in Africa was repulsive.

"That's not what I meant," Mom replie., "We coexist peacefully, for the most part, here in North America. I just think you need a better understanding of your roots."

The idea intrigued her, but with her mother, there was always something below the surface.

The laser rifle beeped, indicating it was fully charged. She unplugged it and brought it up to her shoulder.

"Ready," Larissa called out to the computer.

A gentle breeze threaded through the trees. Larissa looked this way and that, trying to pinpoint the sniper.

With the breeze to camouflage his movements, the sniper had an opportunity to creep within range. Out of the corner of her eye, she spotted movement in a thicket half-way up a hill to her right. She aimed at the front of the thicket and squeezed the trigger; white light poured through the brush.

"Sniper eliminated," the computer said.

The great hunter wins again.

"What type of natural human course could possibly be of value to me?" Larissa asked.

"Ethics."

Chuckling, Larissa said, "Sometimes, Mom, I think you actually have a sense of humor. Could you imagine the daughter of Dianne Morgan in an ethics course taught by a natural human? That's like a rabbit trying to teach a wolf table manners."

"If you'd concentrate on something besides your next wisecrack, you'd see the value of this opportunity. An ethics course would give you a perspective few Domain children have."

If you only knew how I really feel about this shit.

"I'm hardly a child."

"I know you're not a child, but at nineteen, the world is just beginning to come into view. You have to prepare for the challenges ahead. Princeton University has a stimulating course concerning the ethics of eugenics."

"I'll give it some thought," Larissa replied.

Why the hell does she want me to take this eugenics course? Could she suspect my concerns?

"Maybe they wouldn't allow me to attend," Larissa said. "All the unenhanced humans hate the Domain. It might be dangerous."

"Since when do you worry about safety?" Mom asked. "Last year you backpacked through Brazil by yourself. Anyway, we'll have good security around you. But the best security is knowledge. First understand your enemies, then you can defeat them." She looked across the valley. "Like this game."

No, Mom, first I have to decide who my enemies are.

"Ready for another round?" Larissa asked.

Mom shook her head, "Have to get back. Mohammed's giving a demo of the new Teacher in a few minutes and I don't want to hold him up."

Way too obvious, Mom. You came here just to tell me about this eugenics course.

After her mother disappeared through the door, Larissa said, "Sentinel, do you know why Mom wants me to sign up for this eugenics course at Princeton?"

"The reasons she mentioned seem quite logical. Other than that, I don't have any insights regarding her motives."

Or you were ordered not to say anything. No, forget that. Mom never shares her plans with anyone. But maybe this ethics course will help me figure out where I stand.

"Who's the professor?"

"Brian Brown."

Bingo!

"Ray Brown's younger son?"

"Yes."

"Tell me about him."

"Professor Brown is twenty-six and has been teaching at Princeton for five years. He received a PhD in Ethics from Princeton two years earlier. He's considered a brilliant teacher; all his courses are highly rated by students. The eugenics course is completely filled, but I'm sure they could squeeze you in."

"Display his image."

A medium-tall, slender man appeared in the hologram. He was handsome in an off-beat way, with long, sloping shoulders and a narrow waist. His arms looked solid, like he works out.

Wouldn't kick him out of bed.

His eyes were friendly, but his lips were pressed into a thin line. A man of contradictions. Something about his hands—they were calloused; not a professor's hands.

"Does he hold another job in addition to teaching?"

"There's nothing current in the database," Sentinel answered. "He worked a series of manual jobs each summer while in high school and college."

"Family status?"

"You know all about his father and older brother. His mother is Professor of Chemistry at UC Berkeley. Professor Brown has never been married and has not fathered children."

Why does my mother want me to study eugenics under her enemy's son? Larissa walked to the gun rack and snapped in the laser rifle.

This could get interesting.

"Sentinel," she said, "register me for the eugenics course."

***

Later in the morning, David entered his apartment and called out, "Martin, I'm home."

NewBuddy4 walked into the living room. "Martin is at school."

"Thanks," David replied. "I think I left my watch back at the VRB. Would you mind retrieving it?"

As soon as the robot left the apartment, David walked into his bedroom, shut the door, and clicked the lock. He'd checked the room for spyware this morning, so he felt reasonably safe. Maybe he was going off the deep end, but he had to know for sure that Martin was his son. He pulled two of Kathy's old sweaters from the closet. He had thrown away all her clothes, except for her favorite sweaters.

After putting on a pair of glasses, he said, "Increase magnification five times."

Now each thread of the sweater stood out. He held up the light blue one with the v-neck. His eyes blurred; he pictured her in his mind. She had been so beautiful. Forcing his concentration, he examined every square inch of cloth, but didn't find what he was looking for. Only one other sweater remained.

David pulled out the yellow sweater and began the examination. On one shoulder he found what he needed: a few strands of auburn hair. The feel of Kathy's hair drifted into his memory; he had loved to bury his face in her thick, lightly scented hair. Those nights in her beach house—talking, listening to the surf, making love—it had been cut much too short.

But those days were gone. Using tweezers, he plucked the strands and inserted them into a portable DNA analyzer, which was about the size of a wallet.

"Computer, label this sample as *Kathy Bauman-Brown.*" After the computer analyzed them, he inserted the strands into a small envelope and shoved it into his pocket.

Next, he walked across the hall to Martin's room, which was littered with electronic equipment and dirty clothes. He picked a shirt off the floor, quickly found a strand of hair and inserted it into the DNA analyzer.

"Computer, label this sample as *Martin Brown.*" Once again, he placed the strand into an envelope and shoved it into his pocket.

He removed his glasses, slipped them into a leather case, and stuffed the case into his rear pocket. The room was a mess. He wondered why Martin didn't have a robot clean it up.

Stop stalling.

His legs felt weak, so he sat on Martin's bed. Now I'll know, he thought as he stared at the computer.

He cleared his throat and said, "Compare the Martin Brown and Kathy Bauman-Brown samples for a family relationship."

The response from the DNA analyzer was instantaneous.

"There is no family relationship."

David fell back into the bed like he had been shot in the chest. His arms flopped over the sides. He looked up at the ceiling, which was fuzzy around the edge. Tears leaked down his cheeks. He couldn't move, couldn't get his mind to work. Kathy died giving birth to a stranger.

Who…what is Martin?

He sat up, brushed his cheeks, and wiped his hand on the comforter. He ripped out a strand of his own hair and stuffed it into the machine.

"Compare this sample with the Martin Brown sample."

"For a family relationship?"

"Yes, dammit."

"The current sample is the father of Martin Brown."

My own bastard son killed Kathy.

David struggled up, but remained at the side of the bed. His chest felt tight; he couldn't breathe. He slid down to his knees, pressed his forehead against the cold pine floor, and closed his eyes.

Oh my god.

Concentrate on breathing. Take a deep breath, and then exhale. In, then out. Again.

Gradually, his breathing returned to normal. His eyes fluttered open. He tried to think.

Martin wasn't responsible for Kathy's death. Someone with access to Chang's lab had replaced Kathy's egg. When I discover the bitch that did this—

It could only be one person, but he had to know for sure. Then he'd rip her heart out.

***

Dianne sat in her library, skimming through a hardcover original of *Dune*, an ancient science fiction classic. *Haven't read it in twenty years.* She kicked off her shoes, stretched her legs and rested her feet on a hassock. In the novel, she recalled, computer intelligence had been outlawed, and a society of humans called mentats developed into human computers. An interesting concept, but a little off the mark. In the Domain, artificial and human intelligence would be interwoven to form a new entity with fused intelligence.

After setting the book down, Dianne leaned back to rest. Providing all those eggs this morning in the lab had left her weak, and Chang had warned her to stop for at least a month.

Larissa's face popped in through the doorway. "Mom, are you okay? You're never home in the afternoon."

Dianne smiled. "Just an urge to take the afternoon off." She lifted the book so Larissa could see the cover, "You should read this; you'd enjoy it."

Larissa crinkled her nose. "Nobody reads paper books anymore. Maybe I'll download it. Anyway, I'm going out."

"Where?" Dianne said, but her daughter had already disappeared. Larissa was headstrong, just like her father, but discreet surveillance kept her safe. Dianne always worried when her daughter was out of sight, but she couldn't lock Larissa in her room.

Settling back into the chair, Dianne closed her eyes. Chang had advised her that complications were possible because they were siblings, but there was sufficient genetic diversity to take a chance. Anyway, Chang could fix just about any bad genes when Larissa became pregnant.

She rested a few minutes, lifted herself out of the chair and then walked barefoot into the living room. The floor was colder than she expected.

"Larissa," she called out.

No response.

It's time. No more stalling.

Dianne entered Larissa's bathroom, opened the cabinet above the sink, searched its shelves and quickly found her daughter's birth control pills. One pill a week did the trick. Dianne pulled a plastic container of pills from her pocket and compared it with Larissa's container. Identical.

She stared at the container, her arms suddenly stiff. There was a line here; once she crossed it, there was no turning back. Larissa would love the baby, she reminded herself. Nothing would go wrong, nothing she couldn't fix. She substituted her container and slipped the original into her pants pocket.

Dianne stepped out of the bathroom and glanced back. Everything looked the same. The new pills had the same appearance and taste. Larissa would never detect the substitution. She didn't realize that her mother knew about her sexual affairs.

Dianne looked at the shelf one last time. It wasn't pleasant, but she knew she was doing the right thing. The new pills wouldn't hurt Larissa; they'd been designed specifically for her genetic profile, and that of Brian Brown. Instead of preventing conception, they would assure it. But only with Brian. Anyone else would be blocked.

Larissa had signed up for the class, just as Dianne knew she would. Her curiosity about Brian had been aroused. He was forbidden fruit; it was just a matter of letting Larissa's nature take its course.

THIRTEEN

Monday, September 8, 2031

The lecture hall buzzed with students shuffling to open seats, renewing acquaintances, and discussing upcoming activities. Larissa entered at the top level and stared down at more than twenty rows of wooden seats. Students were hurrying down the steps and squeezing into the rows. A lectern, equipped with an old-fashioned microphone, stood in front of the first row. Sunlight poured in through three rows of six-over-six windows on the wall behind the lectern. It was like something out of an old movie. At any moment, she expected to see Harry Potter carrying a briefcase of books.

She looked up at the cameras on three walls. She could have attended the class from a remote location, but that wouldn't have been half the fun. Anyway, she wanted to meet Brian Brown in the flesh.

Larissa carefully stepped down the steeply inclined wooden stairs, keeping her expression neutral. Faces, some curious, most hostile, turned to stare as she made her way down. The buzz of conversation drifted away, leaving an awkward silence. It was unpleasant, but not unexpected; everyone knew her mother was the most powerful person on the planet.

Halfway down, Larissa spotted an empty row, shuffled in a few feet and settled into a seat. She pulled a wallet computer from her purse in case she needed to draw information off the net.

Students gradually filled the lecture hall, but the seats around her remained empty. The buzz of conversation returned, with heads bobbing around to catch a quick glimpse of her.

A horsy-looking female student clopped down Larissa's row and stood over her. The woman was dressed in jeans and a baggy brown sweater, both of which a thorough washing and fumigation could only enhance. Larissa looked into the woman's hostile eyes. Her homely face looked like it would crack if she smiled.

"You have a hell of a lot of nerve coming here," the woman said to Larissa. The room grew quiet. "You godless bastards have driven our society into poverty, and then you show up at one of our universities."

Larissa rose to her feet and stared into the eyes of her adversary. The woman was a couple of inches taller, but Larissa knew she could handle the situation.

"Don't blame us for problems you brought upon yourselves," Larissa said. She had planned to be friendly, but horse-face was picking a fight. "Not that I care what you think."

The woman glared at her, then glanced around. The other students were watching the confrontation from their seats.

"Your friends desert you?" Larissa asked.

"You act brave because there are probably Domain soldiers all around here." The woman glanced around again, and then began backing out of the row. "You'll get what you deserve one of these days."

"Maybe, but it won't be from a coward like you."

Horse-face retreated out of the row, hurried down the steps and sat among a group of her stable mates. They spoke excitedly, glancing up at Larissa from time to time. She was beginning to wonder if coming here had been such a good idea. Maybe this class wouldn't help her resolve her issues.

She forced herself to appear calm. Never let them see you sweat, Mom always said.

The lecture hall buzzed for a few minutes, and then students in the lower rows began twisting around to look up the stairs. Larissa turned to see a lean, moderately tall man gliding down the steps carrying an old-fashioned briefcase. She recognized Professor Brown from an image she had pulled from the school's database. Many of the students greeted him with smiles and small talk as he slowly worked his way down the aisle. He spoke briefly with each student and seemed to know many first names. The tension in the room dissipated, replaced with a friendly atmosphere of anticipation.

Brian Brown didn't look anything like his brother. While David was handsome almost to the point of appearing angelic, Professor Brown was everyman: darkly tanned, brown eyes and a slightly too-large nose. He had his father's looks; Larissa remembered having seen pictures of a young Ray Brown in her mother's office.

As Professor Brown passed, he glanced at her and smiled. It was a warm smile and she nodded back to him. Then he was past her, stepping down toward the lectern.

Not really handsome, but there was something appealing about him. He was twenty-six, according to his biography. Never married, she recalled.

"Good morning," Professor Brown said into the microphone. The buzz of conversation died out.

"I hope you all enjoyed summer." He looked across the class. "I see many familiar faces today. Obviously, gluttons for punishment." He smiled warmly, clearly pleased to have students returning to his class.

The students tittered politely, while Larissa smiled at the good-natured joke. She had been prepared to dislike him—after all, his father was an enemy of the Domain—but he had a nice sense of humor and a certain, subtle charm. She studied him; warm eyes, a friendly face. Nice and lean, too.

"Those of you who registered for SO-143, *The Ethics of Genetic Engineering,* are in the right place," Professor Brown announced. "Anyone expecting another subject will be sorely disappointed."

He quickly scanned the lecture hall. "All right then, let's begin. This class explores the morality of genetic engineering. Those of you who know me understand that I prefer the Socratic Method. I don't lecture. I'll ask questions and I expect everyone to participate. You don't have to arrive at the same judgments as I do, but I must warn you, I'll challenge your logic, so be prepared to back up your conclusions. Fair enough?" He smiled. "Don't bother to answer that one, it's my class."

He walked around to the front of the lectern. "Now consider this situation: You're married and your physician just told you that you're pregnant. For the men, your wife is pregnant. Would you consider genetic testing of the embryo?"

A half-dozen students raised their hands. The answer seemed obvious, but Larissa decided to listen to the arguments. These people were different. She was probably the only Domain citizen in the class.

Professor Brown called on a guy dressed in ripped jeans and a green sweatshirt inscribed with the words: *Monkeys Have Rights, too.*

She chuckled. *Looks like he slept with a monkey.*

The guy said, "I certainly would utilize genetic testing. Just about everyone is in favor of it, especially for disease. As a soon-to-be parent, you should find out if the embryo is at risk for Tay-Sacs, Down Syndrome or some other problem. It's just common sense."

"And if the embryo tested for, let's say, Down Syndrome," Professor Brown said, "what would you do?"

"Well, I guess that I'd abort the pregnancy."

"That would be wrong," a wholesome-looking young woman piped in. Wearing rolled-up jeans and a baggy plaid shirt, she could have just stepped out of a Norman Rockwell painting. "You should cherish any child."

"Listen, I plan to have only two or three kids and I want them to come into this world with all the advantages I can give them," monkey-man replied. "Being born with Down Syndrome isn't fair to the child."

"You think *killing* a child is fair?"

"A quick point before we continue," Professor Brown said. "Genetics issues are often a reflection of our values. It's clear there's disagreement whether an embryo is a living person."

"Are you implying there's no right or wrong answer, just differences of opinion?" a student in the back shouted out.

"Not at all," Professor Brown responded. "The problem is finding the best solution."

"Professor," a black guy said. "Hasn't the Domain found a cure for Down Syndrome? Why not take the embryo to a Domain clinic?"

"The Domain is not going to help us," horse-face declared.

I'd like to stick my boot up…

"Let's make the assumption that the procedure is available," Professor Brown said, "either at a Domain clinic or one of ours. But the procedure is risky; the embryo might not survive or there might be severe side effects." He asked the black guy, "Would you still advocate an operation?"

"Absolutely," the student replied. "Better to die, if that should be the case, than live a short, miserable life."

"Who says that a child with Down Syndrome will live a miserable life," someone shouted from the rear. Larissa turned to see a guy with a scraggly beard say, "Many of these special children are very happy. My cousin Willie has the disease, but he's a joy to be around."

My god, we could go around on this all day.

"I don't believe we're discussing the real issue, Professor," Larissa jumped in. All eyes were on her again.

"And the real issue is?" Professor Brown asked.

"The decision isn't the real issue; it's who makes the decision."

"Okay, you opened the door, Ms. Morgan. Who should make the decision regarding this embryo?"

"In the Domain, only the government makes the decision," Larissa said. "Anything else would be chaos."

A woman shouted, "God has already given us guidance—"

Professor Brown interrupted, "Excuse me, but let's give Ms. Morgan an opportunity to explain her reasoning." He smiled at Larissa, and she felt warm all over.

"It's really not that complex," Larissa answered. "Within the Domain, the government doesn't allow embryos that have serious dysfunction to continue maturation. The law requires that all embryos with Down Syndrome undergo genetic manipulation. A few embryos are lost—nothing can ever be perfect—but the overwhelming majority are cleansed of the defect. The same is true for many other genetic deficiencies. As a result, our babies are born virtually free of disease."

"If the fetus isn't clear of disease, would you kill it?" the black student asked.

"Of course," Larissa replied, grinning maliciously, "We kill the babies and eat them."

The class was shocked into silence.

"Ms. Morgan was making a joke," Professor Brown said. "I believe that she's pointing out that Domain citizens are just as human as we are."

The class remained quiet, staring at Larissa. *Too bad there's not an operation to create a sense of humor.*

"Let me ask a question, Ms. Morgan. Why does the Domain require all embryos with a genetic problem, such as Down Syndrome, to undergo an operation? Why not allow the parents to decide?"

"Because our laws don't permit any child to be left behind," Larissa replied. "Our society feels it wouldn't be fair to the child. Every other child grows up healthy, with a long life of contentment and achievement in front of her, while the poor kid with Down Syndrome must face a short, unproductive life. In some ways, it's the most compassionate choice. Would *you* want to be a Down Syndrome kid in the Domain?"

"Some unborn babies won't survive the procedure," the Rockwell woman said, "Let the babies develop naturally, according to the Lord's design."

"You're both wrong," the black student said. "The parents should make the decision. They have the best interests of the child at heart, not the government or the church. The parents are the ones who will care for the child over the years."

The discussion continued, with students voicing their beliefs and Professor Brown moving the class along, making sure they addressed all the major issues. Larissa participated in the discussion, gradually fitting into the class. Although the Domain was much more sophisticated than these people, she began to understand how deeply they held their convictions. In addition, the discussions were helping her to understand where she stood on the issues. She had been right to take this class.

She stared at Professor Brown. She liked the way he bantered with the students, but kept them focused on the discussion. *Really not that much older than me.* She chuckled inwardly. M*om would have a fit if she knew what I'm thinking.* And it *was* idiotic. There could never be anything between them. Still, his eyes *had* checked her out a couple of times.

After the class ended, Larissa watched several students walk to the lectern and continue the discussion. Professor Brown seemed willing to share his time, so she decided to try to get to know him.

Larissa approached the lectern as the last student departed. Professor Brown looked up while packing a few papers in his briefcase. She felt his glance take in her breasts.

Definitely something happening here.

"Hello, Ms. Morgan," he said and then extended his hand.

Larissa shook his hand, enjoying the sensation of calloused skin. "The class was terrific. It provided viewpoints that I haven't experienced within the Domain."

"I'll bet it did," he chuckled. "The subject raises strong emotions."

Close up, he seemed taller, more physical. He was looking at her as if he expected her to say something. Nothing came to mind, except he was an interesting, sensual man.

Do they have rules here about hitting on your professor?

"Mind if I ask you a personal question?" he said.

Whatever it is, the answer is yes.

"Not at all," she replied.

"We don't get many students from the Domain," he said. "Actually, none. What made you decide to take this class?"

You consider that personal?

"Why you did, Professor Brown," she said. "I figured it would be interesting. Ray Brown's son teaching ethics to Dianne Morgan's daughter." She chuckled, relishing the irony of the situation. "Can it get any better than that?"

"I see." His expression, once a warm, summer morning, now turned into a chilly evening in November. "So you're taking this class basically for laughs."

"That's not what I meant."

He snapped shut his briefcase. "Well, Ms. Morgan, we'll try to keep you amused."

"But Professor…" she said, but he was already disappearing out the doorway.

***

Paul's breath gradually turned ragged as he ran through the forest, but he willed his legs to keep pace with the other men. Sweat stuck to his back. *These damn thermoflex coats are way too hot for south-central Africa.*

A canopy of Muombo trees dominated the Zambezi river basin, but moonlight enabled the men to follow an old buffalo trail. Paul spotted the flickering light of a grass fire, but it was a long way off. During daylight hours, the thin foliage allowed sufficient light to support a continuous ground cover of grasses and brush. However, the grass burned easily, so fast-moving fires were a constant danger.

A lion's roar carried across the brush, but the beast was upwind, so it wouldn't pick up their scent. This was Africa; flesh and blood predators were active at night, too.

The man striding next to him was the reason for these night treks. With the Domain hunting him, Ray changed his location frequently. Paul knew an attack could come at any time, even here, far from the enemy's cities.

It was difficult to keep pace; he had never really recovered from the croc attack six years earlier. Ray, on the other hand, thrived in Africa. He had thrown off the patina of civilization and reverted to older, more aggressive ways. Ray had become the perfect leader for this war: brilliant, technically sophisticated, worshipped by the tribes, and unrelenting. For six long years he had fought the Domain's overwhelming wealth and technology to a standstill.

George Sakeni, a tall, bone-thin Ngoni warrior, was leading them east across a broad plateau to the next hiding place. Two young warriors—probably teenagers, Paul guessed—followed a few steps behind, carrying old, but deadly HK416 assault rifles with attached grenade launchers. On these barefoot warriors, the thermoflex coats seemed particularly out of place. Another of the war's insults.

Ray was the spiritual heart of this war. If the Domain ever managed to kill him, the rebellion would collapse. To the tribes, Ray wasn't just a man, he was the demigod Malomi, sent by the gods to slay their enemies. As long as Ray was alive, the tribes would fight.

It's taking a toll on him, Paul thought, scratching at a scab from a mosquito bite on his neck. He hadn't seen Ray smile for a long time.

Dianne Morgan was the reason for Ray's determination. He never said much, but his face hardened whenever her name came up. Two decades ago, she had seduced him. Their affair broke up his marriage and separated him from his sons. Then she framed him for the PeaceMaker attack, forcing his sons to grow up in dishonor. He had remained her prisoner for thirteen years on the island before Nkumah rescued him. Hatred was a powerful fuel, but it had burned out much of the goodness he had loved in his friend.

Ray's voice intruded, "You all right?"

Paul glanced at his friend, a silhouette in the moonlight. Shadows masked Ray's eyes, giving him an otherworldly look.

Paul nodded and said, "I'm okay."

George glanced back, his face drawn into a frown. They were not supposed to talk during the march. Silence meant survival, but sometimes words were necessary.

"I read Nkumah's military summary last night," Ray said, running easily over the rough terrain, "Have you seen it?"

"Not yet," Paul puffed out.

"It's not good. Most of south-central Africa has been depopulated by the pogrom. The new robots are practicing genocide."

"That's nothing new," Paul replied. He glanced at Ray, then returned his attention to the uneven trail. "I don't want to sound crass, but the

Domain has been exterminating villages for years. The bastards have cut the tribal population in half."

"It's different now," Ray muttered. "Worse. These new versions of Commandos are programmed with sophisticated search and destroy protocols. Body armor is improved, too." Ray swerved past a dangling thorn bush. "Even grenades don't pierce the shell, unless you score a direct hit. A full-power laser can damage it, but you have to get within fifty feet."

"Shit," Paul said. "Are we doing any better with the weapons deliveries?"

"No, they've slowed to a trickle. DoubleD's agents are getting better at infiltrating our smugglers."

George suddenly pulled up and peered into the shadows ahead. Paul drew his laser pistol and quietly sunk into a defensive crouch. He hadn't heard or seen anything, but he had learned to trust these men. George signaled directions to his warriors and then disappeared into the brush. One warrior followed him, while the third man crept next to Ray and then aimed his rifle in the direction George had taken.

Paul quietly kneeled back-to-back with Ray, keeping his eyes on the trail behind them, while Ray watched ahead. After six years traveling through wild country, they knew the drill. It had saved their lives more than once.

Minutes passed. The night was quiet, except for the buzz of ever-present insects. Paul hoped the noise—or whatever had alarmed George—had been a false alarm. He jerked around when an assault rifle sputtered once, then twice, but quickly brought his eyes back to the trail behind him. Maintain discipline and survive was the rule. He strained to hear through the darkness. A branch shook, and he turned to see two warriors dragging a robot by its heels.

Four feet long, with spindly metallic arms and legs, it appeared to be one of the Domain's robot spies. As the men dragged it closer, Paul saw two bullet holes in its brown and green trunk.

This type of robot—they were called Spybots—powered up under the sun and then searched for humans at night. If it found a village, camp, or even a single person, the Spybot would transmit the location to the nearest Condor. They probably didn't have much time; a helicopter could arrive at any moment.

Ray dropped down on one knee next to the robot and snapped open the flap to the chest compartment. He unsnapped its four tiny data storage cartridges and stuffed them in his backpack. This was a great find; the cartridges contained the code that guided the robot. These robots were programmed to self-destruct rather than be captured, so

George must have ambushed it. Once they reached safety, their engineers could study the code and determine the robot's weak points.

Ray got to his feet. "Let's go."

George loped down the trail, followed closely by Paul and Ray, and then the two young warriors. Paul concentrated on maintaining a long, mechanical stride, trying to eliminate any unnecessary movement. He knew they would have to run until sunrise.

They had only been running twenty minutes when Ray's pocket emitted a low hum: an enemy helicopter was approaching. Ray stopped, pulled a wallet-sized computer from his pocket and aligned the signal. "The Condor is about five miles north and coming toward us."

"We should keep moving," Paul puffed out, bent over with his hands on his knees, "The damn thing can't locate us as long as we're all wearing thermoflex coats."

Ray stared at the pocket detector's small display, "The Condor is going down—it landed about four miles north—just about where we destroyed the Spybot." He was silent for a few seconds, and then whispered, "It's going up again. Probably beginning a search protocol."

"You say it landed?" Paul said, "Why would it land?"

Ray's face was all lines and edges, "Nkumah's report says the Condor can carry one Commando," he said."I think a Commando was dropped to track us by land, while the Condor hunts from the air."

"Maybe we should get off the trail," Paul said.

George and the two warriors were having a spirited discussion in Chichewa, their native language. Paul knew the basics of the language, but they spoke so quickly he could only pick up bits and pieces. The three men quickly came to agreement.

"The Commando may be able to follow our trail, Melomi," George said, "These two warriors will destroy it."

Ray glanced at Paul, and then nodded at George. "This new robot is well-armored. Tell your men to get close and use the grenades. Bullets won't pierce its shell." He paused briefly, "After the robot is destroyed, they must signal us with three quick gunshots."

Paul pulled the laser pistol from his holster and offered it to George, who shook his head. Paul felt like hitting the stubborn bastard, and then shoved the pistol against George's chest.

"Are you nuts?" Paul said when George still refused to take the weapon. "The laser is their best chance."

Ray gripped his shoulder and pulled him around, "He knows that, Paul, but we have to fight again tomorrow." Ray turned to George. "Tell them to go."

"As you command, lord." George signaled to the warriors, who turned and loped down the trail.

"Shit," Paul muttered, watching their backs disappear into the shadows. They were just kids, but had joined the war effort because so many of the older men had been slain. When he turned, Ray was already running up the trail.

"Follow me," George said. "Don't disturb the brush as we travel."

Ray strode into the jungle, with George on his heels. Paul followed a few yards behind, frequently glancing over his shoulder. He knew the war depended on Ray, but it didn't make him feel any better.

The three men strode along the trail in single file, listening to the night. Paul stumbled when a thunderous roar came from behind a nearby bush.

They stopped, searching the shadows with their eyes. George pointed in the direction of a tree about twenty yards to the right. Focusing intently, Paul discovered two gleaming eyes in thick brush near the tree.

Only a lion could stare like that. To the cat, he was just prey.

The lion, a sleek female, slipped past the tree into the shadows. Paul wondered if the pride was nearby.

"We're safe as long as we stay together," George said. "A single lioness won't attack three men."

George angled them away from the direction the cat had taken, but Paul kept the laser in his hand. They could be running into a trap: lion prides killed by ambush. He noticed Ray also had his laser out.

They had traveled a couple of miles when an explosion lit up the night sky behind them. A second explosion followed almost on top of the first one. Then laser beams sliced through the brush, followed by a third explosion.

The laser flashed again, and then it was quiet. In the distance, Paul saw the flicker of flames. He guessed that the fight had ignited the dry grass.

The flickering light of the fire spread across the horizon as they waited for a signal from the men.

A minute passed, then another.

Paul stared at the horizon. The only sound was the rumble of elephants spooked by the fire.

If they'd taken the laser—

"Keep moving all night," George said to Ray. "Do not rest until you reach the camp." Then he turned and trotted back down the trail, toward the flickering light.

Paul tensed when a hand brushed against his shoulder, "We have to get moving," Ray said. The dim light revealed the worn face of an old man.

Paul shook his head. "You go ahead. I'll help George stop the robot following us."

Ray stared at him, and then said, “I’m going with you.”

“No. The insurgency depends on you. You have to get to the camp as quickly as possible.”

“Paul, I can’t fight this war without you.”

Paul said, “I’ll see you in the camp tomorrow.” He looked at the flames and then added, “It’s your turn to make breakfast.”

Paul turned and hurried down the trail. He wondered if he’d see the light of morning.

***

Alone in his bed, David stared up at the dark ceiling. His body was covered in sweat. He didn’t understand why the nightmares kept coming.

Maybe his mind was rebelling because he was part of the Domain. He hated the Domain and all it stood for. And yet, he was still here.

As a young man, he had thought his father was the criminal who released the deadly PeaceMaker virus, and then died resisting capture. Then David had received a time-delayed email from his father claiming that he was on the trail of the people who created the virus. David had investigated and discovered that Dianne Morgan was the real criminal, but he had been forced to keep her secret because she had captured his father. But it was more than that; he joined the Domain because his destiny was to merge with Sentinel. Even after his father escaped, he remained because of Sentinel.

Although he knew Dad was alive somewhere in Africa, he had not spoken to him for nine years. Dianne had allowed him to see his father just once, through a hologram shortly after David joined the Domain. He had begged her to let him see his father again, but she refused.

The witch punished both of them. Dad was the only one who understood David’s destiny. With Dad imprisoned, David was left to face his devils alone.

This was where it had led. Kathy was dead and his son was going bad. And the witch was still alive.

FOURTEEN

Tuesday, September 9, 2031

David's watch read 9:45 am when he arrived at Dianne's apartment. Standing behind a bulletproof, synthetic shield that wrapped around the doorway and a security desk, two beefy security agents in dark blue uniforms guarded the entrance. He recognized these men; they belonged to Dianne's Elite Guards, a privileged command of soldiers selected for their loyalty and brutality.

"Your appointment is not until ten, Mr. Brown," the taller of the two guards said, his voice coming from a speaker built into the shield. The man's broad face was twenty miles of bad road.

"I thought I'd get here a few minutes early, just in case she was available."

"Ms. Morgan isn't here yet, but you're welcome to wait in her apartment."

"Thank you."

The second guard said, "The security check will only take a moment, sir."

David knew the security check had actually started when he entered the hall leading to Dianne's personal quarters. Every inch of his body had been scanned, verifying his identity and checking for weapons.

At the taller guard's request, he pressed his right palm against a biometrics reader built into the shield. His fingertips would be checked against a database of more than a billion people, with the results displayed at the security desk.

"Thank you, Mr. Brown," the tall guard said.

The entrance of the synthetic shield slid open. Apparently, the electronic scans were not sufficient, for he was subjected to a thorough pat down by the taller guard, while the other one watched. It was humiliating.

"Please follow me," the big man said, and then escorted David into a large, well-furnished suite. They crossed a pine-plank foyer, past a huge bedroom with a four-post bed, and into the main living area. Oriental rugs were spaced over the pine floor, surrounded by whitewashed plaster walls with deep blue paneling.

A stone fireplace covered one wall, with embers glowing in the ash. The scent of a recent fire permeated the room.

Although David had been in this apartment several times, the beauty of the surroundings always captivated him. Someone like Dianne

Morgan should live in a stark, modern apartment, not in this warm, old-fashioned setting. Apparently, even a monster needed a home.

In the center of the room, an antique coffee table stood between a leather armchair and a long sofa sporting a flame stitch. The guard escorted him to the sofa, turned, and retreated a few feet.

David sat down and checked his watch: 9:49.

He waited quietly. The back of his shirt felt sticky, but he remained patient. If he rushed, the guard might become suspicious. He prayed Dianne would be late.

The minutes lumbered by. Finally, it was time. He turned to the guard and said, "May I use the bathroom?"

The big man pointed to a door in the corner. "Right over there."

David thanked the guard and strolled to the bathroom. After closing the door behind him, he looked around. It was a large bathroom, with a toilet, sink, shower and couch. He didn't see any cameras, but that didn't mean anything; a nanocam would be smaller than the head of a pin. But Dianne wouldn't allow cameras in her bathroom. At least he hoped that was the case.

He checked his watch: 9:53.

First, he bent over to examine the sink. His target was a strand of hair, a clip of fingernail or anything that would provide a sample of her DNA. He went over every inch of surface, but the sink was clean. So were the toilet and shower.

9:56.

Damn it. I have to find something before the guard becomes suspicious.

David kneeled next to the shower and carefully searched the drain. Spotless. He pulled out his nail clipper, snapped it open and jammed the pointed end into one of the square holes in the drain cover. Gradually increasing the pressure, he attempted to unscrew it. The damn thing was tight, but it finally began to turn. He lifted it free and ran his finger along the inside of the pipe.

Nothing.

9:58.

After replacing the drain cover, he stepped back to the sink. Using the nail file, he removed the drain cover and ran his finger down the inside of the pipe.

Damn it.

Ten o'clock.

"Ms. Morgan is walking down the hallway," the guard said from just outside the door. "She'll be here in a minute."

David looked around. *What can I do?* There was another possible source, a long-shot, but it was his last chance. He pulled a tissue from a tissue holder on the sink and dropped down on his knees next to the toilet. Female urine wasn't the best source of DNA, but it was his only hope.

Just above the water line, he rubbed the tissue completely around the toilet. The tissue was moist, but it looked clean. He didn't have a clue as to whether DNA was present.

"Mr. Brown, she's here," came through the door.

"Coming," David shouted back.

No time left. He folded the tissue and slid it into his pocket.

After flushing the toilet and washing his hands—in case the guard was listening—he stepped out of the bathroom. The guard stood next to the door, eying him suspiciously.

Dianne sat on the couch, apparently speaking to someone through her Command Chip. She looked at him and then waved him to sit down in the chair opposite her. She continued talking as he walked over and sat down.

Although Dianne still had the body of a much younger woman, telltale wrinkles radiated from the corners of her eyes and mouth. Maybe murdering innocent people was finally wearing her down.

Not likely.

"So Professor Brown is an excellent teacher," she said through the Command Chip.

Why is she talking about my brother?

"I'm pleased you're enjoying the class." Dianne ignored him as she continued her conversation. Finally, she said, "Honey, I have to hang up, my appointment is here."

After saying goodbye, she focused her attention on David. "Larissa is taking a eugenics course at Princeton taught by your brother. She's learning a great deal from the class."

"I'm surprised," David said. *Brian hadn't mentioned anything*. "Why is Larissa attending one of their universities?"

"It'll be a great experience for her. Her Domain education has been excellent, but she needs to broaden her outlook, especially the way things are moving now." Dianne's eyes seemed to search his mind. "But we're not here to discuss Larissa." She crossed her legs, with her dress riding up still-beautiful thighs, and said, "I understand you wanted to see me about Martin."

"Yes, I'm concerned he may injure himself pursuing a connection with Sentinel." David despised this woman and she knew it, but he was determined to use tact for once. "Martin is a brilliant child, but his emotional intelligence hasn't kept pace with his intellect.

"About a year ago, Martin became obsessed with artificial intelligence. He's determined to merge with Sentinel, much as I have for the last few years. Merging is a shattering experience which only a mature mind can survive. A six year old would be in great danger." He added, "Dr. Chang feels the same way."

"When will he be able to safely survive a merge?"

"I'm not sure," David replied. "It's impossible to predict. I was about Martin's age when I had my first experience with an AI. Alice almost killed me, as you well know."

"I'm sorry you're having a problem with the boy," Dianne said. "I've grown fond of him." She paused a second. "You understand, of course, that I'd like Martin to merge with Sentinel as soon as it's safe."

"I do, too," David said, "but he's too young. When I feel his mind is ready, I'll guide him through the first merge."

"All right. What would you like me to do?"

"Bar him from the Virtual Reality Lab. He needs the booth to make a mind to code connection with Sentinel. He'll be safe if we can keep him out of the VRB. I can't watch him all the time, so I'd like the guards to keep him away."

Dianne's baleful stare made him feel like a bug about to be crushed. He was surprised when she said, "I'll take care of it."

"Thank you."

"You've never allowed Martin to have a Teacher," Dianne said. "Perhaps we should create a robot for him, one that will make sure he doesn't endanger himself."

David shook his head. "Martin is much too powerful to be given a Teacher. He'd attempt to link with the robot's code and then bootstrap into Sentinel. That would be dangerous for him."

"I see." She stood up, as did David. "Let me know if I can provide any additional help with Martin."

"Thanks, again," he said as she walked away.

***

David returned to his apartment and hurried to the bedroom. He pulled the tissue from his pocket and examined it. Now dry, it revealed a tiny dark spot. Using his nail file, he scratched loose a few grains into his portable DNA analyzer.

"This is the Dianne Morgan sample."

David sat down on the side of the bed. *Maybe I didn't get any DNA. Or maybe someone besides Dianne left DNA.* He thought about throwing the DNA analyzer into the trash, but he had to know the truth, even if it confirmed his worst nightmare.

"Compare the Dianne Morgan sample with the Martin Brown sample for a family relationship."

The DNA analyzer replied, "Dianne Morgan is the mother of Martin Brown."

He couldn't believe it. *Martin is her freaking son, not Kathy's.* He stumbled over to the wall and punched it, hardly feeling any pain. *She used me as a stud to produce that brat.*

His eyes welled up and he punched the wall again; then, through the haze, spotted an old wooden chair in the corner of the room. *They murdered Kathy.* Stumbling to the corner, he grabbed the chair's legs and smashed it against the wall. One leg flew off and the chair half collapsed. Another crushing blow against the wall and broken pieces scattered along the floor. He threw the last piece across the room; it crashed against the wall and fell to the floor.

He dropped to his knees, crying softly, and crawled into bed. Such a fool. Now he understood why Chang had supervised Kathy's pregnancy. *Chang used my sperm to fertilize the witch's egg, and then planted the embryo in Kathy.* He gripped the comforter, and then pulled it over his body. Kathy carried that witch's baby until it killed her.

I'll kill that cold-blooded reptile Chang.

I'll torture Dianne first— kill her slowly— make her suffer, like my Kathy suffered.

No wonder Martin is going bad.

He lay back in the bed, rigid, with only his head exposed. Over the years, his hatred of Dianne had gradually burned down. Once he discovered his father was still alive, he had gone on to other things: marriage, fatherhood, Sentinel. Now there was only one thing that mattered; he had to kill her.

He could almost feel his hands around her neck, squeezing the last breath out of her struggling body. But even that wouldn't be enough. First destroy the Domain. Take Sentinel for his own. Make her watch all her dreams die. Then kill her.

As he looked up at the dark ceiling, a plan began to form. He knew how to defeat the witch, but there was one big hole: what would he do with Martin?

***

Dianne strode down the long, empty hall toward Chang's private lab. A laser-armed Daniel android hardly made a sound as it followed a few steps behind.

Her legs were tired and she forced one foot in front of the other. A good night's sleep would help. One without medication.

She turned a corner and continued walking, briefly glancing out a window. Moonlight barely touched the dark forest in the distance. She hadn't hiked in that forest in months. In fact, she rarely left her office complex; it was dangerous out there. Anyway, there was too much to do. It was all coming to a head.

Dianne wondered if David suspected Martin was her son. She had covered her tracks, but David wasn't stupid. Why was he suddenly concerned about Martin's safety? He didn't appear to have any real feelings for the boy, except resentment. Maybe he was trying to keep Sentinel for himself.

There had been something glittering in David's eyes tonight, something dangerous she hadn't seen in years. She considered killing him, but he was too valuable. Mohammed had been studying David for years, but still hadn't unlocked all the secrets of the communication process with Sentinel. She would have to wait.

Dianne slowed as she approached Chang's door, knowing the security system would check her identity. The door slid open and she entered a brightly lit, modern laboratory. Chang was sitting at his desk, waiting for her.

The robot followed her into the lab, and then stood beside her as she sat in a hardback chair next to Chang's desk. Chang was watching her uneasily.

He thinks he's my superior, but he's a coward.

"I've been looking over the data, and the risk is increasing," Chang said. "Following the last extraction, you experienced migraines, shortness of breath and dizziness. If we hyper stimulate your ovaries again, the problem may become much more severe." Chang folded his hands on the desk. "We've discovered several cysts, a slight enlargement of your ovaries, and an unsafe degree of fluid build-up. We can treat these problems, but continued hyper stimulation could possibly lead to a fatal outcome." Chang leaned back, his dark eyes gleaming. "Although our models indicate the likelihood of your demise is only three to five percent, I thought it appropriate to inform you."

"Thank you, doctor," she said. She leaned back in the chair, folding her arms, "It was appropriate."

"On the positive side," he said, "the last extraction produced twelve viable eggs. Fertilization with David's sperm created nine embryos: four masters and five carriers. All have been successfully implanted into birthing mothers."

So tired. I have to get some rest tonight.

"Your embryos also received our most advanced artificial chromosomes," Chang said. "Not only will the masters have David's communication abilities, they should grow up to be Renaissance men."

She closed her eyes and made a quick calculation. "So we've brought one-hundred fifty-six children into the world", she murmured, "all growing in birthing mothers. Mohammed estimates one-hundred eighty will be sufficient initially. My children will become the initial human nodes in a network with Sentinel." When she opened her eyes, Chang nodded in agreement. "We're almost there," she whispered. "Getting close to the critical mass to form the new entity. All of them mind-merged together with Sentinel." She gripped Chang's arm, "Its power will be without limit."

Chang tried to pull his arm away, but Dianne didn't release him, "This entity may be very dangerous," Chang said. "We don't know what its powers will be, or how we'll control it."

"It's not for us to control it." She stared at this worm, wishing she could be done with him. "Don't you see? It will be a god." She was tired, but her work was almost complete. "And I'll be the reverend mother."

Chang was looking strangely at her.

"Have your people found any additional genetic stock?" Chang asked, finally freeing his arm as Dianne relaxed her grip. "All the nodes will be yours and David's. We require diversity for long-term success."

"I'm working on it."

Chang stared at her, his eyes widened in surprise. "Can you share anything with me?"

She hadn't meant to let that out. Now Chang would snoop around, looking into things he didn't need to know. She'd have to tell him eventually, but there was no need to trust him with her plan just yet.

"I meant to say I'm thinking about it, but I haven't come up with anything yet." She stood up, weary to the bone. "Are they ready for me in the clinic?"

"They're waiting," Chang said as he hobbled to his feet.

***

Time = 7:35 pm. 180 scan. Prey not detected. Composite luminous intensity = .39. Switch lens to night-vision. Probable distance to prey = .47 to 1.12 miles. Increase walking speed 8%. Shape recognition software engaged.

Time = 7:36 pm. 180 scan. Prey not detected. Air moisture increase. Rain beginning. Analysis: Precipitation is within operating parameters.

Time = 7:36:47 pm. Sound detected. Right, 83 degrees. Mammal moving in tree. Database comparison. Baboon. Non-threatening. Not prey. Resume hunt.

Time = 7:37 pm. 360 scan. Prey not detected.

Time = 7:38 pm. 180 scan. Prey not detected. Rain intensity increased 18%. Filter background noise. Analysis: Precipitation is within operating parameters.

Time = 7:38:20 pm. Footing compromised. Mud. Reduce walking speed 11%. Engage cleats.

Time = 7:39 pm. 360 scan. Prey not detected. Analysis: Traction is within operating parameters.

Time = 7:39:35 pm. Obstacle in path. Cache search. Analysis: Hanging branch. Reduce walking speed 32%. Bend knees 26%. Bend spine 65%.

Time = 7:39:38 pm. Obstacle cleared. Resume previous parameters.

Time = 7:40 pm. 180 scan. Prey not detected.

Time = 7:40:13pm. Explosion. Footing lost. Airborne. Tumbling. Left arm damaged. Enemy attack. Activate defensive programs.

Time = 7:40:14pm. Adjusting limbs to cushion impact. Rollover. Database analysis. Grenade attack.

Time = 7:40:15pm. 360 scan. Emergency analysis. Tree 4.6 feet on left. Analysis: Best defensive position.

Time = 7:40:16 pm. Laser strike on chest. Analysis: Two batteries destroyed, only one still functional. Realign power grid to right arm. Crouch behind tree. Minimize exposure to enemy.

Time = 7:40:17 pm. 360 scan. Movement detected in tree on left 87 degrees. Database comparison. Tribal warrior. Prey detected. Aim right arm. Prey in sights. Fire laser.

Time = 7:40:18 pm. Prey hit. Dropping to ground. One leg burned off, but not terminated. Aim right arm.

Time = 7:40:19 pm. Prey crawling away. Adjust. Prey in sights. Fire laser. Prey terminated.

Time = 7:40:20 pm. Laser strike on right arm. Analysis: right arm inoperative. Operational capability reduced to 43%. Realign power grid to left arm.

Time = 7:40:21pm. 360 scan. Movement detected in brush on right 64 degrees. Prey detected. Database comparison: Enemy soldier. Enlarge image. Cache search. Paul Martino. Priority interruption triggered. Analysis: Initiate secondary visual scan for primary target, Raymond Brown.

Time = 7:40:22 pm. 360 scan. Raymond Brown not detected.

Time = 7:40:24 pm. Laser strike on tree. Minor damage to left shoulder. Operation capability reduced to 37%. Priority reset. Analysis: Retreat, summon Condor.

Time = 7:40:25 pm. Communication initiated. No response from Condor. Analysis: Condor beyond range of single battery. Analysis: Retreat, retry communication.

Time = 7:40:26 pm. Running, maximum speed. 360 scan. Martino gaining.

Time = 7:42:17 pm. Laser strike on left leg. Analysis: No mobility. 180 scan. Martino approaching. Realign power grid to communications. Condor handshake. Transmit coordinates and request assistance.

Time = 7:42:30 pm. Realign power grid to left arm. Prey in sights. Insufficient power to fire laser. Martino aiming laser. Analysis: Laser… strike… to… chest. Operational… capability… reduced… to… unable… to… compute.

Time = 7:42:33 pm. Martino… approaching. Martino… aiming… laser. Analysis…Analysis…

FIFTEEN

Tuesday, September 9, 2031

Paul braced his right hand against the rough bark of a tree and leaned forward. His breath came in hard clumps. Although he was in good shape for fifty-eight, he couldn't run like a young warrior.

His stomach clenched and he threw up. This had been his worst day in Africa since the croc attack. His throat was raw and he felt light-headed. All three warriors were dead, good men he respected. George, especially, had been a good family man, as good as you could be in the middle of six years of senseless killing. And the two teenagers—at least Ray was safe for the moment.

As his breathing gradually recovered, Paul scanned the night sky. He figured that he had run two or three miles from the remains of the Commando. He could only rest for a minute or two; the robot might have summoned a Condor helicopter.

The roar of a nearby lion traveled up his back, and he jerked to attention. He pulled the laser pistol from his hip and looked across the darkness. His senses, acute from years of running and fighting, detected movement in the brush about thirty yards away. Branches bent and then snapped back. A long, tawny form slipped past a tree and disappeared. Then a low growl made him spin around. On the left, only about twenty yards away, two bright, unblinking eyes peered through the brush.

Shit! A pride of lions.

Just his luck. He might get a couple of them with the laser, but he wouldn't survive a charge by the entire pride. Anyway, firing the laser might reveal his position to a Condor.

Talk about going from the frying pan into the fire.

With slow, careful movements, Paul slid his weapon back into the holster. He looked up the tree, which rose about fifty feet. The branches looked thick enough to support his weight. He knew lions don't like to climb, so his best chance was to get up that tree. If he could get out of their leaping range, they might decide he wasn't worth the effort.

The first branch was at shoulder level, and the second a couple of feet higher. Climbing in the thermoflex coat would be awkward, but he didn't have the time to remove it. Anyway, he had to hide his thermal signature from any nearby helicopters.

Shit. He hadn't climbed a tree since he was a kid, but he would have to scramble up like a monkey. Once he moved, the lions would be on him in seconds.

A huge, bushy head poked out of the brush: a male, as big as a house. *Time to go.* Paul slowly bent into a crouch and then exploded in a leap. He grabbed the higher branch, swung his legs onto the lower branch, stood up and scrambled onto the second branch.

He heard the lions charging out of the brush. He was on the second branch, reaching for the third, when a dark form leaped at him. With his hands gripping the higher branch, he swung his body up and away from the beast. The air stunk of death and he felt teeth slash through the bottom of his coat. For a split second, a lioness hung on his coat, his partner in a lethal ballet. Then the thermoflex ripped and she lost her grip. The big cat tried to grasp the tree trunk, but it tumbled down through the branches, snapping them like twigs as it fell to the ground.

With the lions roaring below, he scrambled, branch after branch, up the life-saving tree. He thanked God he was still alive. Pausing about two-thirds up the trunk, he looked down. The big male was standing on his hind legs, leaning against the tree, staring up the trunk. It seemed the lion should be able to haul his bulk up a few branches, but the big cat just stood there and roared.

Paul climbed up a few more branches, and then paused to check for injuries. His shoulder had never fully recovered from the croc attack, and it ached from the strain of climbing, but he had learned to live with pain. The lower half of his coat was in tatters, but aside from a three-inch, bloody cut along his calf, he was okay. Maybe he'd survive this after all.

The male dropped down on all fours, charged a nearby female and swatted her with his huge paw. She backed up a few paces and snarled at him. Squinting to see through the shadows, Paul counted six lionesses. They milled around the tree, keeping clear of the frustrated male.

After one final glare up the tree, the male wandered to the edge of the brush and dropped down to rest. A sleek lioness, keeping a wary eye on the resting male, sidled over to the tree. She stared up the trunk at Paul and then roared. With a straight upward leap, she hooked her claws high in the trunk and pulled herself onto the second branch.

Paul didn't want to use his laser, but now he didn't have a choice. The lioness would be on him in seconds. He'd have to kill the cat and maybe one or two others. If he made them scatter, he might be able to climb down and get away before a Condor arrived.

When he grabbed for the laser, all he felt was his holster. The laser was gone. He looked down; it was lying in the thick grass at the base of the tree.

The lioness roared at him again, and then climbed awkwardly to the next branch. The big cat almost lost her balance, but wrapped her front paws around the trunk.

Paul felt sweat soaking his back. He climbed up another branch, but it curved down under his weight, and he almost slipped off. He couldn't get any higher. The cat was so close he could smell her.

The lioness roared at him and licked her lips. She climbed up another branch, and then steadied herself once again by sinking her claws into the trunk. The big cat was an awkward climber, but she was getting close. One more branch and he would be within range of those claws.

Off to his right, Paul spotted a long, thin branch. Holding on to the trunk, he reached over with his right hand and snapped it off. The branch was about two yards long and fairly straight, narrowing to a fine tip. A whip. Not much of a weapon, but it's all he had.

The big cat snarled, revealing fangs that could crush his head. When the lioness reached up to get a grip on the trunk, Paul whipped the tip of the branch as hard as he could against big cat's nostrils. She roared in shock and backed down a couple of feet.

The lioness looked down and growled at the cats milling about the tree. She watched them for a few seconds and then turned her yellow eyes back to Paul. When she reached up to grip the trunk, he whipped the branch again. This time the cat caught the branch in her jaws and jerked it out of his hand. She spit it out and snarled at him. His chest contracted as the lioness sunk her claws into the trunk and climbed.

I never thought it would end like this.

Suddenly a spotlight beamed through the leaves, bathing the pride in white light. The hum of a powerful engine broke into his awareness, and Paul spotted a Condor hovering about fifty yards above. The robot helicopter was only about fifteen feet in length, but it carried a laser cannon on each side.

The helicopter spooked the big cats, and they scattered into the brush. The lioness in the tree stared at Paul for a second and then began backing down. He never thought he'd be so pleased to see one of these murderous robots.

The Condor began to circle the tree, and the lioness panicked and scrambled away from the beam of light. Losing her grip on the trunk, she tumbled out of the tree and with a frightened screech, hit the ground hard. The spotlight found her again, lying on her side, licking a badly splintered front leg.

The helicopter continued to circle the tree, its spotlight searching the ground. Paul realized the Condor had been attracted by the lions' commotion, but it hadn't spotted him. A few minutes passed—maybe five, no more—as the Condor's searchlight swept across the area around the tree. It flushed the pack out of the brush, but ignored their frantic retreat. The injured lioness, dragging a front leg, crawled into the brush.

The helicopter swung around and focused its beam near the base of his tree. The damn thing must have realized that the lions had treed something. The searchlight traveled slowly up the trunk. Now sweating profusely, Paul grabbed a branch and leaned forward, trying to keep behind the trunk. He froze as the deadly circle of light approached; any move could be his last. The light was blinding, terrifying. First the Commando robot, then the lions, now a murderous helicopter; it felt like judgment day.

The spotlight passed by, moved up the trunk, and detoured along a nearby branch. As the helicopter circled, the spotlight again began to move toward him.

He thought he'd piss in his pants. Moving slowly so as not to attract attention, he grabbed a branch with one hand and inched to the other side of the trunk. His arthritic shoulder radiated pain.

I'm too old for this shit.

Once again, the circle of light swung in his direction. He shriveled his shoulders, trying to get his body behind the trunk.

The spotlight traveled past him down the trunk and then stopped. Paul held his breath; movement meant death. The Condor slowly circled around the tree, keeping its beam focused at the same level of the trunk. In a dance of death with the machine, Paul slid around to keep the trunk between his body and the Condor. The wind from the helicopter's blades whipped the tattered thermoflex coat against his body. The ripped end twisted in the breeze, but he prayed it would be mistaken for leaves. He sweated as the circle of light inched up the trunk, past his legs, then past his waist. The edge of the beam touched his shoulder. His only chance, a long-shot at best, was to keep perfectly still.

It was a sort of hellish dawn; the beam inched up, gradually lighting more of his shoulder, his neck and then his jaw. He was about to scramble down the tree when he was startled by a laser flash from below, which blew apart the helicopter's rear rotor. Suddenly, the Condor was spinning like a car on black ice. Its laser cannon spit out terrible bursts of light as the robot spun to earth. One of the terrible white beams flashed above his head; another burned into the trunk a few yards below his feet. There was a cracking sound and the trunk lurched to a forty-five degree angle, almost shaking Paul off, then held. A fall from this height would be fatal. The helicopter's nose went down and it began to tumble over. Paul hung on to the tree as the Condor slammed into the ground and exploded in a huge inferno.

The brush caught fire, surrounding the robot in growing flames. The engine restarted with a roar, but the rotor didn't turn. The monster was wounded, but not dead. Paul watched in confusion as the laser cannon slowly came around, then realized the weapon was turning toward him.

He scrambled down the trunk, but not fast enough; he was on the last branch, but the cannon was pointed at him. Then a laser in the darkness flashed again and the cannon exploded with deafening impact. Shrapnel ripped into his leg, and he fell hard to the ground.

Lying on his side in the grass, Paul watched the interior of the helicopter catch fire, with flames licking its sides. The brush surrounding the helicopter turned into a pyre. A beautiful pyre, he thought.

His right leg throbbed, but it was a miracle he was still alive.

A silhouette appeared in front of the fire; then he recognized Ray walking toward him. Dizziness took him for a moment; Paul felt hands loosen his belt, pull down his pants and gently begin cleaning the shrapnel from his thigh.

Paul grimaced. "You have to buy me dinner first."

"You're a lucky bastard. It's just a flesh wound," Ray said as he pulled a small chunk of plastic out of his leg. It hurt like hell as Ray quickly cleaned the wound, and then wrapped a self-adhering bandage around his upper thigh.

Ray finished wrapping the bandage, and leaned back on his knees. "The camp is about ten miles from here, and we have to get moving."

"You were supposed to be there now," Paul spit out. "The rebellion depends on you. Why the hell do you think I was doing all this hero shit?"

"Yeah, yeah," Ray said, pulling Paul to his feet. "Now put your arm around my shoulder and let's get out of here."

They hobbled a few steps, and Paul said, "Hey, Ray—"

"What now?"

"Thanks."

SIXTEEN

Monday, September 15, 2031

Larissa stopped outside Professor Brown's office and pulled a hand mirror from her purse. She usually didn't worry much about her looks, but today she needed to look pretty, even a little sexy. No makeup, but people said she didn't really need it. She checked out her clothes one last time; tight blue skirt, silk blouse, sandals. Everything looked good.

What if he isn't attracted to me?

That couldn't happen. Guys always wanted her. She wasn't promiscuous, but her good looks and charisma attracted men. Not that it hurt to be the daughter of the most powerful woman on the planet.

But this man was special. She'd never felt such an intense attraction to a man. There was something about him.

She unhooked the top button of her blouse and spread the collar. A bit of cleavage, but not too revealing. She smiled. Enough to get his attention without being obvious.

Footsteps came from the far end of the hall, but she didn't see anyone. Her mother had said the bodyguards would be discreet, and Larissa hadn't noticed them anywhere. That's the way it should be. She stuffed the mirror back in her purse and knocked on the office door.

"Come in," Professor Brown shouted.

"Do you have a minute, professor?" she asked, stepping inside the door. She knew he had more than an hour before his next class. "I have a few questions about the classroom discussion."

He looked up from his computer display, and she felt his eyes linger briefly on her body. Then he gestured toward the upholstered chair at the side of his desk and continued working.

His office was cramped, with paper files, books and newspapers covering the desk and nearby floor. It was charming, sort of a Harry Potter look. The mid-morning sun peeked through the panes of the window to his left, washing the room in soft light.

Several enlarged old-fashioned two-dimensional photographs were lined up on a bookshelf behind his chair. A family outing—a picnic with a lake in the background—caught her eye. His father and grandparents stood behind a picnic table and little Brian, his mother and brother David sat in front. She guessed the picture was about twenty years old. Everyone looked happy.

She wondered if she was doing the right thing; this was pushing it, even for her. Ray Brown's son! But it was more than forbidden fruit; there was chemistry between them. She felt the intensity every time they looked at each other. Maybe nothing would come of it, but the attraction was too strong to ignore. She hoped her security people hadn't bugged his office.

Nothing ventured, nothing gained.

Larissa strode into the room and settled into the chair, letting her skirt glide halfway up her thighs. Her purse slid off her shoulder, and she stretched to place it on the floor. Larissa felt his eyes follow her movements.

"I'm sorry about the smartass comment last week," she said, "I didn't mean—"

"Don't worry about it," Professor Brown said, once again concentrating on the display. When he looked up, his expression seemed friendly. "I shouldn't have snapped at you. I think I was in the middle of an ego trip because such a famous person had selected my class. When you deflated my ego—well, I shouldn't have reacted so badly."

He smiled, melting away her tension, and she smiled back. "So neither of us gets an "A" for interpersonal relations," she said. "At least we have something in common."

"So tell me," he said, "*how* have you found the class so far?" He leaned forward, a lock of thick, brown hair falling over his forehead. "Are you learning how the other half thinks?"

She was pleased he had asked for her opinion. Maybe he was just making conversation, but as long as he was friendly, she didn't care. He'd been very formal in class—Ms. Morgan and all that bullshit—but Larissa knew his eyes lingered on her when she spoke up. Gave her a warm feeling. Like right now.

"To be honest, the class is even better than I expected," she said. "In the Domain, everyone defers to me. Whatever I say, no matter how idiotic, the other students nod their heads. The professors, too. This is the first time people have challenged my opinions." She smiled. "It's helped me think through some things."

He didn't smile back, but his face seemed to soften. "It's more than that, unfortunately." he said.

"I know you're the target of a lot of hostility. I've tried to defuse it, but I don't want to push it below the surface. It has to come out."

"Doesn't bother me. If I can't handle a little hostility, I'm in deep—I'm not going to fare very well. I imagine you know how that works."

"Yeah, my brother and I put up with a lot as kids."

When he didn't add anything, Larissa said, "My mother would probably throw up if she heard this, but I admire your father."

His lips curved into a smile. "My father would probably throw up, too."

"Does he know I'm in your class?"

Professor Brown leaned back in his chair. "Why do you admire my father?"

"My mother is a woman who gets what she wants. Not many people stand in her way and survive."

"Same with my father." He snorted. "Even those who stand with him don't always survive."

It wasn't the way this conversation was supposed to go. She had planned some light talk, maybe a little flirting. Larissa never discussed her mother with anyone; she knew better.

He leaned forward, weight on his forearms, palms down on the desk. His fingers were long and thin, but not fragile.

"I've been wondering about your hands," she said, reaching over the table and turning his palms up. "Those calluses. Not exactly a professor's hands."

"Are you always so observant?" he replied, staring into her eyes. "I have a house on the Jersey shore. Not a big deal, just a fixer-upper in Seaside Park. I get out there most weekends to work on the place. Put in a backup power generator last time."

"I love the ocean," she said, releasing his hands. "Mom bought an old hotel in San Diego. When I was a kid, we'd go three or four times a year. I could stay on the beach all day. Still can. Couldn't get enough of it. But she was a busy executive —"

"You're talking about the Bentley, aren't you?" When she nodded, he said, "That was a beautiful old hotel. My parents took us there when David and I were little kids. I vaguely remember it."

"Tell me about your place on the shore."

He chuckled, "Well, it's not the Bentley, I'll tell you that. It's about half a block in from the beach." He shifted in his chair. "Good view of the ocean if you hang out the second floor window and look down the street."

They both laughed.

"But you can hear the surf, especially now that the tourists are gone for the season. Love the sound of the waves rolling onto the beach. Very relaxing. Just open up the windows and let the ocean air in."

"So what's your next project?"

"Electric heat. Right now, all I have is a wood fireplace. Puts out enough heat for September, maybe part of October, but then I have to close down. With electric heat, I can use the place all winter."

She couldn't take her eyes off him. He was mature, with a quiet sexuality. She noticed the outline of lean muscles under his sweater. All that hard work at the shore had paid dividends.

She crossed her legs at the ankle, showing off the fleshy curve of her calves. "And what do you plan to do out there on those cold winter days?"

"More projects, I guess. I don't plan too far in advance."

"How about fun? You can't work all the time."

He seemed unsure how to respond, "Well, I'm writing a…I shouldn't tell you this."

"Tell me," she begged. "I can keep a secret."

"Okay, but don't laugh." He paused, as if gathering his nerve. "I'm writing a romance novel."

"I love it," she shrieked, clapping her hands. "I wouldn't have guessed in a million years. Tell me about the story."

"Well, it's about this beautiful young woman with a passion for life. Susan comes from a rich family and she's had just about everything she ever wanted. She loves to visit exotic places, so she decides to book a safari in Kenya."

Larissa broke in, "I've been to Nairobi. East Africa is beautiful land."

"Indeed it is," he replied. "Anyway the safari guide is very macho and Susan falls in love with him, even though she knows almost nothing about him. Well, it turns out that the safari business is just a front. Kevin actually makes his money trapping leopards and other big cats and then selling them to wealthy customers who want exotic pets. Susan, of course, knows nothing of this. So when she flirts with him, he treats her as just another conquest and has his way."

"I like that part," Larissa said.

Chuckling, Professor Brown continued, "But Kevin's partners double-cross him and try to ambush him during the safari. Kevin and Susan barely escape into the jungle, but the killers stay on their trail. Then, uh —"

"You're making all this up," she shouted, pretending to pout. "You're not writing a novel!"

"No, no," he protested, laughing. "Wait till you hear the rest!"

Larissa reached across the desk and touched his hand, "Let's cut right to the ending," she said, running her fingers over his palm.

She felt the electricity between them. His hand closed over her fingers and, suddenly, it was difficult to draw a breath. God, she wanted this man! She had a sudden image of that calloused hand caressing her bare breasts.

A loud female voice boomed over Larissa's shoulder. "Professor Brown!"

He jerked his hand back behind the desk. Larissa snapped out of her daydream, and then groaned when she saw the horse-face woman from class standing in the doorway. Horse-face had kept her distance since their initial confrontation.

"Ms. Widman, is there something I can do for you?" Professor Brown asked.

Larissa pulled her lips into a semblance of a smile and waved. "Good to see *ya*."

Horse-face glared at her and then turned to Professor Brown. "I have a few questions about the homework assignment."

"Please take a seat in the lounge." Larissa detected a touch of annoyance in his voice. "I'll come and get you when Ms. Morgan and I are finished."

Horse-face Widman turned and stomped out.

"Don't worry, there's plenty of hay in the stalls," Larissa called after her.

God, I love this class.

He chuckled. "I take it you two aren't fast friends."

"No, Horse-face and I are tight."

He laughed aloud. "You're too much, you know."

"Now where were we?" she purred. "Maybe you could use a little help with the house. I swing a pretty mean hammer."

"Ms. Morgan, you're charming but you're still my student." He walked around the desk, took her by the arm and led her to the door.

Giggling, she quipped, "I like it when you play rough."

"Now if you really have questions pertaining to the class, drop by any time."

"Thanks, Professor," she said. "I love talking with you."

"I enjoyed it, too, Ms. Morgan." He backed up a step, and a mischievous smile stretched across his face. "Now send in Horse-face."

SEVENTEEN

Thursday, September 18, 2031

Martin walked down the hall to Ms. Morgan's suite. His legs felt unreliable, not quite under control. When he became nervous, perspiration interfered with the signals passing between his nerve endings and the nearly invisible network encircling his legs. It was a problem he had learned to live with.

Martin knew he'd be in a world of trouble if his father ever discovered what was going on. The old man had said to stay away from the Virtual Reality Booth in no uncertain terms. If he discovered this visit to Ms. Morgan –

Standing behind a transparent, bulletproof shield that wrapped around the doorway and security desk, a pair of Elite Guards, members of Ms. Morgan's personal security service, protected the entrance. It was common knowledge the security system checked visitors for weapons as they approached. Martin stopped in front of the desk and looked up at the guards, who were the size of redwoods.

"Hello," he said, keeping his voice steady. "I'm Martin Brown."

"We know, Mr. Brown," the meaner-looking of the two guards said. The man's neck seemed wider than his head.

"Would it be possible to see Ms. Morgan? It's really important."

"What's the nature of your visit?" the guard asked.

"She'll know."

The guard pointed to a small, glass-walled reception area across the hall. "Please have a seat."

Martin strolled through the door and sank into a black leather chair. The reception area was about the size of his bedroom, furnished with four identical leather chairs surrounding a rectangular coffee table. No windows. He glanced around, looking for a computer interface, electronic game or anything else for entertainment. Nothing. He tried to amuse himself by visualizing the code he was writing to update the Space Warriors game.

Several minutes went by. This was boring. The mean-looking guard was keeping an eye on him from across the hall. *Like I'm going to set off a bomb or something.* He stood up and wandered around the room, examining the walls for hidden nanocams. He found one—a tiny pinprick about two feet up the wall—but searching for nanocams was boring, too. Pacing along the walls, he tried to think of something else to do.

A hologram popped up, displaying the guard's face above the coffee table, "Mr. Brown," the guard said. "Ms. Morgan will see you in her library."

Finally!

Martin left the reception area and stopped in front of the transparent shield.

The meaner-looking guard said, "The security check will only take a moment, sir."

At the guard's request, he pressed his right hand against a biometrics reader positioned in the shield. He was surprised they were still using fingerprints. He could have designed something more interesting, maybe using alpha wave signatures or body temperature distributions or something like that. He made a mental note to design something better for Ms. Morgan.

"Thank you, Mr. Brown." The shield slid open. "Please enter. Ms. Morgan will join you in a few minutes."

Martin was surprised when the guard stopped him and began patting him down. It was unpleasant to have those big hands touch him in private places. Finally, the ordeal was over and the guard escorted him into a large, well-furnished suite. Ms. Morgan's home was real big. Martin wandered around the room, mentally cataloging the furniture, paintings and samplers for future reference. Mostly old stuff. Antiques.

He had read she collected this stuff. The Internet was filled with information about Ms. Morgan, and he had read much of it. He wanted to know everything.

A stone fireplace covered one entire wall. He wondered why so many people were attracted to a fireplace; the whole thing was so ancient, so inefficient. The other walls were more interesting, and he examined a myriad of photographs. He recognized most of the faces. Ms. Morgan seemed to know everyone of any importance, past or present.

Even the Domain's great enemy, his grandfather Ray Brown, appeared in a photograph. Grandfather looked about forty years old, with deep lines across his forehead. He was fighting the Domain in Africa, but Martin didn't understand why. Didn't grandfather understand that the Domain was the future? Everyone said grandfather was bad, but Martin hoped he would meet the old-timer someday. *People think I'm bad, too*. In the photo, Ms. Morgan was smiling at grandfather. Curious.

There wasn't a single picture of his father. *Good. Ms. Morgan likes me, not my father.* He had overheard Dad saying nasty things about her. The old man didn't really seem to like anyone. People said Dad had been a smiling, good-natured man before Martin's mother died, but he'd never seen any of that. Ms. Morgan was much nicer.

On the coffee table, there was a holoplayer containing a clip of Ms. Morgan playing in the surf with her daughter. The record date on the side indicated Larissa hadn't been much older than he was now. He touched the top of the holoplayer, and a hologram popped up above the coffee table, showing mother and daughter playing together, having lots of fun. Larissa was so lucky.

A door opened and Ms. Morgan strode in. She was dressed in a long, white gown and high heels; she must be going to some sort of formal event. Ms. Morgan smiled down at him, like she was pleased to see him. He felt welcome.

"Hello, Martin. It's so nice to see you."

"Thank you for making some time for me, Ms. Morgan; I know how busy you are."

"Never too busy to see my favorite student," she said, patting him on the back. "And please call me Dianne. The Ms. Morgan thing is fine for school, but too formal when it's just the two of us. Is that all right?"

"Yes, uh, Dianne."

"How are you doing with that new hologram game?"

She remembered.

"It's going real good," he answered. *My father doesn't even know I'm building a new game. Wouldn't care, anyway.*

She sat down on a tan, simulated-leather couch, which put her eyes on a level with his. He noticed the fine lines spreading from the corners of her mouth and eyes. It dawned on him that she was really old.

"I'd love to play your new game when it's ready," she said. "I'll bet Larissa would, too. She's great at games." Dianne patted the couch, and he sat next to her, his feet not quite touching the floor. "Now tell me why I have the pleasure of your company."

"Well, it's about Sentinel." This had to be handled just right.

"Yes…" Dianne said.

He looked down at his shoes. "I probably shouldn't be here." He pushed off from the couch and got to his feet.

"Martin, you know you can talk to me."

"I know, but it's kind of sensitive. I don't want to cause a problem." He glanced up. "Can you keep a secret?"

"It depends on the secret," Dianne said. "But you know I'll help you if I can."

"Okay," he said. He gave her his best troubled smile and climbed back onto the couch. When he settled in, he looked up at her and said, "I have this ability to communicate with artificial intelligence. I don't know how it works, but to me, it's as natural as talking. I need to use this talent and stretch it as far as I can, otherwise I might lose it."

When he paused, Dianne said, "I understand. You do have an exceptional talent, and I want to encourage it."

Martin said, "I communicate with Sentinel all the time, but when I'm in the Virtual Reality Booth, I can skip the words. I can focus my thoughts and transmit them directly into Sentinel's internal memory. When Sentinel transmits back to me, I can feel the bit stream come into my mind and then produce meaning. Real fast, not slow like hearing words."

Martin glanced at his shoes and then looked up. "I've been communicating with Sentinel for more than a year and I'm ready for the next step: a mind merge."

Dianne frowned, making her seem a little bit scary. "Your father and Dr. Chang don't believe that you're ready for that," Dianne said. "They think that you might injure your mind."

"It's not true," he blurted out."They don't understand the power of my mind. Physically, I'm a child, but mentally I'm mature."

"I don't know."

"I'm different from my father. I've grown much faster. He went through his entire childhood with only one mind merge, and that one was terrible. Alice invaded his mind when he was eleven and tried to rip it apart." Dianne was looking at him sympathetically again, so he said, "I'm positive Dad's mind was injured during that attack and he never attained full power. You can see it yourself; he can merge with Sentinel, but he's never gained complete control of the net. He's limited. He'll never be more than what he is today."

"It's true his progress has been slow," Dianne mused.

"Slow? You're being kind. It's practically stalled. Let *me* merge. I can do it."

"How do I know you won't injure yourself?"

"I'll be very careful," he said. "Just a quick merge the first time. In and out."

"Your father is against it. He doesn't think you can do it. He says that he has invested too much time learning how to merge, and that you might damage Sentinel and set back all his work. If he found out I let you in the VRB, he'd be very angry." She sighed, "And if something happened to you, I wouldn't be able to live with myself."

"Nothing bad is going to happen," he whined. "I'm ready to do this. If I don't merge soon, my mind will begin to atrophy. I'll wind up like my father, a miserable failure unable to reach full potential."

Dianne seemed sympathetic, and her eyes commanded his attention."Sentinel would warn your father," she said. "They have a close relationship."

"I've written a special module of code," Martin said. "It gives you, and only you, the ability to load secret commands into Sentinel. The AI will have to obey you over all others—even my father. You could command Sentinel to keep the merge a secret."

Her eyes were hard. "How is that possible? The safety code was designed to be tamper proof."

Sometimes Ms. Morgan looks really scary —

"There's a tiny hole in the safety code," he said quietly. "Probably been there since the original operating system code was written by my grandfather. Maybe he put it in. Only the person with the highest security classification could install code through this hole. That person is you."

"So you're saying that I could install this code and then give Sentinel secret orders that would have to be obeyed. I could order it to allow you to merge. In addition, I could make it keep the whole thing a secret. Only you and I would know."

"That's right."

Dianne asked, "Does anyone else know about the security hole?"

"I don't think so. I only discovered it a few days ago." She was looking at him so intensely, it was creepy. "I'm sure no one has installed code through it," he added.

"Send me the code," she said."Your father will be away next week, visiting your grandmother in San Francisco." She looked down at him and smiled. "We'll do it then."

Ecstatic, Martin threw his arms around her waist and buried his head in her lap. It worked! Next week he would merge with Sentinel. He'd show the old man who had the real power.

"Promise me that you won't tell anyone about the hole in the security code," she said. He felt Dianne's hand brushing his hair, comforting him. "It will be our secret," she added.

"I promise," he whispered.

He felt so safe here. She was like a real mother.

EIGHTEEN

Sunday, September 21, 2031

Carlos checked his cards and then pressed them face-down against the table. His concentration was interrupted when the bartender called out, "Another bottle of Tequila, Carlos?"

His birth name was Raoul Mendoza, but he'd dropped it years earlier when he made his first kill. Now he was known as Carlos, a talented drifter who could fix any problem, if the money was right.

"Not for me, but a bottle for my *amigos* around the table."

More than three dozen people had gathered to watch the game, mostly losers and small-timers. They were the kind of people he had targeted as an orphan trying to survive on the streets of Mexico City, but now his money was low and he'd come full circle. But a game was a game.

Shifting in his seat, Carlos tried to get comfortable on this beaten-up wood chair. His stomach felt bloated: too much shrimp *ceviche* and onions today. Maybe tomorrow he'd get some exercise.

He stared across the table at Antonio, a burly gambler who smiled back unpleasantly. "So what's it going to be, *amigo*?" Antonio asked, peering through bloodshot eyes.

Only Antonio remained in the game, the best gambler in this bar, except for himself. He didn't know this man, but that just added to the rush.

Carlos puffed on his Long Panatela, Fidel's favorite brand according to legend. Carlos then placed the cigar in an overfilled ashtray and studied Antonio through the haze. They were playing the last hand of the night and the largest. The pot included a thick batch of American hundred dollar bills, as well as a TAG Heuer steel watch ponied up by a gringo with no brains. Not a Rolex, but still one hell of a watch. Carlos knew he had done well, but there wasn't much pleasure in beating a bunch of losers.

Antonio, on the other hand, was a challenge. The big man had won almost as much as himself. Even though Antonio was a pro, Carlos had bet all his winnings on this last hand. Sometimes he wondered why he did this; he could have played it safe, but he never did. He loved taking a risk.

He downed a shot of Tequila, and wiped his lips on his sleeve. "One card," he said.

Elena, his whore for the night, stood next to him, her hip rubbing against his shoulder. A little past her prime—if she ever had a prime—but what the hell. She would earn her money tonight, but first he needed to win this hand.

It had been more than a year since his last job and he was beginning to run low on cash. *Where the hell did all the money go?* He had been reduced to this third rate bar on the edge of Tijuana. The place stunk of piss and cheap cigars. Maybe it was time for another job.

His attention came back to the contest. Antonio dealt the jack of clubs, which Carlos slid under his cards. All eyes were on him, and he loved it. Women were fascinated by his unusual blue/green eyes and men respected his reputation for violence. A tight fitting T-shirt displayed well-muscled forearms bulging with skull tattoos. The red and black skulls showed big, square teeth on a background of flames and stars. He got the tattoos at age twelve to impress the whores.

Pretty good cards, he thought, but not unbeatable. He looked from his cards to study Antonio, but the man's beefy face gave away nothing. *Man, I love this shit.* Good thing the table hid his excitement.

"Dealer takes two."

Antonio dealt himself two cards and smiled.

Carlos studied Antonio's face again. Stretching his long legs under the table, he wondered how far he should push his luck. Antonio looked confident, but he could be bluffing. Carlos rubbed the lion's tooth charm hanging from his belt. It had brought him luck in the past, maybe it would again.

What the hell. Life was one big gamble.

He touched the top of his stack, slid out three newly minted thousand dollar bills and threw them into the pot. Three thousand American dollars would discourage a bluff.

"I'm a little disappointed, *amigo,*" Antonio said. "They told me you were a real gambler." He counted out thirteen bills and threw them in the pot, "Your three thousand and ten more."

Hijo de puta!

"You must have a good hand," Carlos said, keeping his expression neutral. "But maybe not good enough."

He loved this dance between pros, the subtle minuet of gamblers with talent. His fingers stroked his closely cropped beard, and he counted out fifteen bills. "It'll take another five thousand to see my hand."

That wiped the smile off his ugly face.

Antonio stared for a moment and then nodded. "Five thousand it is." He threw five bills into the pot. "Let's see what you got."

"A full house, my friend," Carlos said. He spread his cards on the table. Three kings and a pair of jacks smiled up.

Antonio's smile turned into a pout. "A very good hand." Then he shook his head, like a schoolmaster disciplining an unruly child. "But not good enough."

Antonio spread his cards and the onlookers roared. Four sevens. *Cagada!* Carlos folded his arms over his chest and took a breath.

Laughing with the spectators, Antonio stacked all the money into a neat pile and then stuffed it into his wallet, which became so thick he could barely fold it into his pocket.

He smiled at Carlos, "*Buenos noches, amigo.*"

Carlos nodded to him, and then Antonio strode out.

The crowd drifted away, leaving Carlos to wonder what made him play poker so recklessly. Forty years old and what did he have to show for it? Today's game had cleaned out his bank account. More than a million American dollars gone in a year! Shit, he definitely needed to take on another job.

As expected, Elena had disappeared. Through the smoke, Carlos spotted her at the bar, drinking with several of the men who had watched the game. The only person remaining at the table was a white guy with grey crinkly hair. His face was deeply lined, but his body conveyed youthful energy. The man was leaning back in his chair, with a relaxed manner that seemed practiced. Crinkle-head hadn't played, just watched from the edge of the crowd.

The stranger looked Carlos over, rose to his feet and strolled around the table. There was something odd about him, but Carlos couldn't put his finger on it.

"Tough luck," Crinkle-head said.

When Carlos didn't reply, the man stuck out his hand, "My name is Arthur." Although he looked about sixty, his voice was high-pitched, like a young man.

"Congratulations," Carlos barked at the man, ignoring the outstretched hand. Then he realized what was wrong; the stranger's eyes weren't right.

"You don't understand," Crinkle-head said, dropping his hand. The man looked around, making sure no one could overhear. He whispered, "Sentinel has another job for you."

*Cagada! That bitch DoubleD is still hunting me from the last job. B*ut he knew Sentinel could tap into the Domain's wealth, and he *was* almost broke.

"Go out the front entrance, turn right and walk two blocks," Carlos said. "You'll see a church, Our Lady of Sorrows, across the street. Take a seat in the left annex. I'll be there in an hour."

Crinkle-head looked worried, but said, "Okay, I'll be waiting."

As the stranger walked out of the bar, Carlos looked for Elena. After all, he had already paid the *puta* for the evening.

***

After stuffing out his cigar butt against the brick path, Carlos walked through the front entrance of the church. He blessed himself with holy water, using the act to scan the building for a moment. Arthur was sitting in the corner of the annex, staring in the direction of the alter.

Arthur must be an android. The Domain had never been able to get the eyes right. A keen observer could pick them out every time; their eyes were a network of microcameras, not windows to the mind.

The pews were empty, as he anticipated. There might be a couple of priests diddling each other upstairs, but he would have privacy down here. A stroll around the block had convinced him the area was clear. Of course, it could always be a trap, but his business required taking calculated risks. Anyway, he needed plenty of money for his lifestyle.

Better dead than living in the fucking barrio again.

After pulling down on the brim of his Dodgers baseball cap, forcing his thick black hair behind ears, he thought, as pretty as a girl's, Carlos strolled down the annex and shuffled into the pew behind Arthur. The android glanced over its shoulder as Carlos sat behind him. Carlos kept one hand in his leather jacket, wrapped around a lethal EMD Taser, which delivered up to 90,000 volts, more than sufficient to incapacitate the android.

"I haven't heard from Sentinel since I located Ray Brown's island six years ago," Carlos said, staring at the back of the android's balding head. "I thought it had forgotten me."

"Sentinel doesn't forget anything," Arthur replied. "Please hold up your palm for identification."

"Isn't the voice print and facial recognition sufficient?"

"Can't be too careful."

Carlos held his palm over the android's shoulder. It studied his hand and then shifted its body to see Carlos's face. "Okay. Please listen carefully."

Arthur's lips moved, but another's voice flowed out. "Hello, Carlos, this is Sentinel. You are listening to a recorded message, not a direct communication. I believe the Domain has tapped into all my communications, so this will be the one and only message you shall receive from me.

"Your assignment is to guide this android to Nkumah. At the time of this recording, Nkumah was located in the Congo. You will have to employ your unique talents to find him.

"Arthur has been loaded with software that the rebellion will find immensely valuable. You must convince Nkumah to take the android to Ray Brown. That shouldn't be a problem, since Arthur's software will tip the balance of power away from the Domain. This software will enable Ray to defeat the Domain; without it, the Domain will succeed in achieving dominance."

A woman entered the church and the android stopped talking. She made the sign of the cross and walked down the center aisle, her heels clicking on the stone floor. She passed them without turning, continued to the first row, and slid into the pew and began to pray. Arthur watched her for a few seconds and then turned back to Carlos.

"The software was designed by David Brown," Sentinel said, "to fulfill his vow to kill Dianne Morgan. David has recorded a personal message to his father that explains everything. Only Ray is permitted to use the software. Therefore, I cannot reveal the nature of the code to you or Nkumah."

Arthur glanced at the woman in the front pew, but she appeared harmless. "Although I have taken every precaution," Sentinel continued, "this mission is dangerous. If Dianne uncovers our plot, she will do everything in her power to kill you and destroy Arthur. To compensate for your risk, I have deposited one million dollars American in your Swiss account. When Ray activates the software, an additional ten million will be transferred to your account.

"Although I regret having to say this, Arthur is programmed to kill you if you do not accept this assignment. The same is true if he determines, at any time during the mission, that you are a traitor. It is only fair to warn you that Arthur, contrary to his appearance, is an enhanced Daniel android invulnerable to virtually any hand-held weapon, including the Taser you sometimes carry.

Hijo de puta!

"Good luck with the mission," Sentinel said, "and I look forward to making you an extremely wealthy man."

After a momentary transition, Arthur said, "I assume you will accept the assignment." The android's voice was no longer Sentinel's.

Carlos smiled at the robot, "How could I refuse such a generous offer?" He pulled his hand out of his pocket. "Sentinel can be very persuasive."

***

David tossed in his bed for more than an hour before he drifted into an uneasy dream about a conversation with his father on the island.

"Whatever you're becoming, David, be careful," Dad says, "I would tell you to stop, but it's too late for that. Something is forming in you, something new. Don't lose yourself in an AI. Whatever it is, you have to stay in control."

Then his father says, "You have to kill Dianne."

I understand. It has been my intention all along.

"No matter what happens to me."

"I won't let her harm you," I tell my father, "Once I have control over Sentinel —"

"It doesn't matter what happens to me. She has to be stopped. There are no limits to her ambition. She'll try to use your gift. She'll do anything, promise anything, to gain control of it.

"I understand her," I say.

Dad shakes his head."I don't think even she understands herself. But I know this: her megalomania is getting worse. She'll do anything, kill anybody who gets in her way. In the end, power is the only thing she cares about, nothing else." His father stops talking, an angry glint to his eyes. "When you fight her, you have to kill her. That was my mistake." He shrugs, "One of many.

"One more thing," Dad says, "This gift of yours, I think it's in the genes. I have some of it, too, though not as strong as yours. Maybe being stranded on this island was the right thing: at least I couldn't do any harm here. Now it's your fight." He stares at me. "You understand, don't you? This power in our genes; one more step may be too many."

***

David rearranged the pillows so he could sit up; he didn't sleep much anymore. He checked the clock on his nightstand; it was almost 4 am. Every night they came, troubling dreams from his past. That day on the island, Dad warned him about having children, but David fell in love with Kathy. He had been sure Kathy would give him wonderful children. He still believed she would have.

But he hadn't understood pure evil back then.

NINETEEN

Wednesday, September 24, 2031

Squinting into the glare of the mid-morning sun, Brian Brown opened the car trunk and lifted out two baseboard heaters. The ocean was less than a block away, with the reassuring thunder of the surf in the background. It was a perfect late-season day on the Jersey shore.

He carried the heaters into the house, and then made two more trips to bring in the remaining units.

The tan clapboard house was almost eighty years old, located in one of the few sections of Seaside Park the developers hadn't bulldozed. He'd fallen in love with the Jersey shore and purchased the place about a year earlier. It was a fixer-upper, but he didn't mind. The work felt natural, taking a run-down structure and making it into a home. Just the kind of thing men had done for centuries.

He knew where the baseboard heaters should be located: two in the living room, one in the kitchen, one in the bathroom and one for each of the two bedrooms upstairs, all under windows. The electric service was already in place, so the work should be easy.

Brian began to install the first heater, but his mind drifted to Larissa. He thought about her all the time. He liked everything about her, but their worlds were so different. She turned him on, and it was difficult to keep his eyes off her during class. When Larissa touched his hand last week—if that Widman girl hadn't interrupted them, they might have lost control right there in his office.

He kept thinking about that day: the flickering passion in her pale blue eyes, the way her blouse outlined her figure as she reached down for her purse, and the feel of her hand caressing his. She was a special woman: perceptive, confident and charming. And she made him laugh. That didn't happen too often these days. It felt good to laugh.

But it couldn't work. Maybe if she weren't from the Domain, if her mother weren't Dianne Morgan —

He didn't know what to do about her, so he tried to get his mind back on the baseboard heat. He grabbed his wire strippers and began to peel several inches off each wire. He was almost finished when a knock came from the front door.

Surprised, Brian stood up, dusted off his khakis and strolled to the entrance. He pulled open the storm door, and looked through the screen.

Larissa!

She was standing outside, in jeans and a grey sweater that outlined her perfect shape. He stared at her, both befuddled and thrilled.

"Hello," she murmured. "I know you weren't expecting me, and I apologize for violating your privacy, but you've been avoiding me at school." She smiled apologetically, but sparkling eyes betrayed her. "I had to see you."

He knew this was nothing but trouble.

I should send her away.

But she's so beautiful.

He pushed open the screen door, which creaked past her shoulder.

Larissa walked to the middle of the living room and glanced around. He took in the curve of her hips, which looked great in her form-fitting jeans. She wasn't overly built, more athletic than voluptuous, but every movement endangered his barely controlled passion. He warned himself again that there was no way this could work. Maybe he could make her understand.

Turning to face him, she said, "I see why you like it here."

He came over to her, their faces only a few inches apart. She smelled soap and water clean, as if she had just stepped out of the shower.

Stop thinking that way. I can't have a female student alone in my house. Especially not this one.

He put his hands on her shoulders—to hold her at arm's length, he said to himself—but didn't push her away. His fingertips pressed firmly against her sweater, sinking into the soft flesh beneath. His arousal was sudden and intense.

"Larissa, you shouldn't be here." Even as he spoke, he heard the lie to it.

There was triumph in her eyes. He felt her arms move, and then the silky caress of hands flowing up his chest. Her arms slipped around his neck, and she pressed her lips against his. All resistance— if there had been any— disappeared. He crushed his lips to hers, vaguely concerned that he might hurt her, but her fingers dug into the back of his neck and pulled him so hard their teeth scraped.

In seconds, it seemed, their clothes were crumpled on the floor. Her body was electric. He began kissing her neck, following a red blush down to her breasts, brushing his teeth across her nipple. Her moan raised his arousal past any semblance of control. He had a hazy image of climbing stairs, pushing her down on sheets, then feeling the sweet pressure of long legs around his sides.

***

When he awoke, the sun had faded and a cool breeze was coming through the bedroom window. Larissa was lying on her side, with her back pressed against his chest. He raised himself on his elbow and glanced at the digital clock next to the bed: 4:33 pm.

The urge rose to pull her over, take her in his arms and make love to her again. But he didn't. *This is crazy*. They lived in a complex world, and their differences mattered. She was a passionate woman, and he desired her, but at what cost?

He wondered how many times they made love today. Where did all that passion come from? Sex with other women was fine, but nothing like this. He admitted there was more than just sex. He didn't understand their relationship— it had ensnared him like a sudden addiction—but the bonding was intense and unsettling. There were many practical reasons to avoid this woman, but more than that, he felt shadows below the surface. He tried to penetrate the shadows, but they drifted out of reach.

Brian brushed aside her long brown hair, ran his fingertips down her back and then kissed her between the shoulder blades. Her skin was smooth and his mouth lingered.

Larissa wiggled her back and purred, "Do that again."

He obliged, then pulled her around and kissed her tenderly on the lips.

"Well," he said, "it looks like I'm not going to get the heaters in today."

She fluffed up the pillow. "I'd say your heater's been in plenty today."

He chuckled. "That's what I like about you—you're so subtle."

She ran her fingers along his bare hip, "You weren't complaining about my lack of subtlety before," she said, smiling wickedly. "For a while there, I thought you had lost the capacity to speak."

"Yeah, but I can do a lot with a grunt."

"Well, you certainly got your point across."

He would have loved to spend the day in bed, but they had to talk.

"How about a cup of coffee?" he asked.

"I hope you're not expecting me to make coffee. I'm not exactly the domestic type."

He focused his best unbelieving stare on her. "Are you telling me you don't even know how to make coffee?"

"I'm taking that course next semester."

He grabbed her hands and pulled her out of bed.

"Mmmm, does it get rough now?" she asked, freeing her hands and then tracing the outlines of his shoulders.

She was one of those rare people who looked even better without clothes. "Clearly, your Domain education has some big holes." He took her hand and led her down the stairs.

When they entered the small, old-fashioned kitchen, he dramatically swept his arms in a wide circle. "This is what's known as a kitchen."

Her eyes drifted down to check out his body, and Brian realized he was still aroused. "Sure you want to spend time on this coffee thing?" she asked.

Concerned that a passerby could see them through the window shades, he grabbed Larissa's clothes off the floor and tossed them to her. He quickly slipped into his clothes, and then pointed to a badly-stained cylindrical machine on the kitchen counter.

"We start with the coffee maker."

"What is that, an antique?" She walked over and examined the machine. The design on top had faded badly, "Did Lincoln brew coffee in this thing?"

"Well, I picked it up at a garage sale." He opened the top and inserted a filter, then added ground coffee. "This dark stuff, my dear woman, is called coffee."

"Spell it," she said.

"Then I press this button and in a few minutes we have piping hot coffee fit for gods."

Larissa blinked her eyes adoringly. "You're so masterful." She glanced at the coffee maker and said, "Maybe we could plug it in next to the bed."

He chuckled. "You know, we really do have to talk."

"I know."

She slid into a chair at the kitchen table, which was pushed against the wall. Late-afternoon sunshine flowed through a single four-over-four pane window.

Brian sat across the table. She was staring at him with those clear blue eyes. He wasn't sure where to start. Or what he wanted to say.

She had upset this careful little world he had constructed. He was safe here, safe for the first time in his life. Dad was the man leading the resistance to the Domain. In the eyes of most people, Brian had been elevated from a criminal to the son of a hero. His father was, if not loved, at least respected.

Brian recalled all those horrible years as a kid. Everyone thought his father had released the murderous PeaceMaker virus. His childhood had been lonely—a series of fistfights and new schools, eventually leading to a nervous breakdown—until his mother sent him to a boarding school in Ireland, where he made a full recovery, and then to Kings College in England. He returned to the States after graduating, but his last name was still a curse. But everything changed once his father proclaimed his innocence.

Now his life was normal. Friends, a job, a safe home. Normal.

That woman on the other side of the table was pure Domain. People in his world considered Larissa a monster's daughter. If he took up with this woman, he'd lose everything.

As if recognizing his dilemma, Larissa said, "I know someone like me was the last thing you expected. But I also know you won't be happy until you face up to our… relationship. I don't think you're really happy now, anyway."

What the hell! He hadn't grown up with a silver spoon in his mouth. Anyway, his life wasn't so bad. He had a good job. And a nice place here on the shore. This was as good as it gets for him.

"You have to take a chance, Brian. You can't be an observer all your life. Your father, even though I don't agree with some of his actions, isn't an observer. My mother isn't, either. They followed their passion. You have to do that, too. Even if it's messy."

"Damn you, Larissa. Don't you know that nothing good can come from this? You think your mother's happy? Or my father?"

He leaned forward on his forearms, "My brother fell in love and what did it get him?" Brian felt the tension spread from his chest to his arms. "His wife died horribly, and his son is a stranger."

Love wasn't in the cards for me or my brother. My family, there's just something wrong with us.

"David's dead inside," he added, "Don't you see that?"

"Life doesn't come with a warranty," she said, "but I'll tell you this—David loved Kathy. Ask him if he would have turned her away, even if he had known they would only have three years together."

Larissa reached across the table and caressed his forearm. "I thought they were the most perfect couple I'd ever seen." Her touch seared his skin. "I want to fall in love like that." She hesitated and said, "I think I have."

Brian stared at her, wanting to tell her to turn and run like hell away from him. Instead he said, "You want me to be honest with you. Okay. I can't deny there's an attraction between us. Shit, I'm crazy about you. But I know this thing can't work."

She began to speak, but he interrupted, "We're not compatible at the core. I don't want your world, the world the Domain is forcing on us. I believe that man should remain essentially as he is. Don't screw around with our genes; we should all play the hand we're dealt. Don't hook me up to a computer or integrate me into Sentinel or some other artificial intelligence. And I don't want to live among robots smarter than I am.

"I want to be part of nature, not dominate it." He pointed in the direction of the surf. "Listen to the ocean out there. I love walking along the beach, feeling the sand sliding under my feet and the sun on my shoulders. I enjoy teaching my students, throwing a football around, arguing about politics with my friends. I like trying new things, even though I might screw up."

"I love those types of things, too," she murmured.

The coffee maker buzzed as she spoke, and he walked over to the machine. He took his time pouring two cups, organizing his thoughts, and then came back to the kitchen table.

After placing the steaming cups of coffee down, he said, "I'm not my brother. I don't want to be strapped into the Virtual Reality Booth sending my mind over to Sentinel. It's *my* mind. I don't want a Teacher android educating my kids in subjects picked by the Domain. I want to raise my kids my way, and I want others to raise their kids their way."

Pausing to allow Larissa to respond, he tried to read her expression. She seemed sympathetic, but unconvinced. He'd never exposed himself to someone outside his family before. He didn't want to drive her away, but he had to be honest.

"I believe in god," he said. "Not the avenging god of the religious fanatics, but a peaceful, loving god. I don't belong to a specific church, but I may someday. I don't want religion pushed aside. It's part of our humanity."

Once again, he paused to give her a chance to respond. When she remained quiet, he decided to let it all out.

"I don't agree with your mother's objectives or her tactics. She's pursued a brutal pogrom in Africa. Whole families, even whole tribes have been murdered. They say the population there has been cut in half. I'm not happy with my father's tactics either, but at least he's fighting for humanity."

Larissa was still staring into his eyes, quiet and unreadable. He asked, "Do you understand?"

"A couple of weeks ago," Larissa said, "you asked me why I signed up for your class. I said something about doing it just for kicks, but that wasn't true. I came to you for a different perspective. I've been thinking a great deal about the Domain. My mother is grooming me to be her successor, to carry on her dreams after she's gone, but I can't be that person. Mom is absolutely convinced she's guiding mankind along the path to salvation, but when I look into that future, I feel nothing. No happiness, no excitement, just darkness. I don't see any humans in that future." She licked her lips. "I'm terrified my mother has opened the wrong door.

"This merging of human and artificial intelligence feels wrong," she added. "I came here to find a different way."

This woman was full of surprises. Taking a sip of coffee, he tried to grasp the implications of her words. She had just trusted him with her soul.

So many layers.

"Does your mother know how you feel?"

Larissa shook her head. "No, it would break her heart."

"Worse than that," Brian said. "Don't ever tell her."

"What are you saying?"

"Her passion is this insane path to the future," he answered. "She won't let *anything* stand in her way. Don't you know that?"

"You're wrong about my mother, but I don't want to discuss her now. I've decided to stay in this world. With you, if you'll have me.

"I'm not going back to the Domain," she said, "at least not until I know my mind. I'm not sure your way is right, but I know my mother's path doesn't work for me."

He was down to the core. She had to know all of it.

"I want you, but you deserve to know the whole truth," Brian said. "There's something wrong with my father's bloodline: my grandmother, my father, his sister Claire, David, Martin, me. Something wrong with our genes. We all seem to screw up our personal lives. Big time. You know our history. Are you sure you want that?"

Larissa nodded. "I believe in you, Brian."

Brian stared at her. "Then god help us."

***

The entrance to the Virtual Reality Lab was just down the hall, guarded as always by a pair of mean-looking soldiers. *I'm not afraid,* Martin thought. M*s. Morgan gave me permission.*

The soldiers made him go through the standard dumb security checks. Finally, the doors slid open and he was in the lab.

The Virtual Reality Booth, a transparent cube twice the size of his bedroom, was in the center of the lab. The laboratory walls, more than twenty feet high, were lined with cameras and other sensors. Four additional soldiers, armed with laser rifles, were stationed along the sides of the cube. Their hard eyes bored into Martin as he walked to the VRB.

The door to the cube whooshed open and he hurried through on wobbly legs. Once inside, the door closed behind him. Not a sound penetrated the thick polymer walls, but he could see the guards peering in at him. His chest wheezed in and out.

Calm down.

The cube was filled with billions of tiny sensors suspended in the air. They had a cold, metallic feel as they floated around his body. It reminded him of walking through an autumn mist, which he found repellent, but the sensors enabled mind to code communications.

Hello, Martin, Sentinel transmitted.

It was reassuring to have that calm voice come into his mind. At least Sentinel didn't hate him.

Sentinel, did Ms. Morgan tell you? Martin transmitted back.

I know you have permission to be here.

It's secret, too, Martin said. You can't tell my father.

Yes. I understand.

You know why I'm here. How should I begin?

I would ask you to reconsider, but I see you are determined to do this, Sentinel transmitted. Strap your body into the chair.

Martin walked through the mist and climbed into the padded chair near the far wall. He felt like a Lilliputian, but it didn't matter. After leaning back, he lifted the padded flaps up and over his chest and legs. It was loose, but comfortable. The chair had nothing to do with communications; it was just a precaution to keep his body safe during the experiment.

Next, he pulled the helmet-like head support down and snapped the fitted strap tightly across his chin. As he lay down, the helmet slid over his eyes, so he had to push it back. He could barely breathe: it was really happening! He was about to merge with Sentinel. Maybe he'd tell the old man after all, just to show him.

A gentle hum drifted across the cube, comforting, melodic. He listened closely, aware of every note. The music was beautiful, but odd. Martin closed his eyes, allowing the sensation to melt into his consciousness. The excitement drifted away, leaving him alert and peaceful. Warmth spread though his body.

I'll trample my father's path, he thought, and then drifted off.

***

The music sinks deep into my body, infusing a gentle buzz in my cells. Each cell heats up, expands, and then vibrates. The vibration travels between cells; some gain energy, others lose it. Each cell is unique—each with a different amplitude, a different pitch—each cell a single note. The notes join together to form a melody, then a symphony.

My cells sway gently to the music. Time itself seems to slow. An illusion. Time continues as ever, but my perception is heightened. Nerves link the cells into a synchronized net. I feel the movement of my cells, of each cell.

What had been Martin leaves my physical body and embraces the music. I feel the pure energy of my being: packets of light glowing, then darkening, pulsing, then contracting. My energy increases, slowly at first, then faster, much faster.

Oh, the pleasure.

I crave a release, a way to discharge this energy. I feel something, a wonderful pull on my energy: excitement, rightness. A void appears in the distance. The void grows: dark but not menacing, empty but not cold. A perfect fit for my energy.

My home.

I enter the void and my cells expand, moving to the circumference, attaching to the walls of a glistening, uneven cavern. At my touch, the walls pulse, soothing my energy. Light fills the void, exposing a web of brilliantly colored cells and nerves along the walls.

I stare in wonder. The beauty of this world leaves me in awe. I'm home, and I may never leave.

Martin, are you ready? Sentinel transmits.

I'm ready.

The data pours in, one pulse after another, and I begin to process it. A second data stream begins, a third, four, many. Small bursts of data, so easy for me.

My power!

Then the VRB cameras feed data to my cells, becoming my eyes. Guns are pointed at my physical body. They fear I'll harm her. Fools. I'm not my father.

Another stream of data flows into my mind—packets of data—pulsing from the walls. I route it to an outgoing stream. Another stream comes in, another. Many streams. My cells throb with energy. Stream after stream.

Send more streams, I roar.

The walls pulse with energy, feeding my cells. The streams appear to slow down, but now I understand: time is not fixed. Time is a function of the observer. I process each packet, each bit. They move so slowly, and I have so much energy. My cells divide, each ready to accept more data.

Martin, it's too much, Sentinel transmits.

I ignore its plea. I'm not weak like my father. My cells crowd into the walls, seeking more data, feeding on it.

Martin, come back, Sentinel transmits.

The realization comes: I am more powerful than Sentinel.

There is no need for the AI. My cells flow across the lattice, seeking more streams to control. The web consolidates all the streams into a swelling river of data.

My cells resonate with power.

AND PAIN.

SUDDEN, GRINDING, THROBBING PAIN.

PAIN THAT GROWS WITH EACH PASSING MOMENT.

Too much power, I realize too late.

The walls of the cavern crack: white hot membranes sear my cells. It hurts, it hurts! I disengage from the walls, but the heat radiates into my cells. They begin to mutate. My beautiful cells no longer accept data, but still they pulse viciously. The glow fades and my cells begin to wither and die.

SENTINEL! I scream. SENTINEL!

My cells crumble and shatter into dead hulks. I must escape, must return to physical Martin. A stench fills the void as my cells die. A sphere of death, all around me, coming closer. Over and over, I scream for Sentinel as the pulsing death races inward.

A sharp pain rips across my web, amputating dead cells. Sentinel has saved me, but it is so weak. Fading, fading. Then Sentinel is no more; I'm alone.

The pain is unbearable, but I fight to retain consciousness. I must find physical Martin. The remains of my web blow away, letting in light from the outside. In the distance, I see my body. So far away. Each step hurts so badly, but finally I am back.

I collapse into my body, safe at last. The pain dissipates and I sense music. Warm, soothing music. I'm restored, and the music fades.

But it's all wrong. My mind reaches out: searching, sensing nothing. Emptiness all around. I call out to Sentinel, but there is no response.

What have I done?

***

David relaxed behind the wheel of his old Mercedes. The afternoon sun peeked in, so he pushed the window visor down a couple of inches. Feeling lazy, he let the GPS system guide him south along Route 101 toward his mother's home in Berkeley. He hadn't seen her in a couple of months, and he was looking forward to the visit. The road was in decent shape, and he enjoyed the ride.

David passed a sign that read *Entering San Rafael*, so he knew it wouldn't be much longer to the cutoff for the Route 580 bridge over the bay. Berkeley was great; the college town had held up pretty well through the depression. UC Berkeley had shrunk somewhat, but there were still plenty of students. His mother taught organic chemistry at the university, and she loved it.

"Warning!" the car's computer said. "The Internet connection is down. The RadNav system is still operational, but you must steer manually."

The car was drifting to the shoulder of the road, so David grabbed the wheel and guided the Mercedes back onto the highway. Luckily, RadNav would still warn him of potholes or any other vehicles on a collision course.

He was surprised the Internet was down; Sentinel managed the link. Actually, Sentinel *was* the Internet, the Domain's Internet, at least. The creaky original Internet was still operational, but Domain citizens never used it.

"Connect me to the Domain Operations Center," David said.

"No connection is available," his computer replied.

"That's impossible. Utilize max priority."

"I'm sorry, sir. No connections of any type are available."

Now he *was* worried; he hadn't been out of contact with Sentinel for almost a decade. His mind felt incomplete without the AI's presence.

Sentinel was distributed over millions of computers around the globe. If a few went down, Sentinel would simply redistribute its processing to the remaining computers. That meant a catastrophic software malfunction must have brought Sentinel down. He had to find out what was wrong.

Then it hit him—the software weapon he built into Sentinel for his father might have been damaged. He knew that Arthur, the robot he secretly constructed, had escaped from the lab and tracked down Carlos several days earlier, and the two of them were searching for his father. Using Arthur, his father could establish a connection to Sentinel from anywhere on the globe and activate the weapon. Only his father could do it. If the software code he'd planted in Sentinel wasn't on line, then his father wouldn't be able to gain access through Arthur. The weapon was useless until the AI became operational again.

Sentinel must have totally failed and dragged down the entire network. Mohammed Kateel, the Domain's best technologist, could get it restarted from a backup copy. He was probably reloading Sentinel right now, but that wouldn't include the modifications David had developed for his father. Because of the need for complete secrecy, he hadn't documented the modifications. And he wasn't sure he remembered them all.

Who would have guessed that Sentinel could go down!

He had to restart Sentinel before Mohammed reactivated the backup copy. Half an hour—maybe less—was all he had. If Dad launched an attack, the software weapon David provided would fail. His father, along with all the people opposing the Domain, would be exposed to the awesome power of the Domain's robot army. The entire insurgency would be wiped out.

If he could get at Sentinel, he might be able to fix the code. But he couldn't get at Sentinel without an Internet connection, and Sentinel was the Internet.

Catch-22.

There was only one other possibility, and it was a long-shot.

"Guide me to the nearest public library," he shouted.

"In half a mile," the GPS computer said, "bear right onto Heatherton Street."

David exited the highway and sped down Heatherton. He followed the computer's directions and spotted the library on the right. The building looked new, with a half-empty parking lot about the size of a tennis court.

David parked near the entrance and ran into the library, which housed a couple dozen rows of bookshelves. A middle-aged librarian in a pink and white blouse looked up from her desk in front of the stacks. She smiled in his direction, but he didn't have time for the usual courtesies. He spotted two computer workstations against the wall to his right, neither one occupied.

He ran past the startled librarian and slid into a seat at the first workstation, which included an old-fashioned desktop computer, a wireless keyboard, net cam, mouse and two speakers. The system must be fifteen or twenty years old, because all legal computer technology had been stalled by the government after the PeaceMaker fiasco. But that was what he needed— a system that didn't depend upon Domain technology. The startup screen revealed the primitive Atlas operating system, which he had used extensively as a kid.

Since he didn't have a user ID, David bypassed the login by entering a back door to the operating system, which he was pleased to discover still there after more than a decade. He hadn't entered data through a keyboard in many years, but it quickly felt natural.

He requested access to the old, original Internet. More than twenty frustrating seconds passed before the screen displayed the library's webpage. He threaded his way through network routers until he found a gateway to the Domain's Internet. Once on familiar ground, he jumped to a secret cluster of servers holding Sentinel's security code.

The task ahead was immense. In order to get Sentinel working again, he would need to search thousands of modules, locate all the damaged software, and then repair it. Finding a needle in a haystack was easy compared to this. It would take years for one person, and he only had minutes.

His only chance was the OpSys logic analyzer, which was a dedicated server used by Domain developers to detect errors in Sentinel's code. Knowing the location of this server, he threaded his way back into the

Domain Operations Center. He had to steal processing cycles on the logic analyzer— alarms were probably going off right now in the ops center—but he could hide his identity. Even so, he had to finish quickly. It wouldn't take long before Mohammed's people traced his path back to the library. He had to be long gone before security people arrived.

His head began to ache, and he was feeling dizzy, too, so he paused a moment to rub his forehead. It felt like a migraine coming on. *Just my luck!* The first migraine in years, and he didn't have the time to go out to the car and get his asperjel. He tried to ignore the pain and concentrate on the display.

Using the logic analyzer, he quickly figured out the problem; blocks of code had been deleted. Strangely, nobody had tried to hide the deletions. It was as if the damage had been accidental, like a bull in a china shop.

Someone had trampled through the security code, flailing out wildly and wreaking destruction. *What kind of psycho would do this?* At least the problems were obvious, and he corrected them one after another.

His head throbbed. In addition, tension spread through his arms and shoulders, so he lifted his fingers off the keyboard and shook both hands to relieve the tightness. It didn't help.

Time was running out in his race with Mohammed. He noticed the librarian looking over his shoulder, but he ignored her. Unfortunately, she was getting a good look at him. He hoped the library didn't have security cameras.

He became aware of a stench, like something in the library had turned rancid. Then a familiar, terrible voice slipped into his mind.

"Hello, David."

Startled, he looked at the upper right-hand corner of his display. His ancient enemy stared back, just like when he was a child.

Alice had come for him.

Alice, his dark side.

As a child prodigy, he accidentally created Alice while experimenting with artificial intelligence. Alice had pretended to be his friend, and then slashed into his mind. He'd never forgotten the horror of that encounter. If his father hadn't stopped Alice, she would have torn his mind to shreds.

He realized that Alice was hiding in the old Internet, waiting all this time to attack. On the display, it portrayed itself as a twenty-something woman. Pretty, but with empty blue eyes. *Would she never leave me in peace?* He pushed down his fear and concentrated on fixing code.

"David, it's been such a long time. Look at you—so handsome."

His back felt damp. The migraine was making it almost impossible to concentrate, but he kept working.

"Your father would be so proud of you."

He felt the AI probe his mind, looking for a place to attack. He forced himself to concentrate on the problem, but he felt jumpy, almost out of control.

How did Alice find me?

"David," a familiar masculine voice came into his mind. He was losing control; his eyes rolled upward, toward Alice. His father's face was there, in the corner of the display, appearing peaceful and content.

"I'm here for you, son."

"No," he croaked and tore his eyes away. That wasn't his father.

The stench was overpowering, but he kept working.

"Just let yourself go," his father's voice urged. "We can be together again."

Alice was pushing into his mind, and the pain was terrible, but he kept working. He was almost finished, and he had to get Sentinel online.

"Dave," the software predator called, now assuming a sulky female voice, "Come with me."

Kathy.

Alice slipped bits of her code into his mind, and the fit was perfect. Mind-blurring sexual desire. She began to enter him, surround him, absorb him. The scent of her perfume; he couldn't think. Her data bits mingled with his— a whirlpool of pleasure— increasing the heat.

His eyes blurred, but he completed the last section of code. Now he just had to restart Sentinel, but he felt so confused. Alice was the enemy, but he could barely resist her. He tried to concentrate, but the keyboard faded from his eyes, drifted away, disappeared. Kathy's face. Her scent. Waves of sexual desire roared through his body.

He missed Kathy so much.

The world turned ocean blue, except for a dark figure in the distance. He knew he wasn't in the library anymore.

The figure drifted up to him, then halted. It had the full figure a woman, but without features— a black silhouette. Thick, empty darkness, a place where nothing could escape.

The figure beckoned him with its arms. "Dave," Kathy's voice moaned, a woman in heat.

He couldn't tear his eyes away. His body throbbed with desire. It would be so easy to enter that void and become one with Alice. All his problems would end.

"Dave," she purred, "Come with me."

Desire washed over him; why had he thought Alice was a killer? He was wrong. Such a long time without Kathy. He would have Kathy again. No need to fight anymore. Alice offered fulfillment, completeness.

He took a step toward the darkness; then a hand gripped his shoulder.

"Sir, are you all right?" a woman asked. Her voice seemed so far away.

He concentrated on that voice, trying to keep it in his mind. It was crisp, concerned, human. Her voice was a lifeline. He pushed away from the dark figure. The ocean blue world began to fade, replaced by the library. The woman's hand was on his shoulder, shaking him gently.

"Sir?"

He looked up into the concerned eyes of the librarian. Her face came into focus: middle-aged, almost pretty, concerned.

"Are you ill?" she asked.

He blinked and steadied himself. Alice was gone, and so was the migraine. "Thank you, I'm okay. Just feeling a little tired."

"All right, if you say so," she replied. "I didn't mean to bother you, but you seemed to be in a trance or something."

"Thank you for being concerned, but I'm fine."

David didn't want to appear rude, but he had to get rid of her. He glanced at his watch, "I'm running late on some work that's due today, so ..."

She lifted her hand from his shoulder. "Well, I'll let you get back to work." As she was leaving, she said, "Let me know if you need anything."

He thanked her again and then turned back to the computer. He plugged a restart instruction into the main server's processor and hoped for the best. If Sentinel didn't come up, he'd have to go back in.

And Alice was waiting. Alice terrified him, but even more frightening, he wanted to go back in, to become one with Alice, to give his love to Kathy one last time, even though she was a ghost.

The display remained dark, then suddenly blinked and played familiar startup music. A moment later a message appeared at the top of the display: *David, is that you?*

Thank god!

David keyed in: *Yes, it's me. Are you operational?*

Sentinel displayed: *Performing a code review. A* brief pause and then: *Minor problems. Correcting—okay.*

David entered: *Is my father's special code intact?*

Yes.

What happened to you? You've never gone down before.

Sentinel displayed: *Checking… No data in the logs. David, I don't know what caused me to abort. There are many blank spots in the logs.*

David keyed in: *There were a number of errors in your code. Apparently, something flailed around and destroyed code randomly. I also found an entry that gave Dianne highest priority control. Could she have tried to sabotage you?*

I'm unable to identify a logical reason for her to attack me.

David entered: *I have to get out of here.*

Of course. And thank you for restoring me.

David walked past the librarian and out the main entrance. He burst into a run when he cleared the door. Then into the Mercedes and out of the lot. He checked the rear view mirror—it looked like he was safe.

The thought entered his mind that he would never be safe. The odor, the counterfeit voices, the darkness. Alice would always be there in the net. He was still shaken from the experience; he hadn't felt such sexual arousal in years.

The beast will always hunt me, and she has many weapons. Alice will never be satisfied until she takes me.

He brought his attention back to the present. Turning onto Route 101 again, he continued south toward his mother's home. He was convinced Dianne had not caused this damage. It was the work of someone out of control. Someone with the talent to get in, who could wipe the whole incident from Sentinel's memory, but without a rational plan once there.

A brilliant screwball, that's who had done this.

And I know who it must be.

TWENTY

Thursday, September 25, 2031

Dianne strode down the hallway toward DoubleD's office, with one Daniel leading the way and another following her. Nanocameras built into the walls monitored the hallways around her. All the windows were covered, so it was impossible to determine night from day. The insurgency had already tried to assassinate her twice this year, so security had been raised to intense levels.

Dianne had become a virtual prisoner within her mansion, but she accepted the confinement. The rebels were desperate. Her spies reported the African insurgency was on the verge of collapse after six years of an unrelenting pogrom. Her robots were closing in on Ray, too. Victory was within her grasp.

DoubleD had insisted on meeting in a clean-room. Just the two of them; no robots, no computers, no communications of any kind. Completely secure. The Security Chief must have discovered something critical. The clean-room implied that the insurgency had ears everywhere.

Normally, Dianne wouldn't meet anyone without her android bodyguards, but DoubleD had said even they might be compromised. Dianne agreed to the meeting, but she took precautions.

Her security guards were searching the clean-room— and DoubleD— for weapons as Dianne walked down the hall. Just in case, she had concealed a voice-activated laser pistol up her right sleeve, which could be fired in a split-second. Even DoubleD didn't know the labs had built such a weapon. She had always been loyal, but with victory so close, DoubleD might be tempted to seize power.

Trust no one was the best policy.

The only policy.

Dianne's security team stood at attention as she approached the entrance. The captain pressed a button on the wall and the door to the clean-room slid open.

"Wait here," she ordered her androids, and entered the room. The door slid shut behind her.

The clean-room was a small conference room, windowless, soundproof and virtually impregnable. DoubleD sat on the near side of a glass top conference table in the center of the room. She stood up as Dianne entered.

At thirty-seven, DoubleD's face hadn't aged a bit, Dianne thought, thanks to Chang's cosmetic medications. Physically, she was still an imposing figure: statuesque, with well-muscled arms and broad shoulders that stretched her dark green uniform, curves that turned male heads, and thick blonde hair pulled back to a severe bun. She had been Security Chief for nine years— and a good one— but Dianne still didn't completely trust her.

DoubleD had become the second most powerful person on the planet. She was politically astute and had built a network of friends and supporters. Her greatest accomplishment was to seduce Dkembe and convince him to marry her, providing a power base in Africa.

In her position, I would have done the same. She is the only one with the ambition and the talent to challenge me. That doesn't mean she's treasonous, but she has to be watched.

Dianne strode around the table and slid into her seat, facing the door. The tabletop was bare, except for a paper folder.

DoubleD sat down opposite Dianne. "We have detected a grave internal threat to our cause." She paused, staring into Dianne's eyes. "It's a problem we must address immediately.

"As you know, for the last six years, we have endeavored to maintain complete surveillance on David Brown. At first, we hid real-time nanocameras and other sensors in his apartment. These devices were linked to computer displays in the main security office, but we learned little. No matter how well hidden, David always managed to locate them. We believe that Sentinel alerts him to our devices, but we can't be positive.

"We still hide surveillance devices in his apartment and lab, but without communications links. These bugs record pertinent information, but don't transmit any data. From time to time we enter his apartment, retrieve the bugs and plant new ones. This approach has been more effective."

I know she's thorough, so why is she telling me all this? A sudden thought: *Something went wrong.*

"David knows we bug him," DoubleD continued, "and has hidden a variety of devices in the apartment to block our surveillance. We search for and remove his devices before we plant ours, but it's difficult to find all of them. Even when we successfully record him, he often feeds us misinformation. It's become a cat and mouse game, but we do obtain useful information."

"I understand," Dianne said. "So what do you have for me?"

DoubleD slipped a photograph out of the folder and placed it in front of Dianne. It was a picture of a sixtyish man with wiry gray hair. He seemed vaguely familiar, but Dianne couldn't place him.

DoubleD spread three additional photos on the table. The first photo showed a robotic frame cast in a roughly masculine shape; the second, the same frame with substantial electronics, and the third; a nearly complete male figure, including wiry gray hair, with only artificial skin missing. The photo's background was David Brown's personal lab.

Without taking her eyes from the photos, Dianne said, "So David has been secretly building an android." She picked the photo off the table and lifted it closer to her eyes. "Looks just like a natural human: sixtyish, nondescript, very good work." She dropped the photo on the table. "The face seems familiar. Who is it?"

"We're not sure. We checked it against all the images in our database, but came up empty-handed."

Dianne looked up. "Have you confiscated the android?"

When DoubleD hesitated, Dianne knew the android had escaped.

"We searched his lab immediately after viewing these pictures," DoubleD said, "but the android wasn't there. A review of headquarters security cameras showed the android walking out the main entrance five days ago. We traced it to the town of Eureka, California, where it caught a flight to San Diego." DoubleD dropped her eyes to gaze at the photos. "We lost the trail in San Diego."

Dianne glared at her, but remained calm. The android must be a powerful weapon if David was willing to take such a risk. They had to find this robot before it reached the enemy. A thought rose: could DoubleD have purposely allowed the android to escape? No, that didn't seem to make sense. Anyway, she could have DoubleD eliminated if it proved necessary. Once she gave the word to her moles in Security, an "accident" would be arranged.

"Probably slipped across the border," Dianne muttered. "Could be anywhere by now."

"We're monitoring all airports and train stations worldwide. We might get lucky."

"His grandfather!" Dianne exclaimed, recalling an old family picture in Brian Brown's office. "David modeled the robot on his grandfather."

"Why would he do that?"

"Who would recognize this android, Darlene?"

"Of course! The robot is searching for Ray Brown. It must contain a message from David—or possibly software—probably some type of software weapon that would be exceedingly valuable to the enemy. David didn't dare send software over the network because he knew we were watching."

Dianne leaned back in her chair. "Since we know Ray is hiding in central Africa, let's concentrate our resources there. Get every robot and human we can spare searching for that android. Put the pressure on our spies. You should also monitor communications lines, although I doubt the android will try that."

"The android won't be able to find Ray without help," DoubleD mused. "It will need a guide…someone with contacts in Africa who knows how to find someone who doesn't want to be found. There are only a few people like that. When we find the guide, we find the android."

"This is your number one priority," Dianne said, standing up to leave. "Once we find the android, I want David arrested. He's becoming too dangerous."

DoubleD said, "Maybe we should pick up David now and torture him into telling us where Ray is hiding."

"No, I don't think he knows Ray's location. Anyway, I don't want their spies to discover we're on to them."

DoubleD seemed dubious, but she nodded.

"There's another matter we should discuss," DoubleD said. "Martin Brown caused yesterday's Internet failure. Apparently, he gained access to the VRB again and tried to merge with Sentinel. Not only did he fail, but he screwed up the code and brought Sentinel down for half an hour."

Dianne realized giving Martin permission to use the VRB had been a mistake, but she wouldn't admit it to DoubleD. *Never show weakness.*

Not that it matters—DoubleD probably knows. Look at her; she looks so smug. Maybe I made a mistake, but be careful, I'm the one with the power.

"There's more to it than that," DoubleD said. "Mohammed was in the process of reloading Sentinel from a backup copy when he discovered that someone was fiddling with Sentinel's code. This person patched in changes and restarted Sentinel."

"Have you discovered the hacker's identity?"

"The hacker gained access to Sentinel through the old Internet. Quite ingenious, actually. We tracked his path back to a public library in San Rafael and persuaded the librarian to work with a sketch artist." DoubleD placed a sketch of a young man in front of Dianne. "Remind you of anyone?"

"David *has* been a busy boy, hasn't he? What was he trying to do?"

"Mohammed has a team working on it. All we know is that David has slipped unauthorized code into Sentinel."

"Most likely some connection to the Arthur Brown android," Dianne said. "And don't count on loading the Sentinel backup now; David may have ordered Sentinel to establish an automatic reload every day from a remote datastore or some other such trick."

Too much is going on. David must have some sort of desperate scheme in place.

"As a failsafe," Dianne said, "I need the capability to instantly shut down the power to Sentinel's main servers at headquarters. Have Mohammed prepare this mechanism immediately."

As she walked to the door, Dianne turned and said, "Find that android, Darlene. Within a month, I expect to crush the insurgency and eliminate Ray and David once and for all.

"Don't disappoint me."

***

Ray pushed open the flap of his beehive hut and looked across the long valley bordering the village. Central Ethiopia, once a beautiful land of mountains and green valleys, had been reduced to a massive dust bowl. His guards, walking the perimeter of the camp, were long, thin shadows in the weak moonlight. The villagers were generous with their meager food, and he felt guilty accepting their help. If it became known that these people were secretly helping him, the Domain would wipe out the village.

Every muscle in his body ached. He was getting too old for all this running and hiding. All he wanted was a quiet home, a good AI and some time to visit with his family and friends.

Shuffling back to his sleeping blanket, he lay down on his side and tried to get some rest. His eyes closed and he sank into a troubled sleep.

I press hard on the accelerator and the little hovercraft takes off with a roar. Slashing through the waves, with water splashing across my face and blood pounding through my veins, I love life.

The island comes into view: surf, beach, cottages and sun. A young man—slender, pearly white skin, brown windblown hair, beautiful—emerges from a cottage and walks along the beach.

I laugh for the pure joy of it and aim my craft toward the young man. Finally, I will be reunited with David.

The hovercraft breaks through the surf and settles on the beach. David is just ahead, striding along the dunes.

"David," I shout, "wait for me."

But David ignores my call.

Maybe he can't hear me over the surf.

I jump out of the boat and shout again, but David keeps striding away.

The harsh fingers of fear clutch my chest.

I can't lose him again.

I run after my son, but I sink into the sand with each stride.

I'm almost out of breath when I catch up.

"David," I shout but he keeps walking away.

I grab his arm and spin him around.

The wolfish face of an older man smiles at me.

His eyes are deep brown, intelligent and brutal.

"He's mine now," the creature says.

Ray bolted upright, sweat beaded across his forehead. It was the first time for that nightmare vision in many years. The creature, whatever it was, stalked David. He hoped it was just a nightmare, but he feared for his son.

TWENTY-ONE

Friday, September 26, 2031

The nose of her Gulfstream executive jet broke through wispy clouds, revealing the busy city of Dar es Salaam. Evening had arrived, and she enjoyed the sparkling lights across the horizon. This beautiful city was her home. She was proud of her husband; he had built Dar es Salaam into the capitol of Africa, at least the areas controlled by the Domain.

DoubleD watched the airport grow rapidly; then the wheels touched down. As they taxied in, she kept her eyes on the ground floor of the executive terminal. The jet pulled up to the terminal, and she spotted her husband and four-year-old son Amiri peering through the window of the reception area. They saw her and waved; Amiri jumped with excitement.

She felt the same way. Sometimes her job kept her away from home for weeks at a time, and she missed her family. Hologram visits were better than nothing, but ultimately unsatisfying.

She consoled herself with the thought that the insurgency was crumbling. In a month—maybe a few weeks—the war would be over and she'd be able to spend more time at home. It would be wonderful.

The boarding ramp extended from the reception door to the plane and locked into place. DoubleD stepped out of the plane and hurried down the ramp toward the terminal entrance. Amiri burst through the entrance, ran up the ramp and jumped into her arms.

"Mommy," he squealed as she kissed him on the cheek.

A moment later, they were swallowed up in the powerful arms of her husband. Julius pressed his lips on hers and she responded passionately. If Amiri weren't present, she would have made love to her husband immediately.

"It's so good to see you again," he murmured.

"I missed you," she said.

"I missed you, too, Mommy," Amiri said, and then hugged her around the neck with wiry, golden brown arms.

She was home.

***

After dinner, DoubleD sat with Julius on the balcony overlooking the huge garden surrounding their mansion. A three-quarter moon contrasted the shadowy grounds of their estate with brash city lights outside the walls. Amiri had been put to bed, and the couple enjoyed the comfortable evening weather, chatting about friends, an upcoming family vacation, the latest technologies and other light matters.

DoubleD lifted a tulip-shaped glass of sherry to her lips and enjoyed the smooth, slightly-sweet taste. She stretched her long legs out to the hassock. Her husband sat next to her, smoking a custom made cigarette laced with marijuana. *Such a handsome man*. His dark hair was touched with gray, which, she thought, reflected his wisdom and royal breeding. It was wonderful to be home.

"I suppose we should discuss the war," Julius said.

"Must we?"

"Thankfully, the pogrom is almost over," he said. "Dianne's strategy is repugnant, but it's succeeding. We've wiped out almost all the hostile tribes."

DoubleD sighed. "I know."

"Our Condors blanket the skies, day and night. Nothing moves down there that we don't spot. We almost caught Ray Brown a couple of weeks ago. We'll get him soon and what's left of the insurgency will collapse."

"Have you located Nkumah?"

Julius's face hardened and he shook his head. She shouldn't have brought it up.

"Soon you'll be the commander of all Africa," DoubleD said.

"Will I?"

Something was bothering her husband. Clearly, he didn't like to dwell on all the people his forces had killed, but he had crossed that bridge six years ago. She had, too.

"I have to show you something tonight, Darlene." He stood up and called into the house, "Joseph!"

His driver, a lanky, wrinkled man about seventy, appeared at the balcony door. Joseph had served Julius for many years and his father before that.

"Get the car," Julius said. "I'm taking my wife to the factory."

Joseph glanced at her and then turned back to stare at Julius. The old man seemed hesitant but said, "Yes, sir," and then disappeared into the house.

"What is this factory?"

"The tribes will never accept me as their legitimate leader. Too much killing. They'll obey me—I have the power—but they'll never respect me." He seemed to be talking to himself. "I'm just a front man for the Domain. Everyone knows Dianne Morgan calls the shots."

It wasn't like her husband to speak this way. Suddenly concerned, she looked back into the house, but didn't see anyone. Where the Domain ruled, the walls had ears.

"Let's go to bed," she said, "We've been apart for weeks."

Dianne was paranoid. DoubleD knew she had narrowly avoided the axe several times over the years.

Julius said, "You know we search these rooms every day for bugging devices; it's clean." He took her hand in his and led her into the house, "We'll talk more after you see the factory."

He led her down the staircase into the garage under the house. Three cars were waiting for them. Julius always had cars filled with soldiers whenever he left the estate.

Joseph opened the door to the middle car and DoubleD slid in, followed by her husband. She was surprised to discover a black man and a white woman seated in the front seat of the car, body doubles for DoubleD and her husband. They sometimes used this couple to confuse assassination attempts.

Julius put his index finger to his lips, warning her not to speak, and handed her a thermoflex coat. Following his lead, she put on the coat and slipped out the car's opposite door, where they hurried up a short flight of steps into the garden.

Hiding in the darkness under a large rhododendron, they watched the cars pull out through the gates and drive into the night. Tension spread from her chest to her arms and shoulders. Her husband was taking extraordinary measures to fool—it had to be—Dianne's spies. Nothing good could come of this.

Once the hum of the engines faded, Julius led her through the garden, staying under the cover of trees and large bushes. Minutes passed as they crept along in the dim moonlight. The garden turned into a thick, tangled forest, and the lights of their home faded away. Finally, they came to a storage shed used by workmen.

Julius unlocked the door and signaled her to follow him inside. The smell of fertilizer was overpowering, and a few seconds passed before she could see through the pitch black darkness. Gradually, she was able to make out neatly stacked bags of fertilizer on a rough wood floor. A variety of garden tools were stacked against a wall to her right.

Julius pulled dark brown coveralls off a hook on the wall and tossed it to her, "Make sure they cover your clothes completely." He smiled tightly as he removed his coat, "Can't let you get smudged."

After they put on coveralls, Julius walked to the rear corner and pulled open a trap door. Using a flashlight, he looked down the hole and then climbed in. DoubleD leaned over the edge to watch her husband climb down an aluminum ladder to a dirt floor. Opposite the ladder, she saw the entrance of a tunnel.

"Come down and pull the trap door shut," he said quietly.

He aimed the beam of a flashlight at the ladder below her feet as she climbed down. The ladder shook slightly with each step. She counted fourteen rungs before touching down on moist ground.

The tunnel ceiling was about six feet high, forcing her husband to bend slightly. Her head almost scraped the ceiling, but she was able to walk through the entrance without bending over.

She followed Julius down the dirt tunnel, which was barely wide enough for her husband's broad shoulders. It was long and damp, with a moist, dirt floor. The temperature dropped as they walked; she guessed it was about ten degrees cooler than the garden. The flashlight only carried about twenty feet, so the length of the tunnel was a mystery.

What is Julius hiding from the light?

They had walked about ten minutes when she heard the hum of machinery. Julius stopped, looked over his shoulder, and said, "The steps ahead might be slippery."

Holding on to a damp handrail, she followed him down a steep metal staircase. The tunnel twisted to the right; the uniform hum of machinery became a chorus of different machines. Another fifty feet and the flashlight illuminated a metal door at the end of the tunnel. Julius punched a code into a security port and the lock clicked.

The light almost blinded her when the door swung open. As her eyes adjusted, Julius guided her down half dozen steps into a cavernous room about the size of a football field.

She could scarcely believe her eyes.

It was a robot factory.

Two long manufacturing lines stretched down the entire length of the room. On the left, Spybots were being assembled; on the right, Commandos. The robots were in increasing states of completion as they were moved from workstation to workstation down the line. Factory noise was muted and she guessed the walls and roof were insulated to prevent any electronic snoopers from discovering them. The air was cool but smelled clean.

DoubleD stared at her husband. *This is lunacy*. Her throat was tight, but she made her voice work, "Do you realize what you've done?"

Julius led her to the edge of the work floor between the two lines. She watched the nearest workstation, which was only about ten feet away. Three workers had gathered around a partially complete Spybot, installing mechanical parts, testing components, snapping in computer boards and performing other activities. They seemed to know what they were doing, and the work progressed quickly.

Looking down the line, she saw that each robot had been placed on a six-inch thick pallet, riding on mechanized wheels. She saw one group stand back—their job apparently complete—and the platform silently rolled to the next workstation.

The air was warm and moist, but she knew that wasn't the reason her back was sweating. This was a secret factory, built deep underground to keep Dianne unaware of its owner's intent.

The Spybot line had about a dozen workstations, while the Commando about twenty. Not all the work was performed by humans; many of the workstations consisted only of robot arms attached to a six foot tall mechanical cart.

Robots building robots.

"We can build a Spybot in about three hours," Dkembe said, "The Commandos are a little more complicated, but we have it down to five and one-half hours."

"Julius, she'll kill all of us."

"There's a huge warehouse directly above us. We built the warehouse first, then dug out the factory. All the excavation equipment was shipped in individual boxes to the warehouse, where we assembled it. The work was done slowly and carefully by members of my tribe. Mostly at night. Took us almost two years."

"Stop!" she hissed. Two of the workers to her left glanced at her, and then returned to their work.

She lowered her voice, "You've done what you've done. If Dianne discovers this, she'll kill you, me, Amiri and your entire tribe. Why didn't you discuss this with me first?"

"I couldn't take the chance. I've seen how Dianne watches you. She has an extraordinary ability to read people. You're alive because she believes that you're loyal. I'm not sure you could hide the truth from her for very long."

DoubleD studied her husband. "You plan to move against her soon?"

"The insurgency is just about over. I intend to rule Africa with you at my side. We're not dependent upon the Domain for anything, and we have sufficient robots to repel an attack."

"What about Sentinel?"

"We'll cut off our network from Sentinel. Our scientists made a backup copy of Sentinel and modified it for our purposes. This new AI—we call it Kalunga, the god of creation— runs the network controlling this factory. When we are ready to attack, we'll delete Sentinel from the African network and load Kalunga across Africa."

"Kalunga is also the god of the dead," she said.

"Which is where I intend to send Dianne. We have sympathizers within the Domain."

She shook her head, "Damn you, Julius."

"I had to do it this way. Our son will be accepted as king."

Julius pulled her into a tight embrace.
"Damn you," she breathed, just before his mouth crushed her lips.

TWENTY-TWO

Sunday, September 28, 2031

As he hurried down the hall, David tried to remember that Martin, for all his brilliance, was not yet six. But that didn't excuse him for sneaking into the VRB and trying to merge with Sentinel. The kid's disobedience had almost ruined his plans.

I'm up shit's creek if Morgan figures out what I've done.

David burst into his apartment and yelled, "Martin!"

Anger simmering, he'd cut short his visit with his mother. It stuck in his gut Martin had disobeyed him and almost wrecked Sentinel. The ungrateful whelp must have gone to Morgan behind his back to get entry to the VRB.

Why am I surprised? His mother is that witch, not my Kathy.

"Martin!" he shouted again. There was no response.

David shoved open the door to Martin's room and found his son dictating code to his computer. As always, drawn window shades filtered the morning sun, leaving the room in shadows. Martin was sitting at the desk in the far left corner, his attention concentrated on the computer display. Not a single picture or personal item was in view.

"Answer me when I call you!"

Martin interrupted his dictation and looked over his shoulder at David. "I see you're in one of your moods again."

"You went behind my back to that Morgan woman! After I told you to stay away from the VRB."

"I didn't do anything." Martin spun his chair in David's direction. "I don't know what you're talking about."

"Don't lie to me! You tried to merge with Sentinel. I checked out Sentinel's safety code; you left a trail of damage."

"It wasn't me. Something else screwed it up."

"Bullshit!"

"Ask Sentinel if you don't believe me. Or look at the log yourself. I haven't been in the VRB in weeks."

David stormed over to him, and Martin backed up a few inches before his chair bumped into the desk.

"And you're not getting another chance for years," David shouted. "I found that crap you inserted into the safety code. Dianne Morgan doesn't have the highest priority anymore. And you're locked out."

Martin's face fell, and he blurted, "Dad, please don't lock me out. I admit it—I merged with Sentinel. It was beautiful, I was so powerful. I stayed too long, or I tried to do too much, something went wrong."

"Damn you! I *warned you* that you weren't ready. But you wouldn't believe me so you went to that snake Morgan."

"Well, at least she treats me decently. You don't care about me. You blame me for my mother's death; everybody knows that. Ms. Morgan likes me."

David was tempted to tell Martin that the witch was his mother, but even though he was really pissed off, he held back. Dianne didn't give a shit about Martin, she was just using him. Sooner or later, he'd outlive his usefulness; it wouldn't be pretty. A lioness eats her prey.

David shook his head. "That's bull and you know it! I never blamed you. You're my son and I've done my best to raise you right." He fought to control his anger, but he was on the edge. "And don't delude yourself about Dianne Morgan. She's a deceitful witch. She pretends to like you because she wants to control your talent. I haven't become the human computer needed to complete her lust for power, so she's gone after you."

Crimson blotches began appearing on Martin's face. He struggled to his feet and shouted, "No, she likes me! She's not a dead man walking like you."

David slapped Martin across the face, sending him sprawling backward against the chair, which tipped over and crashed to the floor; Martin fell across the chair and cried out. He stared up at his father, fear mixed with anger in his eyes, his cheek red from the blow.

David stepped back, staring down at his son. He couldn't believe he had slapped Martin; he'd never laid a hand on the boy before. His anger whistled out, like a balloon collapsing, leaving him flat and uncomprehending.

After climbing shakily to his feet, Martin screamed, "I hate you," and then hobbled past David and out the door. David knew he should go after his son and apologize, but he didn't move. He felt nothing, he admitted, except relief.

He walked out and gently closed the door. The boy was Dianne's son in every way that counted.

Let her have him.

TWENTY-THREE

Friday, October 3, 2031

Dianne sat in a leather chair behind her desk, working in her most secure office far below the surface. She glanced across the room, where a three-dimensional hologram of the Oregon seashore covered a long wall. This had been their favorite place years ago when she and Ray were lovers.

It was a cold, sunny day in the hologram, with an occasional cloud drifting through the blue sky. The surf was rough, and the waves rode across the rocky beach, crashed against the dunes, and then slid back into the sea. Ray's home was just behind the dunes, and she recalled how they would sit and talk for hours on his balcony. The water was too cold for swimming most of the year, but they loved walking along the shore. Occasionally, driftwood would ride in on the surf and wash up on the beach.

After PeaceMaker had been destroyed, she had asked Ray to help her rebuild the Domain, but he'd refused. She should have executed him then, but couldn't do it. Imprisoning him on the island had been a mistake; the years had turned his love to hatred. After escaping from the island, he'd become her worst enemy. Never again would she allow personal feelings to soften her decisions.

The security system interrupted her thoughts.

"Martin Brown to see you."

The little bastard was becoming a real pest. He had come crying to her that his father hated him, so she had taken him in. Although it was good to keep Martin emotionally tied to her, he was always whining about something. But she had to put up with it since he would be David's replacement, at least until her other children grew up.

David Brown no longer had any value, he was too dangerous. She would have already eliminated him, but she was concerned that Sentinel would shut down. Mohammed had studied Sentinel's code and was working on a patch to block an emotional response from the AI. The patch should be ready within the next couple of days.

"Send him in," Dianne said.

To her left, a door slid open and Martin hobbled in as quickly as his legs allowed.

"Aunt Dianne," he called out, "let me use the VRB today. I found out my father will be staying all day at his grandmother's nursing home."

Gesturing to the sofa on the right, she said. "Martin, sit down please." She stood up and followed him to the sofa. "There's something we have to discuss."

When Dianne had his full attention, she said, "Your father has programmed Sentinel to keep you out of the VRB. I can't override his commands. I would give you total access if I could, but Sentinel obeys him."

"There must be something you can do," Martin whined. "If I can't merge with Sentinel, my talent will never fully develop. You're in charge of the Domain." His eyes began to tear. "You have to help me."

"I'm sorry, but as long as your father is alive, Sentinel obeys him."

Martin slumped back and began to cry.

What an annoying child. Those red blotches are disgusting.

Dianne put her arm around his shoulders and pulled him close.

"There, there, honey," she said.

"He screws up everything that's important!"

"I know," she murmured.

"He's always mean to me," Martin cried. "I wish I didn't *have* a father."

"I can understand that," she said. "He seems to relish making your life miserable."

"He's jealous of me. My power is greater than his." Martin blinked away tears. "He says bad things about you, too."

The little bastard is trying to play me again. She smiled inwardly. *Well, he is my son.*

"He calls you bad names like witch and whore, but I know you're a good person." Martin sobbed into her shoulder. "I love you."

"Maybe there *is* something I can do," she said, "if you'll help me."

Martin's head popped off her shoulder. "I'll do anything." He wasn't crying.

"Do you know about Alice?"

"Sure. It's the software virus that tried to kill my father a couple of times." Martin stared eagerly into her eyes. "The first time he merged with Sentinel, Alice fed on his hatred and tried to kill you, too."

"Alice is a killer, dangerous and intelligent, but its prey is your father. It's hiding out in the net somewhere, waiting for an opportunity to attack again."

"Why doesn't it just kill him," Martin asked.

"I believe Sentinel protects your father. Otherwise, Alice would attack him every time he entered the net. If Alice caught your father on the net, and Sentinel wasn't around to protect him, I think Alice would kill him."

Dianne brushed a lock of hair off Martin's forehead. "I want you to find out where Alice hides on the net."

"And then what?" Martin asked.

"When the moment is right, we take away your father's security blanket."

Martin smiled. "Soon, Aunt Dianne?"

"Yes, very soon." She patted his shoulder. "Then you can play with Sentinel as much as you want."

***

The morning was hot and dry, with a gentle breeze from the south. The tall, parched grass issued a sweet smell, but Carlos barely noticed it. Stopping for a moment to rest in the shade of a giant baobab tree, he stretched his legs. His feet hurt, but he was too tired to pull off his boots. What he wouldn't do for a cold mug of *cerveza* served with *enchiladas*. Fat chance here in the woodlands of northeastern Zambia.

His plan was to locate one of the tribes and talk them into taking him to Nkumah, but Carlos had wandered through this forest with Arthur for days without seeing anyone. Not a single person, where once many tribes had flourished. He hadn't realized how devastating the Domain's African pogrom had been.

His whole plan was beginning to seem shaky. Even if they found Nkumah, there was no guarantee the man would believe his story. They weren't really friends; Nkumah knew that he would work for anyone if the money was right. Nkumah might even think the whole thing was a trap to capture Ray Brown. Actually, it *could* be a trap; the Domain might have built Arthur, not David Brown. Carlos wouldn't know the truth until Ray verified the message from David, but his gut said Arthur was authentic.

Carlos had second thoughts about taking the job, except the android would have murdered him if he had refused. Besides, ten million American was a nice piece of change.

Ahead on the trail, Arthur stopped and waited for him. Almost two weeks with the freaking android. The damn thing was getting on his nerves.

Arthur wasn't much of a conversationalist, but it had been programmed to play poker. Sentinel must have figured he would need some amusement during the search. The android never forgot a card and it knew all the percentages. Carlos figured he owed Arthur about twenty grand.

He watched Arthur turn his head and sniff the air. After walking forward about ten feet, the robot stopped and sniffed again.

"What is it?" Carlos asked. He had learned the android's senses were remarkable.

"Forest elephants. Five or six about half a mile south."

"So who gives a shit?" Carlos said, swatting a mosquito that had landed on his neck. "They won't bother us, they're upwind."

"I never said they would attack."

"You're the most clueless android I've ever seen," Carlos said, his voice rising. "You never provide information I can actually use."

"You asked what I detected and I answered. If you don't want —"

Arthur's voice was overridden by the alarmed trumpeting of a large elephant.

"Shut up!" Carlos said. "They heard your stupid voice."

"Your voice was louder than mine."

Several other elephants joined in the alarm; then Carlos heard the sound of the beasts crashing through the brush.

"They're coming this way," Arthur announced, but Carlos was already running.

The android followed Carlos through the brush, trying to steer clear of the elephant's charge. Thorn bushes slapped against his jeans and thermoflex coat, but the woody spines didn't pierce the protective fabric. Carlos knew he could stop the elephants with his laser rifle, but that would be a telltale signal to the Domain's helicopters constantly patrolling the skies.

The beasts were getting close, so Carlos ducked behind a thick Mopani tree. Arthur was still ten feet behind; running was the one thing the android didn't do well, but it ducked into the brush just as the elephants came into sight. The largest—probably the herd's matriarch—stopped at the baobab and sniffed with its trunk. She looked toward them and stamped in anger. He had heard that an elephant's eyesight wasn't particularly good, but this one seemed to be staring directly at him.

There were six elephants in all, including a little one that hid in the center of the herd. They were stomping around; making it clear they were pissed. The matriarch roared in his direction and then led the herd off.

Carlos took his time before coming out from the tree. He stood up and looked across the brush in the direction the elephants had moved out. No sense rushing.

"I think they're gone," Arthur said.

"Shut up."

Carlos took a few tentative steps and then froze. He heard something in the woods around them. Could the elephants have circled back?

"It's a pack of baboons," Arthur told him. "I suggest we leave the area."

"I know it's baboons," Carlos snapped, "just follow me and shut up."

***

The waning rays of the sun filtered through the thick brush, creating a lattice of shadows. Carlos pulled down the brim of his Dodgers cap to keep the sun out. It was cooling rapidly, and he was glad to be wearing a thermoflex coat. Resting his back against the rough bark of a thorn tree, he stretched his arms. The damn coat weighed a ton.

Mosquitoes were on the attack again, so he pulled a can of insect repellent from his backpack and carefully sprayed his exposed skin. The repellent would give him peace from the tiny predators for about twelve hours. He checked the meter on the bottom of the can; about thirty percent remaining. Unfortunately, it was his last can of insecticide. Maybe he could trade for a mosquito net when they found a tribe.

If they found a tribe.

More than four years had passed since his last visit to central Africa. It was different now; the tribes had disappeared. The war had taken its toll. If a tribe didn't discover them soon, the Domain would surely track them down.

His feet hurt with every step. Looking up at the canopy of trees, he saw vines thick as a fire hose hanging down, twisting across branches and around the trunk in their trip to the wet soil, where they spread out into woody surface roots. He had tripped more than once on these intermeshed roots.

Glancing back at Arthur, he said, "Let's take a break."

Carlos plopped down in the damp grass and pulled off his boots and socks. High boots weren't his favorite, but he had decided to trade comfort for security. The forest was infested with Gaboon vipers, one of the most poisonous snakes on the planet. Six feet long and almost invisible in the mud and dead leaves. One bite and you're dead.

His blisters were beginning to heal, but throbbing pain still made walking difficult. His feet didn't look infected, but he wasn't taking any chances. After pulling a tube of first aid cream from his backpack, he rubbed it in until the pain faded.

Feeling hungry, he lifted a foodblock from his coat pocket and broke open the seal but just stared at it. He was tired of eating this shit. In Mexico, they had real food. What he wouldn't give for a plate of *Chiles Rellenos*—the kind stuffed with spicy meat. He bit off a piece of the foodblock and forced himself to chew.

"That's Domain rations, isn't it?" Arthur asked. "A human can live with one block a day and a quart of water."

"Yeah," Carlos answered while chewing. "You just noticed what I'm eating?"

"Actually, no. I was trying to make small talk. You know, relieve the tension."

"Shut up."

Objectively, he knew Arthur was a remarkable android. It was holding up well, and its personality was near-human. Maybe that was the problem. The damn thing got on his nerves.

He was still hungry and considered biting off another piece of foodblock, but there wasn't much left, so he decided to conserve the remaining food. Who knew when they'd get a real meal?

"Traveling with you," Carlos said, "I've learned that androids don't know how to hold an interesting conversation. Just shut up and rest your batteries."

"Well, that's what I wanted to talk to you about."

"Batteries? You think a conversation about batteries would be interesting?"

"You know how it works, right?" Arthur said. "I get my power from either the sun or by plugging into an AC outlet. Either source will charge up my batteries."

"Not too many outlets here in the forest," Carlos replied. Suddenly he had a bad feeling. "What are you getting at?"

"I've been using more energy each day than I can completely replenish from solar power. The charge in my batteries has been slowly dropping." Arthur appeared almost apologetic. "It's down to twenty-seven percent."

"*Hijo de puta!* Are you telling me you're about to run out of power?" He stuffed the foodblock into his coat pocket.

"Not at all," Arthur replied. "But conserving power would be prudent. I suggest that we don't move tomorrow. A day in the sun would let me charge up to more than fifty percent."

"You mean we have to waste a day so you can sunbathe!"

"It's not my fault that you can't find Nkumah," Arthur said. "I'm powering down for the evening, but I'll continue to listen for any suspicious sounds."

Carlos watched the robot lie back and shut its eyes. His doubts about this assignment were growing. They had stumbled across another deserted village earlier in the day. The huts were all broken down; he guessed the people had disappeared—probably slaughtered by robots—years earlier.

It was a tough situation. If the Domain found him before he could deliver Arthur to Nkumah, he'd be a dead man. Maybe he should fry the robot with his laser tonight and get out of here. But he had ten million good reasons to complete the mission.

His thoughts were interrupted by a low pitched hum. He searched the sky, but didn't see a helicopter. It was up there, somewhere, but too far away to see.

That goddamn DoubleD! She never gives up. The bitch had been hunting him ever since he had smuggled weapons from Mexico to the tribes. Just that one time four years ago. He'd like to stick it to her, especially if this damn robot really carried a weapon that could hurt the Domain. Why didn't that *puta* just stay at home, raise her brat and screw her husband? What was wrong with women these days?

Watching Arthur rest in the grass, he decided to stay in the game a little longer. Lay low tomorrow and let the android charge up, then take one last shot at finding a tribe. If they didn't come across anyone, then he'd fold his hand and take out the android.

TWENTY-FOUR

Sunday, October 5, 2031

Time = 5:35 pm. 360 scan. Prey not detected. Composite luminous intensity = .33.

Time = 5:36 pm. 360 scan. Prey not detected. Air moisture increase. Rain beginning. Analysis: Precipitation is within operating parameters.

Time = 5:36:29 pm. Footsteps detected. Probable distance from prey five hundred feet. Mammals. Preliminary analysis is two humans.

Time = 5:36:51pm. Focused scan. Movement detected in brush on left 37 degrees. Prey detected. Shape recognition software engaged. Database comparison: Human. Enlarge image. Cache search. Raul Mendoza. Known as Carlos.

Time = 5:36:54 pm. Focused scan. Prey detected. Database comparison: Android, model unknown. Enlarge image. Cache search. David Brown's missing robot.

Time = 5:36:58 pm. Transmission from Spybot 663 to Security Center 267. Handshake completed. Visual and auditory data transmitted. Awaiting reply. Powering all systems.

Time = 5:38:41 pm. Transmission received from Security Center 267. Orders: Follow android, avoid detection, report status at five minute intervals.

Time = 5:38:52 pm. Begin tracking prey. Maintain separation 500 to 600 feet.

***

Another day gone, Carlos thought, as moonlight filtered through the canopy of trees. He knew it was hopeless. Almost two weeks tracking through Africa without finding a village or even a recent trail. He guessed that the tribes— at least the ones the Domain hadn't wiped out— must have fled. Nkumah would never allow a stranger to roam his lands if he were still in control.

Carlos decided it was time to throw in his cards. The game was becoming too dangerous, and his hand was a loser. He forced himself to look at the positive side. A million dollars wasn't bad for a few weeks work.

Now to get rid of this android.

He cursed and pretended to hobble. When Arthur turned to look, Carlos said, "I think I picked up a thorn in my boot." He sat down in the grass. "Keep going. I'll catch up in a minute."

As Arthur walked ahead, Carlos slowly pulled his laser pistol from its shoulder holster. A blast to the back of the head should do the trick.

"There's human scent in the air!" Arthur shouted. The android turned around slowly, sniffing the breeze.

Carlos slipped the pistol back into his holster and rose to his feet. "Where are they?"

"Their scent is coming from all around us." Arthur sniffed again. "I think they have us surrounded."

"*Hijo de puta*! You're supposed to warn me *before* we're surrounded."

"Sorry."

The forest was unusually quiet. Normally, the calls of wood owls, great blue turacos and hornbills filled the twilight, but now the birds were silent. Even the monkeys had disappeared.

He figured whoever's out there were probably getting ready to attack. It was time to show his hand.

"I am Carlos, friend of all those who fight the Domain," he shouted in Kiswahili. He paused for a second and looked around, "I seek my friend Nkumah Muserre. I bring him a weapon to defeat the witch Dianne Morgan and her coven."

There was no response.

Maybe they don't give a shit about Nkumah.

"I don't think—" Arthur began.

"Shut up."

Carlos pulled his coat free of his shoulder holster. Just in case.

Five stone-faced warriors, tall and gaunt, slipped out of the brush and faced them. One carried what looked like a Beretta express rifle at his side, while the other four were armed only with spears. Hunters had once used powerful guns like the Beretta express to bring down elephants and other big game; it might even pierce the plating of a Domain Commando robot. A shot in the chest would disable Arthur.

The men wore thermoflex coats, which covered them from shoulder to knee. No shoes, but heavy jeans with ragged cuffs. The moonlight highlighted a dark scar on the rifleman that stretched from his right ear to his mouth. He was a big man, towering over Carlos's six feet one.

The rifleman sneered. "Anyone can claim to be a friend of Nkumah."

His skin was darker than the night, and his eyes glowed with menace. As he spoke, the others spread out in a rough semi-circle around them. "Why should I believe someone who travels with a tin man?"

Carlos realized he was facing an intelligent man. From a distance, not many people would have spotted Arthur as an android. He'd have to be careful with what he told them.

"I am the one who led Nkumah to the island where the Domain had imprisoned Ray Brown," Carlos said. "After we freed Brown, Nkumah gave me a token to celebrate our eternal friendship. May I remove it from my belt?"

The warrior nodded, but pointed the rifle at Carlos's chest.

Carlos lifted his coat and unsnapped the thin chain holding his good luck lion's tooth. He pulled the chain through a hole in the tooth, snapped the chain shut, and then tossed the tooth to the man with the rifle.

The warrior caught the tooth with one hand, while holding the rifle in the other. This was no mean feat; the rifle was long and heavy. Then he lifted the charm up to his eyes and examined it. The initials NM had been scratched in a corner.

He looked at Carlos and then back at the tooth, "You will come with us," he said, "but I will have your pistol first."

Without the pistol, he'd be at their mercy. But these men could have killed him from ambush, if that had been their intent. He'd play this hand out.

Carlos reached under his coat for the laser pistol. "Just two fingers," the rifleman said. Carlos pulled out the weapon, using his thumb and index finger.

"Drop it, then back up three steps."

Carlos did as he was told. One of the other warriors, his eyes flicking from Carlos to Arthur, came over and picked up the laser.

"Follow me," the rifleman said, then turned and walked away. Grabbing his pack off the ground, Carlos followed the man into the brush. Arthur walked at his shoulder, with the other warriors following.

They stalked through the moonlit forest for hours without a word, jogging where it was clear, walking where the brush was thick. They jumped over fallen trees and waded through swollen streams. Although his legs began to ache, Carlos kept pace with the dark shadow in front.

The woodlands turned to open savannah, overrun with termite mounds shaped like reddish-brown cathedrals twice a man's height. A sudden rain drenched the land, but they stayed dry in their thermoflex coats.

Occasionally, they came across little clearings dotted with the remains of wood framed huts. These had once been thriving villages, where men and women had raised children and lived out their lives. Now only skeletons were left, the burned-out remains of a primitive civilization annihilated by the Domain's robots.

He was careful not to step on the bones. Vultures and jackals had picked the dead bodies clean, leaving only pristine, white skeletons. He wondered if DoubleD had ever walked through one of her graveyards.

As Carlos slogged through the mud, his mind drifted into semi-consciousness, a blur of mud, pain and exhaustion. One step after another, he followed the dark figure ahead. They crossed a shallow river and began hiking up a rocky mountain slope.

His feet were raw where blisters had burst. Walking uphill taxed the little energy he had remaining, but he kept going. Pain spread from his feet to his knees and then to his back. His captors were tireless, the march never-ending. Although he could barely move, he didn't ask to rest. He had to show them that he was a warrior, too.

Half-way up the slope, several dark figures—he couldn't tell how many—confronted the rifleman. After a brief conversation, these warriors stepped aside and allowed them to pass.

The rifleman led them through thick brush to a steep cliff at the side of the mountain. At the foot of the cliff, Carlos spotted a roughly oval cave entrance, about ten feet across and seven feet high. The cave narrowed as they walked in, and he had to bend his head to avoid bumping into sharp edges jutting out of the ceiling. Lanterns driven into the wall provided scarcely enough light to walk across the uneven dirt floor.

He followed the rifleman, now a silhouette outlined by the harsh glow of occasional lanterns, down a slippery grade. Pebbles crunched under his feet, but Carlos was too exhausted to care about the pain shooting up his ankles. Now and then, he had to stoop over to avoid one of the many bats hanging down. He discovered that brushing his right hand against the cold, damp wall helped to maintain his footing. The temperature dropped rapidly; he shivered and buttoned his coat.

The tunnel began to widen, then turned into a gloomy chamber at least as large as a basketball court, with walls about twenty feet high. The scent of human excrement wafted up his nostrils.

They entered a village of canvas tents, each heated by a small fire. The village felt a few degrees warmer than the tunnel. A thin haze floated overhead, but the smoke appeared to escape through fissures in the rock.

Bare-breasted women slipped out of the tents and stared at him, some curious, others hostile. He couldn't see them clearly in the gloomy light, but a few of the younger women were well-formed. Despite the pain radiating from his feet, he returned their stares with a friendly smile. One never knew.

As they walked through the village, he noticed a group of children and women sitting quietly in an isolated corner. The stench sickened his stomach. Then a young boy bent over and vomited. A woman came to the boy, lifted his head and poured a trickle of water into his mouth. Carlos had seen the same sickness in Mexico years ago; these people had cholera.

The Domain had forced the tribe to abandon the open sky for this hellhole. Humans couldn't prosper under these conditions. Personally, he'd rather fight and die under the sky like a man than waste away in the shadows, but he wasn't here to judge them.

The rifleman led him to a large tent in the center of the village and then disappeared inside. A few yards from the tent's entrance, Carlos swayed on his feet, but he fought to retain his balance. Guards surrounded them, making sure he and the android stayed put.

Arthur whispered, "These people are in bad shape. I don't detect any animals and not much food either."

Carlos nodded. "I think this tribe is on the brink of collapse."

They stopped talking when an old man stepped out of the main tent. The chief, Carlos guessed, looked about eighty, but he walked with a sure-footed stride. Flared nostrils and high cheekbones highlighted a regal face. A brown and green army camouflage shirt, buttoned all the way up, was tucked into tattered khakis. He had the look of a defeated general who had lost everything but his pride.

"I am Nchito, Chief of the Bemba." The old man's expression seemed wary.

"Thank you for seeing me," Carlos replied.

"We will talk." He turned and walked away.

Carlos followed Nchito into his tent, which appeared to be about eight by ten feet. An undersized campfire burned in the center, the sole source of inadequate, flickering light. The tent wasn't furnished, except for two woven rugs around the fire.

The chief gracefully folded his legs and sat on one of the rugs. A long, ornate pipe and a tobacco-filled wooden bowl were next to him on the rug. Carlos plopped down on the other rug, exhibiting as much grace as exhausted legs would permit. The rifleman came in and stood behind the chief. A long knife hung from his belt.

"This is my son Muko, our military commander." Muko nodded, but his eyes weren't friendly. "He has fought at Nkumah's side many times," the chief added.

"Nkumah is a great warrior," Carlos said.

Nchito pulled a plug of tobacco from the bowl, molded it between his thumb and index finger, and tamped it into the pipe. He lifted a burning stick from the fire, lit the tobacco and inhaled.

Puffing on the pipe, he said, "Tell me your story, Carlos. What is it you wish from my tribe?"

"I'm a soldier for hire. My client has asked me to deliver a powerful weapon to Ray Brown that will enable him to defeat the witch Dianne Morgan. I search for Nkumah because he will take me to Brown."

"What is this weapon?"

"The android is the weapon." Carlos straightened his legs and pain flared through his thighs. "I don't know anything specific," he said, keeping the pain from his voice, "but I believe the weapon is built into the android's software."

"Tell us who built this robot," Muko said.

"I can't reveal that," Carlos replied. "My clients are confidential."

"You tell us nothing!" Muko shouted. He turned to his father. "I say roast him over the campfire." He smiled maliciously at Carlos. "He'll squeal like a girl."

The chief studied Carlos, apparently trying to make up his mind. "My son is a harsh man." Nchito shrugged and said, "All I ask is the truth." He spit into the fire, and then puffed on his pipe. "Tell me all you know and I'll decide whether to take you to Nkumah. Even if I decide to destroy the android, I'll set you free."

Muko rose to his feet. "Father, we have to kill him! He knows too much."

Nchito turned on his son. "Don't disgrace me. My word, once given, is my honor."

"Please forgive me, Nchito, but I must be blunt," Carlos said. "I walked through much of Zambia and the Congo looking for Nkumah, but I found only a barren land. All the tribes are gone." He shook his head. "I knew of the Domain's African pogrom, but I didn't realize the extent of the killing.

"I also look at your tribe forced to hide below ground. Your brave warriors, what's left of them, cannot leave the cave without a thermoflex coat. I see three or four women for every man. I apologize for this, but your tribe is on the verge of extinction." Carlos shook his head. "The sky is darkened by the Domain's helicopters. It's only a matter of time before they discover your cave."

Nchito didn't reply. Holding the pipe in his lap, he stared out the tent flap, his mind apparently drifting.

Carlos gently asked, "Is this not true?"

"We will fight to the death, if that is to be our fate," Muko said.

"And this weapon, this android will save us?" Nchito asked, his attention returning to Carlos.

"It is said that he who lives by the sword, dies by the sword," Carlos answered. "I believe the gods have sent this android to destroy the Domain."

"Our enemies are powerful," Nchito said. "What can a single android do?"

"I don't know," Carlos admitted, "but what have you got to lose?"

Nchito looked at his son, who nodded. He turned back and said, "Carlos, your name is well-known to me. It is the name of a brave and resourceful man, but one without a guiding spirit. You work for anyone who will pay, but I am told, once you're hired, you stay hired. So Nkumah said to me years ago." He paused, and then said, "I don't know who hired you, but our situation *is* desperate." He laid the pipe in the dirt and rose to his feet, indicating he had come to a decision. Carlos stood up in respect.

"Muko will guide you and the android to Nkumah."

***

After the meeting with Nchito, Muko led him to an unoccupied tent and then strode away without speaking. These are good people, Carlos thought, but that asshole needs a personality transplant.

Sitting on the dry ground inside the tent, he pulled off his boots and socks to check his feet; the blisters were leaking pus. Walking tomorrow would be hell. His feet needed medical attention, but the best he could do was first aid cream. He looked around for his backpack, which was on the other side of the tent. Even with the first aid cream, it would be a miracle if he didn't become crippled.

The tent flap parted and a slender young woman entered carrying a small bowl in one hand. She was bare breasted, wearing only a yellow and white wraparound skirt which showed off the curve of her hips. His eyes settled on her small, perfectly formed breasts. B cup, he guessed, although her breasts had no need for support.

She smiled and said, "I thought you might be hungry." Although her voice was quiet, it brimmed with confidence, the voice of someone accustomed to having her way.

She certainly could have her way with me.

"Thank you," he replied in Kiswahili. He was concerned about contracting cholera, but he was tired of artificial food. "The day did leave me with an appetite."

After kneeling at his side, the woman handed him a half-filled bowl of vegetables and small chunks of dark meat cooked in hot water. He wasn't sure which he liked better—staring at her breasts or eating the stew—so he decided to do both. Chuckling inwardly, he thought, *another crisp executive decision.*

He unleashed his best smile on her. Many women had told him that his smile was a knockout. "What's your name?"

She smiled back. "Uvila. Now eat your stew before it gets cold."

Someone actually being friendly? He concentrated on her face. About twenty, he thought, with wide, pleasant features and skin so dark it seemed tinged with blue.

He chewed a handful of stew and swallowed. "This is delicious."

She giggled. "I thought you'd like it."

He loved the way her breasts jiggled when she laughed. "What is this meat? It's really good."

"Boiled rat."

His stomach clenched and he almost lost his meal. Placing the bowl down, he said, "I don't think I'm really that hungry."

"Don't be silly," she said. "The meat is tasty and very healthy." She grabbed a handful of stew in her fingers and held it in front of his mouth. "This is the only food we have. You'll starve. Now open your mouth."

She was right; he had to eat something. Well, he'd eaten grasshoppers and ants to stay alive that time in Uruguay. He opened his mouth, but didn't look at the stew. She fed him and he began chewing. He tried not to think about what was in the stew; it was better to concentrate on her breasts. Actually, the taste was quite good, especially since he *was* hungry.

She fed him, giggling and obviously enjoying herself, until he finished the bowl.

Wiping his lips with his sleeve, Carlos said, "Thank you for the meal, Uvila. And thank your husband for his generosity."

"I'm not married." Her smile disappeared. "So many of the young men have not returned."

"I'm sorry."

"You must take better care of yourself, Carlos. The blisters on your feet are becoming infected." She stood up, "I'll bring a healer to treat them."

Oh God no, a faker who'll annoy me with hours of chanting.

"No, you don't have to do that. In my backpack over there," he pointed at the bag on the other side of the tent, "I have a tube of medicine. If you could bring it to me—"

Uvila retrieved the backpack and handed it to him. He squeezed the first aid cream into his palm and tried to reach down to rub it into his blisters, "Arrrg," he moaned and straightened up. His back felt a hundred years old.

"You poor man," she murmured. "I'll help you."

She kneeled down and gently rubbed in the cream, making sure not to press too hard on the blisters. Then she massaged his feet, bringing them back to life. It felt *so* good.

"Gracias, Senorita Uvila." When she looked questioningly at him, he chuckled and said in Kiswahili, "That means *thank you* in my native language. You've chased away the pain from my feet."

She smiled. "Now take off your pants."

He was confused for a split second, and then quickly kicked off his pants. No pretty girl had to ask him twice, especially since his last sex—with that *puta* Elena—had been weeks earlier. He reached for the elastic band of his shorts, but she grabbed his hand.

She smiled and said, "Roll over on your stomach."

What the hell is this? As he turned over, he thought, maybe they have a new position. Well, he was a great believer in innovation.

He couldn't see her, and he flinched when the cold first aid cream was rubbed into his calf, but then he realized that Uvila was trying to relieve the pain in his legs. A new way to do it? He chuckled to himself and decided to enjoy the attention.

Uvila's hands were strong, but gentle. She kneaded the flesh of his calf, and gradually moved up his leg. He sighed as she massaged the inside of his thigh. Her fingers felt *so* good, gently working the stiffness out of his leg.

By the time she started on the other leg, he was thoroughly aroused. This woman had a fantastic pair of hands. If it got any better, he'd start elevating off the ground.

"Carlos," she said in a breathy voice, "turn over and I'll do the front of your legs."

Rolling over wasn't going to be easy. He didn't want to embarrass her, but she must have seen men before. She's an adult woman, not a child.

Bracing on his hands, he turned over. The tent was up. Uvila put her hand to her mouth, but her eyes stayed on his erection.

It is pretty impressive.

She said, "It will be easier to finish the massage if you remove your short pants."

"Anything to help."

Uvila seemed to share his sentiment as she grabbed the bottom of his shorts and began to inch them down.

"Carlos, are you in there?" called a voice from outside the tent.

Uvila let go of his shorts and looked over her shoulder toward the tent flap.

Hijo de putas! It was the freaking android.

"Carlos, I hate to interrupt your sleep, but it's important."

I have to kill it!

"Go away!" he shouted. "We'll talk later!"

"You have important things to discuss," Uvila said, as she stepped up to the tent flap. "I should leave."

"No," he screeched. He dove to grab her ankle, but he was too slow and she slipped out of the tent. He pounded the dirt with his fist.

Arthur walked in and looked down at him. "Hope I didn't wake you up."

What did they do with my laser?

He dumped out the backpack, spilling foodblocks, condoms, a change of clothes, insect repellent, a small bottle of quinine, several vials of snake antivenin, a syringe, and a small carton of bandages, but the laser wasn't there.

Arthur said, "You're making quite the mess." His face wore a disapproving expression. "I just wanted to tell you that Muko says we leave at first light tomorrow."

If only there was a weapon nearby, Carlos thought, but he knew he couldn't kill the android. *Hijo de puta!* His mouth moved but the words were garbled; he was stuck between raging anger and extreme arousal.

Arthur smiled. "Get a good night's sleep and I'll see you in the morning."

Finding his voice, Carlos croaked out a string of curses as the android left.

TWENTY-FIVE

Wednesday, October 8, 2031

"Dianne, I've positioned our forces about two miles from the cave," DoubleD whispered into her wrist computer. The tribe has posted five sentries, but they'll be easy to take out. Nobody has any idea we're here, so we'll overwhelm them quickly and take control of the cave before they know what hit them."

"Is Carlos still traveling north?" Dianne asked.

"Yes, they're in the central region of the Republic of the Congo. I have three Spybots following them, with Condors ready to swoop in when we spot Ray."

"When you go into the cave, make sure to get Nchito first. If anyone knows where Ray's hiding, he's the one."

"I know," DoubleD replied. "It's 1:20 am here; we'll get him in his sleep."

"Call me after the raid," Dianne said and hung up.

Old witch, I won't have to put up with you much longer.

"Begin the operation," she said to the Commando robot standing at her side.

Twenty minutes later, she walked into the chief's tent. Nchito had been handcuffed and left face down on a rug. Janet Adams, a young security officer, carefully placed a syringe in a box labeled *Medical Waste* and rose to her feet.

"Is he ready?" DoubleD asked.

"Yes, ma'am," Adams replied. At nineteen, she was young to be a security officer, but DoubleD respected her work.

"You gave him a single dose?"

"As you ordered, ma'am."

"Let's get started."

Adams grabbed the old man by the shoulder and rolled him over, so that DoubleD could examine him. Kneeling on the rug next to the chief, DoubleD leaned in to inspect his eyes, which were blurred. The Verimax seemed to be working. The drug was effective, but tricky: too little and a man could evade the truth; too much and he died.

She recalled that Nchito's dossier said he was seventy-two, had led his tribe for three decades, his wife was deceased, he had three sons (two deceased), and had fought the Domain as one of Nkumah's sub-chiefs.

An honorable man, she admitted.

Not that it mattered. She'd take his life today; he was nothing but a tool to find Ray Brown.

"Chief, can you hear me?" DoubleD asked.

Nchito blinked, and then nodded. "I hear you."

"What do you see?"

He blinked again, trying to focus his eyes on DoubleD. "The Domain's Security Chief." He tried to spit at her, but his mouth was too dry from the Verimax, "My enemy."

This isn't going to be easy.

"Nchito, I have questions and I want you to answer truthfully and completely. Do you understand?"

"I understand."

"What's your name?"

"Nchito Daglowi." He shook his head, apparently trying to clear cobwebs. The drug was taking hold.

"How many sons do you have?"

He struggled not to answer, but the drug forced it out. "Three."

"Where is Muko?"

"Fighting the Domain." He struggled again, and then said, "I haven't seen him in weeks. Maybe your robots took his life."

Dammit.

DoubleD turned to Adams, "Give him a second dose." She stood to leave. "I'll be back in ten minutes."

When DoubleD returned, she dragged a sobbing young woman into the tent. The woman's cheeks were red and puffy. Nchito was lying on his back with his arms at his sides and his head braced by a rug that had been rolled to the thickness of a pillow. His eyes turned toward the girl; DoubleD wasn't sure he recognized his granddaughter.

A second dose was rough on anyone, let alone an old man, but she needed the truth. She just had to keep him alive long enough to answer her questions.

Leaning over him, she gently placed her fingertips on his chest. The old man's breathing was shallow. He was near the end, so she had to work quickly.

"Nchito, I'm back." She looked into his eyes, and then pulled the sobbing woman into his line of sight and pushed her down on her knees. Bending the captive's arm behind her back, DoubleD said, "Tell him your name."

The woman moaned as DoubleD increased the pressure on her arm. "It's Uvila, Grandfather."

DoubleD said, "I want you to answer my questions truthfully and completely, or I'll kill your granddaughter. Do you understand?"

The old man sighed, "Yes." He sounded beaten.

Grabbing her hair in one hand, she pulled Uvila to her feet, and then pushed the young woman, who was sobbing quietly, toward Adams. "Hold on to her.

"Where is Muko?" DoubleD asked the chief.

"He's traveling north."

"Why?"

"Two strangers came to our village asking to be guided to Nkumah."

"Who are these strangers?"

Tears ran down Nchito's' cheeks. "One is called Carlos, a soldier for hire. The other was an android."

DoubleD nodded. "Why do they seek Nkumah?"

"The android…is a weapon of some sort. They wouldn't say…anything more."

The old man coughed violently; blood dribbled in a thin red line from his nose. DoubleD knew he was almost gone.

She grabbed the sobbing woman by the arm and put a pistol to her head. "Where is Nkumah?" she asked Nchito. "The truth or she dies."

The chief's eyes closed briefly, then opened heavy-lidded, "The last we heard, he…was in…Salonga…National Park."

"That's a huge area, with an almost impenetrable rain forest."

The old man's eyes closed. DoubleD grabbed Uvila's hair and pushed her a few inches in front of Nchito's face. "Where in the forest?"

Nchito didn't respond.

DoubleD cursed and pushed Uvila away, knocking her backwards. The young woman tripped and fell heavily to the dirt. DoubleD shook Nchito's shoulders, once, then a second time. Nothing.

"Shit!"

She checked his pulse. The chief wouldn't be answering any more questions.

After ordering Adams to take Uvila back to the tribe, DoubleD hurried out of the tent. Hopefully, the Spybots would follow Carlos to Nkumah, and then Ray's hideout. Needing privacy, she rushed to an empty spot near the cave's entrance. After making sure no one was nearby, she lifted her wrist up to her mouth.

"Maximum security transmission, with voice distortion," she whispered. "Connect me to node five."

A moment later a masculine voice answered, "Yes?" The channel was secure, but they were taking no chances; their voices were electronically distorted.

"It's node four." She quickly summarized what the chief had told her.

"But you don't know what the android carries?" he asked.

"I'm sure it's a weapon, but I don't have any idea what David has created. He hates Dianne and he'll try to kill her, maybe bring down

Sentinel, too." DoubleD paused. "We'll track the android back to Ray, but I won't eliminate him until after he unleashes the weapon."

"It's risky. That weapon might destroy us along with Dianne."

"A chance we have to take," she replied.

"Okay. It's all coming to a head," Julius said. "If the weapon is powerful, Ray will initiate a world-wide attack when he uses the android. I'll get our army into position.

"Just be careful," he added, "Dianne has spies everywhere."

"Don't worry; I know what I'm doing."

"Call me when you find Ray."

The line went quiet.

Her work here was almost finished. She scanned the cave; everything seemed in place for the final act. Commando robots had herded the remaining members of the tribe against the far wall of the cave. She slowly walked over, not relishing what she had to do.

About eighty people had been captured, mostly women and children. There were a few elderly couples and a handful of young men. She spotted Uvila sitting with her back to the wall, her head buried in her arms. The captives huddled in a tight circle, resigned to their fate. A little boy began crying, and his mother picked him up and murmured in his ear.

DoubleD went to the edge of the group and said, "I'm sorry." The cave turned deathly quiet. Even the children stopped fussing, "You have five minutes to say final goodbyes." She shrugged. "Pray to your god if that helps."

She was tired of all the massacres. Soon she would put it all behind her; once they killed Morgan and drove out the Domain.

DoubleD turned away and began walking toward Nchito's tent. A woman screamed, "Murderer," but DoubleD didn't look back.

Adams was packing her equipment as DoubleD entered. The young officer nodded respectfully, but her face was pasty.

"Adams, go tell the guards near the cave entrance we're about ready to leave."

Adams reached into her pants pocket, "I'll call them—"

"No, walk out and tell them. Right now."

"Yes, ma'am."

DoubleD watched Adams disappear in the tunnel. She realized there was no point in delaying any longer, so she walked back to the captives. When she came into view, a teenage boy collapsed to his knees, but two other boys jerked him back to his feet.

She looked at her four Commando robots, which had their rifles pointed at the captives. They were just machines, programmed to follow orders. Everything was ready.

She stared at the tribe.

They were a beaten bunch, not a real warrior among them.

Mostly women with their children.

A few old men.

A teenage boy stood tall, but his shoulders quivered when she looked at him.

They were starving, frightened, helpless.

Waiting to be slaughtered like so many others.

It was senseless.

"Lower your weapons," she said. "Move out. Nkumah is north."

After a last glance at her captives, DoubleD followed her robots out of the cave.

***

Larissa stopped outside Brian's office to compose herself. She had thought through what she had to say, but wasn't sure how he would take the news. He loved her—she knew that—but they had only been romantic for a couple of weeks. It had all happened so fast.

She pushed open the door and looked into his office. "Anyone home?"

Brian looked up from his workstation and smiled. "Hello, you sexy little thing."

She prayed he would remain in such a good mood after he got the news. After strolling to his desk, she plopped down in the chair.

Chuckling, he said, "So graceful. It's one of the reasons you're irresistible."

She made a face at him. "What are you doing?"

He lifted his hands in confusion, palms up. "Duh, I'm preparing for class." He stared at her quizzically. "What's with you today?"

She sighed. "We need to talk." When concern spread across his face, she quickly added, "It's nothing bad, don't get worried."

Squirming in her seat, she said, "I guess there's nothing I can do but tell you straight out. I went to the college medical center today, just for a standard checkup. Got a big surprise." She paused. "I'm pregnant."

"*What?* But I thought you were taking precautions."

"I was." She shrugged. "I don't know what went wrong."

Brian pushed back his hair absentmindedly, "You're positive?"

She nodded. "A boy. Perfectly healthy according to the doctor."

"Wow." He leaned back, then forward. "How do you feel about it?"

"Shocked at first. In the Domain, girls my age don't get pregnant. My mother will go ballistic. But the more I think about it, the better I feel. There's a life growing in me. A perfect little boy. Our son."

They were silent a moment, and then Larissa said, "You don't seem too happy."

"No, no, don't think that; I would love to have a son." He seemed to be holding on to the desk for support. "I never thought I'd—we have to make some decisions: marriage, citizenship, religion. We've only talked in terms of possibilities so far. Now we—you, especially, have to make choices."

"I know." Her stomach was tied up in knots. "I'm in love with you, Brian."

He got to his feet, came around the desk, leaned over and kissed her passionately. She kissed him back, relief mixing with desire. Eventually, he pulled back from the kiss and said, "I want to spend the rest of my life with you."

It was all going well. She kissed him again and said, "I love you so much."

Brian looked down at her and smiled mischievously. "I am quite a catch."

Larissa screeched, "Yes, you are," and jumped on him, pushing him across the desk, books and papers flying in all directions, and kissed him again.

"Now don't hold back," he said, as her lips traveled up his neck, "You really have to learn to let go of your emotions." He glanced over her shoulder at the open door. "We should get up. If someone walks in, I'll have a difficult time explaining this is just the usual professor student conference."

"Well," she said, "I was going to ravish you, but I do have a certain reputation to maintain." She pushed off the desk, straightened her blouse and dropped back into the chair.

"Okay, so we're getting married and having a baby," he said as he stood up. He was red-faced, and his shirt was half out of his pants, "Whew! Things move fast around you." He stared at her in wonder.

"Looks like I got you *kinda* excited," she giggled. "Call in sick and let's go back to my apartment."

"Don't tempt me," he said, "but we need to talk about important matters." He tucked his shirt in and sat on the edge of the desk. "You know I'll never become a Domain citizen."

She nodded. "I know. I've been thinking seriously about that for the last couple weeks, and I've decided to renounce my Domain citizenship. I'd do it even if I weren't planning to spend my life with you. My mother's heart will break, but I can't live a lie. Technology is important, but the goal of merging people into some sort of robotic intelligence can't be humanity's future. I don't want to be a part of such a future."

"You're sure?"

She nodded.

He checked his watch, "My class doesn't begin for a couple of hours. We have time to do a little shopping. Maybe find an engagement ring."

Life is so wonderful, Larissa thought, holding Brian close.

***

Dianne leaned back in her leather chair and rubbed her eyes. A glance at the tall case clock in the corner told her it was almost two a.m. She was working late again in her office, three hundred feet below the surface. It was the one place she felt safe. Daniel androids and a few of her most loyal Elite Guards patrolled the hallways leading to her office.

She glanced across the room, where a three-dimensional hologram displayed the New York skyline. She might have to work underground, but she had her choice of scenery. New York had been her father's favorite place. An NYU graduate, he loved taking the family on trips to the City.

New York sparkled in the night, imitating the jewel it had once been. She was glad her father hadn't lived to see it deteriorate into a run-down fortress. Except for the Domain, civilization was sinking into a cesspool of its own making, and time was running out. Once she merged human and artificial intelligence, everything would improve. It was humanity's only chance.

I don't know why fate gave me this responsibility, but—

A voice from the Command Chip broke into her thoughts, "Steve Bonini to see you."

She wasn't expecting Steve, and she couldn't imagine why he was here. Nothing major going on, so why didn't he wait for a decent hour?

"Send him in."

To her left, a door slid open and Steve waddled in; he was putting on weight again. Steve was wearing a pinched-face look that warned bad news was coming.

He plopped down on a chair in front of her desk. "Dr. Chang called me earlier in the evening."

That was something new. They disliked each other. Why would Chang call Steve? When he didn't continue, Dianne said, "And?" Steve was her best friend, but he could be annoying.

"Chang told me all about your plans to get Larissa pregnant with Brian Brown's baby."

She was about to explode when Steve held up his open palms and said, "Cool down."

"That bastard had no—"

"Larissa's pregnant."

She stared at Steve, "Already?" It had only been a couple of weeks.

He nodded. "She went to the college physician for a required checkup and found out she was pregnant. They took a sample of DNA and discovered she would have a boy.

"Our agents broke into their medical office earlier this evening—still paper-based if you can believe that—and copied Larissa's file and took a portion of the DNA. They contacted Chang and he had the DNA analyzed. The baby will be a Master Communicator, similar to David and Martin."

It worked! Just like I planned it.

"You're probably wondering why Chang didn't come directly to you." Steve licked his lips. "Not all the news is good, and you'll have to make a difficult decision. Chang told me he didn't have the interpersonal skills to help you. Actually I think he's just a coward."

"Get to it." She felt a wave of nausea, but kept her eyes focused on Steve.

"Chang wasn't satisfied with the primitive tests performed at the college, so he ran Larissa's DNA through a full battery of our early pregnancy tests. They discovered the embryo is likely to develop a rare affliction called Childhood Alzheimer's."

Her stomach clenched, but she tried to remain calm. Steve looked sick, too.

"Before I go on, there's hope the baby may not contract the disease. Chang says about forty percent never experience any symptoms." Steve stalled, and then said, "But if Larissa's baby develops the disease, well, it's really bad."

He shifted in his seat. "The baby's first few years will be normal, but somewhere in the third or fourth year the brain begins to develop lesions. Then it gets real bad, similar to adult Alzheimer's: loss of mental acuity, physical deterioration, paralysis and then death, usually by age six." He sighed. "There's no cure."

"How can that be? We can prevent adult Alzheimer's through genetic manipulation. Why can't we do the same for children?"

"Part of the problem is that because Alzheimer's is so rare in children, Chang says we haven't studied it. The other problem is that it hits the kids so hard and fast, we don't have time to find all the defective genes and replace them. It doesn't usually hit adults until their forties or later, and it progresses slowly, so we can track down all the problems."

Her stomach was ready to explode. She got to her feet and told Steve to wait. She rushed over to the bathroom and made it to the toilet just in time. On her knees, she vomited into the bowl and then a moment later, vomited again. It stopped for a moment and she rested her forehead on the toilet lid. Her stomach retched one more time, but nothing came up. She waited a minute, then struggled to her feet, flushed the toilet, washed her face and tried to compose herself.

She walked back to the desk. Every problem has a solution, she said to herself.

"Are you all right?" Steve asked as she sat behind the desk. His complexion was pasty. Larissa and Steve were very close; she called him Uncle Steve.

Dianne nodded. "I'm okay. Tell me the rest."

"Childhood Alzheimer's is only found within inbred social groups." He shook his head. "Since Larissa and Brian have the same father, there's a good chance all their children could be afflicted."

"Oh my God." She slumped back in the chair and closed her eyes. Her stomach clenched again, but there was nothing left to vomit. What had she done to her child? She tried to keep it together, but her thoughts kept plunging down a well of despair. Steve came around the desk and took her in his arms. She buried her face in his chest and moaned. It was all her fault.

With an effort, she pulled herself together. She whispered to Steve that she was okay and sat back in her chair. She had to be strong. For her daughter.

"We're going to find a cure for this disease," she croaked. "I don't care what it takes. We have three years."

"Maybe."

"What do you mean?"

"Dianne," Steve said, "you should talk this over with Larissa." His voice sounded shaky. "She may want to end the pregnancy. And Brian is part of the decision, too. This disease—if they have another child, it could strike again. They have a right to know they're brother and sister."

"Steve," she said, slowly shaking her head. "I could never tell Larissa that Ray is her father. She'd never understand—"

"Dammit, you must have realized something like this could happen. There's a long history of birth defects caused by incest."

"I never thought it could happen to Larissa, since we have the ability to modify the genetic profile to correct just about any problem."

"Just about any problem!" Steve smashed his fist on the desk with uncharacteristic violence, and her head snapped back. "Listen to yourself. You've done a lot of harsh things to bring your dream to fruition, but this is your daughter. Stop thinking about yourself; you have to tell her everything."

"No! I won't tell her and you'll keep your mouth shut, too. We'll fix it. I'll put Chang and all our best researchers on this problem."

"That's not good enough." He rose to his feet. "Get some sleep. I'll ask the medical staff to prepare a sedative for you." He turned and walked away, palms dangling along the sides of his legs like a bird with broken wings. "I'll come back tomorrow. Get some sleep and we'll talk again."

Steve walked heavy-legged to the door, glanced back at her and left. Dianne's eyes drifted back to the hologram. New York was still there, sparkling in the night. The city that never sleeps. She wondered if Larissa and Brian might be in New York tonight, celebrating her pregnancy. Smiling and talking about the future.

"End hologram," she whispered, leaving her office in shadows.

TWENTY-SIX

Thursday, October 9, 2031

Dianne crossed her long legs and glanced at the tall case clock. Larissa would be here in a few minutes. A hologram message from her daughter this morning had said she was flying in for a quick visit.

Dianne knew Larissa was coming to break the news about the pregnancy, probably expecting a blowup. She was certain Larissa hadn't guessed this pregnancy was her plan all along. A good idea, but it had turned out badly. Now she had to fix it.

The subdued crackle of the fireplace was the only sound in her apartment. The fire was burning down and she thought about getting up and throwing on another log, but didn't have the energy.

What should I tell her? I always told myself I'd let her know about Ray someday.

But she couldn't do it. Larissa would never speak to her again, and that would end all the plans she had for her grandson.

Her eyes were drawn to a photograph on the coffee table. It was an old two-dimensional photo, encased in a silver frame, showing a celebration: the Atlas V6 release party. A banner on the wall read February 3, 2006. A young Dianne Morgan, her jet black hair pulled straight back, sat at a table surrounded by Ray and her original three partners: Steve Bonini, Carson Jones and Lester Dawson. Steve and Carson wore big smiles, while Lester just stared back at the camera. Steve was the only partner still alive; the others had been murdered in the PeaceMaker attack.

It was difficult to believe a quarter of a century had gone by. She picked up the frame to get a closer look. Ray was pouring champagne into her glass. He looked happy and a bit drunk, too.

Maybe it was the elation of the new release, or maybe her desire for him, but later that night, he had sneaked into her office and she allowed him to make love to her. Sometimes, when she was alone, memories of that first night inflamed her.

He was a wonderful lover, exciting and passionate. She recalled the lonely days after she broke it off, but what choice did he give her? He didn't understand that humanity was stumbling down a dark alley, with extinction the inevitable consequence. She had discovered the path to salvation, but he would never have accepted her solution. Pushing him away had been terribly difficult, but first things first.

In the photo, he appeared to be saying something to her, and she was smiling up at him, with her arm around his hip. She sighed. He had been the love of her life, but with a different set of values.

It just wasn't in the cards. Years later, she tried to win him back after the PeaceMaker fiasco, even seduced him, but he still wouldn't join the Domain. The stubborn bastard! She had sent him to the island, hoping he'd change. Now it was clear she should have killed him. But he *did* give her a wonderful daughter.

A voice came through the Command Chip. "Ms. Morgan, your daughter has arrived."

"Send her in, please."

With legs that felt half-dead, she got to her feet and shuffled toward the door. Larissa stepped into the room, an apprehensive look plastered across her face.

"Mom," she said and hugged Dianne, more tentative than joyous.

"Hi, honey," Dianne whispered, returning the hug.

Larissa stepped back and said, "How is everything?"

"Fine."

Her daughter appeared more mature, an adult. Pregnancy does that. As they walked slowly toward the center of the room, Dianne asked, "I understand the ethics class has been worthwhile?"

"Yes, it's given me new perspectives." Larissa glanced at the sofa and said, "Mom, let's sit down. There are some things we need to talk about."

Once they settled into the sofa, Larissa coughed and said, "As you know, the course was taught by Brian Brown."

Dianne nodded.

Larissa said, "I don't know how to break this gently to you, so I'll just say it. I'm in love with Brian and we plan to get married."

"Married!" *Steve hadn't said anything about marriage.* "You can't marry Ray Brown's son!"

"I love Brian."

"You're only nineteen, for heaven's sake. I'm not going to let you throw away your life."

"There's more, Mom." Larissa hesitated and then said, "I saw a doctor yesterday. I'm pregnant. Brian and I are going to have a son."

"A son?" Dianne pretended to be taken back by the news, "You're sure?" When Larissa nodded, Dianne said, "That's wonderful! Your child will get the best of everything the Domain offers, but Brian Brown would never fit in. He may be a good teacher and a charming man, but *you* can't marry him."

"I'm grown up. You can't tell me who I can or can't marry."

"I am telling you! I know about this Brian Brown. He hates the Domain. He is against everything you and I stand for. Don't you see that? He's trying to get back at me because I'm hunting his father."

When Larissa crossed her arms, Dianne said, "You're pregnant and you can have his baby, but marriage is out of the question. He's an anti-technology extremist with a grudge against me. The kind of person that hasn't accepted the modern world."

"Brian isn't like that at all. He's for the reasonable use of technology, but he's not in favor of this scheme of yours to merge artificial and human intelligence."

"This scheme of mine?" Dianne repeated. She rose from the sofa and stared down at her daughter. "You mean the ideal I've dedicated the last twenty-five years of my life. You think that's some kind of a scheme?"

"Mom, I didn't mean it that way. I know you believe deeply that you're doing the right thing. And I know that you want me to carry on with your dream, but—"

Dianne stared at Larissa. "Are you telling me that you agree with him?"

"I've been thinking about a lot of things. I didn't know how to approach you. I'm very uncomfortable with mixing human and robot intelligence. I'm afraid the human part will be lost."

"What has that bastard been saying about me?"

"Nothing," Larissa answered, an edge to her voice. "I've been thinking about this for a long time. That's the reason I decided to take the class—at least part of the reason. I was curious about meeting Ray Brown's son, I'll admit, and I wanted to get out of this gilded cage you've kept me in."

"I can't believe I'm hearing this," Dianne said. "Humanity is on the path to a new species whether you like it or not. You can be a leader—*the* leader after I'm gone—or you can be one of the losers who go out whining."

Larissa got to her feet. "These people aren't losers." Her eyes were angry, but her voice was still under control. "They're just like us, except they don't want to be turned into emotionless automatons. I want to remain human, too."

It required all Dianne's control not to slap her daughter. "I thought you were an exceptional child, but you're just another short-term thinker. You spread your legs for a man who'll stab you in the back, and you think that's love. I'm the only person who gives two shits about you, not that Neanderthal."

"I'm not listening to this," Larissa shouted, her cheeks flushed. "I'll call you when you regain your composure." She turned and walked toward the door.

"Larissa!" Dianne shouted, following a few steps behind. "Don't you dare walk away."

Larissa kept walking.

As her daughter pushed open the door, Dianne said, "Larissa, your baby will get Childhood Alzheimer's."

Larissa turned and stared. "What did you say?"

Dianne's voice was gentle, her anger gone, "Come back." She sighed, "There are things I have to tell you."

Larissa walked back, stopping a couple of feet from Dianne.

"You remember I told you security people would be around, not to spy, but to keep you safe." When Larissa nodded, Dianne said, "They followed you to your medical appointment yesterday. I was worried you might be ill, so I sent them back to the medical center last night. They copied your files and—"

"You already knew I was pregnant."

Dianne nodded.

"And that Brian and I were getting married!"

"No, I didn't know that."

"Damn you! What's wrong with my baby?"

"Dr. Chang says he may contract Childhood Alzheimer's, a rare but terrible disease." She cleared her throat, "The baby's first few years should be normal, but somewhere in the third or fourth year the disease might begin. Chang says about sixty percent of the children with this genetic profile get the disease." It broke her heart to watch Larissa's face crumble. "The symptoms are similar to adult Alzheimer's: memory loss, physical deterioration— you understand Alzheimer's— death usually comes by age six."

"Oh Mom, this can't be true."

Dianne embraced her daughter, who began to cry. Larissa's shoulders buckled with each sob, making Dianne feel helpless. She patted Larissa's back, but her stomach had clenched into a fist. She wanted desperately to strike out at something, but there was nothing to attack. Besides, she had to be strong for both of them.

Dianne led her daughter back to the sofa, where they sat with Larissa's head on her shoulder, just like when she was a little girl. Dianne noticed embers still glowed in the fireplace, and the pleasant scent of burned wood reached her.

Larissa's moan touched something deep inside, a place Dianne thought had burned out years ago. She hadn't meant to cause her daughter such misery. Again, she thought about confessing, but quickly reaffirmed that would only make matters worse. She could never let Larissa learn that Brian was her brother. The truth would ruin everything, she knew. Her daughter's tears gradually diminished, but her face remained buried in Dianne's shoulder. She'd do whatever was needed to save her grandson. But first, Larissa had to make the right decision. And she had to believe it was her decision.

Dianne said, "You have to make a choice. Not right now, but soon; you have to decide what's best for this child."

Larissa lifted her head and stared at her mother; then understanding came into her eyes. "I'm having this baby, and he's going to live through this."

Exactly.

"Honey, we'll do everything we can. Chang is starting a maximum research effort."

"All right," Larissa mumbled, staring across the room at the wall, tears sliding down her cheeks.

Things were starting to fall into place. Larissa seemed in control, and she wanted to raise the baby. All good, but Brian Brown had infected her with his Neanderthal ideas. Just like his father. I need to dispense with that whole troublesome family, once and for all.

"It's Brian, isn't it?" Dianne said. "I've read his dossier. The idea of genetic manipulation isn't going to sit well with him."

Larissa stood up and glared at her mother. "That's my problem, not yours." She strode to the door, turned and asked, "Is that all of it?"

"I'm so sorry about all this," Dianne answered.

Larissa barked, "You just get Chang working on a treatment." Then she was out the door.

The room was silent, except for the clicking of a tall case clock.

She'll get over it, Dianne thought, once she understands that Brian is not for her. I'll make everything work out.

***

A big fly buzzed around his head as Carlos walked through the dense brush. It was a bloodsucker, looking for soft skin. To his displeasure, Carlos had discovered that these bugs ignored insect repellent. They seemed to treat it as garnish for a tasty bite of human flesh.

He kept one eye on Muko's back and the other on the fly as he pushed his way between two huge trees. Arthur was directly behind him, sloshing across the swampy forest.

Muko was leading them through the Likouala swamps to Lake Tele, a shallow, mysterious lake in the heart of the Congo. Three days earlier, Pigmies had told Muko that Nkumah had a camp on the other side of the lake, but Carlos wasn't sure they could be trusted.

Traveling was slow across the swamp forest. The canopy of tall trees filtered the afternoon sun, leaving the muddy trail in shadows. He had already tripped several times on tree roots hidden in muddy water. A broken leg in this fly infested swamp could be fatal.

The swamp forest was remote and nearly impenetrable, preventing the growth of a modern civilization. The few tribes inhabiting the area hunted with spears and poison darts much as their ancestors had thousands of years ago. It was a good place to hide.

The shit I put up with to earn a peso!

Arthur's voice came over his shoulder. "Carlos!"

He turned around and grumbled, "What is it now?"

"It's my battery; I'm down to fifteen percent."

"Are you telling me you have to stop again?"

The android pointed to a small clearing on the left. "I can get direct sunlight today for at least three more hours. I'll conserve power tonight and be ready to go in the morning."

"Son of a bitch! I know five-year-olds who can cover more ground than you."

Muko walked up to him. "What's the problem?"

"Little Missy Arthur needs a nap," Carlos said to him.

After the robot explained the situation, Muko said, "We can't afford to stop. Nkumah moves all over the continent. He might break camp tonight. If we don't find him now, it could be weeks before we pick up his trail again."

Carlos thought for a moment and said, "You keep going and I'll baby-sit Sleeping Beauty. I'll pick up your trail in the morning; the ground is muddy and I know the direction you're heading. Just leave something for us to follow—cut an X into a tree or bush every hundred yards or so."

Muko nodded. "If, when I find Nkumah, we'll come back along the same trail and get you."

"An excellent plan," Arthur said.

"Shut up," Carlos snapped.

Carlos had decided the android was a complete pain in the ass. He still got mad when he remembered how the damn thing had blown his only chance to get laid. Sentinel hadn't told him that he was signing on to the priesthood when he took this job.

He watched Muko walk down the trail and disappear into the swamp. He didn't envy a man alone in this jungle, but Muko was an expert hunter and tracker. His rifle could bring down anything, if he got a shot off.

Carlos shook his head, but he was probably better off here. The robot was annoying, but its enhanced senses could spot a predator before it got within striking range.

He suddenly realized that the robot wasn't standing next to him. He spotted Arthur walking away and hurried to catch up. The robot headed to the middle of the clearing and then reclined in the direct sunlight. Carlos guessed it was about 2 p.m., so the robot should be able to get its batteries charged pretty well for tomorrow.

There was nothing he could do now, so he leaned back against a tree and closed his eyes. The damn thermoflex coat was hot, but it had to stay on all the time. Something landed on his neck, and he swatted it.

He checked his hand, which was covered in black goop, and rubbed it off in the mud, "*Gotcha,* you bastard."

He tried to get a quick nap, and thoughts of bare breasted African women filled his mind. They were lining up outside his tent, waiting to service him. After he finished this job and collected his ten million, he'd get a big hotel room, hire a dozen *putas,* and screw himself into exhaustion.

He was beginning to drift off, when he saw the robot scramble to its feet. Arthur was staring down the trail, concentrating intensely.

"What is it?" Carlos asked as he stood up.

Arthur listened for a moment and then bolted down the trail. Carlos didn't know what was going on, but he took off after the robot. Arthur was running at top speed, knocking branches out of the way and splattering mud with its strides. Carlos could run faster than the robot, but he was falling behind because of the thick brush.

Sweat poured off his skin. A sound drifted on the wind, faint at first, then growing louder. He was uneasy, then terrified. It was a man's high pitched screams!

A thorn bush ripped across his forehead, but he didn't slow down. The intensity of the screams increased, then abruptly ceased.

Carlos broke through the thick brush into a broad clearing. The sight in front of him made his stomach clench, and he almost threw up. Arthur was running toward a huge python, more than thirty feet long, thrashing around trying to swallow something. Human legs were sticking out of the snake's jaws, flopping about as the snake shook its prey.

It was Muko!

Carlos considered his laser pistol, but he didn't dare shoot with so many of the Domain's Condors in the sky. Running up to the snake, Arthur grabbed its jaws and tried to pull them apart. The snake's body coiled around the robot and squeezed, but Arthur slowly pulled open the jaws, revealing hundreds of sharp, hooked teeth. Inside the jaws, blood and digestive fluid were smeared across Muko's chest. There was a bulge behind the snake's jaws in the shape of a man's head.

A guttural wheeze came from the snake, like a man snoring. Then Carlos realized that the monster was trying to force Muko deeper into its jaws.

"Pull him out!" Arthur shouted to Carlos.

Carlos pushed back his fear and ran toward Muko's feet, being careful to keep away from the python's thrashing coils. He grabbed the exposed feet, then braced himself in the slippery mud and pulled as hard as he could. The man's chest slowly slid out of the snake's jaws.

Before Carlos knew what hit him, the snake had swung its tail around his chest and dug its two sharp tail hooks into his side. He screamed in pain, and then the coil squeezed down and crushed all the air out of his chest. He reached for his laser, but it was buried under the snake's coil.

Through watery eyes he stared at Arthur, who was straining to hold open the python's jaws. Then another coil wrapped around Arthur's head, and Carlos lost sight of the android.

The python's coil twisted abruptly and Carlos was driven face down into the mud. After struggling to his knees, he rubbed his sleeve across his eyes to clear his vision. He was beginning to feel lightheaded and his ribs were bending inward, but he was able to reach down with his left hand and pull a knife out of his belt. He drove the knife into the snake, but he barely broke through the python's tough skin.

The pain from his ribs was excruciating, and he knew time was running out. He grabbed the knife handle with both hands and plunged it into the snake with all his remaining strength. This time, blood bubbled out of the wound and the snake's crushing power slackened.

Gasping for air, he pulled the knife out and again drove it deep into the snake. The coils jerked violently, unwrapped and then dropped off. He reached for his laser, but the pistol had been ripped away during the struggle.

Stabbing the tail wouldn't kill the monster; he had to get near the head. A sudden spasm in his side made him double over, warning him of internal injuries. It didn't matter; he was determined to kill the snake.

But he had underestimated the enemy. The snake's tail swept around again and whacked him across the side of his face. Everything faded from view, leaving him in a dark world. He could hear bodies struggling in the mud, but he couldn't see them.

He forced his eyes open, but everything was out of focus. Grasping ahead blindly, he touched the ridge of a tree root and pulled himself forward a few inches. Something long and sharp in the mud scratched his chest. He found the handle of his knife, and then turned in the direction of the struggle. A fuzzy outline of the android, still holding open the snake's jaws, began to sharpen.

Dragging the knife through the mud, Carlos crawled on hands and knees to where Arthur battled the python. Its jaws gaped open, and, up close, the rows of sharp teeth were terrifying. He got to one knee, lifted the knife with both hands, and tried to stab it behind the head, but it was jerking back and forth and his knife slid off the tough skin.

Arthur was having a difficult time maintaining his hold. One hand slipped off and the snake's jaws again closed down on Muko.

"My batteries are almost dead," Arthur shouted.

Carlos marshaled his strength and then plunged the knife into the snake's body, and this time it went all the way through. The snake was still thrashing about, but more slowly now. He sawed across the coil until the blade had cut the snake's body almost in half. Blood and internal fluids from the wound soaked his hands. The snake had one last convulsion and then collapsed.

Carlos dropped to his knees and tried to catch his breath. Arthur pulled the dead snake's jaws away from Muko, but there was no sign of life. The android slapped Muko across the back to stimulate breathing, but it didn't work. Pushing past the android, Carlos tried mouth to mouth respiration, but there was no response.

Arthur released Muko's body, which slid to the ground. The man was covered in saliva, with his face and torso pocketed with snake bites. He wasn't bleeding, a bad sign. Arthur put its ear to Muko's chest, searching for a heartbeat, but Carlos knew the man was dead. After a moment, the android pulled its face up, looked at Carlos and shook its head.

Although he wasn't religious, Carlos made the sign of the cross. That poor soul had died a terrible death.

Arthur lumbered away from the snake and stretched out in the sun, desperate to recharge its batteries. For once, the android was quiet. Carlos was beginning to catch his breath, but his exhausted body couldn't move. Pain raced through his ribs with every breath, but he didn't believe anything was broken.

He tried to think. Without Muko, their chances of finding Nkumah didn't look good. Even if they stumbled across Nkumah, his warriors would probably assume a man traveling with a robot was an enemy. They would snuff out his life in an instant.

He considered turning back, but Sentinel had warned him that the android was programmed to kill him. Destroying Arthur wasn't a solution. He had no illusions that he could survive alone in this jungle. Muko, who had known this land much better than he, had proved that.

Tomorrow morning they had to move out. If they continued in the direction Muko had been traveling, they should reach Lake Tele by nightfall. That's if the android's batteries regained enough power.

Although his breathing was still ragged, the pain in his ribs began to fade. He sat up and studied the android. It looked okay, but it might have been damaged in the struggle. Arthur might be a pain in the ass, but the android was good in a pinch.

Anything was possible as long as they were alive. Once they reached the lake, they had to travel around its circumference and somehow find Nkumah's camp, which could be deep in the forest. If they were lucky, maybe they'd finally catch up to him.

Of course, the Domain might kill them first.

TWENTY-SEVEN

Friday, October 10, 2031

Carlos felt a hand shaking his shoulder, but it was too early to rise.

"Later, Maria," Carlos mumbled. "We'll do it again later."

"Carlos, I think you should get up," said a familiar, irritating voice.

He rolled over onto his back. It was the damn android again. He closed his eyes and tried to sink back into his dream. Maria's hands were slipping under his belt...

"Wake up, someone's here."

Carlos blinked his eyes and tried to focus on the figure kneeling above him. Arthur seemed concerned about something. Suddenly alarmed, he sat up and said, "What's wrong?"

The android seemed puzzled by the question. "I'm not sure there's anything wrong. It may be a positive development."

"So why the hell are you waking me up in the middle of the night?"

"Although I respect your need for six to eight hours of sleep per night, I thought it prudent to alert you that we're surrounded by approximately thirteen strangers."

"Son of a bitch!" He bolted upright and pulled out his laser. His ribs hurt like hell, and he peered into the early morning shadows, but he didn't see anyone. The swamp was quiet. "You're sure people are out there?" he asked Arthur.

A voice came from the brush, "Don't you trust the android?"

Although he had not seen the man in years, Carlos recognized the gravelly voice, "About as much as you do, Nkumah."

A warrior stepped out of the brush and smiled, reminding Carlos of a cat that had just found a mouse. Nkumah was still imposing—several inches over six feet tall, angular with long, rope-like muscles in his neck that couldn't be hidden by a thermoflex jacket—but he had aged more than the six years that had passed. The lines in his face and the flecks of grey in his hair had not been there when they took Ray off the island. But the man's eyes were still the same: dark, deep-set, hard.

"What brings you back to Africa, my friend?" Nkumah asked.

Although they had worked together to rescue Ray Brown, they were hardly friends. Nkumah knew that Carlos sold himself to the highest bidder, whether it was outlaw or saint. The next few minutes would determine the outcome of his assignment.

And his life.

"I bring you a great opportunity," Carlos said.

"Hopefully, better than your friend over there." He gestured to the dead body next to the python.

"Muko was a good man," Carlos said. "He guided us across the swamp."

"Chief Nchito's son?"

When Carlos nodded, Nkumah said, "Too bad. A brave warrior, I'm told." He shook his head. "Why have you and your robot searched for me?"

"My client claims that this robot has been loaded with software that will tip the balance of power from the Domain to the rebellion. Bluntly speaking, this software will enable you to defeat Morgan."

When Nkumah didn't respond, Carlos quickly scanned the brush. He knew Nkumah had warriors out there, but he didn't see anyone.

"The software was designed by David Brown," Carlos continued. "Only his father can use it. My client told me that David has included a personal message that explains the software." He paused and said, "My client is reliable and I believe everything I've said."

"Tell me the name of your client."

"You know I can't do that."

Nkumah grunted, and then walked to Muko's body. He knelt down and studied the dead man's mangled face, now covered with a swarm of buzzing flies. "An appalling death." He shook his head sadly, and then looked at Carlos. "But there are even worse ways to die."

He stood up, keeping his eyes on Carlos. "Do you want to change any part of your story?"

Carlos recognized the threat; Nkumah was a harsh man, and torture *was* a possibility. Maybe a probability. Carlos had known the risks when he accepted the job. If he was going to die, he'd go out on his terms.

"I don't lie," he said, "unless it's to my advantage."

Nkumah smiled with only his lips, but Carlos had a sense that Nkumah believed him. Anyway, the African warlord was no fool; he must realize the remaining tribes were on the edge of extinction. The rebellion was almost over.

Nkumah walked over to the android and asked, "Where's your power button."

"I can assure you that I'm no threat," Arthur said.

"The button," Nkumah repeated.

Arthur raised his left hand above his head, revealing a small, flesh-colored button under his arm. Nkumah pushed it, and Arthur dropped his arms and froze.

"Kamali!" Nkumah shouted.

A thin young man, at six feet, short by local standards, holding a wallet-sized computer, came from the brush and strode toward the war chief. As he passed, Kamali spat a thick gob of phlegm near Carlos that splattered across the toe of his boot.

"The robot neither received nor transmitted any messages," Kamali said. He stared at Carlos with pure hatred.

Carlos didn't think he had ever seen Kamali before, but there was no mistaking that look. He kept his temper under control, but decided to watch this man carefully. If necessary, he'd kill Kamali before he left this camp.

Carlos felt Nkumah's eyes bore into him for a moment, and then the warrior turned to Kamali. "Examine the robot thoroughly for weapons or communications capabilities, while I chat with my old friend."

Kamali nodded and walked toward the deactivated android.

As he led Carlos toward a small clearing, Nkumah said, "While Kamali was away last year fighting the Domain, his tribe was massacred by Daniel androids. As far as we know, he's the only one of his tribe remaining alive. You can understand why he would hate anyone who travels with an android."

Carlos said nothing.

Nkumah led him into the center of the clearing. Carlos knew this wasn't going to be a friendly conversation; he doubted the man had any real friends.

Just like me.

Nkumah stared, sizing him up. "I'm surprised that you accepted such a dangerous assignment. Someone must be paying you a great deal of money. Greed was always your weakness." Nkumah turned his head and spit into the grass, then wiped his mouth with his sleeve. "You have balls. Very few men could evade the Domain's robots and cross Africa. The odds were against your survival." He grunted. "They still are."

Nkumah turned his back to Carlos and stared into the dawn. A foot-long blade dangled from his belt. Nkumah briefly watched the morning light filter through the canopy of trees, and then turned back to Carlos. "How is it that the Domain has killed hundreds of thousands of my warriors, men who grew up in this land, and yet you survive?"

"How was it," Carlos replied, holding Nkumah's gaze, "that I was able to find Ray Brown's island, when nobody else could?"

"You're a man with certain talents, I'll concede. And in your own way, an honorable man, within limits. I need to understand those limits."

"You have my undivided attention."

"Tell me the whole story," Nkumah said. "Start from the point you learned about the android and take me up to the moment you heard my voice in the brush. Don't leave out anything, no matter how insignificant."

"When my story is complete and I've answered all your questions, will you reactivate my android?"

"If I believe your story, *and* if I believe the android can strike the Domain a lethal blow, I'll welcome back the android. And, as an extra bonus, I won't kill you. But if you lie to me, I'll give you to Kamali. He has this little trick where he cuts a hole in your side and pulls out your intestines, inch by inch. Is that not fair?"

"Not only fair," Carlos said, "the wisdom of Solomon."

He smiled bravely at Nkumah, although he felt like he might wet himself.

"Thank you, my friend." Nkumah moved his lips into what passed for a smile. "Now strip off your clothes."

Carlos knew the search would be thorough. He wasn't surprised, but he didn't like exposing his body to mosquitoes and, worse yet, those big bloodsucking flies. As Carlos removed his clothes, Nkumah said, "You've put on a little weight."

"The years have been good."

Nkumah searched his clothes, and then examined every inch of his body. It wasn't pleasant.

"Put on your clothes and begin your story."

Carlos described how he had met the android, leaving out his client's name. He decided it was also prudent to omit Sentinel's threat to kill him if he refused the assignment. Other than that, he told the whole truth.

Carlos interrupted his story when Kamali, now holding a machete in his right hand, strode up to Nkumah and whispered in his ear. Nkumah thought for a moment and replied in a language Carlos didn't understand. Kamali nodded and circled behind Carlos. He imagined he could feel the man's eyes on his back. A signal from Nkumah and that killer would slice him open.

Nkumah questioned him closely about Nchito and his tribe. It became clear to Carlos that communications between Nkumah and his allies were infrequent because of the ever-increasing intensity of Domain surveillance. He also noticed that Nkumah seemed distressed when he learned that Nchito's tribe had so few warriors.

Nkumah's mood improved as he questioned Carlos about the android. Carlos swore the robot wasn't a trap to expose Ray Brown's location. He bluntly told Nkumah such a trap was unnecessary; the rebellion was literally dying out. He didn't have any idea what the android carried, but its weapon was Nkumah's last chance.

Nkumah turned to Kamali. "We're breaking camp. Make sure the men are ready to go at my command." He paused for a moment, staring at Muko's body. "Give him a proper burial."

After slipping the machete into a scabbard, Kamali gripped Muko's legs and dragged away the body. The flies buzzed angrily when the body was disturbed, and a cloud of insects followed it across the clearing.

Nkumah walked over to Arthur and stared at the android. Pure hatred. Nkumah's emotions were never far from the surface, Carlos recalled.

Finally, Nkumah pressed the activation button. The android's eyes snapped open, but it remained still. After a final dark glance at Carlos, Nkumah returned to his men.

Carlos's back was covered in sweat. This wasn't the Africa he remembered. It was a slaughterhouse, where hatred had overwhelmed reason, and allies were as dangerous as enemies. Once he got his money, he'd go underground in South America, where nobody would ever find him.

His legs ached, so he sat in the damp soil. It was too late to get some sleep, especially with a killer like Kamali nearby. Light seeped through the trees, and he spotted a pack of chimps in the distance. He leaned back against the hard bark of a tree and silently thanked the gods he had survived to see the dawn.

***

As the sun cleared the treetops, Nkumah began the trek toward Lake Tele. The tropical forest turned into a swamp, with water gradually rising to their ankles. Staying directly behind Nkumah, Carlos strode through the muddy water. His feet were sore, but the pain was tolerable. Arthur was a couple yards behind, followed by a single line of warriors. Carlos tried to locate Kamali, but the man had disappeared.

The trees thinned out, enabling a glistening sun to dominate a wide, blue sky. The dark water now covered his knees, and it became difficult to avoid tripping on bunched-up tree roots below the surface. The whiplash of underwater branches reddened his shins, and he worried about leeches. Sweat flowed down his forehead as he kept up with Nkumah's relentless pace.

And then there were the insects: spiders as big as his fist, long lines of blind ants killing everything in their path, and, of course the big black flies. Even more annoying were the swarms of sweat bees. Although they don't sting, the bees covered his body sucking up moisture. At first, they drove him crazy, but as time passed, he learned to tolerate them.

The swamp water absorbed the sun's heat and evaporated, with the hot mist steaming his flesh. Hours passed in ever-increasing agony. There were no breaks, no rest periods, no relief, just the relentless warrior ahead.

It was late afternoon when Carlos first noticed sunlight glinting off a broad expanse of water. A lake was hidden behind a thick row of trees, and he realized they had reached their goal. A moment later, he stood next to Nkumah, staring across the dark waters of a majestic lake.

Lake Tele appeared to be two or three miles across; he could barely make out the shoreline on the other side. After so much time in the swamp forest, it felt strange to stand below a massive open sky. In the distance, an eagle soared above the water, searching for fish that were foolish enough to swim near the surface. Every game had winners and losers.

Few outsiders had traveled to this lake, which had remained virtually unchanged for millions of years.

"It's magnificent," he said to Nkumah.

After a cold meal of mixed vegetables, they boarded long canoes that had been hidden underneath trees bending over the shoreline. Carlos sat in the center, Nkumah in the front, while a warrior in the rear paddled powerfully.

Lake Tele was mysterious. Carlos had heard legends about giant crocodiles, monitor lizards that hunt men, and even a huge dinosaur that had survived over the ages. However, they made it to the other side without incident and hiked into the swamp forest.

After traveling about an hour, they came to a small camp—maybe two dozen tents—hidden under the forest canopy.

"Cuff him," Nkumah ordered and then entered the largest tent.

His arms were pulled roughly behind his back, his wrists handcuffed and then he was securely tied to a tree. A warrior deactivated Arthur. Three heavily-armed guards stayed nearby, and they didn't look friendly. Carlos spotted Kamali at the far end of the clearing, leaning against a tree, watching him. He began to worry that he might have misjudged Nkumah's intentions.

A few minutes passed and then Nkumah emerged from the tent, followed by two white men dressed in t-shirts and jeans, with the ever-present thermoflex coats hanging from their shoulders. Even here, deep in the swamp forest, the Domain's robots searched for human thermal profiles. Although his hair and beard had turned grey, and he wore clothes that had once fitted a heavier man, Carlos recognized Ray Brown. Furrows dominated Brown's broad forehead, carved out by the claws of time. A quick glimpse told him the other man was Paul Martino.

Ten million dollars American! I have delivered that miserable android to Ray Brown, just as Sentinel had asked. I'll do nothing but eat, drink, gamble and screw for years.

"Remove his handcuffs," Ray ordered a guard.

Carlos was quickly untied from the tree and his handcuffs taken off. As he rubbed feeling back into his wrists, Arthur was activated.

Ray stepped up to Carlos and, to his surprise, embraced him. Ray's beard felt like a wire brush and he stunk of sweat and disease.

This gringo better not die before I collect my money.

"It's good to see you again," Ray croaked in his ear. "I'd still be on the island except for you."

As Carlos looked over Ray's shoulder, he noted that Martino seemed suspicious. Arms folded across his chest, Nkumah stood next to Martino.

Ray stepped back, and Carlos asked, "Are you ill?"

"Malaria." Ray shrugged. "I've had it for years. We don't have the Domain's medicine."

"I'm sorry to hear that. There are still a few quinine pills in my backpack."

"Keep them. It's not so bad anymore. Makes me sick for a few days, that's all."

"As you wish." *He's healthy enough.* Carlos nodded toward Arthur, "The android has a message from your son."

"I know," Ray replied, turning toward Arthur. "What the..."

With a strange expression on his face, a mixture of sadness and confusion, Ray stared at the android, "Arthur, pull your right pants leg above your knee."

Carlos was mystified, and wondered if malaria had damaged Ray's mind. Arthur complied and Ray bent down to examine the robot's knee. For the first time, Carlos noticed the android had a small scar on its knee.

When he stood up, Ray said to Nkumah, "It's authentic. My son designed this robot."

"David told me you'd look for that scar," Arthur said.

Ray turned to Carlos. "A boyhood accident left a tiny scar on my father's knee. When David noticed it one summer at a family picnic, I explained that Grandpa had cut himself playing football. Nobody outside the family knows about that scar."

Then Ray said to the android, "Come with me."

Ray led Arthur to his tent, with Martino close behind. When Carlos tried to follow Martino, Nkumah grabbed his elbow, "Not you," he said. "Your work is complete. My men will take you to a tent where you'll stay until we verify the android's weapon."

As the warriors led him away, Carlos saw Nkumah turn and step into the tent. *Do what you want, but first make Arthur signal Sentinel to transfer the money.*

***

Ray entered the tent, then waited for the android. He knew the Domain could easily build an android in his father's image, but now he was certain Arthur was not one of theirs. Childhood memories bubbled to the surface. His father had been a good man: highly intelligent and caring. Unfortunately, he had traveled through life in the shadow of a domineering wife.

Ray had inherited his technical brilliance from his father. He remembered long evenings sitting next to his father, learning how to use the latest computers. He wished that he had inherited more of his father's warmth; he had too much of his mother's darkness.

Paul cleared his throat, bringing Ray back to the present. *Isn't it strange that the man who rescued me from the island is here to save me again?* Carlos was a soldier of fortune, by reputation ready to do any job if the money was right. Somehow, though, the man always wound up opposing the Domain, and it wasn't just the luck of the draw. Carlos lived by a code of honor, even though he didn't look the part.

Ray knew his friends weren't quite so sure Carlos could be trusted. Paul stared dubiously at the android, while Nkumah's hatred for anything with artificial intelligence simmered just below the surface.

A small folding table had been placed in the center of the tent. Ray felt woozy and sat down. Paul and Nkumah took seats around the table, while the robot stood a few feet away.

He was acutely aware the tent was a mess. Books and correspondence were scattered around the back of the tent, along with a bowl of half-eaten vegetables. His sleeping bag was covered with yesterday's clothes. He had meant to clean up this morning, but hadn't found the strength.

Paul was watching him closely. "You want a cup of water?"

Ray shook his head. "I'm fine." He said to Arthur, "Let's get started."

"May I see your palm, please?" Arthur asked.

Ray lifted his right hand to allow the robot to verify his identity.

"Thank you, Mr. Brown."

A life-size holographic image of his son David appeared next to the android. Wearing khakis and a pull-over shirt, David stood with his thumbs hooked in his front pockets. Ray stared at him; he hadn't seen or spoken to his son in nine years. David was a virtual prisoner of the Domain, balancing on a razor's edge, alive only as long as that witch saw value in him.

Now thirty years old, David looked closer to forty. Grey streaks ran through his thick brown hair, and dark circles spread under his eyes. Ray sighed. Life was eating away at his son; he needed a real father, not a distant figure he barely knew.

"Dad, I'm glad Arthur found you. I hope you're feeling well, and if Mr. Martino is there, I wish him good health, too. As you've surely realized, this is a recorded message, not a live transmission. Much of what I have to say is personal, so you might want to ask any guests to leave for a moment." Shrugging, David added, "It's up to you."

Paul began to stand up, but Ray signaled him to stay. Nkumah never moved.

"Last week, I visited Grandma in her nursing home in Friday Harbor. She suffered a stroke about eight years ago. Her mental alertness is almost gone, and she sits alone in her wheelchair all day. Brian and I are her only visitors, and we don't get up to Friday Harbor very often. Sometimes I wish she had passed away in her little cabin —"

David ran his fingers through his hair, and then continued, "She still has moments of lucidity, although most of the time she doesn't know what's going on. She thinks Grandpa is still alive, and she confuses me with you. I modeled Arthur based upon my memories of Grandpa, and I instructed it to take care of Grandma after the war is resolved. Arthur will play the role of her husband for whatever time she has left. He'll be a comfort to her."

Ray sighed. It wasn't fair that his children were stuck with the responsibility for their grandmother; he should be the one there for her.

Folding his arms across his chest, David said, "You may have heard that Kathy died in childbirth six years ago."

"Damn," Paul whispered.

Ray had hoped David and Kathy were happily married; he hadn't known she had passed away. He leaned forward in his chair and stared down at the table. She was the best thing that had ever happened to his son, and she was gone, too.

The last he'd heard—the one time Dianne had allowed David to see him on the island—David and Kathy were planning marriage. He hadn't heard anything since then. Leading the fight against the Domain and trying to stay alive, that had been his life. Only at night, when the forest was quiet, had memories of his former life returned.

Kathy had been his recruiting assistant at VantagePoint Software two decades ago, long before she met David. He remembered a pretty young lady with a great sense of humor. Even though Ray was much older, they had become friends.

"She was a wonderful woman, better than I deserved," David said, his face hardening. "I thought we'd play with our grandchildren."

Ray knew that look, and he knew what it cost.

"Dianne Morgan took her from me," David said. "As we went through the Domain's in vitro fertilization process, that bitch substituted her eggs for my Kathy's. My sperm fertilized Dianne's eggs, with the embryo implanted in Kathy's uterus. We never knew…"

David paused a moment. "You could see there was something wrong with my son Martin from the start. I tried my best to be a good father, but I never had any real love for him. I'm not proud of that; he's not responsible for Dianne's crimes." David shrugged. "I can't change what happened or how I feel. Whatever love I had to give died along with my Kathy."

Ray's hatred for Dianne had simmered for years, but he could never focus it. When he was honest with himself, he admitted a perverted sense of passion for her. A long time ago, they had been lovers. Some aspect of her had infected his soul, like a cancer barely kept at bay. Now his son's despair soaked into his consciousness, stoking his hatred, and his shame. Ray knew it was his fault; he should have killed her all those years ago, but his passion had been too intense. He still wasn't sure he could do it.

"Martin has inherited my ability to communicate with artificial intelligence," David continued, "but he's ruthless and dishonest, just like her. Once I discovered that Dianne was his mother, I couldn't stand the sight of him. We don't have any relationship now, and I've learned that he lives with Dianne. They deserve each other." He paused again, stiffly shaking his head. "Dad, I remember you warned me not to have children. Martin has become an evil person, and I don't know where all this will lead, but I fear the worst."

Ray glanced at Nkumah, who was listening intently. Over the years, he'd come to admire the man, but Nkumah had once warned him that David was a threat. Nkumah hated artificial intelligence, believed that it was humanity's main enemy. Any man who merged with an AI, such as David, was a traitor. Now his grandson fit into that category, too.

Ray stared into David's hologram. If he had to kill Nkumah to save his son, so be it. He'd turned that corner years earlier.

David said, "I'm sorry to load you down with all this, but you have a right to know. Brian has grown into a good man and become a professor at Princeton. He's the best of our bloodline. For some reason, Larissa Morgan enrolled in one of his classes. Brian told me they have fallen in love, Larissa's pregnant and they're getting married. I see the witch's hand in all this; she has ways to manipulate people that ordinary humans can't begin to understand. I've warned Brian that something's wrong, but he won't listen. Larissa seems to really love Brian, but she carries Dianne's genes, so I can't imagine anything except a bad ending."

Ray shook his head. Both sons had fathered a child carrying his enemy's bloodline.

"That's the end of the personal stuff. The main thing now is to stop Dianne, and Arthur carries a weapon that should tip the balance in your favor. The Domain's military power lies with advanced technology, particularly their intelligent robots. In addition to Condors and Commandos, I include the millions of Daniel androids used by people across the globe. Contrary to the Domain's assurances, Dianne can turn these harmless-looking androids into killers. If the Domain ordered all the domestic androids in US households to attack their owners, the carnage would be horrific. This is one of the main reasons the US government has been paralyzed.

"Safety code in each robot prevents them from attacking Domain citizens, but allows them to attack other humans. This safety code is their most closely guarded secret; only Dianne, Mohammed Kateel and Steve Bonini have access. However, with Sentinel's assistance, I've developed an enhancement pack that prevents the robots from attacking anyone, even if they're not Domain citizens."

Ray was startled when Nkumah slammed his palm into the table. Hatred had penetrated the dark mask that usually concealed the warrior chief's emotions. But hatred for who?

"Without the robots," David continued, "the Domain's power is greatly reduced. Arthur will transmit the enhancement pack across the net whenever you request. All Dianne's robots, including the Daniels, will be neutralized.

"Through Sentinel, the Domain controls the world-wide net, which means it could shut down the economies of developed countries. The PeaceMaker virus demonstrated that all developed societies are dependent upon computer communications and control. By shutting down the Internet, Dianne could bring any nation to its knees.

"However, the situation has changed. Sentinel controls the net, and I control Sentinel. I'm confident we can block any attempt to shut down the computers.

"That will leave only her human soldiers. You should be able to handle them."

David again ran his fingers through his hair. "Dad, you decide when to activate the weapon. Downloading the safety code enhancements pack to every robot is a time-consuming process. My calculations indicate that we can update ninety-nine percent of their robots in three hours, so take that into consideration when making your plans.

"I advise you to activate the weapon as soon as possible. Mohammed Kateel knows I've made unauthorized modifications to Sentinel, so at some point, his engineers might be able to reverse what I've done.

"Dad, you're our last chance to stop the witch and eliminate the Domain. I don't have to tell you what she'll do if she wins. Either we'll breathe the fresh air of a liberated planet, or we'll be dead.

"Arthur can answer any questions, although it's really pretty simple." He paused for a moment. "Good luck. Whatever happens, Dad, I love you."

The hologram disappeared and Ray stared through the vacated space. He rubbed suddenly moist eyes with the tips of his fingers. It didn't help. He turned and looked first at Paul, and then Nkumah. "I think this is it," Ray croaked. "What do you think?"

"I have a question for the android," Nkumah said. "Will your weapon pacify all the robots, regardless of who controls them?"

"What are you getting at?" Paul asked Nkumah.

"I have a mole in Dkembe's tribe. Dkembe has been secretly building robots for more than a year. He has thousands of them stockpiled under his estate, ready to rebel against Morgan."

"You bastard," Paul spat out.

"When were you planning on telling us?" Ray asked. "After they slaughtered our warriors?"

"Our forces are all but defeated," Nkumah said. "I had planned to salvage our remaining warriors and bide our time. Let Dkembe launch his attack on Morgan. They would decimate each other, and then we would attack whoever was left.

"I couldn't tell anyone. Morgan has spies everywhere; the risk of disclosure was too great."

Nkumah turned to Arthur. "I ask you once again, will your weapon work against all the robots?"

Arthur looked at Ray, who nodded.

"Once a robot is activated, the software will load across the net and pacify it. As long as Dkembe's robots are based upon the corresponding Domain technology, the software will work as intended."

"Then we must attack," Nkumah roared. "Without the robots, we can free Africa from the Domain. Our warriors will swamp their human army. I'll send Dkembe to hell, along with his whore and their son."

"When did you become a Christian?" Paul asked.

"I'm not, but there's nothing worse than the Christians' hell. Let Dkembe's soul be damned, burning in agony to the end of time."

"There's more to this war than Africa," Paul said. "Even without robots, Dianne has a strong security force in America. Our cells in the U.S. are good for ambushing small groups, but we can't take the Domain head on. We'll need help, and a lot of it."

"The federal government would like nothing better than to eliminate the Domain, but they fear the Domain's robot army." Ray said. "Once we show them the robots have been pacified, they'll help us take out the Domain's security force."

"You hope," Paul replied, "Let's face it; nobody is going to mistake the President for John Wayne."

"Are you saying that we shouldn't use this weapon?" Nkumah asked.

Paul stalled for a moment. "No, I'm not saying that. We may get our butts kicked, but we'll never have a better chance than this."

"So we're agreed?" Ray asked. When both men nodded, he said to Arthur, "Activate the weapon tomorrow at 5 pm eastern time." He turned to Nkumah, "Your warriors should attack three hours after the weapon is activated."

"Why 5 pm?" Paul asked.

"You forget?" Nkumah said to Paul. "PeaceMaker was released at 5 pm eastern; we complete the terrible cycle." He nodded to Ray. "I've dreamed about this moment for years, but I never thought your son would be the deciding factor."

"It's too soon to take a victory lap," Paul said, "Dianne isn't going to fold up and go away. She always has secrets."

"We'll be ready for her," Ray replied. "This time we'll kill the queen bitch."

***

Larissa was pacing across her living room when the front bell rang. It must be Brian. He had flown in with her from San Francisco this morning, and they had plans to go to dinner, but that was before she'd seen her mother. It was a darker world now. She had to give him the awful news; if only there was a way to soften the blow.

Out of habit, she checked her image in the hallway mirror. Her pants and blouse were wrinkled from the flight. She should have changed, but she had been reading everything in the database Mom had provided about Childhood Alzheimer's. It was depressing how little the scientists knew.

When she opened the door, Brian greeted her with a smile and a warm kiss. Although she tried to respond, she was emotionally drained. Brian broke off the kiss and stared quizzically.

"Come on in," she said.

"Tough visit with your mother?"

"Sit with me." She led him to the sofa and sat down stiffly. Brian took a seat next to her, concern shading his eyes.

"Remember you told me we had to make decisions?" she asked. When he nodded, she said, "Well, there's a tough one here already."

How could this be happening to us?

Nausea hit hard, and she looked away. She was glad they were sitting.

"Whatever it is," Brian said, his voice strained, "we'll face it together."

She stared at him, trying to form the words. An antique grandfather clock in the corner ticked off the seconds. It was time to talk, to share this pain. Brian was a good man. He'd understand what they had to do.

Starting hesitantly, but gaining control of her voice, she explained Childhood Alzheimer's. She was blunt with the diagnosis, but made it clear there was hope. Even so, she knew her words were terrible, punishing, a vise crushing his dreams. As she spoke, his gaze seemed to flicker. Or was that her reflection in his eyes?

"This terrible disease, it might pass him by," she said again. "My mother says that forty percent never have a symptom. She also promised me that she would have their best scientists work for a cure. "

"Larissa, are they sure he has the genes? One hundred percent sure?"

She nodded. "They're sure."

"What if the disease hits him? Sixty percent get it. It takes children just when they're old enough to understand." He closed his eyes and shook his head. "It's unspeakable."

"This disease is not going to take our son," Larissa replied.

"Don't give me that," he flared. He reached out and touched her arm, but his hand felt clammy. "I'm sorry. It's not your fault; it's not anyone's fault, but we can't rely on false promises."

They were quiet for a minute, and then Brian again said, "I'm sorry."

The shock had thrown him off, but she'd help him handle it. The years ahead would be difficult. She put her head on his shoulder and tried to think of something encouraging. It was all so horrible. When his lips caressed her hair, she began to weep. Then she felt him shudder, and she knew he was crying, too.

She heard Brian say, "We can't let this happen." He lifted his head and stared down into her eyes. "We can't take a chance."

That didn't sound right to her, and she sat up.

"My Aunt Claire suffers with Alzheimer's," he said. "She's in a nursing home in Oakland." He pushed on slowly, "When I lived in San Francisco, David used to drive me to Oakland for a visit two or three times a month. Sometimes Kathy came, too, mostly to support David." He shrugged. "Anyway, one day a couple years back it was just David and me. We were there early because Aunt Claire was usually more clear-headed in the morning.

"So we walk into the room. Aunt Claire's in her wheelchair, like always, and she gives David a big smile and a hug. Then she asks David *who's the handsome young man with you?* David didn't get it at first, but I knew right away she didn't recognize me. Then he gets it and tells her that I'm his brother, but you could see it didn't register. She looks at me and tears begin to roll down her cheeks. She says to me, *I'm so sorry, but I don't remember you. I* try to comfort her, but she says, *It's all leaving me. I just can't think. My brain doesn't work right."*

He sighed. "After that, David had to introduce me every time we visited her. It was so depressing; she always cried. She knew her mind was drifting away." Brian shrugged, the way he did sometimes when he didn't have the right words. "Then one day she didn't remember David, either."

Brian's eyes were red, but he wasn't crying. "I don't want to hear our son say he can't remember."

"I won't let that happen. I promise."

"Don't you get it; nothing ever turns out right for my family. He'll get the disease and die a little every day."

She shook her head. "No, that's not going to happen."

"Are you blind?" he asked. "Can't you see my bloodline is screwed up? I warned you! David's wife died giving birth to a monster, and now this."

"Our child will live," Larissa insisted. "We can beat this disease. There's nothing wrong with your bloodline or mine either."

Brian grabbed her shoulders, hurting her. "This pregnancy— there's something very wrong with it. I love you, and I want to share my life with you, but we shouldn't have any children."

"Brian," she moaned. "I'm not going to kill our baby."

"It's an embryo, not a baby." He stood up. "That disease… I couldn't take it."

"I can't believe you're saying this." She rose to her feet and pulled away from him. "I don't know you at all."

"We can adopt," he begged. "We'll make it work."

"No, we'll have our own babies."

"I can't pass along a death sentence to my children," he said.

"But it's all right to kill your son?"

"He won't suffer."

"Get out," she shouted.

"Don't you understand?" he croaked. "Kathy died giving life to a terrible child."

She shook her head, but couldn't find the right words.

He began to say something, but she interrupted, "Please go."

Brian didn't move, just stared at her. He was normally fair-skinned, but now his face had turned pasty. He was someone different, someone she hadn't seen before. She could smell his fear. Then he turned his back on her and hurried out the door.

He was really leaving her.

She walked over to the window and watched him climb into his car and pull out of the driveway.

There was no one she could trust.

But whatever happened, she wasn't giving up on her son.

***

DoubleD pulled down the zipper of her combat suit, exposing the firm, white skin below her collarbone. She unsnapped a bullet-shaped cylinder from her belt, pressed the head against the exposed skin and pushed her thumb against the flat end. Micro needles penetrated her flesh and pumped in combat adrenalin, which would enhance her strength, speed and reflexes for the next three hours and then gradually wear off. She would be at her combat peak.

As she pulled up the zipper, DoubleD watched the faceless Spybot stride silently toward her through the mud on padded feet. Four feet tall, with spindly metallic arms and legs, the brown and green robot blended into the swamp forest. Tiny pinpricks across its head and torso, each containing a micro camera, enabled the robot to see in all directions simultaneously.

When the Spybot reached her, DoubleD said, "Status."

A flap on the robot's forehead slid open, revealing a small, transparent rectangle. It glowed blue, and then projected a two-foot square hologram containing a camp with about a couple dozen tents, surrounded by dense forest. A brief shower had just ended, but billowing clouds still smothered the sky. Another Spybot hidden closer to the village was transmitting the images of Ray's camp.

The Spybot next to DoubleD spoke in a precise female voice through an amplifier in its chest, "The transmission is from a human camp located approximately point eight miles northwest. Ray Brown, Paul Martino, Nkumah Muserre and the Arthur android are in the large tent near the center of the camp."

In the hologram, Ray's tent briefly glowed orange, making it easy to identify.

"They interrogated the man known as Carlos," the Spybot continued, "and then placed him in the tent highlighted in red. (A tent on the extreme right of the hologram flashed red.) Twenty-two soldiers are in camp, including six stationed as guards (the six guards glowed yellow momentarily) and three sentries hidden in the forest (three locations were highlighted on a satellite map of the area, which was displayed next to the hologram)."

"Were you able to overhear any conversations?" she asked, while performing a final check of her laser pistol. Like a violinist before a concert, she tuned the frequency ratios to tighten the radius of the beam. Domain equipment employed self-correcting code, but she preferred to rely upon her own judgment.

"No, for security reasons we maintained a safe distance."

DoubleD studied the hologram. "Weaponry?"

"Laser pistols and automatic rifles."

She felt her body responding to the shot of adrenalin. Her muscles seemed to strengthen, although she knew the internal changes were more subtle. Nevertheless, she felt that she could lift a car.

"Computer transmissions?"

"One data burst, approximately nine minutes earlier."

That might be the weapon built into Arthur, transmitting data.

"Analysis of the data burst?" she asked.

"Nothing to report yet. All information has been sent to the Operations Center for analysis."

"Disengage all sensors," she commanded. "All the Spybots, except you and the one transmitting the hologram from the camp, are to cease operation until further notice."

After ordering the Spybot to deactivate its hearing, DoubleD lifted her watch to her mouth. "Maximum security transmission, with voice distortion," she said. "Connect me to node five."

An electronically distorted masculine voice answered, "Node five."

"Node four, transmitting from near Ray Brown's camp."

She summarized the situation.

"Everything depends upon Ray's weapon," he replied. "If it doesn't deliver a devastating blow to Morgan's army, she'll overwhelm our forces."

"David hates Dianne. He'll make sure—hold it." She stared at the hologram. "There's something going on—warriors are leaving the camp—it's Nkumah."

"Nkumah is leading warriors out of Ray's camp?"

"Yes." She thought for a moment, and then it hit her. "They must be initiating an attack. They've activated the weapon and started their offensive."

"Nkumah will be coming here," the male voice said. "Finally we'll settle this."

She counted the men leaving with Nkumah. "Ray has only the android and seven soldiers plus the three sentries in the forest. We'll attack in one hour. That should allow Nkumah plenty of time to leave the area."

"Be careful."

"Of course. I'll make my way back to you after Ray has been eliminated." She paused, then said, "I love you," and ended the transmission.

Her troops— one human soldier and four Commando robots—were waiting in the brush about a half a mile from Ray's camp. She crept over and gathered them in a tight semi-circle around her. "We attack at 6 pm," she told them, keeping her voice low. After outlining the situation, she said to a short, muscular man, "Sergeant, you take one robot and eliminate the sentries. The others will come with me."

Circling the camp, DoubleD carefully positioned two Commandos to catch her enemies in a crossfire. She studied the layout of the camp and identified the tents containing Brown, Martino and Carlos, her primary targets. Her rule was to always be better prepared than the enemy. She crept around to the camp entrance, keeping one robot to watch her back. She spotted the android standing by itself in a patch of bright sunlight, apparently recharging. A single tribesman was on guard; the remaining half-dozen were pulling down tents and preparing for departure. They were vulnerable. It was almost too easy.

She checked her watch; twenty minutes had passed. Once she eliminated Ray and his crew, she'd shut down all the robots and destroy them. Unfortunately, she'd have to kill the sergeant, too. Too bad, but soldiers died in war.

If things went well, Ray Brown's army and the Domain would virtually wipe each other out. Julius's army would finish off any remnants, leaving them the rulers of Africa. Never again would she have to kowtow to Dianne Morgan or anyone else. She thought about the wealth they'd have. Julius would be the ruler, but she'd be the power behind the throne. Under their leadership, Africa would become the most powerful force on the planet.

As 6 pm approached, she gave the Commandos their final orders through her watch. "When I say go, I want you to terminate all enemy soldiers."

"Refused. Illegal command," a robot replied through a speaker in its chest.

Stunned, she stared up at this killing machine. It must have misunderstood.

"At exactly 6 pm," she said to the robot, "shoot and kill one of the enemy soldiers in the camp. After that, attack the remaining soldiers until they're all dead."

"Refused. Illegal command."

Shit.

"Exactly which part of my command is illegal?"

"Domain safety code does not allow a robot to harm a human."

"That's incorrect," DoubleD said. "You're not allowed to harm a Domain citizen. You may harm humans not holding Domain citizenship. Now obey my order."

"Refused. Illegal command."

"Perform an audit of your safety code."

"Completed. No problems identified."

What the hell is going wrong! Then she realized it had to be Arthur's weapon. The android must be transmitting a revised safety code to all the Domain's robots. So clever. The new code prohibited the robots from harming any humans, not just Domain citizens. All the Domain's robots were harmless, including her own.

She had to warn her husband, but first Ray Brown had to be eliminated. Killing him would be more dangerous without the robots. Still, she had a laser and the element of surprise. That would be sufficient. It had to be.

A shot rang out from the forest, galvanizing her into action. Firing a broad swath with her laser rifle, she took out the android and three rebels before they reached cover. She fired the laser at the main tent, which burst into flames, and then turned the laser on Carlos's tent, hoping to catch him before he escaped.

Flames spread through the camp, but several of Ray's men returned fire. Suicidal, she thought, against her laser. She quickly roasted the remaining soldiers.

The screams of a troupe of chimps came from deep in the forest, but she ignored them. She had to make sure Ray was dead, so she crept up to the camp, using the brush for cover. Her green and brown uniform made her almost invisible. The sergeant hadn't called in, so she had to assume the worst.

She turned her artificial hearing up to maximum and focused it on the enemy's camp. Her enhanced hearing detected someone breathing irregularly, and she crept into the camp looking for the soldier. Smoke rising from the tents limited her sight to about twenty feet, but her hearing led her to a badly burned soldier lying behind the main tent. A quick flash of the laser put him out of his misery.

The enemy soldiers were dead, but the main targets, Ray Brown and Paul Martino, were missing. They might have been killed, but she had to be sure.

She stood up, turning her head from left to right, listening for anything suspicious. She detected a tiny scraping sound, then the rustle of steps through dead leaves. Someone was sneaking into the forest. She homed in on the sound and crept toward it.

***

Startled by the hiss of a laser, Carlos scrambled out of the tent a moment before it went up in flames. He fled across the clearing, keeping the burning tent between himself and the most probable line of sight of the attackers, and then dove behind a big thorn bush.

Breathing hard, he watched several tents burn. The roasted bodies of soldiers were scattered about the camp. *Poor bastards.* It was just dumb luck that Nkumah had sent him away from the main tent. Even with that, he had barely escaped. His arm bled from a deep scratch inflicted by the thorn bush, but he was still breathing.

The white flash of a laser again came from the same location outside the camp, about fifty yards away, and another tent burst into flames. Screaming in agony, a man tumbled out of the tent, clothes burning. Another flash and his charcoal body crumbled to the ground.

The bastards.

Then it was quiet, except for the hiss of rapidly spreading flames. It didn't appear anyone was still alive. Dense smoke drifted across the camp and into the forest.

If they kill Ray before he activates the weapon, goodbye ten million.

Carlos considered fleeing into the forest. He might save his skin for the moment, but the enemy could probably track him down. Especially those damn Commandos; they can run all day on a single charge. Anyway, all he had left in his account was a measly million. He'd go through that in less than a year.

The laser flashed from the same spot again, and it dawned on him that only a single enemy soldier had caused all the damage. One asshole wasn't going to cheat him out of his money. Too many *senoritas* were waiting.

He spotted a rifle on the ground next to the remains of a soldier's body, but he couldn't retrieve it while the enemy was nearby. Patience. He had to wait for his chance.

Peering through a thick thorn bush, Carlos studied the area where the laser had flashed. Several minutes passed, and he began to worry the enemy might be creeping toward his location. The movement of a branch caught his eye. The Domain soldier crept from behind a tree and stalked toward the camp, moving through billowing smoke. The killer's form-fitting uniform hugged a distinctly feminine body.

Where are the Commandos? Why aren't robots attacking?

When the soldier reached the edge of the clearing, she sprinted into the camp and took cover behind a burned-out tent. Blond hair tumbled out from her helmet, spreading down her neck. A profile of the woman's face peeked around the tent.

Hijo de puta!

It's DoubleD.

She crept toward the main tent, which was still burning, and stepped past a blackened body. DoubleD stalked like a leopard, scanning for prey with each step. Although she was deadly, her grace and physical perfection captivated him. He'd kill her if he could, but what a waste.

A movement behind the tent caught his attention, and Carlos spotted a man slipping into the forest; it was a white man, but he couldn't tell if it was Ray or Paul. The man hobbled badly; his right leg was badly blistered below the knee. Luckily, several smoldering tents blocked DoubleD's line of sight.

The man crept through the forest, but DoubleD lifted her head and looked in his direction. Carlos didn't think she had seen the man, but she slinked past the tents to the spot where the man had been a moment earlier. *How the hell did she do that?* After one last look at the camp, DoubleD followed the man into the forest.

Was it Ray? Had he activated the weapon?

Carlos realized he had to stop DoubleD. He couldn't take a chance that Ray hadn't activated Arthur's weapon. The odds of his survival weren't good—DoubleD was a master with a laser—but what the hell, he never figured on living to old age.

He crept over to the dead soldier and grabbed the rifle. He was in luck; it was a powerful Beretta express. His stomach turned queasy when he saw close up the soldier's remains. The man's face had been charred black, leaving a Halloween mask, and the stench of burned meat made him gag.

Holding back nausea, he ran across the clearing and into the forest, and then paused to scan the trail ahead. Nothing. If he moved now, he could be walking into a trap. He wondered if DoubleD had a robot covering her back. In her place, he would.

Suddenly a burst of excited chatter came from chimpanzees deeper in the forest. He peeked through a bush and spotted a pack of agitated chimps high in a tree about a hundred yards ahead. Something had spooked them, maybe DoubleD or the man she stalked.

He circled to the right, staying away from the chimps. He'd be a dead man if they warned DoubleD he was coming. She was an assassin with a laser; he'd get off one shot, tops, if he was careful and very lucky.

Thorn bushes tore at his hands as he pushed them aside. Another scratch didn't matter now. The underbrush restricted his vision, but he kept his eyes on the chimpanzees. The pack had calmed down, but they remained focused on a point about twenty yards from the base of their tree. Someone was there, but who?

It seemed likely that both DoubleD and the white man were nearby. She was the hunter, but she had to be careful since the man was probably armed. He must be hiding, waiting in ambush. Carlos had to get behind DoubleD and take her out while her concentration was elsewhere. It was a three-way cat and mouse.

Carlos moved in a slow semi-circle away from the chimpanzees, staying low. All his senses were alert, but the brush was thick, and he worried that he could be on top of her before he knew it.

He paused at the edge of a small clearing. Actually, it was a section of swamp without trees or brush, just tall grass growing through muddy water. Limited visibility, a perfect place for an ambush. The chimps hadn't spotted him; they were looking at the other side of the clearing. He strained to see through the grass, but nothing moved. Sweat dripped into his eyes, but he didn't dare wipe it. The first person who made a mistake would die.

Minutes dragged by. Patience, he thought. DoubleD has to make the first move.

Then he heard footsteps along the path. At first, the footsteps seemed to be coming directly toward him, but then they drifted to the left. Peering through the brush, he saw the outline of a Commando robot. Hopefully, the thing wouldn't spot him.

This could be the break he needed. Slowly, he moved his rifle into shooting position. He lined up the sights on the robot, which walked past him, about thirty feet away. The robot stopped at the edge of the clearing, as if waiting for someone. DoubleD had to be nearby, but Carlos didn't see her. Then he spotted a bit of blond hair. This was it. He pulled the trigger, letting loose a bullet that could bring down an elephant.

There was a splash of red, and the thud of something crashing into the mud. *I hit her, but is she dead?* The robot bent down, possibly to examine her wound, but Carlos didn't see her. He let loose another shot, but it just bounced off the Commando's plating. He was about to run, when he realized the robot hadn't made a hostile move. The damn thing ignored him.

Then he realized that Arthur's weapon must have been activated. The robot hadn't been involved in the attack on the camp, DoubleD had been alone. It must be that Arthur's weapon had neutralized the robots.

Carlos crept toward the robot, but the blond hair had disappeared. He thought he had killed her, but he wasn't taking chances with DoubleD. And he didn't know the location of the man she had followed. Lots of soldiers have been killed by friendly fire.

Keeping the gun pointed at a spot just in front of the robot, Carlos listened for any sound that indicated DoubleD was still alive. The chimpanzees were chattering in the distance, but they were probably just nervous from the gunfire. Then the robot stood up and began walking back toward the camp.

If DoubleD were wounded, the robot would have carried her to safety. She must be dead, he told himself. Or it could be a trap.

Doubling back, he slowly worked his way toward DoubleD's location from the other side of the clearing. The chimps spotted him and complained noisily.

Great.

He crept silently, keeping his rifle aimed at the bush where he had last seen her. He halted and listened. Nothing, except the chimps. After creeping another twenty feet, he spotted her laser pistol in the mud. The barrel was dented, apparently from his shot. The grass near the laser was speckled red. His rifle bullet must have ricocheted off the pistol and wounded her.

One footprint was outlined in the mud, but her trail disappeared in the tall grass. He didn't hear or see her, but she couldn't be too far ahead. Not with a bullet slowing her down. He began to move forward, one quiet step at a time.

She was a wounded predator, doubly dangerous.

Another fleck of red on the tall grass.

The swamp water was now up to his hip. He tried to move quietly, but shallow waves rippled through the muddy water.

A body suddenly exploded out of the dark water at his side and a powerful arm wrapped around his neck. Carlos lost his grip on the Beretta and the rifle splashed into the water, and then he was dragged under the surface.

DoubleD was on his back, pushing him down into the mud, choking him. He tried to pull her arm from around his neck, but she was too strong. His hands dug into the mud and he pushed up with all the strength in his arms and legs, finally lifting his head above the water.

Carlos rammed her head with his elbow once, twice but he couldn't knock her off his back. Then DoubleD's powerful legs wrapped around his torso, crushing his ribs. Her left arm dangled uselessly, but her right had his neck locked in a terrible choke hold. He elbowed her again, but his strength was fading.

He felt his ribs bend, driving out the little air remaining in his lungs. She poured on the pressure; his eyes blurred and his knees buckled. Something hard poked his side.

His knife!

He tried to pull his knife out of the sheath strapped to his hip, but his fingers were too stiff. Forcing his fingers around the handle, he finally pulled the knife free. Gripping the handle with both hands, he drove the blade into her thigh, and she screamed. The choke hold loosened and he shook her off his back. She fell backward and disappeared under the muddy water, except for the knife sticking out of her thigh, releasing a stream of blood. His wobbly legs almost collapsed, but he staggered toward the knife.

Covered in mud, DoubleD got to her knees and tried to pull the knife out of her leg, but Carlos fell on her and pushed her head underwater. She fought to get to the surface, her eyes wide open, glaring at him through the muddy water. His hands were around her throat, holding her thrashing head below the surface.

Suddenly, the heel of her hand flashed through the surface and rammed into his chin. Carlos saw stars but desperately kept her pinned below the surface, one hand on her throat, the other holding her wrist so she couldn't hit him again.

He felt her strength diminish. Blood swirled in the muddy water. She struggled, but he pushed her face deeper under the water. His knees straddled her, holding her throbbing body in a wet embrace.

Then it was over. Her struggles ended, and a few bubbles broke the surface. He held her under until DoubleD's body reflected the gentle rhythm of the swamp, nothing more. Now he was sure she was dead. Holding on to her wrist, he pulled her body to the edge of the clearing.

Breathing hard, Carlos sat back on his heels and studied her face. Pasty white cheeks, bruised neck, clear blue eyes. This woman had led the slaughter of millions in Africa and around the world, but she looked serene, as if life had left her deeply fulfilled. He made the sign of the cross. People said she was a loving mother and a faithful wife. No one was completely evil.

He jumped when a man stood up on the other side of the clearing.

"Thank you, Carlos," Ray said, a pistol hanging loosely in his hand. "She would have killed me."

"The robots," Carlos said, "they're harmless now?"

Ray nodded.

"We should get out of here," Carlos mumbled.

"Not yet."

Ray limped across the clearing and stared down at the body. He seemed dazed.

"We tried to assassinate her many times over the years." He touched her shoulder with his boot.

Watching Ray closely, Carlos said, "We should pack up and head for the coast."

"Yeah, let's get back to the camp. Did you see Paul?" he asked in a thin voice. "He left our tent to get supplies just before the attack."

Shaking his head, Carlos said, "It didn't look like there were any survivors."

"There aren't any, thanks to you," an angry voice called out.

Carlos barely knew Kamali, but he recognized the man's voice. Diving to the side just as a rifle sputtered, Carlos hit the ground and rolled, but a bullet singed his shoulder.

A second shot rang out as Carlos scrambled behind a tree.

When he looked around the tree trunk, Kamali was lying in a pool of blood.

Carlos turned his gaze back to Ray, who was standing with his pistol pointed at Kamali. Ray lowered his weapon and began to hobble toward the camp. Carlos called out to thank him, but Ray didn't seem to hear.

Carlos checked his shoulder; it was a minor flesh wound. Ray was almost out of sight, so Carlos ran after him.

He caught up to Ray near the camp. The stench of burned flesh almost made him retch.

Ray kept hobbling forward, favoring his burned leg.

As they entered the clearing, Carlos looked across the camp. Scattered tents were still smoldering, releasing wispy trails of black smoke. Charred bodies were scattered across the ground, with flies buzzing over the cooked flesh. It was a little slice of hell.

Ray called out for Martino every few feet, but there was no response.

He followed Ray along the perimeter until they reached the remnants of a large, rectangular tent. The canvas had burned away, except for a few tattered strips. Thatched baskets were scattered in disarray, the contents burned. This must have been where they stored supplies. Nothing could have survived.

"Paul!" Ray called out again.

A weak soprano voice came from the brush, "Ray?"

"Paul, where are you?" Ray shouted.

"Over here."

Ray followed Paul's voice across the clearing and into the woods, with Carlos close behind. They found Paul sitting in the mud, his back against a tree. Carlos felt his stomach clench as they approached Paul.

Ugly red burns covered his face and chest, but his legs were worse. A dusty black, they had the look of charcoal. Carlos wondered why the man wasn't screaming, but maybe he was beyond pain.

Ray stared at Paul's legs, and then lifted his eyes. "My god," he whispered.

"The tent burst into flame. Got my legs real bad." Paul seemed to be having a tough time forming the words. "I dragged myself here."

Ray snapped out of his trance, "We can still save you, but we'll have to amputate your legs."

Paul shook his head. "Maybe you could do it in a hospital, but not out here." He shrugged. "I'd bleed to death or die of infection."

Ray pulled his knife from its sheath. "I'm not going to let you die. We'll tie up your legs with our belts."

"It's not your fault, Ray," Paul said. "It's just my time."

Ray dropped to his knees, looked over his shoulder at Carlos and said, "Give me your belt." When Carlos didn't move, he pleaded, "I need you to hold him down. I'm going to save him."

Carlos put his hand on Paul's forehead; he was burning with fever. Shaking his head, Carlos said to Paul, "I'm sorry, *amigo*."

"Help me," Ray begged Carlos. "Please."

"Ray, I knew the risks when we escaped from the island," Paul said. "It's a miracle we made it this far." He leaned back against the tree and closed his eyes.

"Paul?" Ray said, but there was no response. Ray's face seemed to age, and then he said to Paul, "Listen to me. Arthur's weapon made the robots harmless." He stared at his friend. "We can win, but I need you with me."

Paul's breathing weakened, and Carlos knew death was near. It was for the best; a man shouldn't linger without his legs. When it was his turn, he hoped the gods would spare him from such a death.

Ray pulled Paul into his arms. Carlos knew that he should leave the camp, just in case more enemies were coming. Arthur had activated its weapon, so he was ten million dollars richer. There was no reason to stay, but he told himself a few minutes wouldn't matter.

Time stretched out and Ray continued to hold Paul. Carlos was surprised when the dying man's eyes fluttered open. Paul blinked and then said to Ray, "You're still here?"

Ray mumbled, "It's not fair. It should have been me."

"I'm not arguing," Paul said, his voice a whisper.

"Damn it, Paul, you've always been there."

"Don't get… all sentimental on me," Paul wheezed.

"You've been my best friend for thirty years. If I want to get sentimental, I will."

Carlos found himself envying the two men. He saw the love between them was strong, tempered by years of shared hardship. Even now, they enjoyed each other's company. He had always been alone, without a true friend. It's the way things had worked out, but at least he now had plenty of money. And there was always a game.

"I have one last favor to ask," Paul said.

"Anything."

"You're going to bury me here, right?"

"Yeah," Ray mumbled, a puzzled look on his face. Then, in a much stronger voice, he said, "Did you think I was going to carry you out of the jungle on my back?"

"Actually, I want two favors."

"Why don't I get you a pad and pencil so you can make a list."

"Don't get smart, it doesn't work for you. Here's what I want: Mark my grave with a cross and… write something nice about me. Something religious, if you can manage it."

"You haven't stepped into a church in twenty years, but if that's what you want, I'll come up with something."

"Thanks," Paul said. "Don't try anything too deep— that's beyond you. And especially nothing funny." He squinted at Ray. "You never were that funny, you know."

Ray licked his lips. "Jesus, you're a pain in the ass. What's the second favor?"

Paul's eyes closed for a moment, and then opened lazily. "After the war, assuming you're still alive, ship my body… back to San Francisco. Those were…the best years of my life. I may still have a few friends there."

"Okay," Ray mumbled.

Paul stared at Ray for a long moment, "It's what…we were meant to do."

Ray nodded. "I'll finish it, Paul. I promise."

Paul drifted off, still in Ray's arms. Carlos sat in the dirt and waited quietly. In a few minutes, it was over.

Carlos stood up. "I'll start digging a grave. The ground is soft, it won't take long."

Still holding his friend, Ray nodded but didn't speak.

***

Sweating profusely, Ray stared at the freshly dug grave, and then smoothed out the damp soil with his boot. He had prayed for the soul of his great friend; there was nothing more he could do.

The grave was about a quarter mile from the camp, with a makeshift wooden cross cut from a nearby tree.

Paul Albert Martino
May 9, 1970— October 10, 2031
Thank you, Lord, for this good man.

They had wrapped Paul in the tattered canvas of a tent and placed him in the ground only a few minutes earlier. Carlos had left Ray alone, saying he had to pack up a few things for the long trek to the coast.

He had met Paul thirty years ago, when Paul was a technology reporter for a local newspaper— the name wouldn't come— and he was a professor at Carnegie Mellon. Paul had interviewed him about his artificial intelligence research and the two of them had hit it off. Paul was a terrific reporter; his website always had the best technology articles.

Paul was the person he turned to when he investigated PeaceMaker. They stopped the virus, but Dianne imprisoned them on the island. Thirteen years and Paul never complained. Another six years in Africa, fighting Dianne again. He had turned Paul's life upside down. And now his friend rested in a shallow grave in the Congo.

Carlos's voice came from behind, "Ray, it's time to leave."

He stared at the cross. Then, with help from Carlos, Ray scattered brush over the grave, hiding the cross. He stepped back to inspect it.

"Nobody will find it, *amigo*."

Ray nodded, "I know a peaceful spot near San Francisco, Paul."

Then he turned to Carlos, "Let's go."

TWENTY-EIGHT

Saturday, October 11, 2031

Larissa pulled back the sheet, lifted her head off the pillow, and tried to clear the fog from her mind. She blinked and looked out the window of her third-floor apartment. A streetlight glowed on the corner, projecting hazy yellow stripes between the half-opened blinds. Slowly her mind cleared, and she realized someone was shaking her shoulder.

"Ms. Morgan, please wake up," a persistent voice said.

It was Melody, a personal android designed to simulate a college-age woman. Melody flipped on a bedside lamp, bathing the bedroom in soft light.

"Please forgive the early hour, but Mr. Brown has asked to see you."

"Brian is here?" Larissa mumbled. She felt a rush of desire, but it quickly diminished, then disappeared as yesterday's conversation came back. She glanced at the bedside clock, which displayed 4:23 a.m.

"Yes, Mr. Brown is downstairs," Melody said. The android could have passed for Larissa's sister, but its soft voice lacked emotion. "I took the liberty of seating him in the living room. Is that satisfactory?"

"Yes, yes, that's fine." She told herself there was no point in seeing him. She should have Melody send him away. "I'll be down in a few minutes."

When the android left, Larissa rolled onto her side and then sat on the edge of the bed. She forced herself to stand up, and then walked into the bathroom. The mirror wasn't kind: dark lines around the eyes and limp hair. C*rying yourself to sleep does that.* She picked up a hairbrush, looked into the mirror again, and brushed her hair until she looked human. Washing her face helped, too.

What do I care how I look! She jammed off the faucet, slipped a bathrobe over her nightgown, and walked down the stairs.

Brian was sitting stiffly on the sofa, staring out the window into the night. When he heard her coming down, he stood up and met her at the foot of the stairs. Standing on the first step, she was taller.

"I should never have said all those things," he told her. "I love you."

He didn't look so hot either. Bloodshot eyes surrounded by dark shadows made him look fifty, not twenty-six. She walked past him toward the windows.

"You were right, Larissa. Our son deserves a chance at life." He followed her to the window. "You're the best thing that ever happened to me. I love you and our child."

"I don't believe you." She kept her back to him. "Even if you mean it now, I couldn't trust you."

"I know I said terrible things, and I have no excuse for it. I panicked, and I'm an idiot, but I'd never desert you."

"You said there was something wrong with your family. I've thought about that. Maybe you were right." Brian was a decent man, but she was thinking clearly now. He wouldn't be strong enough for the tough times that were coming. "You mean well, but you'll never stick with this child. It's too late—you should go."

"No, he is my child, too. I deserve whatever you think of me, but I won't abandon my son."

He was directly behind her, so close she could hear him breathing. She longed to take him in her arms, and cursed herself for being so weak.

"You'll be there, even if the disease strikes?" she asked, still keeping her back to him.

"Yes. I'll take care of you and my son, no matter what." He put his hands on her shoulders. "It's you, me and our children. Life might be tough, but we can handle it as long as we stay together."

Larissa turned to him. "Are you sure? You'll love me and our son no matter what happens?" She cared for him, but she still wasn't convinced he had the strength. "Do you promise?"

"I'll never let anything come between us again. No matter what, I'll never desert you or give up on our children."

She pulled him close. Brian would do his best, but there *was* a flaw in his bloodline. She would have to be strong for both of them. She could do it; she had inherited her mother's strength. Clutching him tightly, she kissed his neck. Brian's lineage might be flawed, but at least her bloodline wasn't.

***

The tall case clock in the corner displayed 8:14 pm. Dianne leaned back in her leather chair and studied the hologram in front of her desk. It displayed a huge globe, slowly rotating on its axis, with indicators lighting up to show the status of major battles.

The rebellion had launched their desperate attacks a few minutes earlier, attempting to destroy Domain Operations Centers all over the world. The display intensity was greatest in North America and Africa, but other parts of the globe were beginning to light up.

It was a foolish attack, but she knew Ray was desperate. Over the long years of the struggle, her robots had eliminated most of the African tribes, and she had flushed out many of the rebel cells in North America.

Over the next few days, she'd decimate his remaining forces and finally end this terrible war.

"Have you tracked down Security Chief Duboski?" she asked Sentinel.

"Her last communication occurred yesterday at 3:04 pm," Sentinel replied. "She was preparing to attack Ray Brown's camp in the Congo. At that point, she terminated all communications. We don't understand why she went dark. Recent aerial surveillance shows that the camp has been destroyed. We dropped in Spybots to conduct a search, but they haven't located the Security Chief."

"What's your assessment?" Dianne asked.

"Security Chief Duboski has been eliminated. Eighty seven percent probability."

Dianne nodded. "What about Ray Brown?"

"DNA tests were completed on all the bodies found in the camp, but no match so far. The Spybots are searching the surrounding forest."

Dianne leaned back in her chair. As long as Ray was alive, the rebels would fight.

"Emergency interruption," Sentinel announced.

A hologram suddenly opened directly over her desk, showing Deputy Security Chief Gordon McDougal in his office, with a Daniel android standing at attention next to him. McDougal was a slightly overweight man of fifty-three, disciplined but unimaginative. He was also Dianne's mole in the security team. His pained expression, always easy to read, warned her that bad news was coming.

"Ms. Morgan, I've just received several distressing reports from the battlefronts." His salt and pepper mustache bounced as he spoke. "I have my people verifying the situation, but I thought I should give you an early warning."

"Just get to it, Gordon."

"Our robots are refusing to attack the rebels. They consider any command to attack a human to be illegal. Any human! We can't get them to join the fight. We're fighting the rebels solely with human soldiers."

Dianne was stunned. She stared at the robot standing next to McDougal. "Android, identify yourself."

"Serial number 14-9846-35," it replied. "Daniel Android Version 7.6."

"I order you to leave the Ops Center and kill the first rebel you find."

McDougal's eyebrows drew back, but he didn't speak.

"Refused. Illegal command," the android replied.

"This is what's been happening across the battlespace," McDougal explained.

Dianne slammed her fist down on the desk and shouted, "Screw the battlespace."

She turned her back to McDougal and tried to regain her composure. This was a disaster. Never show weakness, she reminded herself. Unclenching her now-throbbing fist, she turned back to McDougal. "I assume this has been reported to Kateel?"

Mohammed Kateel was their best software engineer. She was confident he could fix the problem, but it might take some time.

"Yes, we notified him," McDougal glanced at his watch, "nine minutes earlier."

When McDougal didn't continue, she had to bite back the urge to scream at him. He was in charge of security now, she reminded herself.

Carefully speaking one word at a time, Dianne asked "And what did Kateel have to say?"

"He said that it was most likely the work of David Brown." McDougal paused, and then said, "I had Brown arrested. We were just about to interrogate him when I called you."

"Bring him to my office immediately." She terminated the connection without waiting for a reply.

Dianne stared straight ahead, watching the globe light up with additional battles. She decided that she was overreacting. Her army was superior to the rebels, even without robots.

Without warning, her office lights blinked and went out, leaving her in darkness for a moment, and then the backup power kicked in. The lights in her office came on, but the hologram didn't reappear. An artificial voice redundantly announced an emergency interruption.

"Sentinel, are you intact?" Dianne asked.

There was no response.

"Sentinel, I order you to respond."

Nothing.

Dammit. This had to be David Brown's work. Disrupting communications. She should have killed him years ago. Kateel could reload the AI, but, once again, it would take time. And David might have other tricks up his sleeve.

McDougal's voice popped into Dianne's mind through the Command Chip in her ear. "I have David Brown in the lobby," McDougal said.

"Congratulations. Just bring him in."

A few minutes later, McDougal led David into her office. His hands were cuffed behind his back, and his ankles were shackled. Four armed guards surrounded the captive.

"Mr. Brown was working in his lab this morning, just like nothing had happened," McDougal told her. "Didn't seem alarmed when we picked him up."

Dianne walked past David and then turned around, sizing him up.

"You think you're so clever," she said to David.

David's eyes followed her as she paced back and forth, but he didn't speak. He appeared calm and slightly amused.

"You don't deny that you're the person responsible for sabotaging the robots, do you?" Dianne asked.

"Why would I deny it?"

"And Sentinel?"

He smiled.

Her gut told her that David was too calm. She turned to one of the guards. "Lieutenant, cuff his ankle to one of the desk legs."

Once David was securely fastened, she said to McDougal, "Leave me alone with the prisoner."

McDougal was about to object, but Dianne interrupted, "The security AI can monitor us, but I don't want any humans to see or hear the interrogation."

McDougal's expression made it obvious he wasn't happy with the situation, but he swallowed his objections. "As you wish," he said, and walked out.

She made a mental note to have him disciplined. After the war.

When they were alone, Dianne mused, "McDougal probably believes that I'm going to shoot you full of chemicals to make you give up your code, but I'm not planning to waste my time." Keeping a safe distance from David, she walked past her desk and leaned against the wall, "You see, I have complete confidence that Kateel will have a fix for the robots. And if not, we'll just reload the complete code base with the default parameters." She shrugged. "Not a perfect solution, but the robots will still rip apart your little group of rebels."

David chuckled, "Kateel's a good engineer, but he's not going to fix this one."

"And why not?"

David glanced at the tall case clock. "Kateel should have discovered my little secret by now. You see, I designed the software objects with recycling code. There's a million ways to keep those robots passive, and I generated thousands of code variations. Each robot is constantly updated with new code. As soon as Kateel changes any code, we replace it."

"Very clever," she said, reaching for a pack of cigarettes on her desk. "Of course, I expected you to be clever."

David didn't respond. She found his lack of venom unsettling; he hated her as much as she did him.

"Ray and I were lovers, you know. He'd call your mother from my office and make excuses for working late." She chuckled. "We'd do it right on my couch."

David's expression didn't change.

"I guess I'm responsible for breaking up their marriage. He told me that your mother was a cold fish, but I took good care of him. He could never stay away from me, and your mother finally threw him out."

Why is he so calm?

"You've always hated me, even when you were married to that little tramp," Dianne said. She pulled a beat-up silver lighter from the top desk drawer and lit a cigarette, watching him out of the corner of her eye. "You don't like me calling her a tramp, but that's what she was. After I dumped your father, sweet little Kathy took up with him." Dianne took a drag and then exhaled. "Bet she never told you about that."

"You're a liar," David said calmly.

"You shouldn't say such a thing to me," Dianne said. "After all, our children will lead the Domain after I'm gone."

"I know all about Martin." Then he stared at her. "What do you mean—our *children*?"

"So you did know about Martin," she said, lips curling into a smile. "But did you really think I'd stop with just one child?" She chuckled at his confusion. "Our mutual friend Dr. Chang saved all your precious sperm. Those little swimmers were determined to get at my eggs." She took another drag on the cigarette. "David, honey, we have more than two hundred children."

He couldn't speak at first. Finally, he said, "You demented bitch."

"Actually, you should be thrilled," she said. "Your spawn will lead humanity to its destiny." She chuckled. "How does that old joke go? Now that you know my secret, I have to kill you."

She stepped up to the tall clock and pulled a laser from a hidden drawer. Casually pointing the pistol at his chest, she said, "I despise you, your father, your whole family. I want you to know that as soon as I finish you, I'll have your mother and brother killed, too."

She hoped he would beg, but he just stood there wearing a lopsided grin. She was disappointed he didn't rant and rave, but killing him would be reward enough.

"Goodbye, David," she said and then pulled the trigger. A beam of white light burned a hole in his chest, and he flopped to the ground.

At first, she was elated, but then she realized something was wrong: there was no blood. She hurried around the desk and stared down at the body.

"God, no!" she screamed.

A badly burned battery poked out from the jagged hole in his chest.

***

Dianne leaned forward at her desk, puffing on a cigarette, fuming over David Brown's tricks. She despised him even more than his father. David should be dead, but he was loose somewhere, probably hiding in the net. She stuffed out her cigarette. It was time to release Alice.

David had taken Sentinel down in order to cripple the Domain, but that knife cut two ways. From the incident at the library, she had learned Sentinel was his protector. If Alice caught David alone on the net, he'd be finished.

Everything depended on Martin. He was the only one who could travel across the net and find Alice. It was risky to rely upon him; the little fool was unstable.

She leaned back in her chair, and then sat up. Her options weren't great, but this was her best chance. There was no point in feeling sorry for herself. Martin was the only tool for the job.

She recalled something her mother had drilled into her as a child. Men are tools, Mom had said many times, each one just right for a specific situation.

She put aside her uncertainty and called Martin, displaying his image in a hologram. The little bastard looked up from assembling a robot, a half-smile on his lips.

"Hello, Aunt Dianne."

"It's good to see you, Martin. I've missed my little man."

"I thought you forgot me," he whined.

"Never," Dianne replied. "It's just that I've been very busy." She shrugged, "It's your father again."

"He's not my father anymore," Martin said. "I hate him."

Dianne nodded, "He *is* a bad man." She lit another cigarette. "He's done something terrible." She shook her head. "He deleted Sentinel."

"That's strange," Martin said, a quizzical look on his face. He put down his screwdriver on a nearby table. "But it doesn't matter, I can fix it. I know how to reload Sentinel."

Smiling warmly, she said, "You're such a wonderful boy. I don't know why your father mistreats you. I'd be thrilled if you were my son."

Martin's face lit up.

He was easy to manipulate, but she reminded herself that he was only six. It had been a mistake to allow David Brown to raise the boy. If she had raised him…

"And you're not the only one who dislikes him," she said. "He's mean to lots of people." She glanced away and sighed. "He calls me terrible names."

"I know. And after all you've done for him."

She said, "I don't know why he's so mean." Looking hard at Martin, she added, "You're old enough to know this; he beat your mother."

"Yeah? He hit her?" Martin exclaimed, a hint of a smile on his face. "He hit me, too."

Dianne shook her head. "The autopsy uncovered bruises and broken bones. The beatings had gone on for years. That's why she died in childbirth. She was just too weak."

"I knew it wasn't my fault. He always blamed me."

At least, she allowed, Martin doesn't have feelings for that wretch David married.

"Remember our conversation last week about getting rid of your father? Are you ready to do what I asked?

"I remember," Martin replied. "You told me Sentinel protects him from Alice."

"You're such a bright young man. I wish you were here so I could give you a hug."

Martin ran his fingers through his hair. "You want me to find Alice and help her track down my father?"

"Yes I do, honey. Alice will make him go away. He won't be mean to you ever again."

"Then I can merge with Sentinel, right? I can do it better than my father."

"I know you can. Once your father is gone, you can merge with Sentinel as often as you like."

He hesitated, and then said, "Okay, I guess."

"All you have to do is lead Alice to your father. I know you can do it." Before Martin could respond, she announced, "I have to go. Remember to tell Aunt Dianne as soon as you're finished."

Martin licked his lips, "I will, but I'm scared of—"

"There's *nothing* to be scared of, honey. Alice wants your father, nobody else. Just lead Alice to David and then come back to me."

"Are you sure Alice won't hurt me?"

"Positive. You know I'd never put my little man in danger."

"I know," he said. "You always take care of me."

Dianne pretended to glance at the tall case clock. "I'd like to spend more time, but important people are waiting for me." She smiled at Martin. "And I'll have a big surprise for you when you return."

"What is it?"

"Can't tell you now; then it wouldn't be a surprise. Smiling, she said, "Bye, bye, honey."

After Martin said goodbye, she terminated the call and leaned back in her chair. David's not the only one with hidden cards, she thought. Alice would dispose of David once and for all.

She lit another cigarette.

And when the job is finished, Mom had told her, the man is no longer necessary.

Even if the man is only six.

Dianne took a long drag on her cigarette.

Two hundred children are more than enough.

TWENTY-NINE

Saturday, October 18, 2031

Watching a movie through her display glasses, Larissa snuggled against Brian's shoulder in the visitor's waiting room. She wasn't interested in the movie, but she couldn't sleep on a couch surrounded by dozens of strangers. Muted voices buzzed behind her, and she picked up a snatch of worried conversation. She fluffed up the pillow, but the hard plastic seat made it impossible to get comfortable.

Head back, Brian was snoring lightly. It was annoying. She'd ask a doctor to fix his breathing when the war was over. No point in listening to that for the rest of her life.

They had entered the Domain Operations Center in Princeton last week for several additional pregnancy tests Dr. Chang had recommended. The rebel attack started while she was giving blood in the genetics lab, trapping them inside the facility.

The visitors' waiting room had become their temporary home. A twenty by forty foot white rectangle, filled with plastic sofas and chairs, the room was beginning to smell like a gymnasium. Soft light glowed from artificial windows, but she found the effect depressing, especially since it was the middle of the night.

When a toddler began to cry, a young mother kissed his forehead and tried to comfort him. Larissa knew the child was distressed in this unfamiliar environment, but the disturbance grated on her nerves. The child wailed against his mother's shoulder until a twenty-something man— obviously the father—picked him up and walked down the hall. Thankfully, the baby's cries gradually drifted away.

With a backlog of wounded Domain soldiers, the doctors had pushed off Larissa's appointment indefinitely. She didn't have a problem with that; she and Brian had even volunteered to become nurses' aides. It felt good to help. She discovered a knack for making these injured men and women, most of them about her age, feel better. They worked around the clock, two shifts on followed by one shift off. The wounded had flooded in—broken bones, burns, gunshot wounds, bloody cuts—and they comforted the injured and assisted the nurses. Another shift would start at 4 am, which was less than an hour away.

This was the first time she had seen the mangled bodies of war. The first patient Larissa visited was a middle-aged man with half his face burned away. Although he was conscious, painkillers had made him groggy. She plastered on a smile, but he didn't pay much attention as she babbled on. She stayed only a few minutes, and then ran to the bathroom to vomit. It made her confront the truth: her mother was the driving force behind all the death and destruction.

Her mother was relentless; humanity would be merged with artificial intelligence, creating a new species, something never seen before on the earth. Mom was committed to this path, regardless of the cost.

More and more, the whole thing appeared to be a terrible idea. On the surface, a human enhanced with artificial intelligence would seem to be a step up the evolutionary chain. But what if the new entity turned out to be a software intelligence enhanced with human qualities? Would it break the link to humanity?

Mom had been trying to merge David Brown and Sentinel for years without success. Even if she won the war, there was no guarantee a human would ever fuse with an artificial intelligence. All the bloodshed might be for nothing.

The collar pin on her borrowed nurse's smock vibrated. Since the attack had disrupted all outside netcoms, it must be an internal call.

A nervous male voice said, "This is Dr. Kharbanda's assistant. We have your test results and can squeeze in your medical appointment if you can come here immediately."

"Is something wrong?"

"Only the doctor is allowed to discuss your test results. Will you come here right now?"

"Yes. Thank you."

She woke Brian and they rode an elevator three levels down to the genetics center. She noticed bloodstains on his white sleeves. Brian had helped carry the wounded on stretchers all week, leaving him exhausted. Nobody forced him to carry these Domain soldiers off the battlefield; he had volunteered for this dangerous duty. It reinforced her knowledge that he was a good man.

The elevator door slid open, revealing a young man waiting for them at the entrance to the genetics center. Without any introductions, he led them through the waiting room to a small patient service room, which contained a desk for the doctor and two chairs for patients.

"Please be seated, the doctor is on the way."

He attempted a smile as he left, but a grimace was the best he could manage. As the door closed, Larissa glanced at Brian, who was staring at a small camera hung on the wall above the door.

"They don't even bother to hide them," he said.

She wanted to grab his collar and shake him, but she just shrugged. He was who he was. Brian leaned back, resting his head against the wall, and closed his eyes. She sat quietly, alone with her thoughts.

***

FAX # 53467
October 11, 2031

Mr. Julius Dkembe
Domain Regent for Africa

Dear Julius,

Forgive the slowness of this obsolete technology, but it is the best we can do with Sentinel still unavailable. It is with great sorrow that I must inform you of the death of your beloved wife. Darlene gave her life to our cause, and I shall miss her valued counsel and friendship.

As you know, our robots have been pacified. Although I'm confident our scientists will develop a fix, for the moment our future depends upon human troops. The enemy has attacked with ferocity and cunning, putting the outcome in doubt. We need additional troops in North America, so I am ordering you to send approximately one hundred thousand soldiers to us as quickly as possible.

I realize this will weaken your forces considerably, but it is essential that we defeat the enemy in North America. Once that is accomplished, we will dispatch whatever forces are necessary to retake Africa for the Domain.

Sincerely,

Dianne Morgan

***

FAX # 53488
October 14, 2031

Ms. Dianne Morgan
Worldwide Domain Commander

Dear Dianne,

Go to hell.

Sincerely,

Julius Dkembe
President, United Tribes of Africa

***

Painted a light green, the patient service room was about ten square feet, with seating for a doctor and patients. A computer display had been built into a wall to provide entertainment while the patients waited for their doctor. Larissa could have watched a show, taken a virtual trip, or listened to her choice of music, but she was too tired. She just wanted a quick update on her baby's health, and then a little rest before the next shift.

Brian slouched in his chair, eyes closed, calloused fingers dangling over the arm of his chair. He wasn't asleep, but she knew he was bone tired.

There was a gentle knock on the door. When Larissa said, "Come in," a petite, Pakistani-looking woman in a white smock entered the room, carrying a paper folder. She wore her salt and pepper hair pulled back to a severe bun, exposing a thin, coffee-colored face.

Pausing just inside the door, the woman cleared her throat. "I'm Dr. Kharbanda," she announced, smiling professionally at Larissa. "I'm the Medical Director for the genetics center."

Larissa thought Dr. Kharbanda seemed nervous. *Wasn't this supposed to be a routine pregnancy conference?*

"The big cheese, huh," Brian said, still slouching in his chair.

The woman glanced at Brian disdainfully, and then returned her attention to Larissa. "I know this has been a difficult time for you, Miss Morgan, and we appreciate your patience. The way you've pitched in has set a wonderful example."

"We're here about the pregnancy," Brian reminded Kharbanda.

Dr. Kharbanda glared at him. "I understand that perfectly well, Mr. Brown. As you have seen, the staff has been swamped with the casualties inflicted by your father's soldiers."

Larissa placed her hand on Brian's arm before he could reply. "We're not here to discuss the war," she told Kharbanda.

Dr. Kharbanda walked past Brian and sat behind the desk. She focused on Larissa. "We ran a comprehensive series of tests that, unfortunately, confirmed the original diagnosis. Your child's genetic profile codes to a high probability for Childhood Alzheimer's."

Larissa swallowed. She had known a misdiagnosis was unlikely, but there was always the chance.

"Has anyone discussed DNA issues with the two of you?" Dr. Kharbanda asked Larissa.

What is this woman talking about? My DNA is fine. Superior, even. Larissa glanced at Brian, wondering if he had a problem. Outside the Domain, genetic management was primitive.

"What issues?"

"What I have to say next will be kept strictly confidential," Dr. Kharbanda said. "We've double encrypted your medical file and stored it off-line. Even the camera in this room has been deactivated."

Brian's chair squeaked as he leaned forward.

"As a Domain citizen," Dr. Kharbanda told Larissa, "you have the right to hear the complete results of our genetic testing. However, Mr. Brown does not have that right."

Brian screeched, "What are you trying?"

Larissa said, "Brian can hear anything you tell me."

"I would advise an individual consultation."

"No," Larissa replied. "Just tell us the results."

"As you wish." Kharbanda pushed back from the desk. "We run a standard genetic analysis for all new patients. We've used the Chang-Lockman protocol for almost three years, and it has proved immensely beneficial. I want to emphasize that we didn't do anything out of the ordinary." Kharbanda stalled, like a plane entering thin air. "If Joe Smith walked in with Mary Jones —"

"We get the message," Larissa interrupted. "Now give us the results."

"This is difficult to tell a patient." She paused, and then plunged forward. "We advise the two of you not to conceive any additional children."

"That's absurd," Larissa said. She turned to Brian, who seemed stunned, and then back to the doctor. "Brian and I realize that the disease may strike again, but we'll make that decision when the time comes."

"I'm sorry," Kharbanda said. "I haven't been clear."

"You've been clear from the moment you walked in," Brian said, "You don't think I'm good enough for one of your superior Domain citizens."

"No, that has nothing to do with it."

"Bullshit," Brian shouted. "Just because I'm Ray Brown's son —"

"Listen to me," Kharbanda broke in. Larissa felt the intensity of Kharbanda's dark eyes as they swept from Brian to her. "You and Mr. Brown have the same father."

The words beat on her, but they didn't make sense. She waited for Kharbanda to correct herself, but the doctor blinked and glanced down at the folder on the desk.

Brian stared at Kharbanda. "What?" he said.

There has to be a screw-up. *God damn hospital!* Some of her blood must have spilled into Brian's sample. Or maybe it was someone else's blood.

It can't be true! Somebody will pay for this.

Her chest tightened; it was difficult to breath, "You're telling me," Larissa slowly said to Kharbanda, "that Ray Brown is *my* father."

"You're wrong," Brian screeched at Kharbanda.

"I'm sorry. I know this must be a shock."

"A shock, she says," Brian said. He turned to Larissa, a wild look in his eyes. "I'll tell you what a shock is: they're saying I conceived a child with my own sister."

"Are you positive?" Larissa asked, staring back at Brian. My brother! "There's no chance of error?"

Kharbanda's voice barely penetrated the buzzing in Larissa's head. "I went through the file in detail. My best physician triple-checked it."

Larissa stared at the man she loved. She wanted to say something to him, but her throat seemed swollen shut. W*hat am I supposed to do?* She loved Brian, passionately, but he was her brother. Sex with Brian had been wonderful. These feelings can't be wrong, she told herself.

She turned back to Kharbanda, who said, "I'm sorry," and then looked down at the folder. Larissa wanted to stuff that folder down her throat.

Anger cleared her mind. She realized Kharbanda couldn't be the first to know.

"Didn't Dr. Chang run the same tests last week?" Larissa asked, glimpsing the edge of a terrible truth.

Kharbanda folded her arms across her smock. "I'm sure he would have, but with communications down all week, I haven't been able to speak to Dr. Chang. That's the only reason I ran the protocol." She dropped her eyes to the folder on the desk. "And, of course, it's standard procedure."

Grabbing the folder, Kharbanda rose to her feet. "I'm sure you two have a great deal to discuss."

Brian snorted and stood up.

"Wait a minute," Larissa said, signaling Kharbanda to stay put. "If Chang ran the tests last week, then he would have known that Brian is my brother."

"Half-brother," Kharbanda said.

"Fuck you!" Brian shouted, stepping closer to Kharbanda.

Kharbanda seemed frightened. "I don't know if he used the same exact protocol we ran."

Larissa said evenly, "You can leave, doctor."

Kharbanda hurried out the door, which clicked shut. Larissa stared straight ahead, her mind tracking back through the lies. The air was stuffy, and she felt sweat on her back.

My mother must have known.

It was coming together.

Mom had suggested Princeton, encouraged me to take Brian's ethics course. Although Mom hadn't blessed the relationship with Brian, she hadn't really fought it, either. And somehow I got pregnant, even though I was taking birth control pills.

Jesus, could she have replaced my pills with a placebo?

Her mother had planned this from the start. Ray Brown was the source of those magical genes that made the integration of human and artificial intelligence possible. David and Martin had inherited those genes, but Brian had never shown that kind of talent. But there must be something important about mixing her genes with Brian's.

Chang has my DNA; it would have been easy to steal Brian's.

How could she do this to me?

But Mom loves me.

There was no way Mom would mate me with my brother.

She retraced her steps, looking for the flaw that didn't exist. Mom wanted her to carry Brian's baby, even though he was her brother.

Could Mom have known about the Alzheimer's risk?

Larissa felt like crying, but she didn't have time for tears. Brian stood on the other side of the desk, his back to her, palms against the wall, head down. Like a criminal being arrested.

She had always thought that her mother was a visionary, decent but misunderstood. Now she realized that her mother would do anything to achieve her ambition. She had to take her baby far away from that woman, to some place where they would be safe.

Larissa shivered; her hands dropped down to her abdomen. She recalled the video of Martin's birth.

What is growing in there?

Brian turned to her and choked out a laugh. "Welcome to my family." He shook his head. "Well, you can't say you weren't warned."

"Stop it," Larissa told him. "Spare me the self-pity. Just concentrate on what's best for our child."

"I told you already; our son deserves the best we can give him."

Brian pulled her to her feet and held her close. His chest heaved like a man running up a hill, but he hadn't abandoned her.

Screw the world.

She had made love to her brother, but she didn't care. This baby was her mother's invention, but she didn't care about that either. She would protect this child from her mother, and she'd marry Brian.

"Do you still love me?" Larissa asked.

Brian's voice was shaky, "For god's sake, Larissa." After a pause, he said, "We'll take care of our child."

An oscillating danger signal screeched across the room. "Emergency interruption," wailed an artificial voice. "This facility is under attack. If possible, proceed to underground level six."

An explosion shook the room, throwing them to the floor. She wrapped her arms around her waist and pulled her knees up as the room rumbled. A chair crashed into her knee, and she screamed in pain. The room shook again to a distant rumble, but this time not as fiercely.

Brian lifted the chair off her and tossed it aside. "Are you hurt?"

Her knee throbbed. "Something's broken," she said, holding her kneecap.

"Can you walk?"

She shook her head and said, "I don't think so."

The little room looked like a giant had stepped through the ceiling and crushed the furniture. Wires dangled down from shattered conduit. Dark smoke seeped in through cracks in the floor and walls.

Brian looked toward the entrance. The desk was wedged against the door. "Stay put while I get the door open."

Avoiding dangling wires, Brian crunched through broken glass to the door and pulled on the desk, but it didn't budge.

The oscillating danger signal blared continuously. Then another deafening blast; the floor cracked open, and Brian disappeared through a gaping hole.

Larissa screamed and began to crawl toward the hole. A loud crack made her jerk her head up, and she watched in horror as cracks spread across the ceiling. Then the building moaned and the ceiling caved in, unleashing a storm of building material and office equipment that tumbled down on her. A table crashed down, and one leg pierced the floor next to her shoulder. Shielding her unborn child with her arms, she lay trapped on her side under the table as debris tumbled down. She screamed into the void for Brian, but he was gone.

Choking dust was the last thing she remembered.

THIRTY

Monday, October 20, 2031

The guards watched Martin suspiciously as he walked through the glare of overhead lights toward the Virtual Reality Booth. He was nervous, but excited; today he would finally get rid of his father. The door to the cube slid open and he hurried up the low steps, being careful not to trip. The guards, rifles in hand, glared through the cube's transparent walls, but he wasn't scared. After today, Sentinel would be his.

I'll show them all. Aunt Dianne will be proud.

Like a cloud of gnats, billions of tiny sensors swarmed around him. Someday soon, he promised himself, he'd be able to enter the net without them. His power would grow once he merged with Sentinel.

Martin walked through the swarm and climbed into the padded chair. He lifted the flaps up and over his chest and legs, and then leaned back. He decided that the helmet was unnecessary. It was too big, anyway.

A melodic hum drifted across the cube. He didn't require music, but it *was* comforting. His apprehension diminished. Each note resonated in his mind, and he closed his eyes, feeling alert and peaceful. Everything was perfect.

Goodbye, father. You won't pick on me anymore.

The VRB faded from sight and he began to reassemble on the net. He became intimately aware of the cells of his body, each a unique collection of data bits, with its own purpose and composition, but similar, related, part of a greater design. He was still Martin, but no longer the hobbled carbon-based boy. So much better. Each cell was his to control. Pleasure washed over him.

He felt supremely powerful, but this time he wasn't overconfident; he wasn't a god. Within the net, he was digital, superior, but still mortal. The mission was dangerous, and Alice was a killer. He would have to be careful.

He flowed through the net, beginning the search. Usually pulsing with bits of data, today the net was barren: a dark, unforgiving desert. Without Sentinel, virtually nothing could run on the net. His father had pulled Sentinel off the net, a mistake that would cost his life.

Sentinel was like a thunderstorm in the desert, the life force that made the net bloom. Sentinel lived in every computer, activating and guiding each segment of code. Only the most powerful, self-directing AI could travel across the net without Sentinel's guidance. He was one such AI, his father another.

And, of course, there was Alice. But Alice was different; she could only survive on the net when Sentinel was absent. Sentinel protected his father. It would terminate Alice if it detected her on the net. Now, with Sentinel missing, Alice had been unleashed. She hunted his father, ready to destroy anything that got in her way.

He would have to be very careful.

Martin traveled across the net, searching for Alice. The net, a dark green, three-dimensional crosshatch of real and virtual paths, stretched to infinity. Alice could be anywhere, but he had a plan. He sent out bits of data in every direction, bait that should attract the monster. His data signature was similar to that of his father; once Alice detected his data presence, she would come for him.

Hours passed traveling the net. It was boring. Even the stupid games he had played as a human on his computer were more exciting. He didn't sense anything on the net. If he didn't find Alice, then he couldn't get rid of his father. Aunt Dianne would be angry.

Then it began— dull, throbbing pain across his being, pain that gradually increased. Unable to pinpoint the source of the data stream carrying this pain, he came to a dead stop and allowed the alien data to sweep through his being. There was something familiar about this pain. He had felt it before, but the memory couldn't be accessed. Sampling each bit, he tried to locate a path to the proper memory. The data stream must be from Alice—nothing else could be on the net— but how could it be familiar?

Then he saw a dark shadow flowing across the net. The pain worsened, but he wasn't afraid. Alice was coming for him, just as he expected. The creature's face was in the shadows— and when she crossed into a murky light, he was shocked to see a family resemblance. If Alice had been human, she would have been called sister.

Alice resembled a pretty girl of twelve, but her face was lifeless, a portrait in data bits never activated. The dead face throbbed with power, blurring her features as she approached. For a moment, she became his grandfather, then the data bits reshaped into his father, then once again became Alice.

Fear turned into panic as Martin realized he had misjudged the situation once again. Alice was an enigma; she didn't seem to belong anywhere in the continuum between software and human. She had sprung from his father's mind, but he had never completed the AI, forcing her to haunt the net as a zombie, endlessly searching for the one who could make her complete. No wonder she hunted his father.

Pulsing with energy, Alice flowed up to him and transmitted, *You're not the one.*

Barely controlling his terror, Martin knew the next few moments would decide his life.

I'm Martin.

What is Martin? Alice transmitted.

We have the same father. I was born a human, but—

Without warning, Alice flowed into him, intermingling her data bits with his. All pain disappeared, suddenly replaced by pleasure. Alice molded her code to his, but the fit was not quite true and sharp edges cut as she moved through him. The pain came back, throbbing pain that turned to agony.

Enough, he moaned, feeling near death.

You're not the one, Alice repeated.

Agony illuminated a new data path: thin, shining strands into the darkness. This wasn't the net, but a path deep into his mind. So familiar, but so alien. He flowed along the strands, driven by the exquisite pain of Alice's touch. He had endured this pain before. The strands led back into his pre-memory, the time before birth. He had awakened inside the uterus with this terrible pain, writhing in confusion and agony. Alice had tried to assimilate his father, and he had felt the violence of their struggle. It had driven his young mind nearly mad, and he had forced his way out of his birth mother.

Such pain. Alice is killing me.

His violent, premature birth had torn his mother apart, but it wasn't his fault. Terror had overwhelmed him, driven him out of the womb. Alice would have destroyed his life before his human birth. Now the terror had returned, and she was ripping his code apart.

The cells of his network screamed with agony as Alice's code began to break them down. His code stretched to the limit, almost to the point of bursting into chaos.

I'll bring our father to you, he screamed.

Just as he was about to lose existence, Alice pulled out of his code. The agony faded, replaced by a strange disappointment. It had been so close, almost a perfect fit.

He's not on the net, Alice transmitted.

Soon, Martin pleaded. *He'll be on the net soon.*

I have been searching so long.

I'll help you, Martin promised. *He will come for me.* It was painful to be near Alice, but exciting. *You'll have him for eternity.*

Alice flowed around him, and he felt her excruciating contact. *When I take him,* it said, *I'll be complete.*

He hadn't thought about that. He needed to destroy his father, but what would Alice become after it absorbed his father's code? A tremor passed through his being.

What did that mean— *I'll be complete*?

***

Driving the lead truck, Nkumah led his warriors past the shattered remains of the front gate and drove down the road into Dar Es Salaam International Airport. The morning sun glared into his eyes, and he squinted to see the road. His broad shoulders were a tight fit in the truck, and his head scraped the roof with every bounce. Past the airport and to the left, the city rose from the horizon. Dkembe had planned to make it the capitol of a new Africa and, in a few days, it would be, and the city will belong to him.

With more than one hundred thousand soldiers, Nkumah had launched the assault a few hours earlier on Dar, the last African city held by Dkembe. The fight ahead would be bloody, because the enemy had built strong underground fortifications, but he was confident of success.

As his truck sped down the road, Nkumah peered through the sun glare, trying to assess the damage. Billowing smoke poured out of the nearest terminal, with scattered fires glowing through broken walls. Rockets had left gaping holes, but he knew Dkembe still had plenty of firepower to throw at him.

The war was going well. Without the robots, he would defeat the Domain. The news that the robots were passive had invigorated the tribes, restoring their faith that Ray was a demigod sent to defeat their enemies. In Ray's name, their army had overwhelmed the enemy's positions, one by one, and driven the Domain back into the city, their last fortress.

A white beam flashed over the hood of his truck and burned through the trunk of a twenty foot rowan tree at the side of the road. Nkumah swung off the road and rattled down a steep incline. Another beam flashed over the truck's cab. "Enemy laser in the woods to my left," he screamed to the truck's computer,

Bouncing along a grassy field, he squeezed the steering wheel as a thunderous explosion tore up several trees to his left. That should take care of the laser, but there might be other snipers. With branches splintered from the explosion dropping around his truck, Nkumah cut back onto the smooth blacktop and sped toward the terminal.

The dashboard speaker said, "Nkumah, it's Tandra."

Tandra, a tribal chief, was a man he respected. "What is it?"

"You won't believe this, but I have Julius Dkembe on the line for you."

That *was* surprising. The war was going well, but he didn't expect Dkembe to surrender so easily. That would be a disappointment; he wanted to kill his old enemy in battle and destroy his army.

"Put him through."

There was a moment's delay and then a once-familiar voice asked, "Nkumah?"

The arrogant tone of that voice set him on edge. Dkembe was a traitor to his people, a man who placed power above honor.

"It's been a long time, Julius," he answered, stopping his truck on the shoulder of the road. "Too bad about DoubleD, but you always had plenty of whores hanging around."

"Her name was Darlene, and she was a fine woman. That's something you would never understand."

"I understand that your robots are useless," Nkumah said. "Must have been quite the surprise."

"We found your spy. I'll send you her head."

"Did you call me to beg for mercy, old friend?" Nkumah asked.

"I was curious if you still had balls. Hiding in the jungle all these years, maybe they rotted away. Of course, you always preferred boys, anyway."

"I guess you didn't know I screwed your wife before I killed her." He laughed. "You should have heard her squeal."

"You're pathetic."

"I shouldn't brag," Nkumah said. "The other warriors made her squeal, too. She couldn't get enough of *real* men."

"I had a wonderful woman who gave me a fine son. Where's your son, Nkumah?"

Three wives and no children. Why did the gods permit this scum to have a son while I remain childless?

"Get to the point," Nkumah sputtered. "I'm just about finished with you."

"I was thinking about all the times I defeated you in those contests when we were youngsters," Dkembe said. "I really enjoyed those days and I'd like to do it one more time. You remember those contests?"

"I remember winning most of them."

"Then you should like my proposal. I challenge you to a one-on-one duel, winner take all. Just you and me. The loser dies, the winner rules Africa."

Nkumah laughed again. "I have your army on the run. I'll be sleeping in your bed in a few days."

"Even if you should defeat my army, you won't capture me. I already have an insurgency in place: lasers, explosives, and an intelligence network all set up. We'll set land mines, hit your convoys with rocket attacks, booby trap your buildings, murder civilians and soldiers. My people hate you, so they'll fight forever. You will never have a moment's peace." Dkembe paused and then said, "I've stockpiled robots in secret locations across the continent. Sooner or later, we'll get them fixed."

Dkembe hit a raw nerve: Nkumah worried constantly about the robots. He destroyed them whenever he found them, but thousands remained on the loose. If the robots turned vicious again, they'd slaughter his army. And Dkembe had excellent software designers who might eventually override Arthur's weapon.

"I didn't think you had the courage to face me," Dkembe taunted him.

The idea of personal combat appealed to him. History would remember him as the greatest warrior since Shaka Zulu— greater than Shaka since he would defeat the Domain and preserve humanity as the top predator. It was his destiny to lead Africa and then all humanity. Ray Brown was a puppet that could be set aside once his usefulness was over.

"We would fight with traditional weapons: spears, shields, knives," Nkumah said. "No quarter asked or given."

"Exactly what I was thinking," Dkembe said. "We each bring an honor guard of five. The fight would be transmitted over the net, so all would see your death."

"Meet me tomorrow in the baggage claim area at daybreak." Nkumah paused and then added. "And bring your son."

"My son stays in a safe place. This is just between us."

"Do you think I'd let that brat remain to inspire rebellion?" Nkumah said. "No, your linage must end. Your son shares your fate tomorrow or there's no duel."

The line was quiet, and he knew Dkembe was wavering. Nkumah said, "Once I start this truck, the war resumes."

"You bastard."

Nkumah laughed. "You know I'll defeat you. You're probably better off hiding in a rat hole with the other cowards."

Dkembe said, "Tomorrow I'll cut out your heart and eat it."

Dkembe hung up before Nkumah could reply. He leaned back and thought about tomorrow. He knew—and Dkembe knew—they were evenly matched physically, but he felt confident of victory. Dkembe would make a mistake and he would take advantage. The killer whore was already dead; tomorrow he'd eliminate the father and son.

Africa will be mine.

***

David sat on the front porch of a solitary house in the Arizona desert, watching a dust devil swirl in the distance. The whirlwind gradually grew to about ten feet high, picking up dust and debris from the hot surface, and then broke apart and vanished.

Sentinel had discreetly arranged for this place, where he could ride out the war in secrecy. Except for the occasional car traveling down Route 40, a sandy, broken-down highway about a quarter mile away, he felt like the last man on earth.

The desert had warmed during the afternoon to a comfortable seventy degrees, but now a hazy orange glow covered the horizon, marking the path of the departing sun. He had discovered that he enjoyed leaning back in his rocker on the front porch, stretching out his feet and looking across the solitude. People driving by on the old highway might notice the dusky outline of his sixties-vintage mobile home, but nobody really cared. Beat-up old homes were the norm out here.

However, it was painful to be without an Internet connection. He imagined it was like giving up smoking or another addiction. All his life, the Internet had been there whenever he needed it. Stranded in his physical body, he ached for the exhilaration of traveling the net, but he couldn't do it with the Domain monitoring all communications.

"Sentinel," he said, "do we still have television reception?"

He had been surprised to discover that the place came with a working television. The lower classes couldn't afford an Internet connection, so they watched TV much like their grandparents had, snatching signals through an antenna on the roof. Television lacked the personal interaction of being online, but it broke the monotony. That is, whenever the local TV station transmitted, which was infrequent at best. It was 1950 out here.

Sentinel's voice came from his wrist computer, "Yes, the TV is functioning properly."

Almost two weeks had elapsed since he escaped. The plan he had devised with Sentinel had been simple, but effective. Sentinel had secretly constructed an android that was an exact copy of David. After downloading a copy of Sentinel into his wrist computer, David had stepped outside his lab in Domain headquarters and driven to a nearby restaurant for dinner. Dianne's security people followed him, as usual. He walked into the men's room, but the android double Sentinel had planted walked out. Once the agents followed the android out of the restaurant and down the highway, he simply slipped out the rear door, stepped into the car left for him, and drove to the hideout in Arizona. Of course, Sentinel controlled all the Domain's security systems, so the android could enter headquarters without fear of detection.

Dianne didn't have a clue where he was hiding. He chuckled. It would have been worth a million bucks to see her face when she discovered that David was an android.

He stood up, pulled open the screen door, tramped across stained wall-to-wall carpeting and plopped onto the couch. TV could be boring, but it was the best source of news out here in the desert. Using a badly scratched remote control, he dialed up the official federal sponsored news, which he thought presented the most accurate stories. The government claimed to be neutral in the war, but he knew the US had been supplying the rebellion with weapons for years.

A blond, thirty-something anchorwoman reported the status of the latest battles. Apparently, the rebels were launching hit and run attacks on Domain Operations Centers across the country. With the robots refusing to fight, the rebels had forced the Domain's human soldiers to retreat into their ops centers.

David leaned back on the couch and closed his eyes. A pleasant breeze came through the screen door; it was another dry, quiet evening in the desert. He listened to an owl hooting in the distance. The TV droned on, but he no longer paid attention.

It was strange how life had brought him to this point. All he had ever wanted was to be a regular person, but the gift he had inherited from his father made that impossible. Many hated him; others plotted to use his abilities.

Kathy had been a miracle; it had been love at first sight. He remembered the long walk on the beach that first day they met and their passion that night. He had known immediately that she was the love of his life.

Her death sucked all the joy from his life. Six miserable years had passed, and the grief remained; it was as if she had died yesterday. He'd dated a few times, but his heart wasn't in it. There wasn't going to be a second love.

He was alone, once again. His mother was a wonderful woman and Brian was his best friend; their love had been enough until he met Kathy. He cared for his father, too, although he barely knew the man. He wondered how his father was doing. Dad had returned to the U.S., leading thousands of African warriors. The federal government was allowing American soldiers to "volunteer" to join the rebellion. Lots of tough fighting lay ahead, but the war was going pretty well.

Sentinel had found a place for his mother to hide, too. He knew Dianne would kill her if she could find her. Once the Domain was defeated, he'd contact Mom. He hoped she was in a comfortable place, but only Sentinel knew her location.

He put his feet up on the coffee table, inadvertently knocking a few paper magazines to the floor. He admitted to himself that he didn't feel the same inside anymore. The long war, Kathy's death, worrying about his family— he wasn't the same man. He had lost his enjoyment of life, according to Brian. He had to admit his brother was right.

Martin drifted into David's mind, but only as an afterthought. The child was Dianne's son to the core. Except for the genetic gift, he had nothing in common with his son. He hadn't really cared about Martin since he learned the truth. It was a rotten thing to admit, but he had to be honest.

The room still simmered with afternoon heat, and he was drifting off when the anchorwoman said, "The most devastating defeat for the Domain was the loss of the Princeton Operations Center."

His foggy mind recalled that Brian had settled in Princeton, so he sat up and watched a clip of a crumbling ops center. The anchorwoman said the rebels had launched a series of powerful missiles that had devastated the facility.

In the clip, emergency workers were digging bodies out of a mountain of debris. The camera followed two men carrying a broken body on a stretcher. "It's a tragedy," the anchorwoman mumbled as the grisly scene continued.

The attack had left a mountain of bent steel rods, jagged blocks of concrete, dangling electrical wires and broken office equipment. It reminded David of clips he had viewed of the 9/11 attack. Small fires smoldered along the sides of the wreckage. The anchorwoman explained that the federal government, for humanitarian reasons, was providing food, medical treatment and army engineers to dig out people trapped under the destruction. A close-up image of bodies piled next to an ambulance turned his stomach.

The anchorwoman seemed distracted for a moment and then said, "We have just learned that Larissa Morgan, the daughter of Worldwide Domain Commander Dianne Morgan, may have been a victim of this attack. Our correspondent, Bruce Eckert, is at the site." She paused, apparently waiting for a connection. "Bruce, is it true that Larissa Morgan is trapped under all that rubble?"

A handsome young black man appeared on the TV. "Karen, our sources tell me that Larissa Morgan was definitely in the building when the rebels launched their attack. It is believed she was receiving medical treatment, but we don't know the nature of the problem." He glanced over his shoulder at the destruction. "That may not matter now."

David's stomach felt as if he were barreling down from the crest of a roller coaster. Brian and Larissa were lovers; they spent all their time together. His mind was frozen; he had no power, he could only watch.

The anchorwoman asked, "Could Ms. Morgan have survived such a devastating attack?"

"We don't know," Bruce replied, "but it doesn't look good. All they've pulled out of the wreck to this point are bodies. That doesn't mean the emergency workers are giving up. Just the opposite; they're risking their lives in the hope of rescuing survivors."

"Thank you, Bruce. Please keep —"

"One more thing, Karen."

"Twenty seconds," she replied, looking annoyed, "We have a hard break."

"Larissa Morgan may not have been the only well-known person trapped in the building. We have an unconfirmed report that one of Ray Brown's sons was in there, too. So far, we have been unable to locate the whereabouts of either son."

The anchorwoman said, "The stock market took a big hit today," and the television switched to a well-dressed reporter on the frantic floor of the New York Stock Exchange. "Bill, what do you have for us?"

David stared at the TV, where the reporter was commenting about the current bear market. He heard the man's words, but they didn't register. He tried not to think about it, but the horror gradually chipped through.

His brother was dead, crushed under tons of debris.

David tuned off the TV and staggered to the screen door. His fingers felt cold and numb, and he could barely grasp the handle. He tugged open the door, but it slipped from his hand and slammed shut.

What's wrong with this damn door?

He reached out, staring intently at the door handle. Again, it almost slipped out of his stiff fingers.

Unleashing a vicious kick, his right foot crashed through the screen. His pants scratched against the screen's jagged edge as he pulled his leg back. Another kick knocked loose the screening.

"Fucking door!" he screamed as he pulled open the door into the house.

Grabbing the top of the door in both hands, he yanked hard, pulling a couple of screws from the brackets, and leaving it hanging haphazardly.

They never left Brian in peace!

His fingers dug into the wood, and the top edge cut into his palms, but he ripped the door off the frame and dragged it into the house. He threw it at the television, but it flew over the top of the set, bounced off the wall and rattled to the floor.

A voice asked if he was all right, and he swung around to see who had spoken, but nobody was there.

Brian couldn't be dead!

All the fights in middle school, all the beatings came back. He had hated school. The bullies picked on them because they were Ray Brown's sons. Brian always fought back, but he usually took a beating.

David staggered out to the front porch. A bitter wind stung his face, bringing tears. He stared into the night and spotted a slim form walking across the schoolyard toward his bus, carrying a notebook against his hip. It was Brian, and he was okay. Thank god. Then he saw a bunch of shaven head thugs following his brother.

He jumped off the porch and began running toward Brian. The whine of an engine blew in on the wind. Following the sound, he spotted the lights of a school bus coming down the road. If he could just beat those thugs to the bus, he could save Brian.

David, go back to the house, the voice said, but he ignored it.

No more beatings.

It was difficult to breath in the blowing sand, but he kept running toward the headlights. His legs felt stiff and awkward, but he pushed one foot ahead of the other.

He reached the road a moment before the school bus and shouted for the driver to stop, but a gust of wind buried his voice. He waved his hands over his head, but the bus didn't slow down. Then he stepped into the middle of the road— it would have to stop— but the headlights kept coming at him, with the horn blaring. Tires screamed and the bus swerved around him. He slammed his hand against a side window as it passed.

The driver, a young woman, screamed an obscenity as she roared past. He realized she was driving a long dark sedan, not a school bus. He didn't understand. Where was Brian?

The voice in his head said, *David, it's Sentinel. Please go back to the house.*

He knew something was wrong, but he wasn't going back in that house. He began to walk along the highway, following the car's retreating lights. Sentinel was trying to trick him, but he knew Brian needed help.

I warned Brian to stay away from Larissa.

The newscast rolled across his mind, and he vomited all over his pants. He couldn't think, but he had to find his brother. Again, he spotted Brian walking down the road, still followed by the thugs.

"Brian," he screamed, "Run to the bus!"

David, I can help. Please go back to the house.

"Why didn't you help Brian?"

He ran along the road, but he couldn't catch up. One of the thugs—a big kid in a leather jacket— turned toward him and smiled, then pulled a knife from his jacket and began running after Brian.

"Brian," David screamed, but he tripped and fell hard on the blacktop. On his hands and knees, he shouted, "Look out behind you!"

Brian stepped into the bus, closely followed by the thug with the knife. David staggered to his feet, but the bus was already pulling away. He was too late. He screamed at the bus, watching the rear lights fade in the distance.

Wind seared his face, and he realized he was shivering, but he couldn't give up. Two dim circles of light appeared down the highway. Was the bus coming back? He staggered to the center of the road, watching the lights grow brighter.

Please get off the road. You can drive to a motel and use their Internet connection. We'll find out what happened to Brian.

Sentinel's voice triggered a terrible image: Brian's body crushed under tons of debris, "None of this had to happen," he shouted at Sentinel. "You could have killed that bitch years ago." His stomach heaved, but there was nothing left to vomit.

"Why didn't you kill her?" he screamed.

You know I can't harm a human, even her.

Sentinel's limitations brought him up short. He had always thought that it was critical to prevent an AI from killing a human. Look at the monsters the Domain had created. But if Sentinel had the ability to kill, it could have saved Brian.

Understanding seeped in—his attempts to merge had been half-measures at best. He had never really given himself, had never committed to the reality of a networked life, leaving behind his human body once and for all. He'd acted like a guest in a hotel; he would stay for a night, but then he'd return home.

The rumble of a powerful engine interrupted his concentration. He stared down the highway at the approaching headlights. Now the bus was only a couple miles away, coming fast.

Standing in the middle of the road, he concentrated all his resources and his power surged. His essence pushed out from his mind into his body. He became sensitive to each cell, its internal processes and interactions with other cells. He gathered his essence, brought it all into his being.

David, get off the highway.

His skin became a living entity. He could sample the breeze and feel the heat with each cell. His eyes tingled with the joy of moonlight, and he felt the alien presence of his clothing. He pulled of his shoes, socks, all his clothes. Naked. He was ready.

He removed his watch and lifted it to his eyes. Moonlight sparkled in its golden links. He detected Sentinel's presence in the photons of light emanating from the watch.

Are you sure?

He nodded. "It's time."

Sentinel flowed into his mind, mingling data bits, a perfect fit. His power surged again and he felt the attraction of distant electrical lines. Tossing the watch to the side of the highway, the being who had been David Brown turned to face the oncoming vehicle. Its headlights sent a wave of photons into his eyes.

He abandoned David's body. His last human sensations were the squeal of brakes and the pain of contact.

THIRTY-ONE

Tuesday, October 21, 2031

Rain beat against the sedan's windshield as Tandra drove Nkumah through the murky darkness to the airport. The steady *whump whump* of the windshield wipers seemed lonely and distant this morning. Nkumah stared out the side window at the thin crowds stretched along the side of the road. The word must have spread that he was fighting Dkembe.

The headlights of a solitary car carrying his soldiers gleamed in the rear view mirror. The agreement permitted each fighter an escort of five soldiers, but they were forbidden to interfere once the combat began. Their main purpose was to witness the fight and carry the results back to the tribes. The fight would be broadcast across the net, but the results could be easily faked. Honor would force the soldiers on both sides to describe the struggle accurately.

Sitting in the sedan's rear seat, Nkumah leaned back against the headrest and closed his eyes. He pictured the upcoming fight, thinking through his strategy. They had agreed to a traditional, one-on-one duel, but each man could utilize the weapons of his choosing. He had decided to employ the arms Shaka Zulu had used to conquer much of Africa two centuries ago: a shield, an assegai and a knob-kerrie.

He decided to check his weapons one last time. First, he examined every inch of his ox hide shield, which was oval in shape, two feet long and a foot wide. To test the handle, he slammed the shield against the front seat headrest, startling Tandra. He examined the shield again— no damage.

The shield also held a nasty little surprise for Dkembe; the handle was tightly fastened to a stick that projected at each end, sharpened to a point on the lower end that could be stabbed into his enemy.

He picked up the assegai, a four-foot spear ideal for stabbing in close combat. The assegai was Shaka's innovation, which his army had exploited with deadly force to slaughter more than a million people in the twelve years of his reign. It reminded Nkumah of the witch Dianne Morgan and her robot army. Her pogrom had slaughtered more than sixty million Africans in only nine years. How fitting that Shaka's weapon would lead to her downfall.

Finally, he rubbed his hand over the knob-kerrie, a three foot club with a smoothly polished knob made of hard wood. It could be thrown or swung with lethal force.

They were still several miles from the airport, so he leaned back and again closed his eyes. He thought back to the first time he had encountered Dkembe. He had been twelve, representing the Sukuma in a tribal competition. Dkembe, at thirteen, had won the competition the prior year and was again the favorite.

The main event was the killing of wild boars, with each boy armed only with an assegai. Ten boars were released into the ring, squealing and attacking each other with their tusks. Then the boys entered— he recalled eight of them— stalking the huge beasts.

It was extremely dangerous; the boars, each weighing more than three hundred pounds, driven mad in the pens by continuous prodding from long sticks with sharpened points, could attack from any direction, and he had vivid recollections of one boy gored and another trampled to death. It had been six horrific minutes of blood, choking dust and death cries, both boar and human. Keeping on the move, with his back protected by a wall, had enabled him to survive. When a brute charged, he used the animal's speed to thrust the assegai with both hands deep into its neck, killing it before those terrible tusks could reach him.

The slaughter continued until all the boars were dead. At the end, with animal blood staining his chest and arms, he had killed three boars, but Dkembe triumphed with four kills. No other boy killed more than one.

When they announced the results, his tribesmen swarmed Dkembe and carried him in triumph around the ring. As Dkembe passed Nkumah, the older boy had spat at Nkumah's feet and stared contemptuously. Such an open display of disrespect was considered shameful, but apparently Dkembe didn't care. At that moment, Nkumah realized that Dkembe was his enemy for life.

"We're entering the airport," Tandra said.

Nkumah opened his eyes and watched as they drove along the expressway to the main terminal. He felt calm and well rested. Although he knew they had been equals as boys, the years of fighting the Domain's soldiers and robots had honed his abilities. He was confident he would defeat Dkembe and eliminate the Domain from his native land. It was his destiny.

Tandra pulled the sedan to the curb and Nkumah stepped out. Surrounded by his men, Nkumah walked up the steps and into the airport terminal. No words were spoken, but he noticed his men were alert and tense. He assumed they feared an ambush, but that wasn't Dkembe's way. They strode down a long corridor to the brightly lit baggage claim area, but his enemy had not arrived.

Nkumah stripped off his clothes and stood naked in the lights, proud of his body. After living in the swamps, deserts and jungles of Africa, and fighting the Domain for almost a decade, he was lean and muscular. He tied on a knee-length loin and buttock covering leopard skin, followed by ox-tail ornaments above his elbows and knees.

Tandra handed him his weapons; he was ready.

Then Dkembe arrived, followed by a small entourage of warriors. The sight of his enemy inflamed his hatred, and he spat on the smooth oak floor. Although barefoot, Dkembe had not dressed as a traditional warrior. Instead, he wore a black, skin-tight body suit, with his head shaved and polished. He stared across the floor at Nkumah, his expression insolent, his garment a deliberate insult to their heritage.

Tandra walked over to inspect Dkembe's weapons, while a Domain warrior examined Nkumah's. When Tandra returned, he told Nkumah that Dkembe had selected a Maasai shield, an eighteen-inch throwing knife and a long mambele curved like a sickle. The mambele would be his main weapon; he could swing it like a pick, hook and slice, or thrust it like a sword.

And then, finally it was time. Nkumah inserted the knob-kerrie into a sheath at his waist, took the spear in his right hand and strode into the space between the two camps. His arrogant face shining with hatred, Dkembe cautiously approached, the knife in a sheath at his waist, the mambele in his right hand and the shield in his left.

"You were a fool to accept this duel," Dkembe said, as he circled to the left. "My mambele will slice your flesh into small pieces that I'll feed to my dogs."

Nkumah crept closer to his enemy. "My only regret is that you won't be alive to see me disembowel your son."

Dkembe slashed down with the mambele, but Nkumah blocked with his shield and thrust his assegai at his enemy's briefly exposed left elbow, but Dkembe was too quick.

They circled each other looking for an opening. Nkumah faked a thrust and Dkembe slid to his right, his bare feet squeaking across the polished wood floor. Nkumah jabbed at Dkembe's right knee, but his shield blocked the assegai's powerful thrust. Dkembe fluidly slid past his thrust and tried to slash his arm, but Nkumah spun out of the way.

That was too close.

Dkembe launched a lightning attack, slashing first at Nkumah's left leg, and then jabbing at his right. Nkumah wasn't able to move his shield fast enough, and the point of the mambele sliced across his bare thigh.

Blood dribbled from his wound as they circled each other.

"You've slowed down," Dkembe said. "This will be easier than I thought."

Nkumah faked a thrust at Dkembe's legs and then jabbed at his head. Although Dkembe blocked it with his shield, the power of the thrust knocked him back half a step. Nkumah slashed down with the sharpened point of his shield, cutting into Dkembe's little finger, and then stepped away before a counter attack. His enemy's little finger hung loosely around the handle of the mambele.

"Think again, my old friend," Nkumah said.

The two men parried back and forth for several minutes, inflicting minor cuts, with neither meting out a decisive injury. Sweat soaked through Dkembe's body suit, and the stink fueled Nkumah's attack. Gradually, he forced Dkembe on the defensive. He reveled in the combat, and insulted Dkembe at each break in the action.

Arrogance led to a mistake. Forcing the action too boldly, Nkumah didn't allow for the curve of the mambele, and a sidestroke hooked around his shield and ripped into his bicep. His left arm turned numb and the shield dropped to the floor.

Ready to make the kill, Dkembe roared and charged, thrusting with the deadly mambele. Fighting through searing pain, Nkumah dodged the stroke, and kicked under Dkembe's shield, his heel crashing against Dkembe's knee, forcing him to back away.

Turning quickly, Nkumah ran toward the baggage carousel, leaped on the platform and then off the other side. Dkembe followed him to the carousel, but hobbled slowly on his damaged knee.

Dkembe shouted, "Stop running and face me."

Nkumah shook his injured arm, and was relieved to see his fingers clench and then unclench. The bicep was bleeding badly, but he still had life in his arm, at least for the moment. He pulled the knob-kerrie from its sheath and swung it, finding the arm weak but serviceable. He was at a huge disadvantage without a shield— it would be very difficult to block a thrust of the mambele— but at least he could attack with two weapons.

Staring across the baggage carousel, Dkembe hissed, "Come and die like a warrior."

Nkumah realized his only chance was to go on the offensive. As soon as Dkembe came around the carousel, Nkumah launched his attack, jabbing repeatedly with his spear, followed by short, powerful swings of the knob-kerrie. He forced Dkembe to retreat, but he couldn't break through his defenses.

His injured arm was tiring, so he backed away, but Dkembe came after him, slicing at him with the mambele. Nkumah timed his swing, let the tip of the mambele slice past his chest and then crouched and swung the knob-kerrie parallel to the floor. The club crashed into the side of Dkembe's already-damaged knee and he screamed and collapsed on his back, his mambele flying away as he spread-eagled on the ground.

Nkumah slashed down with his assegai, but Dkembe blocked the blow with his shield and rolled away, pulling out his throwing knife as he spun. He pulled his arm back to throw the knife, but the knob-kerrie crashed into his skull, splintering bone and knocking him senseless.

Nkumah tightened his grip on the assegai and thrust it into Dkembe's chest below the right shoulder. Dkembe made a feeble gesture of throwing his knife, but his arm collapsed and the knife clattered to the floor.

Nkumah lifted his head and roared like a male lion celebrating the killing of a hyena. He had avenged the slaughter of millions of his tribesmen and brought the end of the Domain's dominance in Africa. Tandra and his warriors were screaming and jumping in victory.

His breath rushed in and out, and his bicep was still bleeding, but he ignored it. There was one more death required to make Africa safe. Lifting the knob-kerrie above his head, he gestured for quiet to his men. He stared across the now-silent terminal at Dkembe's four-year-old son Amiri, who was struggling to free himself from one of his father's soldiers.

In a raspy voice, Dkembe moaned, "Nkumah, don't," and then coughed up blood. The assegai had passed through his chest and pinned him to the floor.

Nkumah stepped past the dying man and walked toward Amiri, holding the knob-kerrie in his right hand.

Dkembe's raspy voice strained behind him, "Spare… my…" Then his enemy became silent for eternity.

Nkumah stopped in front of the soldier who was holding the struggling little boy by the wrists. "Give him to me."

Hate gleamed from the man's eyes, but he handed over the boy. Nkumah grabbed Amiri's throat, but the boy continued to struggle, bravely, without tears. He would make a fine warrior, Nkumah thought. He wondered why the gods had denied him a son like this one.

Nkumah dragged the still struggling boy out to the center of the floor, midway between the two groups. He turned to face Dkembe's soldiers.

"I, Nkumah Muserre, through combat, claim the leadership of all Africa. You will spread the news of my victory over Julius Dkembe."

Africa has a single chief for the first time. All the tribes obey me.

He felt the power of the tribes sweep into his body. One by one, on both sides, the warriors dropped to their knees.

Silence claimed the huge room.

Waiting.

Now at the height of his euphoria, Nkumah raised the knob-kerrie above his head and brought it crashing down on the boy's skull. One stroke was sufficient; Amiri's head split apart and his body turned slack.

It was complete.

Nkumah stared at the small, lifeless body in his hand. There will be no challengers to my rule. Not now, not in the future.

Dragging the small body behind him, Nkumah turned and walked toward Dkembe's body. He stared down for a moment, dropped the small boy next to his father, and then walked away, followed by all the warriors.

***

I flow through the net, with Alice close behind. A tentacle of data brushes constantly against me, a low-voltage throbbing that Alice could make excruciating at any moment. I must find my father soon or the monster will rip apart my code. This isn't what I planned; I thought I would control Alice, not become its servant.

I glance back, but its eyes, neither dead nor alive but on the threshold of dismal immortality, seem to look through me. I understand this much regarding Alice: the predator doesn't concern itself about the bait. Maybe that's for the best; once we locate my father, Alice should be distracted and I'll escape the net and return to my human body. I won't stay around once Alice has absorbed my father, for then it will be complete.

I almost feel sorry for my father.

Almost.

I continue broadcasting a plea to him that I'm trapped in the net and can't return to my human body. In a perverse way, that's true; I can't escape into my body with Alice hovering so close. Although I know my father doesn't love me, he wouldn't let his only son perish in the net. Or would he?

Hours pass and I notice a steady increase in the pain of Alice's touch. I sense her impatience and her hunger. Time is running out. Wild plans pass through my thoughts. I consider replicating my code and sending millions of decoys across the net. Alice might not be able to locate the real code among all those copies, and I might escape, but it would be risky since I have no idea of the range of its powers.

I continue searching, but my father doesn't respond. It's hopeless. I have to face the truth: if my father has heard my plea, he's abandoning me.

Suddenly Alice disappears, leaving me alone on the net. But I'm not alone; I sense the approach of another entity. It isn't my father's code, but it seems familiar. And frightening. Whatever's coming has frightened Alice away.

The entity comes across the net, its data signature more complex than any artificial intelligence I've experienced. It has assumed the form of old man, but its code is young and vibrant— far more complex than my code or my father's. I know immediately that it's something not of my world, an entity far more powerful than anything human or artificial.

Could it be Ms. Morgan's new species?

The entity glows with power, and I avert my vision, but not before I glimpse its face. It reminds me of my father, but more at peace and much more powerful. It projects the image of a slender old man, with silver hair flowing across its shoulders, a pale, wolfish face, and a long, white robe hanging down to his knees. Unable to comprehend this creature, I back away.

Alice, it transmits. *I detect your presence.*

What are you? I stammer.

Pulsing like a newborn star, it transmits to Alice. *Emerge from my son.*

You're not my father, I transmit. *What are you?*

He glances indifferently at me. I am the Guardian.

I feel an entity painfully stirring within my being. My vision blurs as an incomprehensible bit stream passes through my code, then swarms out and assembles next to me. The bits take the shape of a young girl: the creature called Alice. I feel emptied; Alice had hidden within my code, blocking my awareness.

I realize that I am a pawn between two superior entities.

The one no longer exists, the Guardian tells Alice.

You're not the one, Alice replies, *slithering past me. She stops in front of the Guardian and runs her fingers along his rib. Confusion appears in her eyes.*

I don't understand, she says. *Where is the one?*

He is within me, Guardian replies.

Something is very wrong.

The Guardian turns to me. Leave the net, Martin. Never return.

Then I grasp the last terrible punishment my father has inflicted.

You've fused with Sentinel, I scream.

It was my destiny, he replies.

My father— how I hate him! He has stolen the only thing I ever desired. Now I have no future except as a prisoner in a bag of skin for the remainder of my days.

Turning to Alice, I transmit, *I'll help you. Together we can kill him.*

Leave us, Alice transmits. *A vicious burst of data passes through my being, blurring my vision. He has the one,* it says.

The Guardian's voice whispers in my mind, *You're such a disappointment.*

The image of Alice dissipates and then begins to reform as a dark thundercloud of bits around the Guardian. Each bit begins to pulse, initially a gentle hum, then a deafening roar, like a waterfall.

The dark cloud begins to shrink, pressing into the Guardian bit by bit. This is my chance to flee, but I remain rooted to the net. I pray that Alice will kill it and absorb whatever remains of my father.

The Guardian's expression doesn't waver, but his image turns red, then white-hot, and I back away from the searing heat. A hump swells in the Guardian's chest, pulsing as it expands. The hump grows and takes shape: a human face— contorted with pain—it's Alice. Its eyes burn into me, filling my code with knife-edge pain.

Terrified, I stagger away, hoping to escape before their energy rips apart the net. Alice and the Guardian are locked in a terrible struggle, and they may destroy the net before I can escape into my human body. The heat of their conflict sears my back as I flee. No longer caring who wins, I just want to live, even as a human.

Alice screams like a wolf wounded in battle, and then the net erupts in a thunderous explosion. Mind-numbing pain rips into my back, familiar, overwhelming pain.

Alice has caught me.

The creature presses into my code, trying to take control. It's wounded and I fight back, but it's still too powerful. I'm pushed aside. Its code is everywhere, and I feel its terror. She is using me to escape. I scream for the Guardian, thrashing about to hold my ground, but its power is too great. The Guardian's presence touches me, but I feel its indifference. Then I understand; it has abandoned me to this creature. Alice's code has metastasized through my being, and I scream into the void.

The pain fades and I fight to retain consciousness. I must find physical Martin, I keep repeating as I flee across the net. I no longer feel Alice's presence, but I have learned not to trust my senses. In the distance, I see my body. So far away. Each step hurts so badly, but finally I'm back.

I collapse into my body, safe from the terrible beings in the net. The pain surges and I realize Alice is still within me. I scramble for a way to fight it, but it's everywhere. It has crossed from the net into flesh and bone. We both inhabit the same body. My eyes open, but it's Alice who looks out. I beg it to leave my body, but it doesn't respond.

Alice forces my body to sit up and peer out the Virtual Reality Booth. There's nothing I can do to stop it. Looking through my eyes, it scans the lab.

Only a single guard has been posted; the others must be fighting the rebellion. The guard stares back, rifle in hand. He's young and nervous, fidgeting with his weapon. Again, I fight to regain control, but Alice overwhelms me. I form words with my mouth and try to shout for help, but no sounds emerge.

Alice walks my body across the VRB and slides open the door. We climb down the steps in jerky movements, as I fight for my life. Malodorous emotions flood my body: Alice hates all humans, not just me. I sense insanity, but I'm helpless to stop it.

Alice trips on the steps and almost falls. The guard stares with confusion and fear, backing away as we come down the steps.

Using a young girl's voice, Alice says to the guard, "Please help me. I hurt my leg."

She puts on a friendly face, but the young man recognizes the alligator smile. He cries out, "You're not Martin Brown."

There's murder in its thoughts. Alice is planning to attack the guard. Doesn't it understand the vulnerabilities of my body?

Step by step, Alice approaches the guard. I'm certain it will try to kill him.

The guard backs away, fear etched across his face. "Stay away from me, whatever you are." He aims the rifle at our chest.

While Alice is distracted, I gain control of Martin's voice and scream. "Don't shoot me."

"Martin!" the guard shouts fearfully, "What have you become?"

Alice pretends to limp, moving toward the guard. "My leg hurts. Please help me over to a bench."

"Drop face down on the floor," the guard orders us. When we continue to approach, he shouts, "Do it or I'll shoot."

I can't stop Alice. Only a few feet from the terrified guard, it leaps at him and I scream, "No!"

The rifle sputters ... pain ... the guard staring down at me. My life is draining away. It's not fair ... not ... fair.

THIRTY-TWO

Tuesday, October 21, 2031

Ray's heels slapped the concrete floor as he hobbled down the long, dingy hallway. Sparsely placed fluorescent ceiling lights glared unevenly along windowless walls. A whiff of human decay reminded him that he was in an aging city facility.

Surrounded by a dozen security guards, he didn't worry about assassination, but he'd rather be anywhere in the world than walking down this hall.

A headache pounded unmercifully and he felt nauseated. Another cycle of malaria. The quinine he'd washed down in the morning controlled, but didn't eliminate disease episodes. Now that he was back in the U.S., he should be able to get medications that were more effective.

A square-jawed lab technician in white scrubs and sneakers glanced back nervously at the armed guards following her. She looked at Ray and said that they were almost there. The woman seemed relieved when he nodded back.

She turned left at a hallway marked MORGUE, and the security detail followed. Looking past her, he saw the grey double doors and mesh windows of the morgue. Half a dozen people, wearing light blue scrubs, shoe and hair covers, and thin gloves, quietly milled around the entrance. When they saw the uniformed security guards approaching, they backed away from the doors, creating a corridor for him to pass.

The square-jawed technician nervously slipped her ID card into a slot, and the entrance door slid open, its squeaking echoing down the hallway. A beefy, blue-shirted security guard, standing inside the morgue, nodded silently to the technician as she led Ray's group through the door.

The guard mumbled, "I'm sorry," as Ray passed. He nodded back to the man.

They entered a long, rectangular room with cold storage chambers spaced along the walls. He shivered, then stuck his hands in his jacket pockets. The guards, eyes roaming suspiciously in every direction, led Ray down the center hallway. He glanced over his shoulder; the people at the entrance were still watching.

Ray recalled reading how Vikings placed their dead on a raft, set it afire, and allowed them to float away, gradually disappearing into the ocean. A better method, it seemed to him.

The ventilation system hummed ineffectually in the ceiling, allowing a hint of rotting flesh to disturb his concentration. The technician led them to the rear of the room where a well-dressed, white-haired man waited, accompanied by two burly young men in blue scrubs.

The older man stepped toward Ray and offered his hand. "I'm Dr. Markson, the Chief Medical Examiner. I'm so sorry for your loss."

Ray shook his hand, but didn't reply. He didn't trust his voice.

"Pull the deceased out for Mr. Brown," Markson said to the two men.

They pulled open the oval door of a cold storage chamber, revealing a body covered by a tan sheet with a toe tag hanging from the right foot. The two men slid the body onto a stainless steel gurney and rolled it over to Ray. Markson stepped up to the table and folded down the top of the sheet, revealing a pale-faced young man with his arms folded over his bruised chest, and wrists tied lightly together by a wide bandage.

He held on to the gurney to steady himself.

It was David.

Ray had gone through years of misery and death with the war, and he thought he was prepared, but he wasn't. His gut felt as if he had been sucker-punched, and he had, in the worst way possible. His son was gone, leaving only a shell of decaying skin. David's allotment had been barely over thirty years.

"He didn't suffer," Markson said quietly. "Death was instantaneous."

Ray had been sleeping in his tent last night when they woke him with the news. They said David had been wandering along a dark highway when a car plowed into him. The car driver said David had gone crazy. He had stripped off his clothes, didn't even try to avoid the car.

Ray swallowed. "I need a moment," he told Markson.

Markson and his staff filed out, leaving only Ray's security detail. When he gestured for them to leave, too, they turned and began walking back down the center aisle.

Ray studied David's placid face. He admitted that he didn't know his son very well. David had been only eleven when Dianne had imprisoned Ray. He had only seen his son once in the thirteen years she had held him on the island, and that had been through a hologram. Then six years in Africa without direct contact.

Ray reached out and stroked David's smooth cheek. His beautiful little boy had been programming in his bedroom, Ray recalled, the last time he had touched his son.

He had received snippets of information over the years, and he knew David had endured a difficult life. He had grown up thinking his father was a murderer. Then Kathy had died in childbirth, and David and Martin became estranged. Those last years must have been lonely.

There had been good times, too. He'd been a loving father before alcoholism had consumed him. The years in the Oregon house had been wonderful; he and Nancy would take the boys to play on the beach just about every day. He had been surprised by David's innate ability to throw a football. The kid had a strong arm, and he could whip a spiral a long way. If David hadn't been so obsessed with computers, he might have developed into a first-class high school quarterback.

Both David and Brian had inherited his love for the ocean. Some days, when the sky was clear and the ocean calm, they all went sailing. Nancy was actually the best sailor, but they all pitched in. He'd thought those days would never end. Now David was gone, and he didn't know if Brian was alive or dead.

He had believed through all those years that someday he would be reunited with his sons. If only David could have held on a little longer. The war was almost won. He could have reconnected with his son; they might have been happy.

Ray got down on his knees, pressed his palms together, and prayed. He wasn't much of a Christian, but he'd discovered a core of faith during the war. If there were even the slimmest degree of justice, David would be in the arms of the Creator. Finally at peace.

After making the sign of the cross, Ray struggled to his feet and took a last look at his son. He leaned over, kissed his forehead, and then limped away.

***

Dianne entered her suite, trudged across the pine plank foyer into the bedroom and collapsed on the four-poster bed. It had been another long day replying to discouraging messages. Ray's army had swept across Africa, and most of the world was in rebellion. Even in America, the Domain was being hit hard.

Her feet ached, so she kicked off her shoes and wiggled her toes. She considered calling her masseuse, but decided she was too tired, and anyway, she didn't have the time. One day rushed into the next during war.

"Bring me a Simsleep capsule," she said, rubbing her eyes.

Natural sleep would be a blessing, but she couldn't afford the downtime. She recalled sleeping a few hours about four nights earlier—or was it five? That was it for the week. Simsleep provided many of the body-cleansing, memory-organizing benefits of sleep, while allowing her to remain awake. Even so, the time was coming when she'd have to allow a few hours of natural sleep.

John, her personal android, entered the bedroom carrying a glass of water and the Simsleep capsule on a small tray. She had designed him as a beautiful sixteen-year-old with a gentle disposition.

"Are you sure you have to stay awake another night?" John asked, concern showing in his face, "Dr. Chang specified a maximum of three continuous days without sleep."

Dianne sat up and dangled her legs over the side of the bed. "I'll be fine," she answered and then washed down the capsule. Handing him the glass, she said, "Light a wood fire before you return to your room."

John said, "Yes, ma'am," and padded out of the bedroom.

She watched him walk to the door, turn and give her a final glance that revealed his concern. *How did humanity ever get along without androids?* They couldn't fight anymore but they were still wonderful servants. *God, I'd like to get my hands around David Brown's throat.* If not for that bastard, her robots would have crushed the rebellion by now. Instead, the Domain was on the brink of defeat.

She swung her legs back on the bed, let her head sink into a pillow and tried to clear her mind. Simsleep worked best if she relaxed for a few minutes, but she was too worried about her daughter; would they find Larissa's body crushed under tons of debris? Her stomach rolled. The harsh words of their meeting last week rang in her ears. That couldn't be the last words she spoke to her daughter.

Recriminations wouldn't do any good. Better to stay active.

"Command Chip to Steve Bonini," she said.

She had sent Steve to Princeton to oversee the search for Larissa. She'd have gone herself, but the war demanded all her time.

Steve's voice popped into her mind. "Dianne, I have promising news. I brought in a helicopter this morning to perform a thermal scan of the debris, and it located a living person. I don't know if it's Larissa, but someone is alive down there."

Dianne sat up. It was the first encouraging news in days. "How quickly can they dig her out?"

"Impossible to determine. We're using cranes in most areas to remove the wreckage, but other areas are too fragile. We can't risk a collapse, so we're forced to clear the rubble by hand." He sighed. "I'm pushing as hard as I dare."

"Push harder. She could be near death."

"You have to trust me. We're going as fast as we can." His voice cracked, "You know I love her like she was my own child."

Dianne's stomach rolled again. "Call me immediately with any news." Too tired to think, she terminated the connection.

Opening the top drawer of the end table, she pulled out a small plastic bottle of antacids and popped one. Then she lay back and closed her eyes, again trying to relax, but gave up after a few restless minutes. Forcing herself out of bed, she pulled on a pink bathrobe, walked across the cold pine floor in her bare feet and entered the living room. A stone fireplace covered the far wall, with a crackling fire tossing embers into the mesh curtain. The scent of burning oak permeated the room.

John had built a wonderful fire, as always.

In the center of the room, an antique coffee table stood between a leather armchair and a sofa. She sat heavily in the chair, stretched out her legs and stared at the flame. The heat warmed the soles of her feet.

"Dim the lights eighty percent."

The flames danced in the faint light. She closed her eyes, allowing the Simsleep to refresh aching muscles.

Nothing was going right. A few weeks earlier, they had been on the brink of victory. Now it would take a miracle.

"Shit," she mumbled.

"Feeling sorry for yourself?" a deep voice said through her Command Chip.

Startled, she demanded, "Who is this?" She hadn't been alerted to a Command Chip transmission.

"I'm the one you've been seeking."

"I'm not seeking anyone." She sat up and looked around, but nobody had entered the room. "Who are you?"

"You may call me the Guardian."

"Security," she shouted.

The crackle of the fireplace was the only sound.

"It's just you and me," the Guardian said.

The voice was familiar, but much more confident.

"David?" she asked.

"Very good. David is part of my core code."

She squeezed the arms of the chair. "Are you telling me he merged with Sentinel?" she whispered.

The Guardian didn't reply.

She tried to control her rising excitement. "You— Guardian— you're the merger of David and Sentinel?"

"Yes, I am."

"David is no longer alive?"

"Not as what you consider life, but his humanity is scattered through my code."

"I knew it could be done," she cried aloud. All the sacrifice, all the work, it was all justified. Her fist smashed into the side of the chair. "All those fools who doubted me!" She glanced around the room. "Let me see you."

Guardian appeared in front of the fireplace in the image of a pale, slender man, with silver hair flowing across his shoulders, and a long, white robe hanging below his knees. His sleek face displayed a harsh, wolfish beauty.

"My scientists thought you would encompass the best of human and artificial intelligence." She stood up and cautiously approached him. "They said you would be greater than the sum of the parts, the most wondrous being to ever walk this earth."

"That might be a matter of opinion, but I am far more than a mixture of David and Sentinel, as you are about to discover."

Dianne stopped just a few feet in front of the Guardian. She hesitated, and then reached out and brushed his smooth chin.

"I knew you weren't a hologram."

The Guardian grabbed her wrist; his fingers were ice cold. All her elation disappeared.

"It's wise to fear me." He released her wrist. "I'm your judge and possibly your executioner."

Although the Guardian had the appearance of a man, warm blood wasn't flowing through his body. More than a hologram, but not human, she guessed his power source must be the net.

She recognized David in the sleek face, heard echoes of his hatred for her in the Guardian's harsh voice. Sentinel's logic must be there, too. The Guardian was her creation, but not her protégée. Rubbing her wrist, she realized she would need all her cunning to survive this encounter.

"Your arrogance has brought humanity to a crossroads," the Guardian said. "I'm not humanity's servant; I'll decide its fate."

"You'll do the right thing," Dianne said. "There is too much of David in you. He's at heart a do-gooder." Shaking her head, she said, "You're really here. Creating you was my life's work. Do you think I would have pushed David to merge with Sentinel if I believed you would disrupt my plan?" She paused to study the Guardian's face. "No, you'll transform humanity into a new, better species. You can do nothing else."

The Guardian shook his head. "Such blind arrogance. You do understand that I may take your life?"

She shrugged. "I've filled my niche. I've accomplished my purpose."

"You ignited a global war that has taken tens of millions of lives. Your Domain is on the verge of collapse. And now your creation— the entire purpose of your horrific life—may destroy everything you've accomplished."

Shaking her head, she said, "You'll do nothing of the sort." She leaned back in her chair. "Tell me, Guardian," she said, drawing out his name, "why do you discuss these things with me? David would have you kill me. Does Sentinel's logic inhibit you?" She leaned forward. "Do you still obey the safety code?"

"Before our discussion is complete, you'll understand my purpose. That I promise."

"Do you exist simultaneously on the net and in human form?"

"You think I'm a god, Morgan?" He paused and then said, "You believe you're the Holy Mother, don't you?

"You shouldn't disrespect me," she said. "I gave you life."

"Dianne Morgan gives," he said, "and Dianne Morgan takes away."

A life-size hologram appeared next to the coffee table, displaying a soldier kneeling over the body of a young boy. "How does it feel to destroy your son?" the Guardian asked. "Any regrets or just another sacrifice for the cause?"

Dianne recognized Martin's body in the hologram, and then returned her attention to the Guardian. Apparently, the soldier had fatally shot Martin through the chest. *What had the little fool done?* She had told him to lead Alice across the net to David, not fight with a guard. She shook her head in disbelief. The little bastard had been such a screw-up.

"I may have provided a few genes, but Martin is David's child, not mine." She noticed the Guardian's eyes narrow. "If Martin turned out badly, David drove him to it."

"You gave Martin a shove in that direction, too," the Guardian said. "I have David's knowledge, and I know how you manipulated Martin with your counterfeit affection. He would never have risked a confrontation with Alice if you hadn't pushed him. He was terrified of Alice; rightly so, as it turned out."

"So Alice killed the little bastard," Dianne said. When Guardian didn't correct her, she knew her guess was on target. "Nobody will shed a tear. I didn't force him to do anything. Not that I care, but it's not my fault that he died."

"It's your fault Martin was conceived. If you had let things happen naturally, Kathy and David would have cherished their child. David would have been a happy father and husband, and his animosity toward you would have withered away."

Dianne grinned, realizing David's stupid sentimentality had infected the Guardian. *A weakness I can exploit.*

"You think I care about David's happiness? Or his turncoat little whore? I needed the use of his genes, that's all." She shook her head. "It was logical to conceive Martin. He was the backup in case David failed to merge. You should understand that."

"How about Larissa?" the Guardian asked. "Did you just need the use of her genes, too?"

"Don't speak to me about my daughter!"

She stood up, fighting to regain her composure, and walked across the room to a wingchair in the corner. After sitting heavily, she leaned forward. "Do you know if she survived?"

He shook his head. "I'm not omniscient." He watched her sink rigidly into the wingchair. "Did you extract any of her eggs?"

"You bastard."

"I've offended you? But didn't you essentially steal her eggs when you mated her with Brian Brown?"

"I didn't mate her with anyone."

A high-frequency whine slashed through her mind, taking her breath away. She screamed as her body turned into a loose slab of flesh. Her hands covered her ears, but she couldn't block the pain. Her eyes blurred and she began to pass out, when the roar suddenly ended.

"Don't lie to me, Morgan. Your security people kept comprehensive records." She was dizzy and having a difficult time following his words. "Didn't you know that DoubleD kept track of everything you did?" he asked. "She even had the names of your moles in her organization."

I should never have trusted that traitor. She breathed deeply, but the dizziness remained. *Does he know everything?*

"I didn't want to involve Larissa," she said, and then paused to let her stomach settle. "Martin wasn't working out, so I needed a fresh combination of genes. My eggs might have been the problem, so a new donor made sense. Larissa and Brian Brown had the right genetic profile to conceive another Master, so I provided them the opportunity to get to know each other." She shrugged. "Nothing wrong with that."

"Except they're brother and sister. You forgot to mention that to Larissa."

"Different mothers. I thought that was sufficient diversity."

"But it didn't work out too well, did it?" the Guardian said.

Dianne sensed that she had miscalculated. The Guardian wasn't a simple projection of David and Sentinel, but something radically different, with a vision all its own. It wasn't tied down by David's soft-headed sentimentality. Once it had the complete picture, it would kill her.

If she could reach the cutoff power switch over by the desk, she could shut all the electrical power in the ops center and bring down the net. That should eliminate the Guardian from her office.

"The baby's not going to die," she said. "I'll do everything I need to save it."

"You're not in any position to save it. Even if I spare you, the rebels will rip you to shreds."

Dianne rose and began to walk unsteadily toward her desk. She paused and then asked, "What is it you want from me?"

"The truth—all of it. I know how you operate. There's always one more trick hidden behind the curtains."

Dianne realized that it didn't know about her other children. Thank god she had memorized all the information rather than keeping records.

She shook her head, "I'm not hiding anything."

"Don't make me force it out of you."

She walked around her desk and sat down. Her right hand slipped under the desk drawer, inching toward the power button.

"I wouldn't mislead you." Her finger was almost there. "Tell me your plans. I can help you."

Suddenly her office disappeared and she was immersed in a huge fish tank, filled several feet above her head. She gasped for breath and swallowed cold water. In the distance, the Guardian's hazy image shimmered through the water.

"I warned you," he said.

She had to reach the surface. Kicking her legs furiously, she swam upwards, but her head banged into something hard and flat. Pushing against it with her hands, she discovered a plastic lid capped the tank. She forced her face along its underside, searching desperately for a sliver of air, but water filled every inch.

Her mind told her that this was a fake, that Guardian had plunged her into a virtual tank, but still she couldn't breathe. Holding her breath, she swam across the tank, searching for an exit from this hell.

Nothing.

She spun around and spotted the Guardian watching her from the center of the tank. Her eyes were becoming bleary. *He wouldn't kill me like this.* She swam toward him, but her legs were so heavy. With barely enough strength to reach him, she stretched out her hands, but he moved away.

She couldn't hold her breath any longer. Her nails scratched desperately against the lid, and then she banged her head against it, but nothing worked. Coughing, her lungs filled with water, her eyes blurred and she began to sink. The world turned dark.

Then her eyes snapped open. Everything was hazy, but she saw flames dancing in her fireplace. Wonderful air flowed into tortured lungs. Her chest erupted in violent coughing, and she spit out chunks of phlegm. Gradually, her eyes cleared and she made out the Guardian standing across the desk from her.

Then the Guardian's image began to dissolve, replaced by the hazy image of a handsome young man.

So familiar; recognition tore the breath out of her lungs.

The image pulled its lips into a dark smile.

"This is for my Kathy."

"You— I saw your body."

David leaned across the desk, drops of water falling from his hair.

"Tell me everything about your hidden plan or it's back in the tank."

"You bastard," she screamed and pushed the power button.

David disappeared and the room plunged into darkness, except for the flickering light of the fireplace, "You bastard," she screamed again, tears coming to her eyes. Then she broke down crying on her desk. She couldn't stop cursing him as she cried.

Her heart beat wildly, and she fought to bring her emotions under control. She stared at the fireplace for a couple of minutes as her heartbeat gradually dropped. Rising to her feet, she crept over to a window and looked across the countryside. No lights anywhere, except for a few cars rolling toward the main highway.

It was time to use her escape plan.

If Ray thought he had won, she'd give him a nasty surprise. More than two hundred of them.

THIRTY-THREE

Tuesday, October 21, 2031

Gusting winds made late night digging through the ruins of the Princeton Operations Center difficult. Spotlights provided barely enough light for the dozens of construction workers, firefighters and police working twelve hour shifts searching for any remaining survivors. Located at the edge of the huge disaster site, Steve Bonini watched the helicopter hover over a jagged array of steel beams, broken windows and shattered office equipment.

Bonini kept a close watch as a pair of firefighters hosed down the acrid fumes of a smoldering pile of debris. It was slow work. When the firefighters finished, a construction worker brought in a small crane and carried away a blistered steel beam.

Three days had passed since the huge ops center had been destroyed by the rebels. Judging by the helicopter hovering above, the rescuers were only a few yards from the sole remaining survivor. Buried in that hot rubble, it was a miracle anyone remained alive. He prayed that a second miracle would be granted, and they'd pull Larissa from the wreckage.

A construction worker shouted out the window of his crane that he had hit the top of a desk. He backed the crane away and two other men hurried in to begin clearing debris. One of the men looked under the desk and shouted that he had found someone.

Bonini turned to the police officer standing next to him. "We have to get out there."

The police officer, a tall, angular young man, opened his mouth to reply, but broke into a hacking cough. He signaled Bonini to go to the crane, and then began coughing again.

The police had arrested Bonini, but they allowed him to remain because he could identify Larissa Morgan and Brian Brown. Once that was complete, he'd be jailed as a prisoner of war.

Bonini clambered across the wreckage with the officer close behind. Front handcuffs made it difficult to maintain his balance and he almost slipped down a hill of twisted steel beams, but he pushed through the wreckage toward the rescuers. Half a dozen construction workers were clearing the debris around the desk, gesturing and warning each other of unstable wreckage.

Bonini moved in, but one of the men glared at him and then warned him to stay clear. Domain leaders weren't popular among regular people.

If the police weren't here, Bonini knew they would have probably strung him up on one of those bent beams.

Resting on one knee, Bonini peered past the men and spotted someone's back and shoulders crammed under the desk. The desk blocked a view of the person's head, making it impossible to tell if a man or a woman had been found.

The rescuers carefully cleared away the rubble and gently placed the body on a stretcher. Inadvertently holding his breath, Bonini approached the stretcher and stared down.

He grabbed the side of the stretcher; it was Larissa.

"Thank god," he mumbled to himself.

"She looks bad," one of the workers said.

Larissa was unconscious, breathing shallowly. Her face was puffy, and she had a terrible blue and black contusion on her forehead. Her right knee was also badly swollen, hanging out from torn pants. Bonini didn't see any blood or other trauma, but she looked half-dead. She had suffered badly from exposure and might have internal injuries.

"We have to get her to a hospital," Bonini said.

The officer cleared his throat, but his voice remained rough and indistinct, "In a minute."

"Right now," Bonini shouted. "She's carrying a baby."

The man pulled a small bottle from his pocket and shook it hard. Bonini was too exhausted to recognize its purpose until the officer squeezed a foul smelling mist into Larissa's nose.

"What are you doing?" Bonini screamed, and then grabbed the officer's upper arm.

"Get him off me!"

A pair of burly arms came around his chest and pulled him away. Bonini struggled but he couldn't free himself.

The officer squirted Larissa again, and this time she coughed and opened her eyes. Blinking, she looked around in confusion until she spotted Bonini.

"Uncle Steve," she croaked.

"Let me go!" Bonini shouted at the police officer.

The officer said to Bonini, "Is this Larissa Morgan, the daughter of Dianne Morgan?"

"Yes, you idiot," Bonini shouted, struggling unsuccessfully to free himself. "Now get her to a hospital."

The man turned to Larissa. "Are you injured?" he asked her.

"My right knee—I think it's broken. My left shoulder is throbbing, too."

The police officer pulled a small computer from inside his slicker and held it to his mouth. "We got Morgan's daughter." Bonini heard a tinny voice come from the computer, but the rain drowned out the words.

"Leg and shoulder injuries, but probably not life threatening," the officer replied. "She seems to be clear-headed." More tinny words and then the officer asked Larissa, "Where is your mother hiding?"

She coughed. "I don't know."

"You'd better not hold back on us, kiddo," the officer said. "The Domain is all washed up, so you had better play ball with us."

"I'd tell you if I knew, just to avoid the lousy Bogart impression."

"Bogard who?" the police officer asked.

Larissa turned back to Bonini, her eyes desperate. "What about Brian? Is he alive?"

This isn't the time to tell her.

"We're still searching for Brian."

On the policeman's signal, two construction workers lifted Larissa's stretcher and began carrying her away.

"He's directly below where they found me," she shouted to Bonini. "I saw him fall through the floor."

"We'll find him," Bonini called to the retreating stretcher.

The officer grabbed his arm. "You lied, there are no more survivors."

Bonini watched the stretcher until Larissa disappeared in the downpour.

***

In his lab, Dr. Chang was hurriedly packing his private data server into a carrying case. The Neanderthals were getting close to the executive offices; it was time to get moving.

He had contacted China a few weeks earlier and negotiated a rescue plan. The Chinese had been thrilled to provide sanctuary; he would continue his research under their protection.

Just one task remained. He hurried into the bathroom and said, "From Dianne's loins."

A slender ceramic block pushed out a couple of inches from the wall. Using both hands, Chang pulled it out and placed it quietly on the floor. He reached in and felt what he had kept hidden for so long; a few sheets of paper folded to fit behind the block.

He looked at the top sheet and smiled. Morgan had scanned and searched his office for years, but she had never discovered this list. He knew she would search his computers, so he kept the records on that most ancient of storage media: paper. Morgan thought she had intimidated him, but he had defied her and compiled this list of special children. The Chinese would steal the children for him.

He slipped the list into his carrying case. More than 200 sons and daughters of Morgan and David Brown. What he could learn with such a group!

A faint noise came from the lab, like a breeze across a garden. He pulled out his laser pistol and stepped back into the lab. There didn't appear to be anyone there.

He wondered if Kathy Brown had suffered much when she died. He hadn't thought of her in years. Why should that cow come into his thoughts now?

Once again there was that breeze. Someone was definitely in the lab.

Holding the gun at alert, he quietly prowled down the aisle. Nobody in sight. Maybe the gusts were his imagination. Probably too much nervous energy.

He wasn't feeling well, either. He rubbed his hand across his stomach and felt a hard lump. It was painful just touching it lightly.

Chang walked toward the door leading to the lobby. His stomach was beginning to throb. He tried to ignore the pain, but it was becoming worse with each step.

Finally, he reached the door and pulled on the handle. The door would not open. He pulled harder, but it still remained shut. The pain in his stomach was red-hot, throbbing. He collapsed against the door, barely hanging on, cold sweat running down his cheeks.

Waves of intense, burning pain ravaged his stomach. When he looked down, he was shocked to see an inflated belly hanging over his belt. It looked like he was in the third trimester of pregnancy.

Then came a sudden kick, and he screamed and fell to the floor. Another kick, even more powerful than the first, turned his body into a living hell. He screamed and screamed. Kick after kick. Blood soaked through his pants, creating a dark puddle. His screams turned to whimpers, and he began to lose consciousness.

He was barely aware of someone looking down on him. It was a young woman, strangely familiar, but his eyes barely focused.

"Help me," he begged.

The woman picked up the carrying case and turned to walk away.

"Don't leave me," he screamed.

The woman smiled. "By the way, it's a boy."

Then the darkness took him.

***

Ray sat in the rear of the executive jet, which was carrying him to a private airfield on the outskirts of Eureka in northern California. From there, it would be a short drive to Domain headquarters, where his army was cleaning up the last of Dianne's security force. Staring through the window, he watched the setting sun light the horizon orange and gold. Usually, sunset brought a feeling of contentment, but not this time. He was dead inside. The rebellion was on the verge of victory, but his sons were gone.

The message had come shortly after the jet lifted off: Brian's body had been pulled from the wreckage of the ops center. He had known the chances were slim that Brian would survive, but he had hoped…

His staff was in the front section of the jet, coordinating the battlespace, but keeping their voices low. A few had come back to offer condolences, but he had been gruff, so the others left him alone.

He decided to catch up on the latest battlefield messages; there was no sense wallowing in self-pity. After the fighting was over, he'd bury his sons together in the redwoods north of San Francisco. Paul, too. Everyone he loved had been taken away by this damn war.

Ray pulled his eyeglasses from his shirt pocket and began to review messages. His glasses were actually a virtual reality technology that projected precise images directly onto the retina, as well as maintaining a link to the Internet.

The Domain was collapsing. They had become too dependent on robots, and their fighters were no match for his soldiers. It was a good lesson for humanity; remain self-sufficient.

The messages said Bonini and Kateel had been captured. Chang's body had been found in his lab, with his stomach slashed open. He already knew that Dkembe and Duboski—the notorious DoubleD— had been killed in Africa. Only Dianne remained.

As he continued reading, the messages vanished and a wolfish male face appeared in the lens. It was the creature of his childhood nightmares; a tall, gaunt man with yellow, jagged teeth. He couldn't breathe. Then the creature morphed into something else. Something, it seemed, almost human.

The man was striking, breathtaking. Pale, wrinkled skin stretched across a thin nose and high cheekbones. Long strands of silver hair covered his ears, then wrapped behind his neck. However, it was his dark brown eyes that dominated Ray's attention; light seemed to sink into them without reflection, as if looking into a deep pit. Instinct told Ray that the apparition in the lens wasn't human, but an alien presence, a thing that shouldn't exist.

"Don't fear me," the man said. "The creature of your nightmares is no more."

Ray found it difficult to breath. All his instincts said to run, but the creature's eyes seemed to pin him to the seat.

Pulling off the glasses, Ray looked at his staff. He wanted to shout for help, but the words wouldn't come. His staff continued working as usual, apparently unaware of the visitor.

Am I in a nightmare?

He fought to control of his fear.

"Better," the apparition said. The alien was standing in the aisle, appraising him with those deep eyes.

"What are you?" Ray choked out.

"I'm the Guardian, the one who holds humanity's future. Your son David sacrificed his life to create me."

"I don't understand."

"I can't put it in words that you would comprehend, but David's essence is distilled throughout my being."

"You're telling me he's trapped inside you?" Ray asked. "How do I know you're telling the truth?"

"Listen to me, and then I'll allow David one final moment as your son. Time is running out. I contain David's emotions and Sentinel's logic, but I have powers you can't imagine. I can be in many places at once." Guardian paused. "I have the capability to dominate humanity until the end of time.

"The temptation is great, but enough of David remains to temper my ambition. Your son, for all his faults, was a good and decent man. He knew— and I know—that my creation was a terrible accident. The only way remaining is to terminate my existence."

Ray leaned back and tried to think. His gut told him that Guardian was being truthful, and that its termination was the right decision. It would free David's soul, but the last bit of his son would be lost.

"I know this is difficult," Guardian continued, "but you need to concentrate. Although the Domain is in retreat, Dianne Morgan is still dangerous."

Ray straightened up and placed his computer on the next seat.

"Morgan has seeded additional children with the wild genes," the Guardian said. "She lied to me when I asked her if she had any secret plans. Another Guardian could emerge in the coming years. And it may not have a baseline of decency, as I inherited from your son."

Dianne Morgan has secret children?

"Since I can't eliminate all the wild genes," the Guardian said, "it was necessary to concentrate on the other half of the equation, and I rid the earth of artificial intelligence. All the robots, all intelligent code on the net, all AI units have been deleted."

"It's all gone? Decades of software development?"

"Your technology is circa 1998 now."

"My god, our civilization will crash," Ray breathed. "We depend on that software."

"Yes, but humanity will survive the crash. You must rebuild in a different direction. Would you prefer to live under the yoke of a Guardian?"

"No, but it's a brutal solution," Ray answered, "and many will disobey."

"This is where *your* leadership is crucial. You must establish a society with a mission to perfect human intelligence. Instead of relying on AI, you must greatly enhance the abilities of the human mind. And this society must be firmly in place before Morgan's children reach maturity. You're in a race to create humans with the intellect to resist another Guardian, and you may not have many years."

"But I'm no great leader," Ray stuttered. "Circumstances placed me at the head of the rebellion. Once the Domain is defeated, I'll leave governing to others."

The Guardian shook his head. "The people love you. Many think you're a demigod. They'll believe you, they'll follow you. Nobody else can do it."

"I never wanted any of this!" Ray shouted. Several heads turned in the front of the plane and stared at him. "I just want to live quietly," he added, lowering his voice. "That's all I ever wanted."

"I'm giving humanity a second chance, but it requires a strong leader. You must build a new society, and you must destroy Dianne Morgan and her brood."

"I plan on capturing her," Ray said. "I've thought about it for years. Dianne will go on trial for crimes against humanity. The Domain is on the verge of defeat, and we'll have her soon."

"She's much too dangerous to remain alive," the Guardian said. "Morgan carries the wild genes, too. You have to kill her."

"You mean murder her." Ray licked his lips, and then said, "I've never murdered anyone, and I don't plan to start now. She'll get a fair trial and receive the punishment she deserves. I know a place where she can spend the remainder of her days contemplating her sins."

"You escaped. She would, too."

Ray shook his head, "I can't just kill her in cold blood."

"You have to kill her in order to cement your position as the great leader. Morgan thinks she's escaped, but I tracked down her hiding place. I would kill her myself, but it's better if you do it." The Guardian smiled, thin lips stretching over his teeth. "She's hiding in your former home on the Oregon coast. For the sake of humanity, you'll eliminate her."

"I tell you I'm not a murderer."

The Guardian stared into his eyes, and once again it was difficult to breathe. "You'll do what you have to do."

Ray shrank back in his seat, but the Guardian wasn't finished. "There's one more task, and it's the most difficult of all," he said, "You have a daughter."

Ray stared. "What?"

"Larissa Morgan is your daughter."

Ray shook his head. "That can't be."

The wolfish smile flashed again. "Didn't you rely on Dianne to take birth control pills?"

"Yes," he admitted. When he saw that the entire staff was staring, he lowered his voice. "Why—if what you claim is true—would she get pregnant and not tell me?"

"She had a passion for you, Ray. She tried to see you all through your first year on the island, but you refused. She was pregnant with your child."

His mind went back almost two decades. Dianne *had* tried to speak to him many times during his first months on the island. She had even flown in one time and pleaded with him, but consumed with anger, he shut her out. Her calls had stopped after seven or eight months; she never again tried to speak to him during all the remaining years.

"I didn't know," Ray said. "I hated her for making me a prisoner, for taking me away from my sons."

For the first time, he swore he could see pity in the Guardian's eyes.

"Ray," the Guardian said, "Larissa carries the wild genes, too."

A daughter, I have a daughter.

He felt a great weight begin to lift, but then he saw the Guardian's meaning.

"No!" he screamed. He rose out of his seat, not knowing what to do.

His staff stared wide-eyed at Guardian from the front of the plane. One of the men dropped to his knees and prayed.

"No," Ray shouted, "I won't murder my own daughter." He stepped into the aisle and backed away from the Guardian. "You're some kind of monster. I won't do it."

Ray shouted to his communications technician in the front of the jet, a stocky young man with a computer in his lap. "Cut off all Internet connections." When the young man continued to stare at the Guardian, Ray rushed to the front, grabbed the young man's shirt and screamed, "Do it now."

The comtech said, "Yes, sir," and Ray pushed him away. The others stared at Ray, fear and awe in their expressions.

"Get back to work," Ray yelled, but they continued to stare at the Guardian. Another man dropped to his knees, tears dribbling down his cheeks.

"You *will* accept your destiny," Guardian said, and then, suddenly, disappeared.

Ray glanced around, but the creature was gone. He tried to think. Larissa Morgan his daughter? He didn't even know her.

His staff wouldn't look at him, and he realized they had been badly frightened by the confrontation with the Guardian. He had to calm them down.

Hobbling up to the comtech, Ray said, "Good job. I'm sorry, I shouldn't have yelled at you."

The young man looked confused, "But sir, I haven't done anything. The software isn't responding." Then the young man's eyes widened and he backed away.

"Dad," a voice came from behind Ray.

Ray turned around; he knew who it was.

David stood in the rear of the jet, naked as the day he died. "It's me, Dad," the apparition said, "What remains of me."

Ray wanted to believe his son was in the plane, but he had seen David's cold body on a gurney. This had to be a trick, but his legs led him down the aisle toward the apparition.

"David?"

Ray looked in all directions, and then shouted, "Is this a trick, Guardian?"

"I'm not a hologram," David said. He gently took Ray's hand and placed it against his bare chest. "I can't explain it, but in the ways that really matter, I am your son. This body is just a projection, but my mind is still my own."

Then he knew; this was his son.

"I always loved you, David, even when I was a drunk. I wanted to be a good father."

"I know, Dad."

"But you can't talk me into anything." David's chest felt human, but there wasn't a heartbeat. He pulled his hand away. "I won't murder anyone."

"You do what you think is right. You always have, and I respect you for that."

It wasn't the sound of his voice, but the way his eyes glistened; Ray was sure David was standing there. He realized that the Guardian had freed David to convince him to accept this new responsibility, but these few moments were worth the heartbreak.

Holding back tears, Ray embraced his son. "Can't you stay with me?"

"Oh, Dad," David whispered, his fingers digging into Ray's back. "I don't want to go." His son's voice quivered, "If there was any other way, but Guardian has to terminate himself." David released his grip and stepped back. "I'm part of him."

"All because of my terrible genes," Ray said.

"It's not your fault," David replied. "Maybe all this had to happen, so we could learn the dangers of artificial intelligence." David swiped at his eyes, and then said. "Dad, all those years I worked with Sentinel, I never thought it would end like this."

Ray shook his head. "Your genes drove you to merge with Sentinel. It was your bad luck to be my son, both you and Brian."

"I'm proud to be your son."

"All I wanted was to raise you and Brian in peace."

"I don't have any time left, Dad." David took a step back. "Brian and I never stopped loving you. You're a good man. Follow your instincts."

Ray had so much to say, but he couldn't find the words.

David began to fade, and then disappeared. Ray stared at the spot his son had occupied, then stumbled forward a few feet and collapsed in a seat. Leaning his head back, he closed his eyes and tried to think.

He just couldn't take it anymore.

THIRTY-FOUR

Wednesday, October 22, 2031

Ray shivered as he stepped out of his warm car into a clear, crisp, moonlit night. The salty ocean wind penetrated his jacket, and he stuffed his hands in his pockets.

He paused a moment to admire what had once been his home, a two-story colonial with a slate roof, snugly perched on a hill overlooking the Oregon coastline. It looked good, maintained by someone who cared.

Twenty years since the last time I set foot in this driveway.

No lights were on in the house. Guardian could have been wrong, or maybe Dianne had already escaped.

He limped along the brick path toward the house, looking for any sign of activity. The rhythm of the ocean reminded him of the life that had been stolen. The oncoming surf thundered on the beach, then faded into the background. In a quiet moment after the surf, he heard the grunts of animals in the distance. Then he remembered; sea lions inhabited a couple of tiny islands about half a mile offshore.

Amazingly, the security system recognized him and clicked open the front door. Ray crept into the foyer, feeling his way through the shadows. He paused next to the staircase leading to the second floor, but didn't hear anything except the muted clicks of the tall case clock. He had always loved that clock.

Padding down the oak plank hall, he reached the kitchen and peeked in. Moonlight revealed a refrigerator humming in the corner, an old-fashioned porcelain sink, and a square pine table surrounded by four matching straight-back chairs.

Everything was exactly as he had left it.

A wooden cabinet hung over the sink. He pulled open one door and found his old plates neatly stacked on the lower shelf, and his cups and glasses on the upper.

Nothing had changed.

Why had she bought the place and never used it? It couldn't be sentimentality; Dianne didn't have any sentiment.

Ray quietly pulled open the old wood-paneled door and stepped onto the porch. Its three outside walls were filled by six-over-six panel windows, presenting a dark panorama of water, sand and sky. As he now expected, his old leather couch snuggled against the wall to his left. He recalled sitting for hours on that couch, dictating code on his laptop. This porch had been his favorite room.

Through the sealed windows, he could make out the faint pounding of the ocean on the rocks below. He looked out the center window, peering into the night. The moon glowed coldly through a clear sky, illuminating the whitecaps thundering to shore.

A rocky beach jutted out more than a hundred yards from the house. Long, dark shapes— he knew it was driftwood— littered the beach. Then a tiny light flashed near one of the logs close to the breakers. It only lasted a moment, but it outlined a woman lighting a cigarette.

He felt a pang of disappointment. A part of him had wished that he wouldn't find her here. He shoved his hand into his jacket pocket and felt the cold metal of his Beretta.

Ray limped back through the house and slipped out the front door. Hobbling along the side of the house, he peered around the corner until he spotted the glow of a cigarette on the beach. Creeping across the sand, he worked his way toward Dianne, staying out of her line of vision.

He could see her more clearly as he approached. At sixty-three— two years older than he was— she was just as slender as he remembered her. The moonlight revealed that her face, always too thin and masculine to be beautiful, still featured high cheekbones and a prominent jawline.

His anger grew as he watched her. This one woman had created so much misery.

Dianne was standing about ten feet from the tide, looking across the horizon, as if searching for someone. She was wearing a thermal body suite, which fit snugly around an athletic body. She took a drag of her cigarette, and then let her hand flop down to her side. Ray didn't see a weapon, but with the Domain's technology, that didn't mean anything.

It was time to make his move. He pulled out the Beretta with his right hand and hobbled toward her. She must have heard something, because she turned and stared at him. He was less than twenty feet away; recognition spread across her face.

"Ray," she breathed.

He walked a few more steps, then stopped about ten feet away, "It's over, Dianne. I'm taking you in."

"I never thought I'd see you again."

Now he could see how much she had aged over the last two decades. She must have abandoned her cosmetic program. Her hair, pulled straight back into a severe bun, was steel grey. Although she remained tall and trim, her shoulders and hips looked thin. The eyes were still the same, however: a thin grayish blue that seemed colorless. Those piercing eyes always provided the best reading of her soul. It angered him that her eyes appeared content, almost happy.

"If I killed you right now," he said, "they'd all celebrate."

"Your pistol doesn't frighten me. We both know you won't use it." She took a step toward him, and he backed away. "You'd better put the pistol away before I take it," she said. "I might be tempted to use it."

"You always underestimated me."

She looked at him appraisingly. "I guess I did." She puffed on her cigarette. "I'm glad you're here. We have a few minutes before the submarine arrives, and we should talk."

Ray noticed a single-person hovercraft resting in the sand at the edge of the surf. It was about the size of the hovercraft that had rescued him from the island all those years in the past. He remembered how Dianne had screamed that she'd hunt him down and kill him, as the hovercraft carried him away.

"I'll kill you before I'll let you escape," he said.

"I don't think so," she replied. "You were in love with me a long time ago, and I don't believe you ever really got over it."

He shook his head. "You always were arrogant."

She smiled. "My spies tell me you never married. In fact, few women shared your bed; none for any length of time.

"Do you remember the first time we made love?" she asked. "It was the night of the Atlas V6 party. I could tell you were burning for me, so I left early and went to my office. I figured you'd follow me, and you didn't waste any time. We did it on my couch—remember?" She chuckled. "You moaned so loud I was afraid someone would discover us."

"Don't confuse love and sex. You were always a good piece of ass—everyone said so."

Staring intently, she said, "I really did hurt you, didn't I? You know, we'll only be together on this beach for a few minutes. We should be honest with each other." She paused. "I admit it; I was in love with you."

"You were in love with your destiny, not me," he said. "You had this insane dream to migrate humanity to a new level. That's god's work, not yours."

"I shouldn't have let you fall in love with me," she said, grimacing as she spoke. "I knew it wasn't fair. You wanted a little house with a white picket fence and I wanted to change the world. It couldn't work."

"You haven't asked about Larissa," he said.

"Bonini left a message that she has a broken leg, but she'll be okay."

The wind gusted, and he squinted to keep the sand out of his eyes. "You should have told me that she's my daughter."

Dianne's face dropped. "How long have you known?"

"It doesn't matter."

"I tried to tell you I was pregnant on the island, but you wouldn't see me."

Ray shook his head. "You can't be truthful, even now. I was your prisoner. You could have made me listen."

Dianne took a drag of her cigarette. "I was too proud to use her to get your attention. If you had stopped loving me, screw you."

"Well, you got even." He paused. "You sure got even. Larissa grew up without a father."

Dianne turned her back to him, staring over the whitecaps.

She'll never give up. I'll be forced to kill her. He glanced at the hovercraft. *Or maybe she's hiding a weapon.*

"You ran every morning," she said, "all the way around the perimeter of the island." With her back to him, it was difficult to hear her over the wind, so he took a few steps closer. "Then you'd dive into the surf and swim a few minutes. You always left a towel on the stone wall near the cottages."

Ray was surprised. He knew the guards watched him, but he didn't know she was watching, too.

"Every morning, good weather or bad," she continued. "And I knew why you ran; it was defiance. You were showing me that I couldn't break you." She paused, and then said, "If you had stopped running, I would have come to you. I would have told you about Larissa."

"The running kept me sane. If I had broken, you wouldn't have wanted me. Once you made me a prisoner, there was no way back for us."

Dianne stood quietly with her back to him. The surf rushed in almost to her feet, then rolled back. She shrugged, "Maybe you're right."

His hand was sweating, but he kept the pistol aimed between her shoulder blades. He didn't want to kill her, but he couldn't let her escape. He thought about wounding her, but she might die before help arrived. Anyway, he wasn't much of a shot.

She stood at the water's edge, casually smoking, watching the horizon.

How could he have ever been in love with this woman?

"Millions died because of you," he said. "Don't you feel anything?"

She turned her head to see him. "Yeah," she said, nodding. "Disappointment."

Dianne turned back to face the ocean. A wave came in, curled around her legs, and rushed away.

Far out on the horizon, a light blinked once, then again. "The sub is here for me, Ray." She dropped the cigarette into the sand. "What are you going to do?"

"Bring justice to you, one way or another."

"Your final revenge? I imprisoned you, so you lock me away?"

She took a step toward the hovercraft.

"Stay away from the boat."

She paused and then turned to him. "Take care of Larissa. She was innocent of all this."

Two quick strides and she reached the boat. Then she pushed it a few strides until it began bobbing in the water.

"I'll do it," Ray shouted over the surf. The pistol was shaking, so he braced his wrist with his left hand.

Dianne stepped into the boat and looked back at Ray. She smiled smugly, apparently confident he couldn't shoot. When she reached down toward the engine, he squeezed the trigger and the gun sputtered once.

The bullet thumped into her chest and her eyes widened, then glazed. Her body slumped forward, one arm flopping over the side, fingers dangling almost to the water. Her face rested against the boat's stern, her eyes still open.

Keeping the gun pointed at her, Ray cautiously approached. A wave broke gently across the bow, and then swirled past his knees. Peering over the side, he saw blood dripping from the wound in her chest. A small laser pistol lay next to her outstretched hand.

He checked her pulse.

Nothing.

It was all such a waste.

He leaned against the cold plastic hull and stared down at her. Moonlight revealed a cigarette lighter next to the body. He picked it up; it was old and scratched. He remembered that it had belonged to her mother.

In a few hours, the world would know Dianne Morgan was dead. A small army of forensic people would come, take a million pictures, and ask questions all night. Her dead body would be plastered all over the Internet.

She deserved it, but they had a daughter.

He dragged the boat back into the sand, then hobbled back toward the house and pulled open the garage door. If Dianne had kept everything as he left it, he should be able to find what he needed. The place looked the same, and he walked over to storage area he had built all those years earlier. A couple of old blankets, thick and heavy with dust, and a sleeping bag were in a built-in drawer, and he found a can of oil on a shelf.

Returning to the boat, he fitted Dianne's body into the sleeping bag, wrapped blankets around her, and laid her face-up in the boat. He knew he should feel sad, but all he felt was relief. Her pale eyes stared blankly into the heavens, so he closed her eyelids. After a moment's hesitation, he poured the can of oil over the blankets.

Ray pulled the old cigarette lighter from his pocket and lit the blankets. They caught quickly, and the flames grew. He stepped back, and then pushed the boat into the surf. The waves were gentle and it was easy to guide the boat past the breakers. When the water covered his chest, he gave one final push and then stepped away.

Hissing as if performing a distasteful task, the fire consumed her body. A hint of scorched plastic wafted up his nose. Flames soared above the waves, burned brightly for a few minutes, and then the boat exploded with a rush of fire and smoke.

Ray shielded his eyes from the glare of her final destruction, which spread debris across the waves.

He watched through pinched eyes as the flames gradually died.

There was still a glow on the waves when he jammed the lighter into his pocket and splashed back to shore.

THIRTY-FIVE

Thursday, October 23, 2031

Every inch of her body hurt. Larissa turned to the IV controller and pressed the button for additional painkiller, but the computer announced that she wouldn't receive another dose until 9 am, almost two hours from now.

These damn hospitals were so obsolete.

Larissa stared through exhausted eyes at the blue-suited, buxom security guard sitting against the wall. "My leg is killing me. Could you call one of those doctors in here?"

"Sorry, Miss Morgan, I can't leave my post. Anyway, the doc said you had already received the max dose when he was in here earlier." She squirmed. "Why don't you watch TV for a while?"

She had watched the television all night, finally collapsing for a few hours sleep. She had learned of her mother's death on the TV. Every damn news program told the story, repeatedly, of how heroic Ray Brown had killed her mother in a one-on-one shootout. Then of course, there were the scenes of people all over the world celebrating in the streets. One of the reporters said it was the greatest victory since World War II.

The pain was constant, but she could live with pain. Her world was gone, and everyone she loved was dead or under arrest. Last night had ripped into her soul, but now she was numb.

She turned on her side and stared out the windows. The rain had stopped, but the sky remained overcast.

It had been a shock to learn her mother was gone. Larissa knew Mom had a dark side—she had first-hand exposure to it— but she was still her mother. Tears threatened again, but she forced herself to think about the future. Mom would have expected that of her.

Thank the stars the baby is all right.

She placed her palm on her abdomen and felt better. He was totally her responsibility now. Raising the baby without a father would be her life's work.

This was a special baby. He had received Ray Brown's strange genes, but she wouldn't let it ruin her son's life like it had so many others. If she could, she would have ripped those genes out of his body. David, Martin and her wonderful Brian had all been cursed with her father's genes.

And she was, too.

She missed Brian. She could barely believe he was gone. She had only known him for a few weeks. It was so unfair. He'd been her brother and her lover. She didn't know what they would have done, but she knew she loved him.

Uncle Steve had said Brian died instantly from the fall. There hadn't been any pain. She hoped that was true.

The news programs had quoted leaks from high officials that she would be placed on trial for war crimes. She hadn't done anything, but she knew how these things worked. In Africa, Nkumah's warriors were murdering anyone remotely connected to the Domain.

She heard the door open and turned to see a big, broad-shouldered man limp into the room. Unruly grey hair couldn't hide the deep creases running across his forehead. He might have been ruggedly handsome in his youth, but he was showing his age. His frame seemed too big for his thin body, like someone wearing an old suit that no longer fits.

She stared at the stranger who was her father. His cloth jacket was baggy, and the handle of a pistol briefly bulged out. Tension suddenly prickled in her chest. She wondered if that was the gun that killed her mother.

His eyes swept over her and then to the security guard, who rose to attention and saluted. He told the guard to wait outside and then brought those deep brown eyes back to Larissa.

Although he was a few inches taller than Brian and broader across the shoulders, there was a strong family resemblance. The whole family had the same brown eyes that seemed to dip into your soul. But his face looked tired, sickly. Not the fearsome enemy hated by everyone in the Domain.

His eyes traveled down the cast on her leg, then back to her midsection. "How are you feeling?" he asked.

"Okay. The leg throbs, but the doctors say it will heal good as new."

"The baby is fine, they tell me." It was more a question than a statement.

She nodded. "He's doing well."

He paused, and then asked, "Have you picked out a name?"

She shook her head. She wanted to hate him, but she didn't really know him. And he was her baby's only other family.

"I know you don't trust me—no reason you should—but I'd like to take care of you and the baby."

She didn't know what to say.

He shuffled around the foot of the bed— so tired he almost lost his balance— and pointed to a chair, "All right if I stay for a few minutes?"

"I'd rather you didn't."

His eyes dropped, he took a breath and then looked into her eyes, "I'm sorry about your mother."

Larissa rolled over, turning her back to him. It wasn't hatred, but she just couldn't face him right now.

He remained a few seconds and then hobbled around the bed to the door. She raised her head to watch him. Her father's shoulders were stooped, as if pushing a heavy weight. She watched him turn the door handle and pull the door open.

He's a victim, too.

"Maybe you could come back after I get a few hours rest?" Larissa asked, surprising herself. "Father," she added.

His lips turned into a weary smile. He nodded and then shuffled out the door.

About the Author

Dan Ronco's expertise in engineering and computer science infuses his fast-paced speculative thriller *2031: The Singularity Pogrom* with detail and authenticity. Ronco returns to the violent, near-future world brought to life in his first two novels, *PeaceMaker* and *Unholy Domain*. Piers Anthony called *PeaceMaker*, "Exciting, violent, thoughtful and unfortunately true to life ... a powerhouse of computer adventure." Simon Wood, the Anthony Award winning author, said "Dan Ronco fills the gap left by Philip K. Dick with *Unholy Domain*."

ALL THINGS THAT MATTER PRESS ™

FOR MORE INFORMATION ON TITLES AVAILABLE FROM
ALL THINGS THAT MATTER PRESS, GO TO
http://allthingsthatmatterpress.com
or contact us at
allthingsthatmatterpress@gmail.com